About the Author

SALLY BEAUMAN graduated from Girton College, Cambridge. As a journalist, she has worked for *New York* magazine and has written for *The New Yorker*. In England, she worked for the *Daily Telegraph* and *Vogue* and was editor of *Queen* magazine. She has published two works of nonfiction, including *The Royal Shakespeare Company: A History of Ten Decades*. Her novels have been translated into more than twenty languages and have been bestsellers worldwide. Her latest novel is *The Sisters Mortland*. She lives with her family in London and Gloucestershire.

REBECCA'S TALE

Sally Beauman

HARPER

NEW YORK · LONDON · TORONTO · SYDNEY

For Alan

HARPER

Two final stanzas, used as epigraph, from "Stings" from *Ariel* by Sylvia Plath. Copyright © 1963 by Ted Hughes. Reprinted by permission of HarperCollins Publishers.

"Encounter," used as epigraph, from *The Collected Poems, 1931–1987* by Czeslaw Milosz and translated by Robert Hass. Copyright © 1988 by Czeslaw Milosz Royalties, Inc. Reprinted by permission of HarperCollins Publishers.

A hardcover edition of this book was published in 2001 by William Morrow, an imprint of HarperCollins Publishers.

FIRST HARPER PAPERBACK PUBLISHED 2007.

Designed by Jessica Shatan

The Library of Congress has catalogued the hardcover edition as follows:
Beauman, Sally.
    Rebecca's tale / Sally Beauman.
        p.   cm.
    Continues the story of Daphne du Maurier's Rebecca.
    ISBN 0-06-621108-5
    1. Cornwall (England : County)—Fiction.   I. Du Maurier, Daphne, Dame, 1907– Rebecca.   II. Title.

PR6052.E223 R4   2001
823'.914—dc21

2001018675

ISBN: 978-0-06-117467-4 (pbk.)
ISBN-10: 0-06-117467-X (pbk.)

08   09   10   11   ❖/RRD   10   9   8   7   6   5

We were riding through frozen fields in a wagon at dawn.
A red wing rose in the darkness.
And suddenly a hare ran across the road.
One of us pointed to it with his hand.

That was long ago. Today, neither of them is alive.
Not the hare, nor the man who made the gesture.

O my love, where are they, where are they going
The flash of a hand, streak of movement, rustle of pebbles.
I ask not out of sorrow, but in wonder.

—"Encounter," CZESLAW MILOSZ, *The Collected Poems, 1931–1987*

. . . They thought death was worth it, but I
Have a self to recover, a queen.
Is she dead, is she sleeping?
Where has she been,
With her lion-red body, her wings of glass?

Now she is flying
More terrible than she ever was, red
Scar in the sky, red comet
Over the engine that killed her—
The mausoleum, the wax house.

—"Stings," SYLVIA PLATH, *Ariel*

Contents

1

Julyan

APRIL 12, 1951

ONE

Last night I dreamt I went to Manderley again. These dreams are now recurring with a puzzling frequency, and I've come to dread them. All of the Manderley dreams are bloodcurdling and this one was the *worst*—no question at all.

I cried out Rebecca's name in my sleep, so loudly that it woke me. I sat bolt upright, staring at darkness, afraid to reach for the light switch in case that little hand again grasped mine. I heard the sound of bare feet running along the corridor; I was still inside the dream, still reliving that appalling moment when the tiny coffin began to move. Where had I been taking it? Why was it so *small*?

The door opened, a thin beam of light fingered the walls, and a pale shape began to move quietly toward me. I made a cowardly moaning sound. Then I saw this phantom was wrapped up in a dressing gown and its hair was disheveled. I began to think it *might* be my daughter—but was she really there, or was I dreaming her, too? Once I was sure it *was* Ellie, the palpitations diminished and the dream slackened its hold. Ellie hid her fears by being practical. She fetched warm milk and aspirin; she lit the gas fire, plumped up my pillows, and attacked my wayward eiderdown. Half an hour later, when we were both calmer, my nightmare was blamed on willfulness—and my weakness for late-night snacks of bread and cheese.

This fictitious indigestion was meant to reassure me—and it provided a good excuse for all Ellie's anxious questions concerning pain. Did I have an ache in the heart region? (Yes, I did.) Any breathing difficulties? "No, I damn well don't," I growled. "It was just a nightmare, that's all. Stop fussing, Ellie, for heaven's sake, and stop flapping around. . . ."

"*Mousetrap!*" said my lovely, agitated, unmarried daughter. "Why don't you listen, Daddy? If I've warned you once, I've warned you a thousand times . . ."

Well, indeed. I've never been good at heeding anyone's warnings, including my own.

I finally agreed that my feeling peckish at eleven P.M. had been to blame; I admitted that eating my whole week's ration of cheddar (an entire ounce!) in one go had been rash, and ill-advised. A silence ensued. My fears had by then receded; a familiar desolation was taking hold. Ellie was standing at the end of my bed, her hands gripping its brass foot rail. Her candid eyes rested on my face. It was past midnight. My daughter is blessed with innocence, but she is nobody's fool. She glanced at her watch. "It's Rebecca, isn't it?" she said, her tone gentle. "It's the anniversary of her death today—and that always affects you, Daddy. Why do we pretend?"

Because it's safer that way, I could have replied. It's twenty years since Rebecca died, so I've had two decades to learn the advantages of such pretences. That wasn't the answer I gave, however; in fact, I made no answer at all. Something—perhaps the expression in Ellie's eyes, perhaps the absence of reproach or accusation in her tone, perhaps simply the fact that my thirty-one-year-old daughter still calls me "Daddy"—something at that point pierced my heart. I looked away, and the room blurred.

I listened to the sound of the sea, which, on calm nights when the noise of the wind doesn't drown it out, can be heard clearly in my bedroom. It was washing against the rocks in the inhospitable cove below my garden: high tide. "Open the window a little, Ellie," I said.

Ellie, who is subtle, did so without further comment or questions. She looked out across the moonlit bay toward the headland opposite, where Manderley lies. The great de Winter house, now in a state of ruination, is little more than a mile away as the crow flies. It seems remote when approached by land, for our country roads here are narrow and twisting, making many detours around the creeks and coves that cut into our coastline; but it is swiftly reached by boat. In my youth, I often sailed across there with Maxim de Winter in my dinghy. We used to moor in the bay below Manderley—the bay where, decades later, under mysterious circumstances, his young wife Rebecca would die.

I made a small sound in my throat, which Ellie pretended not to hear. She continued to look out across the water toward the Manderley headland, to the rocks that mark the point, to the woods that protect and shield the house from view. I thought she might speak then, but she didn't; she gave a small sigh, left the casement open a little as I'd requested, then turned away with a resigned air. She left the curtains half-drawn, settled me for sleep, and then with one last anxious and regretful glance left me alone with the past.

A thin bright band of moonlight bent into the room; on the air came a breath of salt and sea freshness: Rebecca rose up in my mind. I saw her again as I first saw her, when I was ignorant of the power she would come to exert on my life and my imagination (that I possess any imagination at all is something most people would deny). I watched her enter, then re-enter, then re-enter again that great mausoleum of a drawing room at Manderley—a room, indeed an entire house, that she would shortly transform. She entered at a run, bursting out of the bright sunlight, unaware anyone was waiting for her: a bride of three months; a young woman in a white dress, with a tiny blue enamelled butterfly brooch pinned just above her heart.

I watched her down the corridor of years. Again and again, just as she did then, she came to a halt as I stepped out of the shadows. Again and again, I looked at her extraordinary eyes. Grief and guilt rose up in my heart.

I turned my gaze away from that band of moonlight. Rebecca, like all who die young, remains eternally youthful; I have survived, and grown old. My heart no longer pumps very efficiently. According to our Jonah of a doctor, its arteries have narrowed and there are signs of some valvular disturbance with an unpronounceable name. I *might* keep ticking over for a few years more, or I might keel over tomorrow morning. In short, I may not have very much time left to me, and (as the good doctor likes to put it) I should "put my affairs in order before too long." Thinking of this, and remembering my dream, I admitted to myself that, for motives I've always chosen not to examine too closely, I've procrastinated, prevaricated, and (as Ellie rightly said) *pretended* for decades. I've concealed the truth about Rebecca de Winter for too long.

I felt a change come upon me. There and then, I decided to make my peace with the dead. It was a canny piece of timing, no doubt influenced by the fact that I might peg out and join them at any second, I'll admit that. Nevertheless, I decided to record, for the first time, and, leaving nothing out, everything I know about Manderley, the de Winters, Rebecca, her mysterious life, and her mysterious death—and, for reasons that will become clear, I know more than anyone else does, I know a *very great deal*. There in my room, where the moonlight made the familiar unfamiliar, I made my resolve.

It was two o'clock in the morning. When I finally closed my eyes, afraid my dream might return, I could still hear the breathing of the sea, though the tide had turned, and by then was ebbing fast.

TWO

I AM AN OLD SOLDIER; MILITARY HABITS ENDURE, AND once I've finally resolved on something, I act.

"Ellie," I said, over a fine breakfast of bacon and eggs, "we'll walk in the Manderley woods this afternoon. I shall telephone Terence Gray and ask him to come with us. He's been itching to snoop around there, so I doubt he'll refuse."

A tiny silence greeted this announcement. Ellie, who'd been zipping back and forth between stove and kitchen table, dropped a kiss on my hair—a familiarity she can indulge in only when I'm sitting down as, standing, I'm too tall for such wiles. "How smart you're looking this morning," she said. "Very handsome! Is that a new tie? Are you feeling better? You look better. But are you sure that ?"

"Fit as a flea," I said firmly. "So don't *start*, Ellie. He's been angling to go there for ages and I can't stall him forever. Today's the day!"

"If you're sure," said Ellie, in a meditative way. She sat down opposite me, and fiddled first with her napkin, then that morning's mail; her cheeks became rosy. "Maybe he'd like to come for lunch first," she continued in a casual way. "I expect you'd enjoy that. Oh, look, there's a package for you. That's unusual. Makes a change from bills . . ."

Did I have a sense of foreboding even then? Perhaps, for I chose not to open my package in front of Ellie, although there was nothing especially remarkable about it—or so I thought at the time. A stout brown envelope, sealed with sticky tape, containing what felt like a booklet of some kind; it was addressed to A. L. Julyan, J.P., Esq., The Pines, Kerrith. This was unusual, in that most people still address me as "Colonel Julyan," although I retired from the Army nearly a quarter of a century ago. The "J.P." was inaccurate. It's fifteen years since I served as magistrate here. I did not recognize the writing, nor could I have said if it was a man's or a woman's—and one can usually spot a female hand, I find. Women can't resist certain florid calligraphic tricks and flourishes that a man would eschew.

I was pleased to receive it, I'll admit that. I get very few letters these days, most of my former friends and colleagues having turned up their toes long ago. My sister, Rose, a don at Cambridge, writes occasionally, it's true, but her scholarly spider's hand is unmistakable (as well as unreadable), and this wasn't from her. I carried it off to my study like a dog with a bone, my own ancient dog, Barker (so called because he's profoundly silent; he's now too old and toothless to bother with bones), trotting at my heels. There, Barker settled himself on the hearth rug, and I settled myself at my grandfather's desk, facing the leaky bay window, with its view of a lugubrious monkey puzzle tree, a palm, some stunted roses, and—beyond a small terrace—the sea.

I picked up my pen, and began writing down my list of morning tasks. This habit, ingrained since my days as a subaltern, remains with me even now. I still write these dratted lists every day, although they test even my powers of invention. I can hardly write "potter about," or "tidy desk," or "read *Daily Telegraph* until general tomfoolery of the modern world threatens to induce heart failure." I refuse to write "woolgathering" as a potential activity, although that is how I spend too much of my time.

Today, my list was distinctly promising. It read:

1. Rebecca's death: Summarize salient *facts*. State objectives.
2. Draw up "witness" list re Manderley and de Winter family, etc.
3. Organize all confidential material relating to Rebecca, and file p.d.q.
4. Telephone Terence Gray.
5. Open parcel. If contents urgent (unlikely), reply.

For about two minutes, I felt galvanized by this list. Then a familiar panic set in. Writing the name "Rebecca" immediately upset me. I was daunted by that word "facts." Somehow, whenever I consider Rebecca's brief life, and the perturbing circumstances of her death, I find it difficult to retain my habitual objectivity. Facts are thin on the ground anyway; rumour is, and always has been, rife, and, with the best will in the world, certain prejudices seed themselves around.

Resolving to weed them out, I picked up my pen, drew out a sheet of paper, and began writing. At school, I was taught the fiendish art of *précis* by a melancholy beak called Hanbury-Smythe, a man with a Cambridge double first, who had had a briefly distinguished career in the Foreign Office. He had a weakness for the bottle, too, but we won't dwell on *that*. His claim was that there was no problem, no situation, no matter how great its complexity, that could not be summarized in three sentences, and that *reducing* it in this way promoted clarity of thought. One's subsequent course of action, one's objectives, he believed, then became transparently obvious. I think this belief gave him some problems during his spell as a diplomat in the Balkans, but never mind. I was an early convert to the Hanbury-Smythe method, and used it throughout my Army career with conspicuous success.

I employed the Hanbury-Smythe technique now. Not long afterward (well, within the hour) I had produced the following:

The Mystery of Rebecca's Final Hours

On the night of 12 April, 1931, Mrs. Maximilian de Winter returned from a visit to London, arriving at Manderley, her West Country home, some time after nine; at approximately ten P.M., she left the house alone and on foot, walking down to the bay below, where her sailboat was moored. She was never seen alive again.

Fifteen months later, as a result of an unrelated shipping accident, and long after all searches had been abandoned, both her missing boat, which had been scuttled, and her body were discovered. The inquest verdict of "suicide" was controversial, but subsequently, and as a direct result of the local magistrate's ingenious and energetic inquiries, it was discovered that Mrs. de Winter had been diagnosed as mortally ill and had been informed of that diagnosis by a London doctor on the day of her disappearance; thus, a motive for killing herself, which had seemed lacking before, now presented itself and the matter was resolved.

I looked at this glumly: With the aid of clumsy sentence construction and sufficient semicolons, you can always cheat. My summary was dull; although factually "correct," it contained at least eight evasions and one misleading assumption; I could count no less than six *suppressiones veri*, all of them whoppers. I'd got it down to three sentences, and I'd produced a travesty of the truth. Hanbury-Smythe was a donkey and a drunkard and his methods were useless. *The matter was resolved?* Would that it had been! I was not proud of myself. Rebecca deserved better than this.

Deciding to improve on this effort, I opened the desk drawer where I keep the press cuttings relating to Rebecca's disappearance and death carefully filed. It is a thick file that has grown relentlessly fatter with the passing of years—there is something about this case that newshounds cannot resist. They're obsessed with the idea that there was a miscarriage of justice, of course; most seem to believe there was a concerted cover-up (they don't hesitate to point the finger, I might add) and, given Rebecca's beauty and réclame, the story makes undeniably good "copy," as someone said to me recently— it was Terence Gray, I think.

I inspected the cuttings carefully. The Hanbury-Smythe approach having failed me, maybe these professional wordsmiths could give me a few tips. They, along with our local gossips, have contrived to keep the story alive. Speculation about Rebecca herself, and the manner of her death, has never died down, as I'd once naively expected it would. Quite the reverse. Her disappearance and demise are still the subject of frequent articles; most of them—as Gray scornfully put it—are "cuttings jobs," in which by dint of repetition the most dubious information has hardened into "truth." There have been at least two books devoted to the subject, both purporting to contain new and sensational information—and both of them are works of romantic fiction (in my view, at least).

As a result, the "Manderley Mystery," as it's come to be called, has become one of the "Classic Conundrums of Crime"—I'm quoting here from a man named Eric Evans, whom I was once foolish enough to allow to interview me. In those days—it was before the last war—there had been such a deluge of scandal, and it had rained down on my head for so long, that I'd finally decided to break my silence. I would produce proof of Rebecca's final illness, and set the record straight. I know now that this was an error of the first magnitude. No self-respecting newshound is interested in "setting the record straight." What they're after is dirt.

Mr. Evans presented himself to me as an experienced crime reporter, a man with a nose for the truth. He wrote to me on paper with the *Daily Telegraph* heading (almost certainly pilfered, as I came to realize). I did notice that his letter was poorly typed, misspelled and ungrammatical, but I blamed some secretary girl. I believed him, fool that I was, when he spoke of a "crusade for truth." I know I was at a low ebb—the gossip in Kerrith was by then so bad that I'd had to resign my seat on the Bench; even so I should have known better. I realized Evans was a crank within two minutes of meeting him, and ejected him immediately—thus acquiring a brand-new enemy, of course.

The scene of our interview, here in my study at The Pines, went like this:

(A November afternoon, 1936. Colonel Julyan, until recently magistrate for the district of Kerrith and Manderley, and an imposing figure, is seated at his desk. His wife, Elizabeth, whose health is now poor, opens the door, announces the visitor, and retreats. Enter Eric Evans, a man in his fifties, with thinning hair, a pale complexion, horn-rimmed spectacles, a northern accent, and a fanatical look. He is carrying a suitcase, which he immediately opens. It proves to be filled with newspaper cuttings, photographs of Rebecca de Winter torn from magazines, and the handwritten notes for the book that he now announces he is writing on the "Manderley Mystery." He sits down and glares at Barker, the Colonel's young dog, who is growling. Evans does not produce a notebook or a pen, but embarks on his questions at once.)

EVANS: It was murder, wasn't it?
COL. J.: *(after a pause)* I think you'll find the inquest verdict was "suicide."
EVANS: The husband did it. Any fool can see that.

COL. J.: (*calm*) Are you familiar with the libel laws in this country,
   Mr. Evans?

EVANS: Who was Rebecca's lover? Did de Winter catch them *in
   flagrante*?

COL. J.: (*less calm*) I thought you said you worked for the *Telegraph*?

EVANS: There's been a cover-up. You fixed things for your friend
   de Winter. I won't be silenced! It's a bloody disgrace!

(Exit Evans, pursued by a dog.)

Well, no doubt I exaggerate (why shouldn't I indulge in a few fictions? Everyone else has), but it went something like that. And Evans was indeed not silenced. He was indefatigable, if lunatic. Over the years he published no less than sixteen articles on the de Winter case; he wrote a book, *The Lady Vanishes: A Solution to the Manderley Mystery*, which became a huge best-seller. He became the bane of my life, and before finally dying in the war when his bedsit was hit by a doodlebug (yes, there is a God), he created an industry. It was he, single-handed, who did the most enduring mischief. Sex and death are combustible components: Evans lit their fuse without hesitation. The result? Pyrotechnics. He turned Rebecca into a legend and her death into a myth.

In my file, I examined one of his earliest efforts. It originally appeared in 1937, a few months after our meeting. In the interim, someone—I suspect Jack Favell—had been bending Evans's ear. Despite its blatant prejudice, its mind-bending vulgarity, its manipulations, unwarranted slurs, gross inaccuracies, and truly colossal stupidity, it had an enduring effect. This was the article that doomed Rebecca, Maxim, and me to a curious twilit afterlife in which characters that vaguely resemble us eternally perform gestures that vaguely reflect things we actually did or said. It's a dumbshow; it's a fairground mirror, and I—the last of us left alive—am still trapped in front of it, gesticulating away. I don't recognize the people in the mirror, but who cares what I think?

If I were to tell the truth, what a Herculean task lay ahead of me, I thought, rereading Evans's regrettable prose. The trouble was (and I had to admit this), some of Evans's questions were pertinent; he was not without certain primitive skills, and at least his methods made the *background* a damn sight clearer than mine did. *O tempora, O mores*, I said to myself. My predicament can't be understood without quoting Evans, so I will. For better or worse, this was the article that launched the Rebecca industry; it has been much plagiarized since:

On the night of April 12, 1931, one of the most intriguing unsolved mysteries of recent times took place. The events of that night, and the drama of the months that followed, present the investigator with one of the classic conundrums of crime: Who was the lovely Rebecca de Winter, celebrated beauty and hostess, chatelaine of the legendary West Country mansion, Manderley? What were the events that led up to her tragic disappearance that fine April evening, and who was responsible for her death?

At the time of her mysterious disappearance, Rebecca de Winter had been married for some five years. Her husband, Maximilian (known as Maxim), came from an ancient West Country family. He could trace his ancestors back to the eleventh century. Manderley, his legendary family home, overlooking a wild and remote stretch of coastline, had been given a new lease of life, thanks to the taste and energy of his young wife: There were constant parties, entertainments, and fancy dress balls. Invitations there were much sought after, and the eclectic guest list included many famous—and some infamous—names.

Mrs. de Winter, famous for her beauty, wit, charm, and elegance, featured regularly in society periodicals. She sailed (winning many cups at local regattas); her knowledge of gardening was extensive, and the Manderley gardens, redesigned and replanted during her years there, became renowned. She was much loved locally, especially by the de Winter tenants, but some of the old-guard families in this conservative part of the world had reservations. They found her direct manner of speech regrettable, and disliked her often unconventional views. Some expressed surprise that Maxim de Winter (ten years her senior and a traditionalist, it's claimed) had married her. They regarded her as an outsider—and it is true that her background was mysterious. Who were her parents? Where did she grow up? Virtually nothing is known.

Despite the differences between husband and wife in background, interests, and age, the de Winters' marriage appeared successful, although, after her disappearance, tongues began to wag.

The seeds of tragedy, it was hinted, had been sown long ago. Rumor proliferated, but it was to be over a year before, in the wake of a series of shocking and terrible events, the truth began to emerge. Scandal ensued. Yet it is evident that further details remain to be discovered about the events of April 12, 1931, and the tangle of intrigue that led up to them: Manderley protects the secrets of the de Winter family . . . even now.

Let us examine the events of April 12 and the questions surrounding them. That night, Mrs. de Winter returned from a brief visit to London, the purpose of which has never been adequately explained. Had she gone there to see a lover, as some claim? Why, when she had a flat in London where she frequently stayed overnight, did she make such an arduous journey—six hours there and six hours back by road—on the same day? Why, on her arrival home, in a state of turmoil and distress, as was noted by several of the maids, did she immediately set off for the beach below the house, leaving on foot at approximately ten P.M.? Was she meeting someone at the boat-house cottage she kept there (there were rumors it was used for clandestine assignations), or did she simply intend, as her husband claimed at the subsequent inquest, to go sailing—at night and alone?

Whatever the answers to these questions, one fact is incontrovertible: Beautiful Rebecca de Winter, then age thirty, never returned from that final fatal sail, and it was to be fifteen months before her sailboat—a converted Breton fishing vessel with the prophetic name *Je Reviens*—was recovered. When it was brought up from the bay below Manderley, where it had lain hidden for over a year, two terrible discoveries were made. The boat had been deliberately scuttled . . . and trapped in its cabin was the body of a woman. It was hideously disfigured and heavily decomposed. The precise cause of death was never to be determined, and, in the absence of firm evidence to the contrary, drowning was assumed. Astonishingly, when brought ashore, the body was at once identifiable. Everyone present on that macabre occasion knew immediately who this was: On her wedding finger, the dead woman was still wearing the two rings that, during her lifetime, had never left her hand. . . .

Rebecca de Winter had been found at last. What followed was more tragedy—and a travesty of justice to boot. An inquest was hastily convened, and the jury—composed in the main of tenants of the de Winter estates only too willing to tug their forelocks to the deceased woman's husband—brought in a verdict of suicide. Maximilian de Winter, then forty-one, was let off lightly in the witness box by the elderly coroner. The then magistrate for the district, Colonel A. L. Julyan, a lifelong friend of Rebecca's husband, alleged by locals to be a "snob who liked to keep in with the bigwigs," declined to pursue inquiries any further. As he insisted then, and still insists, the matter was resolved.

Yet, consider the following seven facts, any one of which should surely have prompted further investigation, given the unusual nature of this "suicide":

1. Not long after his wife's disappearance, Mr. de Winter had identified the body of a dead woman washed ashore miles up-coast as that of Rebecca: He made this identification, which later proved to be "mistaken," alone.

2. Less than a year after his first wife's death, Mr. de Winter married again, his new wife, whom he met on a jaunt to Monte Carlo, being half his age.

3. His movements on the night of his late wife's death could not be accounted for in full. He dined with his estate manager, Mr. Frank Crawley, who lived nearby, but he could be said to lack an alibi for the key hours—from ten P.M. on.

4. There had been persistent rumors, in neighboring Kerrith and beyond, that his marriage to Rebecca, which was childless, had been a stormy one.

5. The de Winters did not share a bed at Manderley, and Mrs. de Winter frequently spent the night either at her flat in London or at her boathouse cottage, a situation her husband appeared to condone.

6. On April 12, Mrs. de Winter's devoted housekeeper, Mrs. Danvers, who also acted as her personal maid, was enjoying a rare evening off duty. Who in that household knew that Mrs. Danvers—the person who first raised the alarm the next morning—would be absent from Manderley then? Does this absence explain why it was that particular night that Mrs. de Winter disappeared?

7. On the afternoon prior to her disappearance, Mrs. de
   Winter saw a consultant gynecologist, Dr. Baker, at his
   Bloomsbury consulting rooms. It was her second
   appointment. What happened at the first? (Dr. Baker, who
   diagnosed an inoperable cancer, has since "moved abroad.")

These questions, and numerous others, remain unanswered to this day. And Rebecca de Winter did not rest in peace—or so locals claim. After the inquest, she was buried in the de Winter crypt, next to her husband's ancestors. Within hours of that hasty and secretive interment, Manderley was burned to the ground. . . . Accident? Or were more sinister forces at work? Had Rebecca, a victim of injustice, apparently unmourned by her husband, returned from the dead to take her revenge? Had she risen from the grave, as she'd risen from the sea? Remember that boat's name. . . . *Je Reviens.*

In pursuit of answers to these questions, and others, I set off last month to Kerrith, the nearest small town to Manderley. In the public houses and humble cottages of that picturesque and remote place were many who had loved and respected Rebecca de Winter. Outraged by these events, they were all too ready to talk to me, I found.

Within a day, armed with new and sensational evidence, I was in no doubt that there had been a concerted conspiracy to cover up the truth about Rebecca de Winter's death. Standing at last on the storm-swept headland by the ruins of Manderley, I looked out over the dark sea where she had met her end. And I knew, beyond a shadow of a doubt, that Mrs. de Winter had not died at her own hand. I knew the name of her murderer, and the method he'd used. Only one question remained: Why had Rebecca been killed? Might the answer to that question lie in her mysterious past? Turning my back on the haunted ruins of Manderley, I embarked on a quest for the truth about her origins. . . .

He never completed it, I'm glad to say. That doodlebug got him first. By then the damage was done, of course.

I sank my head in my hands. In the fairground mirror in front of which I'm eternally trapped, two ghosts and one clown were gesturing away. That unreliable heart of mine was playing up again. I was feeling distinctly unwell.

THREE

I CLOSED THE FILE OF PRESS CUTTINGS, AND STARED through the window at my mournful monkey puzzle tree. Barker was twitching his legs as he dreamed, and my own dream of the night before had returned. Up it came, like a nasty gas from the marsh of my unconscious. Once again, I saw myself trapped at the wheel of that sinister black car, which seemed to steer and propel itself without my aid. Once again, I was traveling up that endless drive to Manderley; I was driving through a snowstorm; when I applied the brakes, they failed to respond; beside me, incongruous on the passenger seat, that tiny coffin was beginning to move.

I rose from my chair, walked around my room a couple of times, and inspected my books (the room is barricaded with books). I forced that dream out of my mind. I had sat down at my desk feeling energetic and purposeful; now, as had happened so often before, I felt old, seedy, and inadequate, blinded by a blizzard of misinformation that went back twenty years and more.

Eric Evans might claim that he had discovered "new and sensational evidence," but what did it amount to? Precious little. Like the newshounds who'd come after him, he'd raided the pungent rubbish heap of Kerrith gossip; former Manderley staff and suchlike had tossed him a few smelly old bones. But he and his successors had never unearthed any proof as to what happened to Rebecca on the last night of her life. They had discovered virtually nothing about her pre-Manderley past. Even Terence Gray, an historian, not a journalist, but a sharp operator all the same, has got precisely nowhere with such inquiries—at least, not as far as I knew. That didn't surprise me. I was Rebecca's friend. I knew, better than anyone, how well Rebecca had covered her tracks, how secretive she'd been.

Would I be embarking on this task of mine, I asked myself, returning to my desk, were it not for the influence of Terence Gray, that strange young man, recently arrived in Kerrith—a young man who, for reasons unexplained, has been taking such a persistent interest in the circumstances of Rebecca de Winter's mysterious life, and death?

Possibly not. My dreams had certainly taken a turn for the worse since he arrived and launched his interrogations. I drew the telephone toward me: Time to speak to the man and propose our afternoon visit to Manderley—a visit long postponed, which I was beginning to regard as a *test*. How would Gray respond when he finally saw a house that seems to obsess him? (And why *does* it obsess him, for that matter?)

I picked up the receiver, then replaced it. It was still only ten o'clock (I rise early; Ellie and I breakfast early); the invitation could wait. Mr. Gray is formidable. He's young and energetic, and aspects of the man worry me (not least his motivation, which remains opaque). I was beginning to admit that Gray could be useful to me, but before I spoke to him I needed to think. I picked up the parcel that had arrived that morning, weighed it in my hand, decided it could wait until later, and turned my attention to the second of my appointed tasks—my "witness" list.

Unlike the newshounds and Mr. Gray, I told myself, I did not really *need* the testimony of others if I were to write the truth about Rebecca. I was her friend (possibly her closest friend, or so I flattered myself); I'd known Maxim for most of my life. I'd been familiar with Manderley from my early childhood, and the de Winter family had very few secrets from *me*. I am, as Mr. Gray keeps telling me, a prime source—*the* prime source, since Maxim's death. Even so, as my conversations with Gray had shown me, there were one or two gaps in my knowledge—nothing of any great significance, but irritating nonetheless. I've always had a taste for crime fiction—Sherlock, Hercule, and the rest; a bit of digging around, a bit of sleuthing might not come amiss: so—my witnesses. Who might know something that I did not?

Concentrate, concentrate, I said to myself. The injunction was necessary. I am never dilatory, thanks to my self-discipline and my military training, as I said, but I have noticed recently a certain tendency to be distracted. I am seventy-two, which may be a contributing factor. I've noticed the tendency worsens when, as then, I feel forlorn/irritable/uncertain/suspicious/upset—take your pick. Recovering instantly, and at lightning speed, I wrote the following list:

1. Rebecca
2. Maxim de Winter
3. Beatrice (his sister)
4. The elder Mrs. de Winter (his grandmother, who brought him up)
5. Mrs. Danvers (housekeeper at Manderley in Rebecca's time)
6. Jack Favell (Rebecca's ne'er-do-well cousin; her sole known relative)
7. Former staff (Manderley maids, footmen, etc.; many still living hereabouts)
8. Frith (former butler at Manderley; ancient retainer from the year dot)

Not a long list. The fact that the first four candidates on it were all dead might have discouraged some people, but not me. I have letters from them, and I have my memories. In such ways, the dead can speak.

Even so, just to write their names distressed me. I knew Beatrice, who died at the end of the last war, from her childhood. Maxim, who was some ten years younger than I was, I'd known from the day of his birth. That terror of a grandmother of his I could remember only too vividly from my boyhood. She had still been alive during his marriage to Rebecca, whom she'd adored; if anyone had been privy to Rebecca's many secrets, it was she, I suspected—indeed, I'd often thought she knew more about Maxim's wife than Maxim did. I could be wrong, of course.

There were ghosts in the corners of the room. Writing their

names had conjured them up. Barker lifted his great head; his hackles rose and fell. He gave me a soulful and comforting look. We both thought of my former friend Maxim, dead these five years, killed in a car accident he certainly willed, which occurred at the Four Turnings entrance to the Manderley gates. Only months after his long years of exile abroad with that second wife of his had finally ended; only a very short time after he and she had returned to England to live.

I know something about being pursued by the Furies, and I've never doubted they pursued Maxim with their customary efficiency once he left Manderley, though he ceased communicating with me then, and never answered my letters, so I have no way of confirming this. I was not invited to his funeral; that slight hurt me at the time, and still does. I've been loyal to my old friend Maxim—too loyal, perhaps.

The second wife—"the sad little phantom," as my friends the Briggs sisters refer to her—scattered his ashes in the bay below Manderley, I heard. Did she find the idea of his lying in the de Winter crypt alongside Rebecca unbearable? It wouldn't surprise me. Possessive women remain possessive after death. She has now spirited herself off to Canada, or so I'm told. I considered, then rejected, the idea of adding her name to my witness list.

On the few occasions I'd met her, I'd found her vapid; in fact, I didn't take to her, though, given my admiration for Rebecca, I was biased, I expect. True, the second Mrs. de Winter might know more about Rebecca's death than anyone else; I've no doubt Maxim would have taken her into his confidence. But would she ever reveal her knowledge to me? Hell would freeze over first, I thought—and in any case, being practical, I had no way of locating her. According to my spinster cronies Elinor and Jocelyn Briggs, no one in this locality remains in touch with her. She's said to have walled herself up in Toronto (or was it Montreal?) and no one has her address.

I ran my eye down my list again: Not many names left. As Terence Gray has remarked, there's a distinct *paucity* of informants in this case. Of the remaining candidates, several could be quickly eliminated. I had no intention of consulting antediluvian Frith, erstwhile Manderley butler, footman, bootboy, et cetera. I'll admit he was an exemplary butler, but he was also an exemplary busybody, and he had an inexplicably *knowing* way of looking at me that I still resent. He's now in a local nursing home and virtually senile, in any case. Why had I added his name to my list in the first place? Probably because Terence Gray has taken an interest in him, I decided. More fool him. I drew a thick line through the noodle's name. Who else?

In Rebecca's day, in the Manderley glory days, when the house was filled every weekend with distinguished guests, there was a *tribe* of servants, most of them invisible—invisibility, dumbness, and deafness being the mark of the well-trained servant then, of course. Many of them are still alive, and many of them still live in the Kerrith area. Unlike evil Evans and his disciples, who were not above interviewing former maids, asking zealous questions about bedroom arrangements and so forth, I drew the line at female staff: Most were empty-headed gossipers, who knew nothing (not that this prevented them from inventing reams of stuff for the newshounds, rattling on about sheets, shouts, rows, and rapprochements, et cetera). Some of the men-servants, however, Robert Lane for instance, might have a morsel of knowledge to contribute.

I bump into Robert from time to time, as one does in a small place, and he's always struck me as a nice enough chap. Once a young foot-man at Manderley (Footman! How antique that sounds), he survived the last war, and—according to the Briggs sisters, my invaluable local informers—is now married with four children. He has brilliantined hair and works behind the bar in an unprepossessing hotel at Tregarron, a souvenir-ridden, plaster-piskie infested tourist trap some three miles from here.

Robert, once notorious in Kerrith for his weakness for redheads, was rumored to be loquacious. Could this be true? My confidence sagged. Robert might be talkative, but he's never struck me as in the least observant, and I didn't relish the prospect of pumping questions at him across a bar. There was something unspeakably seedy about it; interrogate a man who used to bring me a whisky and soda? Unthinkable! Who else, who else? My list of informants was shrinking by the second. Only two names were left. With a certain reluctance, I considered my next candidate: Mrs. Danvers. A peculiar woman, Mrs. Danvers.

She was an obvious candidate, it's true, in that she was housekeeper at Manderley throughout the Rebecca years, and always claimed to be closer to Rebecca than anyone else. I placed little credence in that claim (whoever Rebecca *was* close to, truly close, it wasn't her). Certainly she knew Rebecca as a child. But as neither she nor Rebecca ever explained where, when, or under what circumstances, this nugget of information had never seemed of any great use. The Danvers woman was an hysteric, as I spotted the first time I laid eyes on her (one picks up useful psychological insights of this kind in the Army); besides, fantasist though she was and therefore of limited use as a "witness," she was unavailable, too. She left the area on the night of the great Manderley fire, and not one person to my knowledge has laid eyes on her, or heard word of her, since. She *might* be in the land of the living (that's certainly Terence Gray's opinion), but more probably she too has turned up her toes.

That left just one other obvious candidate, Jack Favell, Rebecca's black sheep of a cousin, and a singularly odious man. Favell was a cad and a wastrel: He was kicked out of the Royal Navy (how he got into it in the first place is a mystery to me), and, by the time he first started turning up at the odd Manderley party (self-invited, I feel sure), had embarked on a rather more successful career as a sponger. I met too many men of Favell's type during my Army years not to see him for what he was at once; I first met him shortly after he began gate-crashing Manderley events—in about 1928, some two and a half years into Rebecca's marriage—and I loathed him the instant we shook hands. I was shaking hands with my nemesis as it happens, but I wasn't to know that then, alas.

I always suspected Favell had some hold over Rebecca that went back to their early years; apart from Mrs. Danvers, who kept her mouth buttoned, he was the only person, *the only person*, I ever met who had known Rebecca as a girl. . . . Not that he ever discussed that with me. Our dislike was mutual; our exchanges were curt; I doubt we ever exchanged more than three sentences until after Rebecca's death. Nor was I alone in my dislike; Rebecca never seemed to me to be too fond of her cousin (although certain newshounds have suggested otherwise). Maxim loathed him from the first, and didn't trouble to disguise it. He and Favell were chalk and Cheddar, of course. Maxim, like myself, had standards: Favell, loose-mouthed, a heavy drinker, given to swearing, overfamiliar to women, was never going to be welcome at Manderley—though I always suspected the problems went deeper than that.

Was Maxim jealous of Favell? My wife certainly thought so; perhaps women are quicker than men to sense such feelings. I am not a jealous man myself. My own instinct was that Favell, who liked to cause trouble, told Maxim tales about Rebecca's past that put the marriage under strain—this would have been toward the end, in the year that led up to Rebecca's death. During that period, the atmosphere at Manderley was certainly uneasy. Even Rebecca's considerable acting abilities could not always disguise the marital tension. The whiff of marital tension, in my experience, can always be detected from a long way off.

I know Maxim banned Favell from the house after one disgraceful drunken episode, yet he continued to worm his way in there. I may have mentioned the matter to Rebecca, once or twice. I suspected she'd been talked into lending Favell money, and, if this were the case, I thought someone should warn her off. When I remonstrated with her (anything to do with Favell made me hot under the collar, so I may have expressed myself strongly), Rebecca smiled. My "protective" instincts always amused her, I suspect. She said she knew perfectly well what kind of man her cousin was, and then added in her enigmatic way (Rebecca could be both a sphinx *and* a minx) that, for all his faults, Favell was "accurate." Accuracy? I saw damn little sign of it, although I should admit that I began to see what she might have meant, after her death.

Just thinking about Favell was making me agitated. This happens now, and, since my Jonah of a doctor tells me it's inadvisable, I again rose and walked about the room. Those ghostly presences that have taken to dogging my footsteps were back. They were settling themselves in the corners, settling in for the duration, I expect. Barker growled at them. I tried to ignore them, and failed. I returned to my desk. My hands were unsteady. I re-examined my witness list.

I thought of the last time I'd seen Favell. It was the day that was to prove crucial to the entire case; it was the day after the inquest into Rebecca's death. Favell was not satisfied with that suicide verdict and, in truth, neither was I. I thought it nonsensical. There was no indication of a motive, she had left no note, and I simply could not believe that the Rebecca I knew would ever take her own life. I therefore suggested we do something that was actually very obvious: We should look into Rebecca's movements on the last day of her life; you'd have thought the coroner at the inquest might have had the nous to do that, but he had not.

We examined Rebecca's appointments book (which, fortunately, Mrs. Danvers had kept), and that was how we discovered that, in secret, telling no one, Rebecca had consulted a London doctor—a specialist in women's ailments—at two P.M. on the last day of her life. Rebecca had recorded this appointment in a curious semicoded way, which made me suspicious. This man would have been one of the last people to see Rebecca alive. Why had she consulted him, and not her usual local doctor? What had he told her that last afternoon?

The following day, I drove to London to interview him. I was accompanied by Maxim and his new wife, and Jack Favell—he insisted on being present, and I suppose as Rebecca's cousin he had the right. In fact, Favell was claiming to be rather *more* than a cousin to Rebecca at that point. He was making the most sordid and reprehensible claims about their relationship. Favell was an habitual liar, so I did not necessarily believe him, but I could see that his allegations, if true, gave Maxim a motive for murder. That concerned me. I already had profound misgivings as to Maxim's possible involvement in Rebecca's death.

We spoke to Dr. Baker at his home, not his consulting rooms. It was an ordinary, pleasant house, I remember, somewhere in north London. When the interview was over, we came out into a leafy suburban street. Some poor relic from the first war was playing "Roses in Picardy" on a barrel organ, a tune I can never hear now without experiencing distress. I was in a state of profound shock. Dr. Baker, we'd learned, had seen Rebecca twice: at the first appointment, a week before her death, X rays were taken and various tests performed; at the second, he gave her the results. He had had to tell her that she had a cancer of the womb, and that it was inoperable; she faced a period of incapacity and worsening pain. She had, at best, three or four months to live.

This was not the information I had been expecting Baker to give us. Standing outside his house, I was struggling not to betray the shock and pity I felt. I was brought up to believe that it isn't manly to show emotion and I have an abhorrence of tears as a result.

Had Rebecca suspected she was ill? Or had Baker's diagnosis come as a complete surprise to her? It pained me to think of her concealing this knowledge, and at first I was too numb to think beyond that. Then I realized: The implications of this information were considerable. Now, there was a clear motive for suicide; now, that inquest verdict would *never* be overturned, and the police could have no possible grounds for reopening their investigations—no matter what accusations Favell, or anyone else, chose to make. Maxim de Winter was in the clear, off the hook. I turned to look at my old friend; his sweet little wife had just sweetly clasped his hand. To my horror and disgust, I saw relief flood his face.

I knew then for sure, I think—but I'm recording the truth now, so I'll admit: I had had doubts as to Maxim's innocence before, on two occasions. First, when Rebecca's poor body was recovered, and I'd watched his face as he bent over it to make a formal identification. Second, at that travesty of a funeral Maxim arranged for Rebecca, when he and I, the sole mourners, stood side by side in the de Winter crypt.

I've never discussed that funeral with anyone, not even Ellie, not even my late wife. Yet it will not let me forget it, and winds its way into my dreams at night. Funeral is not even the correct word; it was an *interment*, arranged at indecent speed, immediately after the inquest. It was hasty and it was secretive—in this respect everything that man Evans wrote about it was correct. It was evening, and raining heavily. The crypt, a series of low vaulted chambers with iron gates, is even older than the Manderley church itself, and that is ancient. Once one is underground, the proximity of the river, of the graveyard nearby and in places directly above, can be felt; the glimpses one gets of dead de Winters in lead-lined coffins laid to rest on either side, the recent coffins still intact, the older ones not—well, it is not a place in which anyone would ever want to linger. And on that occasion I . . . but it doesn't matter what I felt. I'll say only that I'd had the very deepest affection for Rebecca, and I was close to breaking point.

The crypt was bitterly cold, and the walls ran with damp; the electric cables, fed through underground in heavily corroded metal tubing, kept shorting, so, as we stood there, listening to the words of the burial service, the lights flared, then failed, then flared again. The vicar, as uneasy as I was, was gabbling the prayers. I had been standing with my head bent, but at one moment, sensing movement from Maxim, who was standing beside me, I looked up. For a brief second, as the power surged and the lights flickered, I met Maxim's gaze—or at first thought I did. He was white-faced and visibly sweating despite the chill; he was not looking at me, I realized, but slightly over my shoulder, at air, and whatever it was that he saw in the air, it left him transfixed. I will never forget his expression, and the agony I then saw in his eyes. When I say that I felt I was looking directly at damnation, I do not exaggerate. I fought in the first war; I fought in the trenches—so I can speak with some authority: I recognized that expression because, God help me, I'd seen it before on the faces of other men, now long dead.

I looked at him, appalled, for what can only have been an instant, though it felt hours long; then, with a hissing, crackling sound, the lights flickered and dimmed again. Before the prayers were over, while the words *May she rest in peace* were still being spoken, Maxim tried to leave. He attempted to push past me. I put my hand on his arm to restrain him, and found he was shaking. He could not meet my eyes then—and he could not meet them now.

Standing in that suburban street, I knew with every instinct I possessed that Rebecca had not killed herself. I *knew* Maxim had been involved in some way in her death. I think I was bewildered, still in shock, my mind not operating well. As I looked at him, I was already imagining some mitigating circumstances—a violent quarrel, perhaps. Could he have struck Rebecca, could she have fallen and fatally injured herself? Could it have been manslaughter? I couldn't believe Maxim capable of premeditated murder. He was my friend, an honorable man. . . . I still believed in honor then, of course.

To this day, I believe that if I'd drawn Maxim to one side at that exact moment, and asked him for the truth, he might have told me. He was in a desperate state, very close to the edge. There were a few minutes of silence. I looked along that leafy road. We had reached what I can now see was the definitive moral turning point of my life. I was about to make a decision that has haunted me ever since. If Favell had kept his mouth shut at that crucial point, perhaps everything would have turned out differently. Who can know? I certainly don't.

Favell *didn't* hold his tongue—he was incapable of it. To be fair to him, I believe he was genuinely shocked, too—he wasn't without feelings for Rebecca. He'd been walking back and forth in a dazed way, saying he couldn't believe it, that he needed a stiff drink. Then, in a way that sickened me, he asked whether Rebecca's cancer was "catching"—a suggestion typical of the man, and typical of the foul way in which he thought. Having failed to get a rise with that remark, he rounded on Maxim and on me. Was that the first time the term "cover-up" was used? I know Favell, in his sneering way, congratulated Maxim on being "off the hook." I know he was quick to suggest that the doctor's information must have delighted me, too, since my old friend was in the clear now. I know he insinuated that I'd hush things up, that the "old boy" network would take care of its own. I was a snob who valued my invitations to Manderley; I could be relied on to protect a de Winter, he said.

I was deeply angered. Loathing Favell, detesting him, his code, and everything he represented, I made my decision there and then in that street. There was a clear motive for suicide; there was no evidence of murder, let alone proof. You cannot put a man on trial for a facial expression; you can't condemn a man because you believe you've seen guilt in his eyes—not when the crime of murder carries the death penalty. So I decided: Let that be an end of it. I would make sure Dr. Baker's information was circulated. Beyond that, I would take no further action. All over. Draw a line under it. Let the matter be laid to rest.

It wasn't, of course, as I should have foreseen. But all those newshounds, all the Kerrith gossips who found other reasons for my actions were very wrong. To them I was at worst a toady to the de Winters, and at best too loyal to my friend. They were all so sure that it was Maxim's interests I sought to defend, that they never saw the truth—yet it was obvious enough. It was *Rebecca*, not her husband, whom I hoped to protect.

I always knew what would happen if there were any further investigation into her death; I knew her reputation would be thrown to the wolves. I knew it would all come out: all the sordid allegations of love affairs, duplicity, and intrigue that Jack Favell was only too eager to boast about. I knew that if people began to suspect Maxim had killed his wife, they'd look for a motive—and they wouldn't have to look very far. What motive could he possibly have had *other* than infidelity on her part? Secretly, of course, I believed in that infidelity myself. I told myself it had to be true, that Maxim would never have harmed his wife unless given very strong cause. What a betrayal of Rebecca that was.

At that point, when I made my decision, the floodgates of gossip were still closed. Whatever the claims of journalists, there were as yet no rumors of "lovers" or "clandestine assignations"—at least none I'd heard. I wanted that state of affairs to continue now Rebecca was gone. I wanted that more than anything else. *That* was why I tried to persuade everyone that, rather than die a slow painful death, Rebecca had killed herself. I wanted people to remember her as I'd always imagined her: as a beautiful, virtuous, and courageous woman. I wanted *my* image of her to be the one that prevailed.

How Rebecca would have laughed. Her notions of virtue weren't mine, and she was always more realistic than I was. She'd have known that the more you try to silence them, the more tongues wag. Jack Favell was on the telephone to his drinking cronies in Kerrith before I even returned from London. There was never the least hope that I'd stem the gossip, malice, and sheer propensity for *making things up* that are so deeply embedded in human nature. Silence the rumors? I was a Canute, telling the advancing waves to turn back.

There is no law against libeling the dead; there was never a trial, so no advocate ever spoke for Rebecca. She's been condemned to silence for twenty years. She can't defend herself or correct the lies or explain; she has never been able to tell her story, or say *No, it wasn't like that*. That's the terrible thing about being dead, as I realize now I'm old. People can jump up and down on your grave, and you can't do a thing about it. You're gagged. You can't *answer back*. . . . Not unless someone comes to your assistance; not unless some good, wise, indefatigable person ferrets around and comes up with the truth on your behalf.

Could I perform that service for Rebecca? Last night, by moonlight, I'd believed I could. I'd thought I could make amends for my past failures, but now I felt very unsure. A seventy-two-year-old bungler with a dicky heart? A moral fumbler who couldn't even write a truthful account of Rebecca's death, let alone her life? I wasn't exactly Sir Lancelot, was I? Much help to her I'd be, I thought.

By this time—I may as well admit it—I was in a bad way. Introspection is invariably painful, and examining my crimes and misdemeanors in hideous close-up was not how I'd meant to start the day. My eyes were watering, my heart was thumping and bumping in the way it does now—no doubt my blood pressure was soaring as well. Barker gave a low whine, rose, and rubbed his gray muzzle against my leg. Trying to calm myself, and failing, I reexamined my foolish "witness" list, then tore it up. So much for my potential informants. The dead, the damnable, and the downright unreliable. If I was to find Rebecca, it would not be by this route.

My vision had blurred. Forgetting my call to Terence Gray, forgetting the parcel whose contents would later prove to be so extraordinary, I rose unsteadily to my feet. I blundered my way past my desk to the French windows. Outside, it was a cloudless April day on this, the anniversary of Rebecca's death.

I opened the glass doors, fumbled my way down the steps into the garden, and set off down the path. Barker, my loyal shadow, immediately followed me. I made my way between the dog-eared palm tree and the lugubrious monkey puzzle, past my viciously pruned roses, to the crazy-paving terrace at the far end. From there, the ground drops away sharply to that inhospitable cove already mentioned, some eighty feet below; I have shored up this boundary of mine with a low, now-crumbling wall, and on this wall I sat down. I looked down at the sea, azure at its edges, inky farther out by the Manderley headland, then looked back at The Pines, a folly of a house, my childhood home.

Dry your tears, Arthur, I heard my grandfather say, in his gentle voice—and it didn't surprise me greatly to hear that voice, though he's been dead for fifty years. The dead often talk to me now; it's one of age's side effects. Before I was aware of what was happening, I'd surrendered to his tone and I was allowing my past back, letting its currents take me where they wanted—and they took me, as they often do, to the Manderley I knew as a boy.

There, some of the dead witnesses on my list were waiting to speak to me: not Rebecca herself, of course, not yet; the Manderley I was watching existed long before she arrived on the scene. But even so, I knew I'd discover something, if I watched these de Winters closely enough. I've always believed that you cannot understand Rebecca and what she became, unless you understand the family she married into; I've always felt that if I were searching for clues to Rebecca, Manderley was the first place to look.

FOUR

I FIRST CAME TO THE PINES WHEN I WAS SEVEN YEARS OLD, accompanied by my mother and my new nurse, Tilly. It was the late 1880s (that's how ancient I am). We were to stay with my grandfather, a widower, in his house by the sea in what was then, and still is to an extent, a remote part of England—a country about which I had many fantastical notions, but in which I had never set foot. I wasn't clear at the time why we had left India, or why my father had remained there, except that he could not obtain leave from his regiment for another few months, and meanwhile my mother needed respite from the Indian climate. As I now know, but didn't then (such matters were not mentioned, especially in front of a child), she was expecting her second baby, my sister Rose.

At first I missed India; I missed my pet mongoose, and my ayah, whose lilting bedtime songs drift back to me out of the past, even now. The Pines seemed strange after the bungalows in which we had previously lived. I was cold all the time; I'd shiver when I woke to the raucous cry of gulls, and looked out of my bedroom window to the Manderley headland opposite.

I'd soon feel I belonged here, my grandfather said, in his comforting way, for my own father had grown up here and there had been Julyans for generations in this part of the world. There were many ancient families in this region, he explained; because it was remote, tucked away down at the foot of England, families and their houses endured; there were the Grenvilles, for instance, and the Raleghs, but the oldest of all was the de Winter family, who could boast direct descent from father to son for eight hundred years. "Can't all families do that, Grandpapa?" I asked. No, he said. For that you needed sons; without sons, families died out.

Seeing I didn't understand, he gave me my first lesson in genealogy. We came from a junior branch of the Julyan family, he explained, but I should be proud of my ancestors, whose blood ran in my veins. He fetched out the family tree he had drawn up, and showed me a bewildering forest of connections: the marriage to a Grenville heiress in 1642; an alliance to a de Winter sister in 1820; the Julyan men who had served their church, their country, or the laws of their country—and there, right at the end of all those forking branches of landowners, judges, soldiers, and clergymen, was a tiny twig—and that, he said, was me.

My grandfather, Henry Lucas Julyan, was rector of the parishes of Kerrith and Manderley; he became my friend from the day I arrived, and he was one of the very few truly good men I've ever known, kind-hearted, learned, and astute. Before taking up Holy Orders, he had been a distinguished classical scholar at Cambridge, where he first met Darwin, who became his friend. He lived a simple life, dining on plain food, taking long walks, reading, writing, and abhorring any form of show or ostentation. He was an unworldly man—and it may be due in part to his influence that I am unworldly, antique, and unrealistic, too.

He was an amateur botanist of some distinction, and it was he who first introduced me to the pleasures of collecting and cataloging. Before my first summer at The Pines was out, I was already learning about fossils and wildflowers; I began my study of butterflies and moths, and my grandfather taught me how to kill them painlessly and quickly with chloroform. Red Admirals, Swallowtails, Painted Ladies . . . I still have our collection; it is in my study, packed away in specimen drawers. I find I can't bear to look at it now.

My grandfather took me on expeditions along the coast; we explored the beaches, the dark little creeks, the moors inland, and the woods, which were often the best butterfly hunting ground, espe-

cially the woods surrounding Manderley. The de Winters had lived
at Manderley since the time of the Conquest, my grandfather
explained, though the house itself had been altered and rebuilt
many times since then; their unusual name was a corruption from
Norman-French, and was possibly derived from the word "ventre,"
meaning stomach, or womb. Lionel de Winter, the present head of
the family, was my own father's exact contemporary. They had been
friends and schoolfellows, although the friendship, he added vaguely,
had lapsed in recent years—probably because my father had been
away in India so long.

I was taken to Manderley that first summer in England. There, I
met Lionel de Winter, and his wife Virginia; she was one of three
famously beautiful Grenville sisters, known as "The Three Graces,"
my grandfather explained. The eldest, Evangeline, had recently married a shipping magnate, Sir Joshua Briggs; the youngest, Isolda, was
still unmarried—she was very pretty and charming and I would meet
her some time. The middle sister, Virginia, now married to Lionel,
was my grandfather's favorite. I would like her, he told me; her health
was not strong, but she was sweet natured and kind.

Virginia—always referred to by my mother as "poor Virginia"—
was a gentle, soft-spoken semi-invalid; she seemed to spend even
more time lying down than my mother did, and no one explained
why. Poor Virginia always seemed to me like a guest at Manderley;
each time I went there, I half expected to hear that she'd packed her
bags and gone away. She seemed to have nothing to do with the running of her home; all the decisions were taken by her mother-in-law,
Mrs. de Winter the elder, who had been born a Ralegh, and was a
terrifying personage. The first time I was introduced to her, she
looked at my hair keenly and announced it was too long—I looked
like a girl. I must have passed muster, or been judged useful at any
rate, for she summoned me to Manderley again. I was to play with
Lionel and Virginia's only child, their daughter Beatrice, a plump,
bossy little girl whose chief interest in life was horses; I grew to like
Beatrice well enough, but she and I had nothing in common at all.

As time went on, I was summoned more frequently, but I was
never sure how much I liked going to Manderley. I liked those woodland expeditions with my grandfather, but I found the house oppres-
sive and strange. It was very large, very dark, and very old, crouching

along its high-ground position, hidden away by its encircling trees; inside, the huge dark-paneled rooms seemed perilous. They were crowded with furniture, so much of it you could scarcely move; I lived in mortal terror of backing away into some little table and sending its many fiddly ornaments crashing to the ground. Everywhere you looked there were dangers of this kind: staring portraits that spied on your every mistake; tapestries that might conceal some hidden watcher; and—according to Beatrice—at least one ghost, a beautiful ancestress of hers, who crept up behind you in corridors, and who, if you so much as glimpsed her, struck you instantly blind.

I thought it very ugly, and I thought it very *airless*, in fact the question of the air at Manderley obsessed me. My years in India had made me a connoisseur of air. My mother and the other officers' wives never ceased discussing it; there was bad air, and good air, as I knew, and every summer we would retreat north to the hill-stations to escape the "bad air" that brought with it all kinds of ailments and hidden disease.

So, when my nurse, Tilly, informed me, with a wink, that the de Winters needed an *heir*, I thought I understood her. The need for *air* at Manderley was all too obvious to me: Despite the size of the windows, despite the proximity of the sea, I'd never been in a house that felt so stifling. No wonder poor Virginia was an invalid: The air in the house, clammy, thick, reverberant, as if weighted down with centuries of secrets, was enough to make anyone ill. It was a bad, disease-ridden poxy sort of atmosphere; whenever I was there I'd try to persuade Beatrice to go down to the sea, down to the bay where, all those years later, Rebecca died.

Indeed, the house needed an "air," as Tilly said—and a good air, a special air, too, beautiful as the zephyrs my grandfather had shown me pictures of in his books. I used to imagine a zephyr like that whenever I was trapped and hemmed in in that awful drawing room, being teased by the boisterous bullying Lionel, who *would* ruffle my hair, or—worse—being interrogated by that mother of his, the "Termagant" as Tilly had nicknamed her.

Lionel de Winter, fortunately, was often away. He was given to moods, and sulks, and, when I did encounter him, would often complain of how boring his life was here. "Backward, stick-in-the-mud sort of place," he'd say. "Don't you find that? Nothing to do; rains all

the time. I'm off to London next week—lots of plays, parties, good
food and wine. Get away from the old girl's apron strings, if you follow my meaning. . . . I expect you know how that feels, eh, boy?"

And here he might wink, or slap me on the shoulder, man-to-man,
and I would say, "Yes, sir," but I didn't follow his meaning at all. Who
was the "old girl"? His mother, or poor Virginia? Neither of them
wore aprons. I thought Lionel, with his flushed face, his sulks, and
silk waistcoats, was an idiot and a popinjay. I didn't like the tone he
used when addressing his wife—it was very domineering and rude;
my own father would never have dreamed of speaking to my mother
in that way. And I was first hurt, then angered, that he never once
asked after my father, his former friend. He was obviously not in the
least interested in his welfare—but then he showed no interest in
anyone's welfare except his own.

The Termagant was another matter. She was a great deal more
intelligent than her son—I think I realized that by instinct, and very
quickly, as children do. She ruled the roost, and had no intention of
taking herself off to the dower house, Tilly maintained. She felt for
poor Mrs. Lionel, she really did, Tilly said; stuck with a husband and
a mother-in-law like that—she wouldn't be in her shoes, not for all
the tea in China, Tilly declared.

The Termagant was very tall, and her voice was very loud. Everyone, including her son, was terrified of her. She seemed to me to
know only two forms of conversation: either she was barking orders
or firing questions at you: How old are you? Why doesn't that
mother of yours have your hair cut? Do you ride? You *read*? A boy
your age? Lionel never bothered with books—what's the matter with
you? You should run around more. Tell me about India—do you miss
India? Why? When's that father of yours coming back? Is he ill?
Everyone in India gets ill sooner or later. He isn't? Then he's a lucky
man. . . .

And then would follow a diatribe, for she seemed to hate the very
idea of India—for no very good reason, I think, beyond the fact that
it was outside her circle of influence. She was fiercely dismissive of
what she called, with a wave of the hand, "abroad." One memorable
day, when Virginia's sisters came to tea in the Manderley gardens,
and Evangeline spoke of her recent honeymoon in France, and
pretty, charming Isolda sighed and said wistfully that she would love

to travel, Lionel's mother called them fools. "What fools you are," she said, gesturing across the lawns toward the sea: "You'll see nothing lovelier than this, however far you travel. Much better to stay here."

Evangeline gave her a cool look and raised her eyebrows; poor Virginia sighed; pretty Isolda made a face the instant her back was turned. When the elder Mrs. de Winter was called back to the house shortly afterward, the three sisters laughed.

"What an old *beast* she is—how can you put up with her, Virginia?" Isolda said, tossing back her curls.

"You should make a stand, darling—she's a monster," said Evangeline crossly.

"Hush," said poor Virginia, glancing at me and Beatrice: "*Pas devant les enfants.* Little pitchers have big ears. . . ."

I agreed with Isolda: Mrs. de Winter *was* an old beast—and that first summer, how she harped on the subject of India! I think she knew I resented it and that drove her on: dirt, disease, dishonesty (she was especially fierce on disease, looking at me as if I might be carrying half a continent's germs on my clothes). I would slowly inch away from her height, and her cold blue eyes, while all my precious memories of India shattered one by one under her terrible fusillade. That's when I would long for my zephyr, pray for my zephyr. That's when I would hang my head and screw up my eyes and conjure her out of the air. My zephyr (I can see now) bore more than a passing resemblance to Virginia's sister Isolda, with whom I was fiercely in love from the age of seven to nine: She was a glorious creature with long flowing hair; she swept into the stuffy room, shaking the heavy curtains with their fringing and frogging, fluttering the tapestries, rattling the doors. This was a zephyr powerful enough, and merciless enough, to topple the Termagant, and silence her forever more.

My grandfather used to say that I shouldn't mind, that Mrs. de Winter meant well, that her bark was worse than her bite, and so on—but my grandfather was a saintly man, and one of the limitations of saintliness is a tendency to excuse or underestimate such people. I thought Tilly was much nearer the mark when she declared the woman was a Tyrant and a Tartar; when she added that the Tartar's son, apple of her eye, wasn't no better than a Tomcat, I found it very interesting, indeed. I had noticed the tomcat sniffing around.

"I've heard tales about *him*," Tilly would say, rolling her eyes at our housekeeper, Mrs. Trevelyan (the source of quite a few of those tales, I suspect, Tilly's being from London and Mrs. Trevelyan's being local). I longed to hear those tales, needless to say, and that longing increased as time passed, but no one ever enlightened me. All I ever gleaned (and this was much later, when, desperate for information on this and any other adult subject, I took up a brief and unsuccessful career as an eavesdropper) was that blankets were mysteriously involved—especially the wrong side of them. What did tomcats have to do with blankets? Did a blanket *have* a wrong side?

As to the Termagant's interrogations, I used to believe at the time that my stammered answers were of little account. No matter my reply, the same questions would be asked again on my next visit. I now think that I was being assessed, and that Mrs. de Winter the elder wanted to get the measure of me, even then. She pushed simply to see how far she *could* push before I rebelled.

I never did—politeness and a fear of being rude to any adult were so deeply ingrained in me, so soaked into my very soul, that even when she made me cry, I did so in secret. I think she did this partly from habit—she spoke to everyone in this way—and partly because she gained knowledge by it, which she then stored up until such a time as it might be useful to her. And in my case, many years later, it was—but that particular episode (it was during the first war, in 1915, and it still shames me) I will return to another time.

Meanwhile, she was better informed than I had realized, and accurate in some of her suggestions, as I learned. My father was indeed ill, though that knowledge was carefully concealed from me. He contracted an enteric fever in Kashmir, recovered in a military hospital in Delhi, relapsed a few weeks later, and died one month before my sister Rose was born.

For a week, no one told me. I knew something was wrong: Something happened to the air at The Pines that reminded me of Manderley. It was full of whispers, and conversations broken off; doors slammed, feet ran back and forth along the corridors, Tilly's eyes were red, my grandfather's face was grave, and I wasn't allowed to see my mother—I could hear her weeping, but they said she was ill and locked her away.

Finally, my grandfather took me by the hand, led me down here to this terrace above the sea, and explained. He had lost his only son;

then, in the childish egotism of my grief, it didn't occur to me that he, too, had lost someone irreplaceable. Now, when I'm older than he was then, and have had tribulations of my own, I know how much it must have cost him to remain so quiet and so calm. When his explanation was over and my tears were done, he took my hand in his and asked me very gently if I thought I should like to live here now, with my mother, and the little brother or sister who would be shortly arriving, and whether I would let him look after me now that my dear father was gone.

I said yes, which brought on another storm of tears—and that is how I came to live here; that is how my bond with this part of the world was forged. I knew the place both before Rebecca and after her advent. I knew Maxim from birth; I remember seeing him as a baby, being pushed in his pram by poor, doting, proud Virginia. I remember the disbelief that greeted the announcement of his name—Maximilian!—and Tilly's prediction: "That old Termagant named him," she cried. "And she means to get her hands on him. Poor Mrs. Lionel won't get a look in, you mark my words!"

Tilly's prophecy proved correct. Poor Virginia had had innumerable miscarriages, as I know now, but, having produced an heir at last, she did not survive him long. She seemed to wither away, growing sadder and quieter day by day, her thin face lighting up only when her beloved son was brought to her. She died when Maxim was three, and I think (my sister Rose confirms) that Maxim clung tenaciously to the few sad half-memories he had of her.

He resembled his mother to a striking degree. Beatrice might have the de Winter looks, but in Maxim's narrow face and dark, intelligent, watchful eyes, Virginia and his Grenville ancestors lived on. He inherited aspects of her character, too; as a small child, he was quiet, dreamy, and shy, clearly fearful of his father, and in awe of his formidable grandmother. I remember him well as a boy, when my grandfather helped to tutor him in the summer holidays. Despite his obvious intelligence, he was backward at his lessons, perhaps because his grandmother held education in utter contempt, and was forever telling him that books were a waste of time. At Manderley, there was a splendid library, well stocked by some of Maxim's more enlightened ancestors, but the only books she ever consulted were those that detailed bloodstock—human and equine.

The elder Mrs. de Winter liked to imply that books, universities, and so on, were all very well for the likes of me: I had no land or estates, and would have to earn my living in some way. But Maxim would have all *this*, she would say, gesturing around that terrible drawing room of hers: This house, these fields, these farms, that sea were his destiny. All that mattered meanwhile was to get him into the same school every male de Winter had attended since time immemorial; once that small matter was out of the way, Maxim would return home and learn the only lesson that mattered: how to run Manderley.

Maxim was brainwashed in this way, day in, day out. I think that, thanks to my grandfather's influence—and, to a much lesser extent, mine—he did see that there was another world, a world elsewhere. But I always felt he looked at that world somewhat wistfully, as if he might like to investigate it, even yearned to investigate it, but already accepted that it was beyond his Manderley palisade. One summer, when I was at home for the university vacation, I took pity on him. He emerged white-faced from my grandfather's study and his struggles with Latin verbs, and when I asked him where he was off to, he replied he supposed he was going home. He looked lost and dejected, so I took him out in my dinghy and taught him to sail—and that was the first of the many trips we made across the bay to Manderley.

We'd always known each other, but it was that summer that we overcame the disparity in our ages, and became friends. Maxim would then have been about ten or eleven; I suppose that in some ways he looked up to me, and I grew attached to him, recommending books and generally taking him under my wing. My grandfather encouraged the friendship, believing that Maxim was lonely. I think that was true, certainly by the time he reached his midteens.

His father's illness first began to manifest itself then. It took an unpredictable—and unpleasant—form; until Lionel de Winter was finally persuaded to confine himself to his sickroom, visitors to Manderley were not encouraged, and when Maxim returned from school in the holidays, he spent long periods alone. By then, I had left the area, and was in the Army; my sister, Rose, closer to Maxim in age than I was, became his confidante in my stead, and for a brief period just before the first war became closer to him in other ways; Rose used to say—and still maintains—that Maxim was always lonelier than we knew.

How very near those years seem to me now! The lives of the de Winters have always overlapped and interlocked with my own; my study is filled with the evidence of that closeness, with letters, with photographs, invitation cards, all the flotsam and jetsam that, assembled, might tell their story. Thinking of that, sitting on my boundary wall this morning, I told myself that, if there were gaps in that story, they could be filled, so long as my memory did not let me down.

Somewhere there, if I could find her, was Rebecca. If she was to be understood, it was in the context of that family and that house. "Who are you?" I said to her once, not that long before her death, as it happens. "Who *are* you, Rebecca?"

"I'm the mistress of Manderley," she replied, with an enigmatic sidelong glance very characteristic of her. It was wintertime; we were walking one of the coast paths; Rebecca had paused close to the cliff edge; she was always careful with words. "Just like one of those Gothic romances," she went on, with a smile. "Don't you think that suits me? I do. Tell Max I want it on my gravestone—HERE LIES REBECCA, MISTRESS OF MANDERLEY. Or, REBECCA, LATE OF MANDERLEY, that would do. I want a plain stone, Cornish granite, with good, clear, simple lettering. I want to be in the churchyard, with a view of the sea—don't let them hide me away in that de Winter crypt, will you?"

"Anything else?" I said—and I expected more, for Rebecca was a perfectionist in everything. I was not taking this conversation seriously, though I should have been, I see now. Rebecca liked to tease me—I always found it hard to know when she was serious—and she was so young, just thirty. I was twenty years older. If anyone's funeral were on the agenda, it was likelier to be my own. "Flowers?" I went on. "Type of coffin? Hymns? Should I be a pallbearer?"

"Yes, I'd like that. As to the rest"—she looked away and frowned— "I don't care, not really. But I mind about the stone, and I mind about the churchyard. So don't forget, and don't back down when Max makes a face and says it's vulgar and unsuitable. . . ."

"And if I do?" I replied, with a smile.

"You'll regret it. I hate that crypt, and I hate the people in it. I'll come back and haunt you. I'll never rest there."

What could she have meant by that remark? Why would she hate the occupants of that crypt? She had known none of them. Even its most recent arrivals, Maxim's parents, had been there years before her marriage, years before Rebecca first came to Manderley. Did I ask her? If so, I was given no reply.

Five months later, she was dead. The following year, when her body was finally brought up from the sea, she was buried in the de Winter crypt in the little gray Saxon church one mile from Manderley. That terrible interment I've already described: the vicar stammering a hasty prayer; no hymns, no flowers; one so-called mourner, Frank Crawley, waiting by the car, and only Maxim and myself attending the coffin. We buried her in the evening, in the midst of a summer storm. The sky was overcast, with a livid hue on the horizon. She wasn't even laid in what might have seemed her rightful place, next to Maxim's parents, next to Lionel and poor Virginia. Maxim had other ideas. So she was secreted away in the darkest and most remote corner of that unhappy place, a section as yet unoccupied by other coffins, divided from the other ancestral husbands and wives by a thick pillar and a sagging masonry arch.

I hadn't forgotten my undertaking, but in the face of Maxim's anger, I had backed down. It was the first of my betrayals, maybe. And Rebecca did indeed come back to haunt me, but then—in my experience—she was always true to her word.

FIVE

I SAT THERE ON MY WALL ABOVE THE SEA WATCHING THIS past of mine for a half hour that lasted decades; I'd known that if I listened to the dead well enough, they'd point me in the right direction. I felt restored, ready to tackle the next items on my tasklist—it was beginning to get chilly on my wall anyway. We may enjoy the benefits of a Gulf Stream climate here in Kerrith, but spring breezes off the water play havoc with the joints, and April is a cruel month as far as my rheumatism is concerned. I levered myself to my feet. Time to open my parcel, I thought—and I must telephone Gray, too. Barker stretched and yawned (he really is a most indolent dog); together we set off down the path to the house. Delicious cooking smells were wafting from the kitchen: Ellie was making bread.

I inspected my nicely stumped roses for any signs of greenfly (one can never start spraying too soon) and congratulated myself on how neat they looked since I took charge of them. They are so-called old roses of the kind garden snobs approve, and were originally planted by my mother—in 1900, to celebrate the new century. They were scions of the famous Grenville rose collection, from the gardens of their house, St. Winnow's, farther up river from here; the cuttings were made by their gardener, and presented to my mother by one of those three Grenville sisters: not Maxim's mother, poor Virginia, who was dead by then, and not pretty little Isolda who broke my nine-year-old heart, for she had left the area and married—disastrously, people said—so it must have been Evangeline.

Both my mother and my late wife loved and cherished these roses, not least for their "romantic" names, many of them French—in fact, I believe some of the roses had originally come from France, where the Grenvilles had relatives. *Honorine de Brabant, Duchesse d'Angoulême, Cuisses de Nymphe* . . . names that do not sound quite so fine in translation: "Nymph's Thighs." *Preposterous*, I used to think. Despite my protests, the womenfolk gave the roses free rein. They grew into vast fecund bushes that threatened to take over the entire garden; I'd snip bits off when I thought no one was looking—they were viciously thorned and in my view needed hacking back hard.

In June, when they were at their best (the only time they *were* at their best; they looked at their worst for the other eleven months of the year), people made pilgrimages here to admire them. Rebecca, burying her face in one of the flowers—a deep crimson one, I forget its name—once told me that she didn't expect ever to go to heaven, but if she did, it would smell like this. Heaven scent, she said; its color, she added, was precisely that of a Pomerol wine. I looked at her coldly. "Oh really? Which?" I said.

My tone was short. I didn't know her at all well in those days—this incident took place shortly after I'd taken early retirement, and returned to The Pines with my family from my last posting in Singapore. It must have been June, so Rebecca would have been married to my friend Maxim for only three or four months; I'd met her maybe twice. I was suspicious of her, for no very good reason. I was suspicious of most young women, especially charming ones. I remember thinking these raptures were either an affectation on her part or a tease (and if you didn't realize when she was teasing you, she could make you look a complete fool, so you had to keep your wits about you, as I've said).

She and Maxim had arrived at The Pines in the early evening, on that occasion. I think my wife, who liked Rebecca, had suggested she might want to see the garden, and they dropped in en route to some party. I was deputed to show Rebecca the roses; Maxim, who'd seen them a thousand times, remained indoors talking to my wife. I wasn't pleased at this suggestion. I was not in a gallant mood that night. So in the cool of the scented evening air, with the sea whispering in the distance, I marched mutinously up and down the paths, murdering the romantic names with an accent that was anything but French. Maxim's young wife, for some reason, made me self-conscious and stiff. I found her exotic and strange. As I was already discovering, she seemed to have no idea whatsoever of conventional social niceties, and you never knew what odd and unexpected thing she might say next.

As she paused to bend over the roses, every shade from the deepest crimson through soft mauves to flesh pink, I stole covert glances at her. I know nothing about women's clothes, and care less, but even I could see that the dress she was wearing was an exquisite thing; later, with a sigh, my wife would inform me that it was Chanel, purchased in Paris, and the last word in chic. It was made of some heavy slubby material that I suppose was silk, and it was very, very plain—*Understated, Arthur, dear,* my wife patiently said. Above its boat-shaped neckline, I could see the bluish hollows below Rebecca's collarbone; she was wearing a famous de Winter necklace, of pinkish pearls, around her delicate throat, and the dress also was pink—but not any pink I'd ever seen before. It was the softest, palest blush pink, almost the colour of skin; I found I was looking at it hard, trying to find a word for the color, when the right term, *exactly* the right term, suddenly rose up in my head unbidden: *Cuisses de Nymphe . . .*

I reddened, moved off a few paces, and attempted to speed up this rose inspection; I looked at my watch. But Rebecca was not to be hurried. She continued to walk between the roses in a slow intent way, bending over them, inspecting the formation of their petals, and inhaling their scent. She looked serious, intent, and impossibly young. It struck me that for all the sophistication of her dress, and despite her height—she was tall and exceptionally slender—she looked like a child, a very beautiful grave child plucked from some foreign place, and set down here in a country where no one knew her customs or spoke her language or understood her race.

I felt a sudden pulse of protectiveness toward her, which disconcerted me. She turned to look at me, inspecting my face; I had the unpleasant sensation that she could read my mind, that she perhaps found me dull or deeply absurd—she'd given no indication of this, but I felt an obscure need to retaliate. Wishing to snub her, bristling and on edge, I became increasingly curt. She made her remark about roses and wine, and I made my snide reply. It was meant to put her in her place, and of course she knew that. She straightened up from the rose and frowned slightly; her extraordinary and unreadable eyes rested on my face. She told me the name of the wine she'd meant (her French accent, unlike mine, was perfectly correct). She said she knew it well because it was one of her father's favorite wines. Then she left.

That was the only occasion, ever, when she mentioned her father to me, but I wasn't to know then how unusual a remark it was. When she'd gone, I was irritable—and curious. I went down to my cellar (well-stocked), found I had a bottle of the particular wine she'd named, and fetched it up. I poured out a glass, and held it against the rose. It was indeed the same color, and Rebecca had been entirely accurate. Very few women are accurate, in my experience, and even fewer of them know the least thing about wine. For these reasons, I paid greater attention to her than I had done after that.

"Did you check? Was I right?" she said to me the next time I saw her. The occasion was some Manderley garden party. It was several weeks later. It was very hot. Rebecca was wearing another exquisite garment, this time the color of milk; her face, arms, and throat were lightly tanned, which shocked me deeply. Women avoided the sun in those days and prized white skin. It was the mark of a lady, people said. This fashion was about to change, but Rebecca cared little for fashionable dictates—she simply did as she liked. She was not wearing gloves or a hat—and I found this nakedness shocking, too.

"Yes I did. And yes, you were," I said.

I could have pretended I didn't understand her reference—there was no prompting or preamble prior to the sudden question—but I felt obscurely that I was being tested, and I was suddenly very anxious to pass that test.

"Good." She gave a small approving nod, leaving me to decide whether she was pleased at this confirmation of her accuracy or pleased that I'd bothered to check. She slipped her arm through mine—the dress was short sleeved, and her arm was bare. "You thought I was pretentious," she went on. "Don't bother denying it. You had a perfect right to think that—you don't know me yet."

I made some fatuous reply. I can't remember, and don't want to remember, what it was, but it was complimentary and patronizing, and prefixed with a "My dear" that made me sound, and was designed to make me sound, like a pompous old stick. I was just forty-six at the time, not *that* much older than Rebecca's husband, but for some reason found it safer to pretend I was sixty-six. It was a disguise I'd been perfecting for a decade at least.

"I'm glad I was right, though," she continued, ignoring my remark—she knew she had me on the run, I expect. "If I'd been wrong, you'd have dismissed me out of hand. Crossed me off your list. Then we'd never have made friends—and that would have been a sad waste. I want friends. And look—apart from you, there isn't a single candidate."

With a mischievous glance, she gestured toward a group of other guests, standing on the terrace. Maxim and his sister Beatrice were there; I spotted Frank Crawley, Maxim's friend from the first war, now his estate manager; there were several spinsters of the parish, including my cronies, Elinor and Jocelyn Briggs, daughters of the former Evangeline Grenville. There was a clutch of the usual county families; the bishop was present . . . and there were all too many dull old coves wearing panama hats and suits exactly like mine; there was a positive invasion of Colonel Julyan doppelgängers, which depressed me a bit.

I could recognize all the people there; most of them were infernal bores, and I'd been skulking in the shrubbery in a desperate attempt to avoid them. I expect Rebecca knew that. But what happened next? Rebecca returned to her guests, I suppose, for, despite her remarks, she was assiduous on such occasions. I was flattered, though I think flattery was not Rebecca's intention. And we did become friends—for which state, I suppose, I have these roses to thank.

I looked for the heaven scent rose now—was it the third on the left, or the fourth? The labels have long gone, and I couldn't be sure, and besides, thanks to my unconventional pruning techniques the roses look very different now. What were once great billowing bushes bowed down with flowers are now small twiggy affairs that reach knee height. I like flowers in serried ranks, as if drawn up on a parade ground. This taste is not universally shared, of course.

There was a small danger that I might take this failure to locate the rose as an omen: I find I'm now given to seeing omens at every turn; I'm also becoming superstitious. I catch myself walking ostentatiously around ladders, or knocking on wood like some damn woodpecker. This is not a good sign. If softening of the brain (and what an unpleasant phrase that is when one thinks about it) first manifests itself in this way, I'm alarmed. I do not intend to give in to weaknesses of that foolish kind. I stumped up to the French windows in a purposeful way. "Barker—*down*," I said, very firmly indeed, pointing at the hearth rug. Barker walked round the room four times, scratched himself, looked at me soulfully, and, finally, having demonstrated his independence of mind as he likes to do, lay down and went to sleep.

I reached for the telephone to speak to Gray—I'd decided Terence Gray could definitely be useful to me; given his interest in Manderley matters, I could do worse than co-opt him, and make him my assistant on my new "quest." Before I took him into my confidence, though, I'd stick to my resolve, and watch how he conducted himself on our Manderley walk. Then I remembered that I *still* hadn't invited him for this walk. I began to dial his number, then changed my mind. I had forgotten all about my package, I realized, picking it up and examining it. Bound to be bumf, I said to myself, but even so I felt a little thrill of anticipation. I'd have felt a great deal more, had I known what the content was.

Inside the envelope was a small black-covered exercise book, smaller than, but similar to, those once used in schools. It had an unusual detail, in that it fastened shut with its own attached leather laces, which wrapped around its width, and were tied in a neat bow on its spine.

For reasons I then couldn't put my finger on, this notebook looked familiar—and it engendered an unspecific but definite unease. I felt around in the envelope. I held the book by its spine, undid the laces, and shook it; to my surprise, an old sepia picture postcard of Manderley fell out. I saw that this had come loose from the notebook's back page. There was nothing written on the card, however, and there was no letter enclosed with the little book. Curiouser and curiouser: an anonymous offering, then.

I could already see that most, if not all, of the pages were blank. My unease deepening—who would send me an empty notebook anonymously, and why?—I laid it down on my orderly desk to examine it more closely. It was not entirely empty after all: One page, the first page, had been decorated. A small black-and-white photograph had been pasted in.

This photograph, somewhat faded and with sepia tones, showed a small child—a girl. She appeared to be around seven or eight. She had an abundance of tumbled, inky, gypsyish hair, unusually large eyes, very striking eyes, and a suspicion of paint about the lips; they were far too marked and voluptuous to be their natural color. I frowned. I do not approve of women's wearing makeup, and I certainly don't approve of face paint on would-be appealing little girls. This child, to give her the benefit of the doubt, might have been taking part in some amateur theatricals, or had perhaps been dolled up for some fancy-dress party—or so I realized on inspecting the photograph more closely, with my magnifying lens. I then saw that, affixed to this curious child's back, were a pair of wired, gauzy, spangled wings.

Fairy? Imp? Angel? It was impossible to be sure what the costume had been intended to convey, and the child's expression was certainly not angelic. It was difficult to date the picture, too, but from the style of the painted backdrop behind her (some canvas studio artifice by the look of it, featuring lushly unlikely foliage and funereal urns) I decided it had been taken at least forty years before; this little fairy had donned her wings around 1910 or 1912—certainly before the first war.

I did not recognize her. I will write that again. *I did not recognize her.* Now I can see that the resemblance of this child to the woman I knew was evident—hair and eyes were unmistakable even then. Now I can see that I should have made the connection at once. After all, not a day has gone by in twenty-five years without my thinking of her. But, at the time, puzzled, uneasy, and flustered, I could not see the resemblance. Not until I turned the page and discovered the two title words written down in an otherwise empty notebook. They were written in black ink, in a child's spiky hand, the tail of the last letter curling down the page in a long punning flourish: *Rebecca's Tale.*

I was shaken—very shaken. Who wanted to torment me now, and why? I'm ashamed to admit it, but I will: My first thought was that Rebecca herself had sent this, that it was a communication from the grave. I felt dizzy for a moment. I looked at the words *Rebecca's Tale,* and my desk tilted. Could it be her handwriting? Was this, in embryo, the hand I knew so well? I thought it was. I looked at the size and swoop of the capital letters: I thought of that small coffin, that *child's* coffin in my dream.

I was very agitated. My heart started its bumping and thumping routine again. When I was sure I was more composed, I examined the sepia picture postcard. It had once been glued in on the final page, and the glue marks seemed old. I had never seen that particular post-card of Manderley before, and its presence in the notebook puzzled me. As far as I knew, Rebecca had no connection with this area in childhood and had never visited it, so why would she paste a picture of Manderley in a notebook she'd had as a young girl?

The handwriting on the envelope bore no resemblance to Rebecca's, or to the writing in the notebook, as I would have realized at once had the shock been less acute. The postmark was indecipher-able. I examined the very ordinary heavy-duty envelope. It could have been bought anywhere in the country, in any one of a thousand stationery shops or village stores; I had a similar batch in my own desk drawers. I looked at the postmark through my magnifying lens; one of the letters might conceivably have been a "K," though it could have been an "E."

I stared at this evidence. A sudden suspicion came to me, and I at once placed my call to Terence Gray.

I made no mention of the lunch Ellie had proposed: Let the per-sistent Terence (or the Terrier or the Terror, as I sometimes call him) fend for himself. I had mixed feelings toward Gray at the best of times, and at that precise moment was not at all kindly inclined to him. Could he possibly have sent me this? If so, why? I'd get the answers to those questions, I resolved, before the day was out.

"Has something happened, Colonel Julyan?" he asked as I made a few weather remarks. "There's nothing wrong, I hope? You sound very agitated, sir."

I ignored the question. I proposed the afternoon walk, as planned. I said nothing of notebooks anonymously sent, nothing of winged children, and nothing of my dream. As expected, Mr. Mysteryman agreed at once.

"I'm coming over to lunch anyway, sir," he said. "I thought you'd know. Ellie called me earlier. So, I'll see you about twelve-thirty. I'll look forward to it, Colonel Julyan. There's a great deal to tell you. I heard from Jack Favell this morning. He called me from London, and he's agreed to see me at last. Oh, and I went over to see Frith yesterday, at that nursing home you mentioned. . . ."

"You did *what*?" I said.

"I went to see Frith, sir. At St. Winnow's. He's very frail, of course, but you're mistaken as to his being senile. Whoever told you that was *quite* wrong. His memory was excellent. We talked for two hours, and he gave me some fascinating material. . . ."

Material? I hung up. Two shocks within half an hour was too much. Frith, whom I'd crossed off my witness list earlier, is one hundred and ninety years old—and that's a conservative estimate. He was always a de Winter apologist; he never liked Rebecca, whom he regarded as an interloper; in short, the one-time butler is an unreliable witness and, if not gaga, a snob, a snoop, a fossil, and an inveterate nincompoop.

Gray had no business to consult him without my being present, and the fact that he'd done so alarmed me. Gray has demonstrated these unilateral tendencies before (he went off to London to pursue his de Winter researches last week, and I still don't know why, though it's not for want of asking). Now, in the blink of an eye, he was about to see that liar Favell, and he'd *already* talked to Frith. Sometimes, I feel Gray plays his cards very close to his chest. Frith knows a great deal about me, as well as the de Winter family, and if he talked for two hours—*two hours!*—heaven only knows what rigmarole he chose to invent.

Could Gray be devious? That suspicion has crossed my mind more than once. Ellie will have none of it, of course. She claims I read too many detective stories; she says I'm getting unnaturally suspicious, and I'll start suspecting her of plotting next. She is always trumpeting Gray's virtues, chief of which (according to her) are neither his conspicuous good looks nor his unmarried status, but his kindness toward me. "He takes you out of yourself," she says. "It's good for you to have someone to talk to about the past and Manderley and . . . and so on. Especially when he's so interested in the subject himself. Don't be such a curmudgeon. He bucks you up—you said so yourself."

This particular refrain was repeated several times this morning. Ellie had changed her clothes, I noted. In honor of the Terrier, she was now twenty-one, that is, ten years younger than she was yester-day, and ten times prettier to boot. How do women effect these transformations? For once, she was sensibly dressed, not in trousers (she *will* wear trousers) but in a modest skirt and a plain blouse; she was wearing the string of pearls her mother and I had given her to mark her twenty-first. She looked innocent, mischievous, and radi-ant. Her soft brown hair was newly washed; her skin glowed; there was a brilliance to her candid eyes that made me fear for her. I want a happy future for Ellie, and I cannot bear the thought that in the pur-suit of happiness she could be hurt.

Ellen, my Ellie, is all I have left. My wife, Elizabeth, died during the war, after years of illness; my son Jonathan's fighter plane went down, and was never recovered, two weeks before the armistice; my elder daughter, Lily, from whom I was estranged, died in childbirth in Australia five years since, her baby son surviving her for only two weeks. I never refer to this Greekish sequence of events, and I will not do so again here. I will merely state the obvious: I can hope and plan for no one now, except Ellie—and I thought deeply of my dear-est Ellie during the course of the morning as I waited for Gray to arrive for lunch.

I was at a loose end. I pottered about, first in my study, then in my garden, then in the kitchen, where I was a nuisance and got under Ellie's feet. Somehow I could not settle. I was worried about Ellie's future, haunted by that winged child in the photograph; once again I felt old, seedy, and maladroit. My fine resolve of the night before now seemed less and less possible. Write the truth? What was the truth? Perhaps it was not the past, but the present, with which I should concern myself.

Then I was struck by an idea: If I did co-opt Gray, as provisionally planned, if I involved him in my Rebecca "quest," he would of neces-sity have to visit The Pines more often. Ellie would then encounter him more often. That might not altogether please me, but it would certainly please her. We live quite a solitary life and Ellie does not get out much. This magnanimity on my part immediately made me feel perkier. I returned from a sortie to the melancholy monkey puzzle with a new spring in my step.

Terence Gray was just arriving as I reached the house. And Ellie, who had been slaving in the kitchen all morning, making bread and a chicken pie, was informing him—without batting an eyelid—that he would have to take pot luck. I was delighted at this innocent deception. Like father, like daughter, I said to myself. I may be getting on in years, but all my faculties are still intact. I fought in the first war, and was back in harness, breaking codes, in the second. I'm still a wily old fox, I told myself. I felt I was more than a match for Gray, well able to steer him in the right direction, and well able to deal with any unilateral tendencies he might choose to manifest.

It wouldn't take me long to find out exactly what old Frith had told him, I decided—and with that comforting intention (among others) I plied Gray with a glass of my latest bargain sherry (not too bad at all; a bit on the sweet side, but a discovery nonetheless); then, taking his gray-suited arm by the elbow, I led him most affably into my study for a little chin-wag before lunch.

S I X

So how was old Frith then?" I said. No point in beating about the bush. "Learn anything interesting? Warm enough in here for you, is it, Gray? Nasty nip in the air this morning, I thought. Ellie got the fire going for me. How's the sherry? I hope it's to your taste?"

I had installed myself with my back to the fire, which was blazing away in a very satisfactory manner. Gray, as he tends to do when he comes here, was wandering around the room preparatory to settling himself. His eyes rested on my bookshelves, which cover all four walls just as they did in my grandfather's day, and which are stacked floor to ceiling with a fine array of books. Before beginning any conversation with me, Gray likes to make a brief circuit of these shelves—and this morning was no exception. As usual, he began prowling about, peering at titles. I smiled to myself. Some visitors, as I've often observed, like to "read" one's bookshelves, and make all kinds of rash deductions from them as to a man's character, intellectual leanings, and so on. Gray is one such. Since I find the habit irritating, I'd made some alterations to the arrangements of these shelves since his last visit. I'd prepared a little *test* for him and was intrigued: Would he notice, or not?

On the left, as you enter, are the older volumes, leather bound, that formed the backbone of my grandfather's library. Gray, passing by, gave them a cursory look. Beyond them, by the bay window, come the sections devoted to natural history, military history, and the morocco-bound immortals my grandfather taught me to love, first the Greeks and then the Romans. Ellie keeps these dusted, but they don't get read very often, I'm afraid. I was well-tutored by my grandfather, however, so I can still recite by heart great tracts of the *Iliad*. Barker is my only audience for these rousing recitations—and just as well, I expect.

Gray paused by this section, then moved on to the far corner, where these deities join hands with their English counterparts. Here we begin with Chaucer and Malory: His *Le Morte d'Arthur*, much thumbed, was my mother's favorite book, and mine, as a child. I owe to Malory my Christian names of Arthur and (God help us: I keep quiet about this) Lancelot.

Gray dallied by Camelot, then moved more swiftly past all the obvious staging posts: Shakespeare, Milton, Dryden, Pope—all the poetry collections my dead son loved. He paused thoughtfully in the dark corner where the Romantics languish on a high shelf, came to a halt at Housman, and began on the novels. There, on the far wall, we romp through the eighteenth century via Sterne and the incomparable Fielding, dwell at length with Walter Scott, hop over that prissy Austen woman, skedaddle past those blasted Brontës, and finally reach the promised land, viz Dickens and Hardy. As grand finale, we have a seasoning of Russians, one or two German interlopers, and a couple of crafty Frenchmen who, in my opinion (which I never voice, obviously), are unbeatable on sex.

Last, on the returning wall, which need not detain us (though it did detain Gray), we have a bit of a mishmash, namely the books I find useful at the moment. They include Tennyson; Conan Doyle (another Arthur!); Miss Agatha Christie; Shakespeare's *Complete Works*; a volume written by my grandfather entitled *History of the Parishes of Manderley and Kerrith, with Walks*; Bowman's classic 1930 *Great Murder Trials of Our Era*; both of the books on the "Manderley Mystery"; the 1890 edition of the *Boys' Own Bumper Book of Adventure Stories*; and the complete works of Marcel Proust.

It was in this final section that I'd made alterations since Gray was last here. Would he spot the red herrings? Could he spot the *clues*?

He misses very little and has a formidable memory. I caught a glint of amusement in his eyes; he took one of the volumes from the shelf (well spotted, Mr. Gray, you pass the test!) and smiled. Then—as I had also anticipated—he made a casual pass by my desk.

It is orderly, as I've said, and I had left my morning's parcel in a conspicuous position. There was the envelope, and—right in the center—there was the black exercise book, closed, and with its leather ties fastened up. I watched Gray closely. No sign of a reaction. This, unfortunately, did not tell me very much, since a) he may genuinely not have noticed, and b) he is a very cool customer in any case.

He hove to, finally, by the fireside next to me, where he bent down to give Barker a pat and receive in return a malodorous lick. Barker was fonder of Gray than I was at this point; I was reserving judgment. Much depended on how Gray handled his cutlery at luncheon, what he said about Frith, and his demeanor once I revealed Manderley to him on our walk. I had given myself until the end of the day to make up my mind—and I did make up my mind, though not quite in the way I had anticipated, as will become evident in due course.

Gray has excellent hearing, but can affect a peculiar deafness on occasion. This was one of them. Somehow, he heard my inquiry as to the sherry, but not my inquiry as to the perkiness or otherwise of antediluvian Frith. He held up his glass to the light, took a sip, suffered a brief coughing fit, and said, "Hmm, most . . . unusual. Where did you get hold of it, Colonel Julyan?"

"Glad you like it," I said. "The Briggs sisters put me on to it. Some fellow over at Tregarron let them have a case. Fell off the back of a boat, I gather. . . ." I tapped my nose. "Remarkably reasonable. The Briggses were feeling guilty about it, so they seemed quite keen to off-load a bottle or six."

"Black market. Well, well . . . ," said Gray, taking another sip. "The color is remarkable, sir. And the taste . . . I can't find the words to describe it. . . ." He bent down to pat Barker again, which I felt was unnecessary. He wandered off to the window, remarking what a fine day it was. I did not intend to tolerate this.

"So what did old Frith have to *say*?" I repeated, more forcefully this time. "You should have mentioned you were popping over there, I'd have been glad to come with you. Years since I've seen him—must

be fifteen at least . . . Did he talk about Lionel de Winter at all—
Maxim's father? He was devoted to him—he helped nurse Lionel in
his final illness, was there when he died in 1914—"

"Nineteen fifteen, sir. I think."

"Yes. Yes. Had a bit of a tendency to harp on about it, as I recall.
Somewhat morbid, I feel, our old friend Frith."

"Really? I didn't notice that. He did mention Lionel de Winter
once or twice, but only in passing. He's lonely, of course, but he
seemed remarkably cheerful. He's wheelchair bound now, but very
sprightly—keeps the nurses on their toes."

I could imagine that only too well: Frith who had once marshaled
an army of Manderley servants; Frith who could spot a speck of dust
at a hundred paces. The word "sprightly," I found, made me curiously depressed. Only someone young would select it. Gray is somewhere in his thirties. I wasn't sure I liked the word "lonely," either.
Could Gray think of me as lonely, too? That would be intolerable. I
took a good swallow of the sherry; it had a most peculiar undertaste,
somewhere between fish and syrup; it was alarming at first, but was
definitely improving now the air had got at it. On I pressed.

"So, did he mention Rebecca at all?" I said, affecting nonchalance.

"I expect he did. He had a bit of a 'thing' about her, as a matter of fact."

"A 'thing,' sir?"

"Well, he never liked her—I must have mentioned that? Resented
her, in fact. She brought in Mrs. Danvers as housekeeper, and that
put Frith's nose right out of joint. Having a housekeeper that actually
stood up to him—old Frith wasn't too keen on that. Not that Mrs. D.
could be faulted. She ran her side of things superbly—and that
annoyed him even more, I always thought. I hope you bore all that in
mind, Gray. What's more, if you're going to see that blasted Jack
Favell—*are* you going to see Favell?"

"I am. He's finally agreed, after stalling me for weeks. He's now
decided he wants to see me as soon as possible. So I'm going up to
London on Friday morning."

"Well, I hope you remember the advice I've given you all along.
You can't trust Frith—and you *certainly* can't trust Favell. He'll feed
you a pack of lies. You should take his testimony with a fistful of salt.
I've warned you a hundred times, Gray—watch out for the biased
witness!"

"Indeed you have warned me, sir," Gray replied. "And I remember that particular piece of advice constantly. It's never far from my thoughts."

Dry. His manner was dry. His tone was definitely dry. It could be said to have verged on the sarcastic, though I fail to see why. I was about to take him up on this dryness of his when Ellie, somewhat flushed from her exertions in the kitchen, popped her head around the door and announced lunch.

"Ellie, my dear, there you are!" I said. "I was wondering where you'd got to. Let me pour you a glass of sherry."

This innocuous statement was a bit of a blind, I'll admit. I knew only too well where Ellie had been, since meat rationing makes things very difficult, and she makes a palaver about preparing a meal on the occasions—all too rare now—when we have guests. Ellie had been in the kitchen, with her head in the Aga, or with her hands in the sink. She'd been peeling and parboiling and whisking and stirring—and I don't like outsiders to know this. Ellie says I'm being absurd, that scarcely anyone has a cook nowadays, let alone a maid, and anyway she *likes* cooking and cleaning, so why should I try to hide such things? There is no answer to this, other than the fact that such work makes me ashamed, and, no matter how hard I try, I cannot overcome this.

If I were of a different generation, perhaps; if I weren't bitterly conscious that such activities advertise the puniness of my pension, that they betray my pathetic caution with investments, so what was once a good and sufficient private income has been sucked down in the marshland of gilts . . . The long and short of it is that money is a bit on the tight side, and I'd die rather than let Gray or anyone else know this.

Ellie's eyes flew to Gray's face. Her color deepened. Ellie is very protective of me and my weaknesses, and I was pretty sure she was searching Gray's face for the least sign of satire. "I don't think I will have any sherry, thank you, Daddy," she began. "I'm sure it's delicious, but . . ."

"I recommend it," Gray said, and, his eyes meeting Ellie's, he smiled. This endorsement seemed to do the trick.

"Oh, well, why not?" she said, smiling in return. "Just half a glass, but no more, or it will make me indiscreet."

This confession was somehow very charming. I think Gray was charmed—I certainly caught that glint of amusement in his eyes again. His unfortunate dryness of manner seemed to disappear at once, and he warmed up, chatting to Ellie in a polite way about this and that. Ignoring his demurrals, I topped up his glass as a reward. Some ten or so minutes later, Ellie announced that the pie would not wait much longer, and that the first course was potted shrimps—my favorite. With this, my own manner thoughtful, we went through to the dining room (I had vetoed the kitchen) and sat down to a fine lunch.

I'd just been reminded yet again how slippery a customer Gray is. You no sooner impale him on the hook than he wriggles off. It's harder to get a straight answer out of him than almost anyone I know—other than myself. Obviously, he was hiding something. The question was—what?

SEVEN

I WILL COME TO OUR LUNCH, AND OUR SUBSEQUENT WALK in the Manderley woods, presently. The afternoon's events were strange, even revelatory, but they left me in a very perturbed state, and I want to be sure I feel up to the task of recording them—as I must. Meantime, as promised, I see I must deal with a connected matter—Terence Gray himself. I'd intended Gray to play a minor role in my narrative, I saw him as secretary-cum-sidekick, as Watson to my Holmes. But events later that day were to change my attitude. They made me realize that Gray was *crucial* to my Rebecca "quest." I've perhaps been reluctant to deal with the question of the Terrier, or the Terror, but I must now bite the bullet. He must be explained and introduced.

Gray first arrived in Kerrith roughly six months ago, at a time when my own fortunes were at a low ebb. I'd been laid up after suffering episodes of dizziness, and one mysterious collapse. Our good doctor, an alarmist, diagnosed a minor heart attack. I disagreed with this verdict, and still do, but no one listened to me, and I was confined to barracks forthwith.

My "cure" was to consist of horse pills, none of which made the slightest difference, absence of all anxiety, and rest. I've never been a good patient, and this regime made me "difficult," I confess. I was crochety and bored; my anxieties spiraled; it was then I began to suffer from nightmares, and I became very depressed. The situation was not helped by the weather, which was atrocious, one of the worst winters I ever remember, and by what I viewed as Ellie's overprotectiveness. It rained. Day after day it rained, and I sat here by the fire, thinking about Rebecca, trying to think of ways in which I could make amends for my past failures—in short, being feeble and feeling sorry for myself.

I think I made life very hard for Ellie—in fact, I know I did. I wish I could pretend that age and illness evinced sudden nobility of character on my part, but I can't. I turned into someone I disliked, and the more I disliked myself, the worse it was. Ellie grew quite desperate, I think, and I know she consulted my old friends the Briggs sisters, the daughters of Lady Briggs, formerly Evangeline Grenville. The sisters Elinor and Jocelyn are both spinsters, and as I've mentioned, my great cronies and chief informants in this neighbourhood. A plot was hatched. As a result, one teatime in the midst of a howling December gale, a newcomer to Kerrith, Terence Gray, was introduced.

Into my study strode a tall dark-haired young man with a firm handshake, a faint trace of an accent—lowlands Scottish, I thought—and a preadvertised interest in local history. He had been "looking forward to meeting me and hearing my stories of Manderley," the Briggs sisters declared; they had been longing to "get us together." I took this with a fistful of salt. I noticed Gray made Ellie blush when he addressed her, and I was displeased to observe that the Briggs sisters (indefatigable matchmakers, both of them) also noticed this. I came to the conclusion that it wasn't entirely for my own welfare that Mr. Gray had been introduced. I eyed the interloper sternly, refused to be charmed, and was curt.

After he left, Ellie and I had a row—which happens very rarely. I was less than kind about Gray's accent, clothes, haircut, manner of drinking tea, et cetera. I made some anodyne remark— "Not quite top drawer" or "Why doesn't the fellow get a proper haircut?" or something like that, and Ellie hit the roof. She told me I was an unmitigated snob; she said I was living in the wrong century and ought to be ashamed of myself. I was ostracized and my breakfast toast was burned. I had to eat humble pie for a week before she fully forgave me. I initiated inquiries into Gray's antecedents and status immediately, of course.

Gray had fluttered the dovecotes of Kerrith on his arrival, I learned. Initially, this was due to his good looks and his pleasant manners; then came the electrifying news that he was unmarried—thanks to the last war, bachelors of any description are unusual hereabouts, and *eligible* bachelors are rarer than hens' teeth. Not that long after my first introduction to him, I witnessed at first hand exactly how potent a combination of forces this was.

I had had a couple more talks with Gray in the interim; the weather had improved, and so to a degree had my health. I had begun to go out and about again on mild days, and had been prevailed upon to address our local history society by its current secretary, Marjorie Lane, a terrible woman of advanced views, who moved here ten minutes ago from London, who believes herself to be an expert on matters about which she knows nothing whatsoever (including Manderley and Rebecca, of course), and who currently occupies a "bijou" cottage overlooking the harbour, where she paints daubs and makes pots.

"That nice Mr. Gray will be joining us for our meeting," she told me, when, clasping our ration books, I bumped into her in the butcher's (they were keeping a chicken for Ellie—under the counter, of course). "He and I are the *greatest* of friends already—and I've persuaded him to join our society. We need some young blood, don't you agree, Colonel? I know he's looking forward to your talk—as we all are. Have you decided on a subject yet? Is it still a secret? I know Mr. Gray's hoping for your 'Memories of Manderley' or 'Manderley as I Knew It'—may we look forward to that?"

"Not much to tempt one, is there?" I replied, ignoring the question, and indicating the postwar plenty on display—a string of sausages, some scrag-end of mutton, and several skinned rabbits that even Barker would not have touched. The horrid woman gave an arch smile at this.

"*Apparently* not," she replied, with a most peculiar and unnecessary emphasis.

"But there are lots of juicy morsels tucked away—or so I hear, at any rate. . . ."

THE EVENING OF MY TALK ARRIVED. I WENT SPRUCED UP in a tweed suit; I had toyed with the idea of discussing this area's many notable Arthurian connections, but in the end, and with few references to my copious notes, I gave a most entertaining, even erudite, account of the old gibbet sites surrounding our historic town. Terence Gray was indeed in the audience, and his presence caused . . . well, to call it a *sensation* would not be to overstate.

At the end of the meeting there were, as always, refreshments: stewed coffee, well-named rock cakes, and sausage rolls. Ellie and I stood to one side; Mr. Gray was instantly surrounded. A posse of old pussies, led by the Lane woman, closed in. Were they discussing gibbet sites and my revelations concerning them? No, they were not. They had instantly homed in on the question of marriage—never far from their minds at the best of times, of course.

"Why weren't you snapped up years ago, Mr. Gray?" Elinor Briggs piped up, as I advanced from the rearguard, intent on rescue (Elinor has always been quick off the mark). All the old bats bared their teeth in roguish smiles, and I awaited Gray's reply with interest. Would he venture some quip? Make some smooth disclaimer? No, neither. He colored and stammered a defensive answer. Did they lose interest? Far from it. Women cannot resist shyness in a handsome man. The capitulation of Kerrith's female population was instantaneous.

Months later, this pertinent question still remains unresolved, and Gray's biography may be summarized in brief. He hails from Scotland—from the Borders, I think. After attending a grammar school I've never heard of, he won a scholarship to Cambridge (my own alma mater; I was at Trinity prior to Sandhurst; Gray was at some other college. King's? Caius? I forget). He took a good degree (it may even have been a first) in History, and I think became a teacher of some kind until, in 1939, the war intervened. I assume he then volunteered or was called up—but he chooses never to discuss this period and having a respect for such silences myself, I have not pressed him. Recently, there seems to have been some personal crisis, almost certainly involving a woman. Whatever it was that happened, it led him to make changes in his life.

He seems to have thrown in his job, cut all his ties, and come looking for employment in, of all unlikely places, this neighborhood. Once here, despite being ludicrously overqualified, he applied for and got a temporary and part-time position at our county archive library in Lanyon—a position so short-term, dull, and ill-paid that it had remained unfilled for months. There he now works, three days a week, cataloging the de Winter estate papers, deposited there after Maxim's death, as I understand it, by lawyers acting for the second Mrs. de Winter. He rents a tiny cottage on the outskirts of Kerrith, and devotes the rest of his ample free time to what he calls "his researches." He always speaks of these in a very modest way, but I believe there is a great deal more to Mr. Gray than meets the eye and I suspect him of *writing*. In my opinion he has ambitions as an author, and these "researches" are intended to form the basis of a *book*. I have a pretty damn shrewd idea of its subject matter, too . . . but I mustn't get ahead of myself.

When I first began to suspect this, I'd known Gray about six weeks, we had begun to meet regularly and I had warmed to him. He is an excellent listener; he is astute, knowledgeable, persistent, and highly intelligent. I welcomed the idea that Gray might make use of material I could give him. The book I then envisaged his writing was a very general one, rather like my grandfather's inestimable *History of the Parishes of Manderley and Kerrith, with Walks*.

Safe in this belief, I opened up. Then I became aware that Gray's field of interest was narrowing. From concerning himself with a large local area and several ancient family estates, he homed in on one estate in particular: Manderley. I was still so convinced that Gray was a dull dog librarian, whose chief concern was such topics as medieval field boundaries, that even then I felt no alarm. I allowed him to draw me out. More than was prudent, I feel in retrospect.

Then, gradually, I began to notice: Medieval field boundaries were *not* his concern; he was not really interested in the early history of the de Winter family, either. It is a colorful history, with the beddings, bastardy, and amours of the eighteenth century being particularly eventful, but all my stories about these de Winters, including the most colorful of all, wicked Caroline de Winter and her rake of a brother, fell on deaf ears. Mr. Gray's concerns were far more modern.

When I finally realized that—and I now curse myself for being so slow—I at once became cautious, and renewed my own inquiries. Who exactly was Mr. Terence Gray, lately come amongst us? Why had he been so anxious to take that ill-paid minor job—and why had he been so anxious to befriend me? *Was* it truly, as Ellie claimed, that he liked me? I began to doubt his motives and this philanthropy.

The Briggs sisters, Marjorie Lane, and others, filled me in. Terence Gray, it seemed, had a sad and touching background: Orphaned as a small boy, or as a baby (everyone seemed suspiciously vague on this point), he had spent his early childhood in various children's homes. He had then been adopted by a woman known as "Auntie May," a saintly and kindhearted body living near Peebles (or possibly Perth). Auntie May had relations in this neck of the woods and had brought the boy here on numerous holidays, when he had gamboled on the sands, walked the coast paths, et cetera, et cetera, and had formed an emotional bond with Kerrith and the surrounding neighborhood.

After the war, Auntie May had died, leaving wee Terence a small legacy. This legacy gave him a measure of independence, allowing him to return to the scenes of his childhood idyll, and it now eked out his inadequate salary. There were even rumors that enough had been salted away by this prudent Scotswoman to enable Gray to consider buying the property he was renting. The Briggs sisters were particularly warm on this aspect of the story. For reasons beyond my comprehension they seemed to believe that whether or not Gray was sufficiently set up in life to own property would be a matter of concern to me.

"Of course, we've given him every encouragement!" Jocelyn, the younger Briggs, cried. "We think it would be so suitable in every way, don't we, Elinor? He's made the cottage so very snug and charming—and it's only ten minutes walk, less, to The Pines! What could be more convenient?"

"Convenient for whom?" I asked coldly.

"Why, *everyone*, Arthur, dear," said Jocelyn, becoming flustered.

"We mean," Elinor put in, giving her sister an admonitory look, "that it would be delightful if he were to stay here *permanently*. And so nice for you, Arthur, dear! You're such great friends now, and you share so many interests . . ." She paused. "I find it hard to believe he never told you about his childhood. He never mentioned his Aunt May? How strange! Jocelyn and I were counting on you to fill in the gaps—we thought you'd be familiar with the whole story. . . ."

I *was* familiar with the whole story. I had read it, or variations upon it, in countless novels. It had Dickensian echoes that unsettled me. Did I believe in Auntie May, alias Betsy Trotwood? Not being as gullible as the Briggs spinsters, I wasn't at all sure that I did. I thought there might be very good reasons why the Terrier had spared me these details— he couldn't pull the wool over *my* eyes, and I think he knew that.

My suspicions being thus aroused (What was Gray hiding? Could he be *illegitimate*? Ye gods, could he be *married*? Could there be a deserted wife and child in Peebles or Perth?), I took care what I divulged, and I watched with an eagle eye the precise nature of his inquiries. At once, his angle became obvious. Medieval field boundaries? What a dimwit I'd been! Gray was interested in the de Winter family, yes, but his chief interest was, and always had been, Rebecca.

Now why should that be? Once I had marked his interest, that was the question I asked myself. Could there be some small personal link that explained it? I wondered. If Gray's claims regarding childhood holidays could be believed, he'd have been coming here during the latter half of the 1920s, when Rebecca was still alive and at the height of her social fame. If his visits continued into his teens, he might have stayed here at the time of her disappearance, or the subsequent inquest. Details of that were splashed across the pages of the newspapers, and gossip was rife. Had Gray and his Aunt May, staying in a modest boardinghouse, perhaps, heard these stories? Had the seeds of Gray's interest been planted then? It seemed possible. Crime (and punishment) were certainly subjects that interested him.

Finally, exasperated, I asked him straight out. I put this scenario to him. He denied it. He had been aware of Manderley as a boy, he added—how could he not be when every second shop sold postcards showing views of the house? He and his aunt generally stayed farther up river; they used to rent a tiny waterside cottage near the ancient church at Pelynt. He thought he *might* have made a visit to the Manderley church to take brass rubbings of the medieval de Winter tombs on one occasion, but he and his aunt moved in very modest social circles and he could remember no discussion locally of those exalted beings, Rebecca and Maxim de Winter. As for the inquest and the subsequent fire, he thought he could remember reading about them in the national newspapers—but he was at least fifteen then, and the holidays in this area had ceased.

He paused; then, as if satisfied with this thumbnail portrait of an earnest little boy, an infant historian in the making, he changed the subject. On balance, I believed that story about brass rubbings. It was in character. Even as an adult, Gray retains a fondness for churches and tombs, and will walk miles in all weathers to visit them. It goes hand in hand with his passion for old books and documents, for the days he spends trawling through archives, newspaper libraries, and antiquarian bookshops.

This is a man who loves *evidence*—or so I initially thought—a man who delights in reconstructing the past by means of estate records, church registers, the incunabula of birth, wedding, and death certificates; this is a peruser of wills, a disinterer of dusty forgotten letters, diaries, and notebooks—and I could quite see that for such a man Manderley represented a special challenge. Why? Because there were gaps—huge gaps—and the historian in Gray was at once drawn to this apparent vacuum.

When Manderley burned down, the contents of the house were destroyed completely. The fire occurred within thirty-six hours of the inquest into Rebecca's death. It began at night and raged through the building. Everything went: all the exquisite furniture Rebecca had assembled, all those spying portraits that so terrorized me as a child—and all the de Winter family papers.

But the estate records, as I've said, had survived. At the time of the fire, they'd been lodged at the estate office, under Frank Crawley's fussy care; now they had passed to the very archive where Gray works, and—needless to say—Gray was quick to make himself familiar with them. His fascination with this dry-as-dust stuff amused me at first. That a fit, active young man with a good mind should choose to bury himself in these details of acreages, tenant farms, rents, and crop rotations seemed to me absurd. My own interest in history takes a more romantic turn; Malory has left an enduring legacy. I like love affairs, fatal passions, dastardly deeds, battles, and derring-do—and, fool that I was, I felt patronizing toward Gray for the footling matters that so absorbed him. The more he labored away at the coal-face, the less I thought of him.

I can now see that these labors were preparatory; I *suspect* Gray may have uncovered several little gems in those records that no one could have foreseen. He has certainly shown a marked interest in one de Winter tenant family, the Carminowes, whom I remember well from my childhood, and about whom I have long held my own conjectures. Their story is a sad one—three sons dead in the first war, their pretty widowed mother left to bring up her two surviving children herself, and one of those children—the boy, Ben—an idiot from birth.

It was Gray who bothered to follow up on their history, and Gray who discovered that Ben Carminowe, who used to haunt the coves below Manderley, was dead—apparently he ended his days in the county asylum. Maybe it was when Gray began to cross-question me about these loyal de Winter tenants that I first became uneasy. My misgivings soon deepened. Having exhausted the estate papers, Gray turned his attention to my own little archive. The Manderley family records might have gone up in smoke, but what about all that rich information packed away in my study—and in my memory?

It was then that the Terrier's interrogations really started. He wanted to know about Lionel and poor Virginia and the Termagant. He wanted to know about Maxim as a boy, and he became very animated indeed when I let slip that, millennia ago, when my bluestocking sister, Rose, was young and lovely, she and Maxim had for a brief period been expected to marry. "Just before the first war?" he asked sharply.

"Round about then," I said, retreating rapidly. "Probably nothing to it, now I look back. People were always speculating—he was the heir, after all. He and Rose were close in age; they were friends, which was surprising in some ways . . ."

"Why?"

"Because Rose always had her nose in a book, even then. And that wasn't really Maxim's taste at all. Most of the de Winters were philistines, now I think about it, and Maxim was influenced by them. He liked to be outdoors. He sailed. He rode. On the other hand, he was handsome. He was dashing. There was a streak of melancholy even then, even before the war—I expect that intrigued Rose. . . ."

"He was also very rich, of course. One day, he would own Manderley."

I was annoyed. "And you're barking up the wrong tree if you think that would influence my sister," I said with some heat. "You don't know Rose. Rose was a socialist in the nursery. She was a suffragette at six. All Rose wanted to do was to go off to Cambridge, God help us, and spend the rest of her life writing unreadable books with lots of footnotes. Which is exactly what she *did* do. She's now *Dr.* Julyan. She may even be *Professor* Julyan. She's a feminist, a man-hating eccentric, and an embarrassment to the entire family."

"I see you're fond of her," said Gray with a smile. "I'd like to meet your sister. I wonder if she'd talk to me?"

"Not a chance," I said, somewhat piqued. "In the first place, Rose left here donkey's years ago. She skedaddled off to Girton College, and she's been in the Fens ever since. In the second, she's vague and very unreliable. And in the third, she's virtually a recluse."

"A recluse? The Fens? Really? But Ellie said—"

"Unsociable, then," I said, interrupting swiftly. "Forget the whole idea, Gray. Now—what were we talking about? I think we got a little sidetracked. Where were we? Remind me."

"We were talking about Rebecca de Winter. That led you to the subject of her husband, and the type of women that interested him. . . . So I suppose we did sidetrack a little. But as always, sir, it was illuminating."

Dry again! I cast a little glance in his direction. Gray was given to understatement, and I was never sure when he might be needling me. His expression now was perfectly bland and innocent. He steepled his fingers. "As a matter of fact," he went on, "we were speaking of Rebecca's death. Which interests me, as you know. A mysterious life—so little known—and an equally mysterious death. I was wondering, Colonel Julyan, if—"

"Time for my nap," I said firmly. "We'll discuss that another day. *Down*, Barker—in heaven's name what's the matter with that blasted dog? Will you stop that infernal whining and whiffling? *Down*, dammit, Gray is leaving. . . ."

WE DID DISCUSS IT ANOTHER DAY—ON MANY OTHER days. At least, Gray attempted to do so, and I grew more recalcitrant and evasive. The habit of silence is hard to break, and a twenty-year-plus silence on this subject was, on my part, near insuperable. Things were not made any easier by my knowing full well that in Kerrith my failure to cooperate was unusual. Everyone else was only too eager to talk—including those like Marjorie Lane, whose ignorance is total. They were all at it, bending Gray's ear, pouring out to him their unreliable tenth-hand gossip and their frankly ludicrous theories. Not content with unsupported speculation as to Rebecca's origins, how she came to meet Maxim in the first place, et cetera (areas where my own knowledge is infinitely superior), they sank their teeth into the question of her death, just as they've been doing at intervals, whenever they're bored with bridge, or the weather is bad, for the last two decades.

The likes of Marjorie Lane fed him the tuppence-colored versions originally peddled by that wretched Evans man: that Rebecca was having an affair (identity of the lover unknown); that she had frequent assignations in the boathouse below Manderley; that she was murdered—strangled, smothered, stabbed, take your pick—either by the lover, or more probably by her husband who came upon them *in flagrante*; that her body was then dumped in her boat, *Je Reviens*, which was taken out into the bay by the murderer and scuttled.

Marjorie Lane gave these suggestions a twist of her own. In her view, she told Gray (who repeated it to me), Maxim de Winter was a obvious deviant, a homosexual (or "pansy" as she put it) who had been "carrying on" with that estate manager of his, Frank Crawley, and who had then killed his wife when she threatened to reveal his predilections to the world in a divorce court. Her evidence for this was a little confused, but placed great emphasis on the fact that Maxim and his second wife had slept in twin beds—as she had learned on the best authority, that is, from the ex-Manderley maid who changed the sheets on them.

I was outraged when I heard this. I couldn't believe the woman's crassness and audacity. I couldn't believe she'd had the nerve to tell Gray this farrago of rubbish, and I noted she'd never dared mention it to me. "Talk to the Briggs sisters," I said. "They'll soon set you straight. They knew Maxim very well, and they know exactly what happened."

Gray did so. The Briggs sisters, as expected, gave him my "authorized version." Both sisters had been devoted to Rebecca and were quick to defend her. They explained that poor Rebecca had learned from a doctor in London that she was mortally ill; she had returned at once to Manderley, gone out at night in her boat, and ended her own life as decisively and courageously as she had lived it. The inquest verdict of suicide, they added, was correct, and fully justified.

Obviously, this version was influenced by conversations with me; but, unfortunately, the Briggs sisters are not subtle. I've told them a thousand times that, given the doctor's evidence, the suicide verdict could not be *challenged*. They simply cannot see, or remember, that there is a very important distinction between "challenged" and "justified."

I did not expect Gray, who *is* subtle, to accept what they said—and indeed, he didn't.

"Rather an unusual way to kill yourself, isn't it?" he remarked. "To scuttle your own sailboat, and then wait in the cabin to drown? What was wrong with an overdose? Or cutting the wrists in a warm bath? Or jumping off a cliff, come to that? There are plenty of suitable cliffs hereabouts, in all conscience. What in God's name were the jury-men at the inquest thinking of? They didn't even have the information that she was ill, at that point—am I right?"

"Yes. You are."

"Then the suicide verdict is even more nonsensical. Was the possibility of foul play mooted?"

"Briefly. Yes. The coroner raised that issue, as he was bound to do. But there was no evidence given in court that Rebecca had enemies— that there was anyone who wished her harm. There were no signs of violence to the body. . . ."

"The body had been in the water for over a year. It was heavily decomposed—at least so the evidence given at the inquest suggests. Was that the case, Colonel Julyan? You were there, I understand, when her body was brought up."

"Yes. I was. I was present in my capacity as local J.P., as magistrate, and . . . look here, Gray, I prefer not to discuss this. The memories are painful, even now."

"I can understand that, sir." His tone softened, but he continued to regard me intently. "You were her friend. You were also her husband's friend. But—forgive me—I'm still puzzled. I can see the London doctor's evidence gave a motive for suicide—but surely it left a great many questions unanswered. She left no suicide note. She took her life in an unusual way, to put it mildly. *Did* she have any enemies?

People seem to know virtually nothing about her marriage or her circumstances, yet they're happy to pronounce judgment: Either she killed herself and she's a saint, or she was murdered and she's a sinner. Every single analysis of this case suggests the same thing: If she was killed, it was *because* she had a lover—or lovers. But was that true? Where's the evidence?"

"I'm not going to discuss this. We're talking about a woman I greatly admired."

"Then surely, sir, you must believe she had rights? And wasn't one of them the right to have her death investigated as fully as possible?"

"It *was* investigated."

"With respect, Colonel Julyan, I don't agree with you. If Rebecca de Winter *was* killed, then her murderer went free. No sooner was she dead than her character was attacked. The blame began to attach itself to her almost immediately: She was an unfaithful wife, *therefore* she was killed. Given the lack of evidence, doesn't it ever strike you that, as far as she's concerned, there may have been a *double* miscarriage of justice?"

"It happened over twenty years ago," I replied, after a very long pause. "I regret the stories about Rebecca more than I can say, but I'm powerless to stop them. Nothing can be proved now, anyway. Rebecca is dead. Maxim de Winter is dead. I'm not likely to see too many more summers. The world moves on, Gray. You're young. You knew none of these people. I don't understand—why should it matter to you?"

"The truth matters," he replied in an obstinate way. "It matters to me, and I believe it matters to you. . . ."

"Go home. Go home," I said to him. "You're as stubborn as a mule, and you're wearing me out. I've had enough of it. You remind me of—" I stopped abruptly.

Of my son, I could have added, though I didn't. And it's true, Gray does sometimes remind me of Jonathan. He asks the questions my son would have asked of me had he lived, and it's when I notice a resemblance between them—sometimes there is a likeness around the eyes—that I feel most weak, and long to unburden myself to him.

I THOUGHT OF THIS CONVERSATION DURING OUR LUNCH. A week had passed since we had that discussion, and I knew it had influenced me. The final point Gray had made then was indeed crucial: Did the truth matter? Yes, indeed, it mattered if you wanted to live with yourself. It mattered urgently if, as may be my case, there is precious little time left to you.

During lunch, I tried to watch and listen to Gray very carefully. I was trying to assess him. How do you measure a man? I gave him the following marks: nine out of ten for table manners (pretty good, given "Auntie May" and that grammar school); seven out of ten for his suit (it was off the peg, but freshly pressed, and the tie was unexceptional); five out of ten for conversational skills (like most Scots, he's inclined to be taciturn); and ten out of ten for patience—we had reached the pudding stage before he mentioned Manderley.

I had hoped this "marking" process would tell me something, but of course it didn't. Those kind of markers, which I've relied on all my life, made me ashamed of myself. They were utterly trivial, and they were not the signposts I should now be using. *Sub specie aeternitatis.* I might be off to meet my Maker at any second; if so, I'd better reform, and pull my moral socks up.

I was feeling low again, and I was so deep in thought that, if Ellie had asked, I couldn't have told her whether the pudding I was eating was stewed apples or stewed cactus. I was busy trying to decide if I could trust this young man, whether I should confide in him, whether he should be my Watson or not; whether, indeed, there might be an even more significant role for him at The Pines in the future. . . . Then I suddenly realized something very obvious. Terence Gray was my *conscience.* That was my conscience sitting opposite me now; my conscience was wearing a ready-made suit and eating apples and custard.

This idea threw me completely—so much so that Gray and Ellie had been discussing Rebecca's famous fancy-dress balls at Manderley for some while before I even noticed. It was not until Ellie mentioned the costume that Rebecca chose for the last ball she gave, and I heard the words "Caroline de Winter" and "Raeburn portrait" that I surfaced. I saw my opportunity and interrupted.

"Those parties made work for the servants," I said. "Frith used to complain about that. Which reminds me, Gray—what *did* he have to say when you saw him yesterday?"

"Frith? He sent you his respects, sir. He made a point of that."

"His respects?" I looked at Gray closely. "Is that *all* he's sent me recently? He didn't mention sending me anything *else*, I suppose?"

"No." Gray looked mystified. "What sort of thing, sir? I don't quite follow—"

"Nothing, nothing. Never mind. Time for our walk, I think." I rose. "Ellie, for heaven's sake, leave the plates, there's no need for you to deal with them. Someone else can attend to all that. We'll skip coffee. We're missing the best of the afternoon as it is. Barker—where's that damn dog got to? Barker—*heel*."

In the hall, I kitted myself out: hat, scarf, gloves, stick, overcoat. Grasping Barker firmly by the lead I waited in the porch with my conscience while Ellie fetched the car from the garage. I looked my conscience up and down. "Look here, Gray. There's something I must ask you," I burst out. "Did you send me a parcel—arrived this morning? About so big? Brown envelope?"

"No, sir." Gray frowned. "I don't quite understand. If I wanted to show you something, I'd bring it over myself. And if I posted it, I'd enclose a letter."

"Of course you would. Just thought—maybe the letter, or note, got left out by mistake. Never mind. It's not important. Forget I mentioned it."

I allowed Gray to help me down the path to the car. There was one last test ahead for him, and much depended on how he conducted himself at Manderley. Meanwhile, his reactions to my question had surprised me.

When I said I had something I must ask him, he tensed. When I posed the actual question and he denied all knowledge of that parcel, I saw transparent honesty—but I also saw relief.

Now why should that be? Gray had been anticipating a different question, I thought. He had been expecting me to ask him something else.

And whatever it was, the prospect had alarmed him. It was the first time I had ever seen him visibly nervous.

EIGHT

ELLIE BROUGHT OUR MORRIS OXFORD ROUND TO THE front gate, and, with Gray's assistance, I was bundled into it. Given my rheumatism and general decrepitude, it's quite a performance getting me into a car, but in the end we managed it. Gray sat in the back behind Ellie, and Barker sat behind me, occasionally licking the backs of my ears, and panting expectantly.

It was a truly glorious day, and my spirits lifted as we bowled along (Ellie is an impetuous driver). We bounced down the narrow, steep hill that leads into Kerrith from our aerie, chuntered along past the brightly painted cottages that perch by the harbor, and skirted the pier, where the ferry departs up river to villages such as Pelynt, where Gray may or may not have stayed in his childhood.

Coming out on the far side of the town, with the Manderley headland directly opposite us across the brilliance of the water, we passed Golden Guinea cove, where Gray's rented cottage is located, and where, allegedly, smugglers once stored their loot (though it's difficult to find a cove around here where they allegedly didn't). Ellie, practising for Le Mans, spun the wheel; we zipped around the notorious blind bend where, shortly after his marriage to Rebecca, Maxim once wrote off his latest motorcar (and was lucky to survive, as it happened). We began the long climb inland, the road snaking along the

indentations of the creeks, and mounting toward the thick planta-
tions of oak, beech, and Scots pine that mark the farther boundaries
of the Manderley woodland.

Gray was unusually silent, even for him; Ellie was concentrating
on double declutching, and I was drifting about on the seas of the
past, as usual. At 3:15, we reached the crossroads where, as I'd
explained in my history society talk, a gibbet had once stood, and
public executions had provided a cheap form of popular entertain-
ment. We parked outside the now shuttered and deserted lodge at
this Four Turnings entrance to Manderley, and I began on my habitual ritual: searching for the key to the tall gates, which might be in
any one of fifteen tweedy pockets, and which unfailingly turns out to
be in the last one.

I keep quiet about this key in local circles, and have sworn Gray to
secrecy concerning it. It was originally my grandfather's, given to
him by the Termagant, I think, so he could have access to the woods
for his butterfly expeditions. In those days, we rarely used it, for the
lodge-keeper was usually there to let us in; I think I may have used it
on later occasions, once or twice—Rebecca, knowing my love for
these woods, more or less told me to come and go as I pleased. After
the fire, when Manderley was abandoned, I expected the locks on the
gates to be changed, but they never were, so I can use my key still
whenever Ellie, Barker, and I want to walk in a place where we can be
sure of meeting no one—a major consideration in the summer
months, when even Kerrith is now becoming infested with tourists,
and we have to go farther afield to find the lovely isolation that has
delighted me from my boyhood.

Where was that infernal key? I started the familiar process of pat-
ting my pockets. Ellie sighed. Gray wandered over to the gates, and
looked through them to the wilderness, the beautiful Eden, beyond.
Not in my overcoat, not in my jacket, not in my trouser pockets . . .
Gray was inspecting the large notice that hangs drunkenly by the
gates, and has done these twenty years. It was put up by the land
agents who have been responsible for these woods, and for what is
now left of Manderley itself, ever since that disastrous fire.

Originally, they answered to Maxim, during the years of his self-
exile abroad; now, since both Maxim's marriages were childless, they
answer to the remote branch of the de Winters that inherited all this

after his death. Whoever these heirs are—they are domiciled in some vast heap in Yorkshire, I believe, but are said to prefer the several villas they own in the South of France, or their castle in the Scottish Highlands—they take no interest whatsoever in Manderley, and as far as I know have never set foot here. Presumably they're content to receive the income from the tenant farms (still flourishing) and refuse to bother themselves about a ruin. The land agents, I suspect, take a similar view, since they seem to do damn all. Maybe they inspect the place once a year or so, but no effort has been made to manage these woods, or protect the once-beautiful gardens, or indeed to shore up the house itself, although the last of the roof has now fallen in, and the site—as I often say to Ellie—is positively dangerous.

The notice Gray was inspecting, the sole evidence that the land agents have ever bestirred themselves, was battered; its paint was peeling. The words could still just be read: PRIVATE—NO TRESPASSING.

I looked at it with a scornful eye. Such warnings do not apply to me, I have always felt. As an old friend of the family, I am entitled to come here. Maxim would have wished it; Rebecca would have wished it; and the indolent land agents can go hang themselves. With which thought, my hand finally closed over the missing key, buried under a quantity of farthings and fluff in my overcoat pocket. As I drew it out with an exclamation of triumph, I saw Gray give a frown. He turned the iron handle on the tall iron gates; they creaked and—lo and behold—they opened.

Gray seemed less surprised by this phenomenon than I might have expected. I was considerably startled. "Good grief," I said. "Well, I'm jiggered. Ellie—you don't think that we—?"

"Definitely not. We were last here a week ago. I remember, because it was the day Mr. Gray went up to London. And we locked the gates when we left, I know we did. Don't you remember, Daddy? The lock was stiff, and I had to help you. . . ."

Her voice trailed away. She looked through the open gate and along the winding drive, her expression apprehensive. I must admit, I felt a certain apprehension, too. My first thought was that one of the land agents had decided to put in an appearance on this fine April afternoon—and, if so, I wasn't anxious to encounter him. While I felt certain as to my rights here, I wasn't anxious to explain them to some

bumptious tweed-suited twerp who would no doubt be young
enough to be my grandson. He might not understand; he might not
know who I was, or appreciate my claims. . . . I hesitated, suddenly
doubtful of our expedition. The sun passed behind a cloud, the landscape momentarily darkened, and I felt the fingering touch of those
superstitious fears that now come to me without warning. Looking at
the winding drive, my dream came back to me: I saw the tiny coffin
and heard again the small and insistent voice that rose up from it: *Let
me out. I can't sleep. . . . I can't rest. Lift the lid—I must talk to you.*

I shivered; beside me, Barker made a low whining sound, and I saw
that his hackles had risen. It was the anniversary of Rebecca's death,
and I was suddenly afraid. There were worse encounters to be made
in these woods than with some anonymous, unimportant land agent.
They were filled with ghosts, as I already knew. Among these trees, in
the past, I often glimpsed my grandfather and my mother, and if
these quiet figures were just projections of my thoughts, I was the
sadder, for I wanted to encounter them. These were the kindly
ones—that is how I thought of them; today, looking along that driveway, narrowed now by the undergrowth on either side, its center
marked by a spine of grass, I felt that I had been lucky in the past.
Today, the presences I could half sense beckoning from the shadows
were less kindly, and more threatening.

I was about to suggest we go home and postpone this visit when
Gray, having pushed the gate wide, walked through. "Someone's
driven this way recently," he said. "Look, you can see the tire marks."

He indicated a muddy patch a few yards inside the gates, where the
gravel, once raked daily by a battalion of gardeners, had thinned.
Ellie went to inspect them.

"Someone could be here now," she said in a hesitant way. "Perhaps
we should do this another day. It's odd. No one ever comes here. We
never meet a soul. . . ."

She paused. I forbore to contradict her.

"We don't want a scene. . . ." She lowered her voice, though I
could still hear her. "Technically, we are trespassing, I suppose—and
if anyone were to challenge us . . . It would upset Daddy. He tends to
get very fractious and difficult when we come here anyway, but I can't
stop him. He *will* come. He always comes here on the anniversary of
Rebecca's death. . . . And he was so anxious to show it to you."

"I don't think we should worry." Gray glanced over his shoulder at me. "These tracks are probably days old—and if they aren't, and we meet someone, I'm sure I can talk our way out of it. We're not doing any harm, after all. I'll take responsibility. My only worry is the distance. How far is it to the house from this entrance?"

"A long way. It's endless, this drive. We haven't been as far as the house for ages." She hesitated. "We just walk a little way. There's a place my father likes, where you hear the sea for the first time. You can see the house from there in the winter. And last year we brought the car in and walked from the house to the Happy Valley—the place where Rebecca had those wild azaleas planted. It leads down to the sea—but that was before, when Daddy was stronger."

"That's what we should do now," Gray said. "Drive as far as the house—walk, if your father feels strong enough, and then come back." He lowered his voice, and, leaning down to her, said something further that I couldn't quite catch; whatever it was, it seemed to convince her. Ellie turned back to me, her face bright with purpose—that meant she expected me to make difficulties.

I made no difficulties. The word "fractious" lingered in my mind; I wasn't sure if I was pleased or displeased to see Ellie and Gray exchanging these confidences and "ganging up" on me. In any case, I was determined to see the house, though, now I was here, I knew I'd never be able to walk to it.

Gray opened the gates for us, closed them, then rejoined us. Ellie eased the car forward and we entered the cool tunnel of trees, arching up from deep banks that were bright with emerald mosses, harts' tongue ferns, and primroses. My fears, and my ghosts, receded. My past came back to me as we drove in, the way it does now that age has given me the strange option of binocular vision. All I have to do is adjust my invisible lenses, and the distance and the decades disappear; then I can see the past close-up, right in front of my eyes. It's there all the time, of course, on the far horizon of the present—and I sometimes feel sorry for people like Gray and Ellie, who are too young and still too shortsighted to see it.

So I watched myself, in a blue serge sailor suit, run through the trees, the butterfly I was pursuing just out of reach. I watched my mother, stately, dreamy, and gentle, in the mourning she never left off, stoop by one of these banks to examine a wild orchid, its leaves freckled, its petals the startling magenta of methylated spirits. "Look, Arthur," she said, and then straightened, and turned through eighteen years to greet my sister, who came along the drive, lovely in a rose-colored dress, swinging a parcel of books on a strap, and laughing over her shoulder at Maxim. "People ask me why I married Max," Rebecca said to me as more years sped past in the slipstream of her car, low-slung, fast, with its spread silver wings on its long expensive bonnet. She braked hard, and stopped, here on this drive, at this very bend, or the next one. She turned to look at me, her hair tousled from the wind, her skin glowing, and her eyes, lit by the sun, then shadowed as the branches moved above our heads, were exultant, then secretive, as unpredictable as April.

"I tell such lies when they ask me—I despise them for asking me. I say I married him on a whim one rainy weekend, or for money—how they like it when I say that, it keeps them in gossip an entire winter. But you never ask, so I'll tell you the truth. I married him for *this*. Listen. You can hear the sea from here. Walk through those trees, and you can see it. How many flowers can you see? How many birds can you identify? There's a thrush that nests just there, it has six eggs the color of the sky. I saw a sparrow hawk here once. *This* is why I married him. It belongs to me and I belong to it. I knew that the first time I saw it."

"You were already engaged to him when you first saw it," I replied, clinging to the prosaic, as always on the defensive, afraid to meet her gaze because if I did all the rules of my life might fail me. "You were already engaged. Maxim told me. So something else must have influenced your decision. You exaggerate."

"You're wrong. I've known this place all my life. I've seen it and imagined it. And now it's mine—"

"Courtesy of Maxim."

"If you choose to think so. What a literal tiresome man you are today. Here." She stretched out a bare brown arm, reached across, and opened the passenger door. "You shall walk the rest of the way. When you've stopped being an actuary, *if* you stop, we'll still give you tea. No, I mean it. Out you get. I don't allow actuaries in my car, and I don't allow them at Manderley."

"Rebecca," I said, and Ellie, reaching across, patted my hand. "You dozed off," she said. "Look, we're almost there."

I rubbed at my eyes; behind me, Barker made a low, whimpering sound; Gray tensed; the gravel crunched, the trees thinned, and across a wilderness of arching brambles, lit by an April sun, lying crouched along the side of the rising ground, were the broken walls and the bare ribbed beams of Manderley. I wound down my window and leaned out eagerly. In the distance, light glanced on the sea; I could taste salt on the air; a blackbird sang from a bush, and, behind and through its song, I could hear the tide approaching, approaching.

We PARKED ON THE GRAVEL SWEEP, NOW MUCH SHRUNKEN and weed infested, where the carriages of my early boyhood, and later the motorcars, used to draw up on the north side of the house, by its heavy ornamented portico. Here, once upon a time, Frith would descend the steps in state to greet guests. Here Rebecca, returning from her honeymoon and arriving at Manderley for the first time as a wife, had been received by Frith with full Manderley majesty: all the outdoor servants, from head gardener down to the lowliest stable boy, clutching their hats, lined up on the gravel; and in the vast hall beyond, every indoor servant in ranked lines and full livery, jackets brushed, aprons starched, eyes lowered, awaiting their new chatelaine.

"I think Frith *may* have hoped to intimidate me," Rebecca said, giving me a small sidelong glance of secret amusement. "There he was, guarding the ancestral lair. He was longing for me to make a mistake. I nearly did, just for the pleasure of watching his reaction. But I'd promised Max—no tricks! And I kept my word. It was a faultless performance—I wish you'd been there to see it."

"*I* hear you dropped your gloves, so Frith had to stoop and pick them up," I said. "That wouldn't have been deliberate, by any chance, would it?"

"Certainly not. Those gloves were the first present Max ever gave me. They were beautiful gloves, the softest suede—my mother had some like them once. I wouldn't have spoiled them for the world—not even to annoy Frith. I only dropped one, anyway, on the steps outside, when I saw that great tomb of a portico rearing up. It was an accident—truly."

I looked up at the portico now. Its pediment was deeply cracked and sprouting a rich growth of ivy and infant willow herb; one of its supporting pillars, blackened from the fire, still stood upright; the other leaned dangerously. I bent to release Barker from his lead; he at once trotted off in the direction Gray and Ellie had taken, and I followed more slowly.

Later in the year, when the brambles and weeds have had time to recover from winter, to spring up and re-establish themselves with new vigor, it becomes very difficult to make a circuit of Manderley. But in early April, especially in years like this when the winter has been hard and prolonged, it's still possible. Clutching my stick, wary of rabbit holes, I stepped onto the once-smooth grass and made my way around the great ruined northern flank of the house, to its once-famous, long west front, with its heady view straight out to the ocean.

In this central section of the west wing, the most beautiful part of the house, Rebecca and Maxim made their rooms, ignoring tradition and refusing to occupy the more sheltered south-facing bedrooms that had always been occupied by the heads of the family. Here, on the ground floor, was the great drawing room where I first saw her on my return from Singapore; here she came running in from the gardens in her white dress, astonishingly young and three months married. Here, farther along and on the first floor, was the room I never saw but that I know she made her bedroom. "I can always sleep there," she said to me. "I have the windows opened wide. Even in a storm, I open them. I can hear the sea. I can *smell* the sea. It always calms me."

There is no trace of those rooms now. I believe the fire first sprang up in this part of the house—that was what I always heard, anyway—and it was in this wing that it burned most intensely. I touched the blackened stones that were all that was left; I leaned against a crumbling stone quoin that had once framed a window. I peered through into the interior, trying to make sense of the rubble, the charred and fallen beams, the windings of brambles. I tried to reorder it in my mind's eye, to reassemble the walls and restore the dimensions to what they had been, to decide that there was the fireplace, there a doorway, but the chaos confused and saddened me.

I turned away and looked at what was left of a lawn: Over there, under that beech tree, a little boy in a sailor suit had once sat and taken tea with the Grenville sisters, and fallen in love with pretty

Isolda. Over there to my right, I had once watched Rebecca cut great branches of white lilac. She walked toward me now, carrying them in her arms. All this past, so visible to me, so invisible to others. I looked at the sea and the sky, my vision blurring.

For a moment, I felt my age. I felt infirm, my hands trembling slightly. Then Barker, who always senses my moods, returned to my side and pressed his damp gray muzzle against my legs; a breath of salt freshness came to me on the air, and I rallied. I had a reason for coming here today, I reminded myself. Every year on this date, I make this no doubt foolish pilgrimage as an act of . . . what? Contrition? Respect? Sentiment (since I am not, alas, devoid of sentimentality)? But this year I had a secondary purpose—and I was forgetting it.

"Come on, Barker," I said, and set off across the rank tussocky grass toward my daughter and Terence Gray; they had been wandering ahead of me, and had come to a halt at the southwest corner where Lionel de Winter had had his rooms. This extremity of the house was the least damaged. The towerlike structure where Lionel inched out his last hideous years, and where he finally died, was still standing, though its roof had long gone, and owls now nested behind the thick ivy that shrouded it. I looked up at the window that had been his; my younger self, wearing uniform, looked down at me.

The year 1915: I was in England on two days' leave, to see my wife and newborn son; by that evening I would be back on a troopship; by tomorrow I would be back in France; by the day after, or the week after, I would most probably be dead, as so many of my friends were. Meanwhile, I had been summoned to Manderley once more by the elder Mrs. de Winter. I was to be one of the witnesses to her son Lionel's newly revised will; Frith, who was shortly to be promoted to butler, was to be the other. Why me? Because Mrs. de Winter had learned years before how far she could push without my resisting? Or because statistics suggested I was unlikely to survive Lionel very long and was therefore unlikely to talk? Lionel was surely too ill to understand what document he was signing, though his mother claimed otherwise. He died later that same day; I've defied statisticians to live on for thirty-six years—and that action of mine remains on my conscience. Twice in my life, as I'm now bitterly aware, I've allowed myself to be taken advantage of by the de Winters.

This is a part of Manderley that I have never liked. Beatrice once

brought me here as a child, claiming its corridors were haunted, and
we would see some fearsome apparition—a headless man or the
wicked deadly ghost of Caroline de Winter. We saw nothing, but I
felt much, and I've never succeeded in shaking off that childish dread
entirely. I approached it now, even now, with reluctance, and was
relieved to see that Ellie was waiting for me. Gray was no longer with
her; he was already moving off at a rapid pace in the direction of the
sea. I halted.

"Doesn't it look beautiful in this light?" Ellie said, coming to join
me. "Sometimes I think it looks even more lovely like this than it
ever did before. It was splendid then, of course—but now it's so still
and quiet. It's magical. There's a foxes' den under the tower there—
she has cubs, I think. I could hear them. In another few years, there'll
be nothing left of the house. Nature will have reclaimed it for the
birds, the foxes, and the badgers. . . . The ivy will win—and the
brambles."

"Maybe. Maybe," I said. "*Sit*, Barker."

Ellie rested her hand on my arm; the breeze lifted her soft hair
away from her face; it had brought color to her cheeks. For a few
moments, neither of us spoke, and Ellie continued to look toward the
woods, just coming into leaf, the light slanting through their
branches. She looked at the pale pools of primroses; beyond them, in
the cool of the trees, there would soon be bluebells, thousands upon
thousands of them. In the distance, the sea moved and turned,
crested and sparkled. I could feel spring: Its restlessness and promise
were in the air—and I could see spring in my daughter's eyes: Its
loveliness touched me to the heart; it also dismayed and pained me.

Ellie is attuned to me; I think she sensed this, for she gave a sigh
and shook off her reverie. "Well, at least we didn't meet anyone," she
said, the dreaminess leaving her voice as if she had decided, for my
sake, to concentrate on more everyday matters. "I'm glad of that. I
wonder if they employ a keeper now, to patrol the woods? Or maybe
they've sent someone in to look at the house—to shore it up, perhaps? It's so dangerous—those agents ought to have done that long
ago. I think they've finally got around to it. Someone's certainly been
here, Daddy—did you notice?"

"No. What makes you think so?"

"Well, look—" Ellie pointed. "That patch of nettles and briars is all trodden down. And over there—on Lionel's tower—you remember the windows had been boarded up years ago? They're not boarded now. The planks have been been pried off."

"Could have been a storm. During the winter—wind damage. Those boards were rotten."

"No, it's not storm damage. Someone's used a tool to lever the boards off. You can see the marks at the edges. And look, the ivy's all ripped away, and there's mud on the sill. I think someone's climbed in there, and recently, too. Terry said it was probably just children, daring one another, something like that. I told him children never come here—"

She broke off with a frown. Following her gaze, I looked at the window in question; someone had, indeed, forced an entry—and Ellie was right, it was unlikely to be children. Tempting though ruins and deserted places are, not only to children but to others who seek privacy, solitary walkers, courting couples, Manderley has remained strangely unexplored, neither vandalized nor violated.

And both Ellie and I knew why: The atmosphere here by the house, and in the encircling woods, too, has a virgin and forbidding quality. Ancient forces protect it—or so I sometimes feel—and to walk here is to feel one is entering a sanctum. I've felt something similar in the past when I've walked through ruined temples in the Far East, or sacred groves in parts of Greece or Italy. The fact that one may not believe in the deities once worshipped in such places is immaterial; one can sense their powers, and I've always felt it was an unwise man, a foolhardy man, who dismissed or denied them. Call it instinct or superstition; I would not relish coming here alone now, especially after dark, and I would never allow Ellie to do so. I looked at the window Ellie indicated; I looked at my daughter. *Terry* . . . She had never used that name before; when had that change happened?

A faint breeze came from the sea. I thought of that zephyr of my childhood; I gave a small shiver, and turned away from the window; that fearful tendency I've recently noticed in myself was creeping upon me, and it made me irritable. I gestured toward Gray, still in view, but now some distance away. "Where's he off to?" I said. "He seems in a devil of a hurry—he might have waited. . . ."

"He wants to see . . . well, the place where Rebecca's boat went down, I think. The cove. Her boathouse cottage . . ." Ellie gave me an anxious look. "He knew it was too far for you, and he didn't want you upset, so he said he'd just walk down quickly on his own, and then come back."

"Too far? Too far? It's a quarter of a mile at most." I bristled. "Whippersnapper. Who's he to decide what's too far and what isn't?"

"Now, Daddy . . ."

"Anyone would think I was some useless old crock. . . . I brought him here, damn it. He has no right. . . . 'Upset'? Certainly I'm upset. *He's* upset me. Gallivanting here, there, and everywhere. Off to London, God knows why. Off to see Frith, without so much as a by-your-leave. Who told him where Frith was? I did. Writes to Favell, arranges to meet him. And now this. Prowling around, leaving you behind, no manners, wet behind the ears, I've had enough of it. 'Too far'? I'll show him . . ."

Well, I said something of this kind. It went on quite a while. I grew more and more peppery, more and more indignant, more and more confused and heated. All the time I knew that Gray was right; it *was* too far and too steep; all the time I knew it *would* distress me to go down to that cove—I haven't set foot there in decades. The more I knew how right Gray was, how right *Terry* was, the more incensed I became. One second I was Colonel Julyan, wise old bird, the next I was King Lear. The fact that I knew this perfectly well made it all the more painful.

"Daddy, calm down—please don't do this," Ellie interjected at intervals. "This is ridiculous," she said finally, growing visibly upset and losing patience. "Why are you so stubborn? You know what happened last time you went that way. We got as far as the Happy Valley and you collapsed. Oh, for heaven's sake! The doctor's warned you, I've warned you, your own *body's* warned you. You're not well, and it's too far and it's too steep—"

"Leave me alone, Ellie," I cried. "Don't interfere. Since when did I take orders from you?"

"I'm not ordering you, I'm *asking* you. I'm asking you, for once in your life, to listen to me, and think, and be reasonable—"

"Let go of my arm, damn it. Let go this instant. And don't start snivelling, for God's sake. Red eyes and a running nose will do nothing for you, Ellie. If you want to look pretty for Mr. Terence Gray, and I'm sure you do, that won't be the way to go about it, believe me."

"Daddy—stop this. . . ." Ellie let go of my arm, and took a step back. The hurt and the apprehension in her eyes were so acute that I hated myself—and that enraged me further.

"Making him lunch! Making eyes at him at lunch! Don't think I didn't see. Sheep's eyes! You're making a damn fool of yourself, Ellie. It's painful to watch—and he's *not interested*. Look at him, waltzing off at the first opportunity. Bleating away—'Daddy this' and 'Daddy that'—I expect he's sick and tired of it. Damn it, *I'm* sick and tired of it. Leave me alone, and go and snivel somewhere else, for God's sake. . . ."

Color flushed up from Ellie's throat into her face. When she finally spoke, her voice sounded terrible, all breathless and choked. She was very angry.

"That's a hateful thing to say—*hateful*. I wasn't . . . I didn't . . . How can you say that, you of all people? I remember you—sighing and moping and snapping at everyone except Rebecca. It broke mother's heart, and it made me miserable, *miserable*. Make a fool of myself? You made a fool of yourself for five *years*. . . . Well, go if you want. I don't care any more. Go chasing off down to her beach. She never wanted you there then, and she wouldn't want you there now. Maybe you'll finally realize that, you stupid, *stupid* old man. . . ."

She turned away with a coughing sound and covered her face with her hands. I could see she was trembling from head to foot. There was a terrible silence, a silence that seemed to me to go on for a very long time. A crying girl, whom I loved with all my heart; a pigheaded, frightened, indeed stupid old man. Tears came to my own eyes, and I brushed them furiously aside. I watched myself with disbelief, shame, and bemusement as I swung around, slashed at the grass with my stick, and then, without further speech, left her and stalked off seaward.

NINE

I WISH I COULD WRITE THAT I REPENTED AT ONCE, THAT I turned back to Ellie, asked her forgiveness and made my peace with her, but I didn't do that. I went on walking toward the sea, stumbling, shaking my stick at the air and shouting at poor Barker. I was in too great a passion of rage, fear, and self-hate to think, let alone act in any way that was sensible. I just set my face against the freshening wind, and forced myself on, my heart hammering in my chest, and each breath becoming more painful. I can't really describe what it was like. I felt blind and deaf and *maddened*. Ellie's accusations buzzed about my ears; there was a terrible tumult in my head, like the crashing of howitzers.

Not true, not true, I kept saying to myself, but the words wouldn't stay still, others intruded, little jabs from the past: "No fool like an old fool, eh, Colonel Julyan?" And my wife, turning her pale drawn face to the wall, closing her ears to my pleas, excuses, and protestations: "Please don't say any more, Arthur. I'm dying. And I'm no longer interested."

I tried to shut these voices out. They were not the voices I wanted to hear—even, God forgive me, that of my wife, who, in all the long years of our marriage, never said anything to me, even in anger, that was unjust or inaccurate. *"Go away,"* I shouted at poor Barker, who kept circling around me, and getting under my feet, and on I pressed, scarcely knowing where I was, my pace faltering and my chest heaving, until I rounded a thick outcrop of gorse, in flower, and saw that the flowers were *moving*.

I came to an abrupt halt, panting, and passed my hand over my wet face. I looked again, and saw the moving flowers were butterflies, deep in nectar, newly hatched, unwisely hatched—too early. I took another step forward, then stopped, suddenly giddy. Below me, the ground shelved away sharply. I had not taken the right route; the path to the cove below—if it still existed—was somewhere away to my left. But I could see the shingle of the cove, a horseshoe of white below me, and the rocks that guarded the entrance to the bay, the rocks that Maxim and I, in our youth, christened Scylla and Charybdis.

The water was choppy; the tide was coming in fast. There was no sign of Gray, whom I had almost forgotten, but there below me was the small jetty where Maxim and I used to moor our dinghy, and Rebecca later moored the tender for *Je Reviens*. And there, away over to the right of the cove, still sound after twenty winters, was the boathouse where she sometimes slept if she had gone sailing alone at night, as she liked to do; the boathouse she had kitted out as a simple cottage. At high tide, the sea washed right up to its walls, and in storms the spray lashed its seaward window; on the landward side, the trees crept down close to the shore, and from the window that side, where the ground shelved upwards, Manderley was invisible.

In the last six months of her life, Rebecca spent much of her time there. Sometimes she made brief restive expeditions to London, where she kept that flat by the river, but when she returned from one of these forays, she was almost always to be found here, and only rarely at Manderley itself. Whatever other people say—and on the subject of that boathouse and its uses they are scurrilous—I believe it was the only place where Rebecca could be at peace. It was her refuge.

My heart turned over as I looked at it. I made some croaking noise in my throat that brought an anxious Barker to my side. I leaned on my stick, and fought for breath; when the ground beneath my feet began to shift and the sea began moving, so it was close one second and distant the next, I closed my eyes, the giddying ceased, and I was able to focus. There was the boathouse, foursquare, built to withstand storms, with its four-foot-thick stone walls, its low sheltering roof, its small deep-set windows. Smoke drifted from its newly added chimney—if it was not too dark, if there was moonlight, or starlight, you could see it from a distance. In the windows, light burned, making them shine gold; sometimes, if I walked the coast paths at night, as I liked to do then, I would stop at some vantage point, and look at them, and know Rebecca was there, as she had been almost every night that last winter.

I would ask myself why, when her home was no more than twenty minutes walk away—less—she chose to be here. Up there on the higher ground was a thirty-bedroom house, with an army of servants, and every luxury and convenience—a house *she* had transformed and made beautiful. Soft chairs, log fires, exquisite food, scented baths, linen sheets; up there was a house widely admired, copied, and envied, every aspect of which from the paintings and furniture down to the tiniest detail—the trimming on a cushion, the arrangement of the flowers, the placing of the smallest objects—was her creation.

For five years she had organized the machine that was Manderley with a careless grace that concealed a military precision. She over-looked nothing: the invitations, the collection of the troops of guests from the station, the menus, the table settings, the design of each room, the layout of the gardens. She kept meticulous records, so no one would ever be served the same dishes twice, even if a year or more passed between their visits. She remembered which guests liked which rooms; she made sure that the flowers in those rooms, and the books in those rooms, reflected the tastes and interests of the guests concerned. She did all this and more, much more, with a com-pulsive care—yet so well and discreetly was it done that some visitors never realized that her hand was involved, and assumed that she and Maxim were merely fortunate in having such exemplary servants.

And yet now she avoided this lovely place she had made. She appeared on formal, arranged occasions, as she had always done, but when they were over, or when her time was free, she came here, to a tiny single-storey stone building on the edge of the sea. I wanted to know why; I *had* to know why, and one evening in early April, a week or so before she died, I walked along the cliffs as dusk fell, saw the square gold light in those windows, and went down to ask her.

The last of her dogs—and her favorite—Jasper, was with her. Either he or perhaps Rebecca herself heard my feet crunch on the shingle as I approached. At least I assume that, for my visit seemed neither to surprise nor startle her.

I tapped on the door, and then went in. And that afternoon, standing by the gorse, leaning on my stick, with my eyes tight shut, I went in again, and again and again—watching closely, closely, so I knew no detail escaped me. The small whitewashed space was warm; it smelled of wood smoke and faintly of the Turkish cigarettes Rebecca now smoked constantly. There was a red rag rug on the floor, of the simple homemade kind one often used to see in cottages hereabouts; on the small bed to my left, which served as a sofa, Jasper was curled up on a plaid blanket. There was a shelf, with a row of little model boats, crudely made, but charming. There was another shelf with books, cups, and plates, and a small Primus stove beneath it. Next to the bright fire, on which driftwood was burning, stood a small armchair with a worn cover, a chair that looked as if it might once have done service in some maid's bedroom at Manderley.

On the other side of the fire, opposite the sofa-bed, was a deal table, at which Rebecca was sitting. It was piled with books and inks and pens; there was a bright pink blotting pad and an ashtray, in which one of her distinctive oval cigarettes was burning. An oil lamp stood here, its brass brightly polished; it created a warm circle of light in the quiet room, and gave it an atmosphere of pleasant serenity. I looked, and looked again, and looked again. Even now, twenty years later, I still saw what I first saw then: a simple place, that had been made delightful simply. Something, perhaps the bright colors or the little model boats or the small scale of the furniture, made me think of a child's room. It had a comforting ambience that, rightly or wrongly, I associate with that refuge, that palace of play, that had once, at The Pines, been Rose's and my nursery.

Rebecca was sitting at her improvised desk, her face and hair lit by the circle of lamplight. She was wearing her sailing clothes, and they were old but comfortable: trousers, a thick Guernsey sweater. Her hair, which had once been long, she had recently cut short, as was the fashion then. This altered her appearance radically—in fact, I still wasn't used to it, so, each time I saw her, it still took me by surprise. It made her look disturbingly androgynous, boyish yet intensely female; if possible, it increased her beauty.

She looked up as I came in, but neither smiled nor spoke a greeting. I looked at her hands, in the pool of lamplight. They were thin, long fingered, tanned from the previous summer's sailing; she was still, but her hands moved restlessly across the table, moving the blotter an inch, picking up then setting down a pen. They were fine and capable hands. Rebecca never wore gloves when she gardened or rode or sailed; she would have despised the idea of "lady's" hands, I think. I looked at her hands, again and again, down a tunnel twenty years long I looked at them.

On her left hand, she wore two rings on her wedding finger—as she always did, I never saw her without them: a narrow gold wedding band and a thin circlet of diamonds, of the kind called an eternity ring. Her right hand was bare, and its first two fingers were inky.

I could sense Rebecca was preoccupied, and that my visit was unwelcome; I didn't stay long, ten or fifteen minutes at most—and I suppose that I stayed there even less time that afternoon as I stood above the cove. In my mind, I seemed to be there, warmed by the fire, looking, looking, for a long time; in fact, the vision, or visitation, lasted only a minute or so. I now think that, giddy and distressed as I was, I *knew* I was looking for something, and had known all day at the back of my mind that, if I concentrated, I could find it.

So I looked and looked: at the plaid rug, and the books, and the bright fire, at Rebecca's face and her restless hands; then Barker gave a whine—and at last I saw it. Next to the pink blotter, under her left hand: a square black-covered exercise book, in which she had been writing just before I entered, which she quickly blotted and closed *as* I entered, and which she laced up, tying its leather fastenings in a neat bow on its spine, and pushed out of sight before rising. . . .

"*I've interrupted you. You were writing. What were you writing, Rebecca?*"

"*What sharp eyes you have, Grandmama! A letter, I expect.*"

"*You write letters in notebooks?*"

"*Oh, very well. My life story. I felt autobiographical today. I wrote pages! Tomorrow, I'll tear it up, I expect. Or maybe I'll keep it. For my grand-children. For my own children. They can read it one rainy day—it will while away an hour or two, don't you think? I'd like them to know me.*"

"*Rebecca, they'll know you anyway.*"

"*I suppose so. Maybe.*"

I opened my eyes again; I stared at the sea and the cove, which were steady. The giddiness had gone. My heart still ached, but my mind was clear—and I want to stress that point, in view of what happened next. I stood there, certain that I had remembered this conversation accurately, that I remembered the interior of the boathouse, the tone of Rebecca's voice. I was absolutely certain about the notebook, too. The one now lying on my desk at The Pines was identical, and that was why—when I first saw it that morning—it had seemed familiar and made me uneasy. Identical, yet different in one crucial respect: The notebook sent to me was empty. The one I remembered had been written in.

Where was that now? Lost in the Manderley fire? Or saved, and preserved all these years? My mind began to race; an idea came to me.

Someone was calling to me. I looked over my shoulder and saw Ellie running toward me from my left; I looked down at the cove, and saw Gray walking toward the boathouse; I saw him stop, look up at Ellie and me, then turn and begin running toward the path across the shingle.

I looked at the boathouse itself. I had a clear view of the landward window. I have good vision, despite my age (I also want to stress this), and am, if anything, longsighted now, wearing spectacles only for close work or reading. So I could see that window perfectly; it wasn't in the least blurred or hazy. I saw someone move behind the glass. I saw someone raise a hand, catch hold of something, and then drag it across the window. It could have been a remnant of curtain; it could have been a piece of old sacking or canvas, anything. But someone was in there, and someone didn't want to be seen—and I still insist on that, despite the skepticism of Gray and Ellie.

That is what I saw—and I might have had a better chance of persuading my companions had I then behaved less foolishly. Such a great mad hope leaped up in my heart. I thought, She isn't dead. We buried the wrong woman. She's alive. And now at last she's come back. . . . I heard again that voice in my dream: *Let me out, I must talk to you.* . . .

"Rebecca," I said as Ellie reached my side; and then something curious happened, I'm not sure what, but I found myself on the ground. I was lying full length, with Gray's jacket under my head; my collar had been loosened and my scarf unwound and my coat unbuttoned. Gray was kneeling beside me, and bending over me, and Ellie was holding my wrist and saying "It's very faint and unsteady."

"Now, Ellie," I heard myself say in a very odd reedy voice. "Don't *start*—I'll be fine in a jiffy."

"Oh, God, oh, God," said Ellie, and started weeping.

They got me back to the car. *How* they got me back isn't important. It took a long time, and it was awkward and difficult, and we'd never have managed it without Terence Gray. He behaved—and I will say this without equivocation—magnificently. Women are always hopeless in a crisis of this kind, and will flap about being emotional and foolish. Gray remained calm; he allowed me to direct operations, and the fact that he is extremely fit and strong proved invaluable. They settled me down on the backseat, finally, and by then I had warmed to Gray to such a degree that I was glad when he seated himself next to me. I thanked him. I may even have said, "Thank you, Terry."

Back at The Pines, the doctor was summoned. Ellie was being so exceptionally stern that I didn't dare argue, and I hadn't the energy anyway. Fortunately, for once, the good doctor wasn't an alarmist. He examined me; he went into the next room to have a brief talk with Ellie and Gray, and then returned to me with the verdict. A faint. As simple as that. I had overdone it, and then I had fainted.

"I could have told you that," I said, and my voice was improving.

There was a good deal more, of course. I was confined to barracks again, inevitably. I scarcely listened to all that rigmarole about rest and diet and horse pills and a total ban on all agitation and excitement. The point was: It was an ordinary common or garden *faint*. Not another heart attack, *not* a stroke—nothing, in any way, that could have affected, or is likely to affect, my faculties. Just a faint, brought on by temper, by my own inexcusable behavior to Ellie, by distress, by overexertion—and by seeing someone at that boathouse window.

I didn't mention that to the doctor, of course. He is not an imaginative man, and I didn't want him thinking I was losing my marbles.

"Now take care of yourself, Arthur," he said, as he prepared to leave. "Try not to get yourself worked up. Think of this as another warning, there's a good chap. And this time, make sure you heed it."

I certainly will. I don't want to keel over now—there's far too much to do. I have already made a start. (Obviously, rather more time has passed than I indicated at the beginning of this narrative; it's taken longer to write than I anticipated, especially as I seem to tire quite easily. It is, as I write now, a day or so since the events I describe happened—but they are fresh in my memory.)

First: I have apologized to Ellie, made my peace with her, and begged her forgiveness. Ellie has begged mine. I have told her that she spoke the truth to me, and the truth needs no forgiveness. Second: I've decided to trust Terence Gray, and I've already enlisted his assistance. His kindness to me after that foolish fainting fit will not be forgotten. Third: I've made this record of these events, for my own benefit and Gray's, so we can all be clear how this quest began, and I can remind myself, should I need to do so, of the many *clues* I've detailed here, and the state of affairs as they were, at the outset.

Gray is coming to see me in a day or two, when I've had a chance to rest thoroughly. We've already agreed on a division of responsibilities. It turns out that he has a number of "leads"—I think I may call them that—which came out of his discussions with Frith and his recent visit to London. He's going to postpone his meeting with Jack Favell for a few days, until he's sure I'm recovered. He's assured me that he will, at all times, remember the question of *bias*, and, if in doubt, will consult me. I, meanwhile, will open up my boxes and files; I will search my memory, and I will tell him *the whole story*, in interview with him or—if I feel up to it—in writing. Meanwhile, just to be on the safe side (I *might* keel over; you never know), there is this testimony.

To mark the importance of this pact, which we made on the evening of our visit to Manderley, we shook hands, and exchanged certain confidences. Gray told me exactly what he had discovered among all those dusty Manderley estate ledgers (no surprises there: As I suspected, it concerned the Carminowe family) and what he discovered in London at Somerset House and the Public Record Office—and that *did* surprise me. With some emotion, I showed him that strange black notebook sent to me, with its picture of a winged child. Yes, I showed him *Rebecca's Tale*. And, finally, I gave him—this was a great wrench—my key to the gates of Manderley.

"Go back there tomorrow," I said. "And whatever else you do, Gray, make sure you take a close look at that boathouse. Someone was there, I know it. What's more, I'm pretty damn sure I know who it was. . . ."

"Of course I will," he answered gently. "I'll go over there as soon as I can. You mustn't worry about it. Try and forget it for the moment, sir. The pills the doctor gave you should be making you sleepy—I think you should rest now."

"I'm going to rest—I will in a minute. Gray—listen: Someone else is on the same trail as we are, that's what I think. Don't tell Ellie, will you? Ellie will just say I'm imagining it; she'll say I see plots right, left, and center. . . . Well, for once, Ellie's wrong. No, Gray, *listen*: Whoever was there in the boathouse . . . I think it was the same person that sent me the notebook. Someone's out to make trouble—I've got a hunch about it. And, if I'm right, it can only be one of two people."

I gave him the two names. "That's astonishing, Colonel Julyan," Gray said politely. "Very ingenious. I'd never have thought of that, sir. Now—I mustn't let you talk any more. You've had an exhausting day, and Ellie's very concerned about you. I promised her I wouldn't stay long. . . . You really must sleep."

His gentleness and the obvious concern in his face touched me. I think Gray doesn't like to betray this more sentimental side to his nature, because he then bent down to straighten my eiderdown, so I couldn't see his expression. (I should have explained—I had been packed off to bed by this time, so this conversation was taking place in my bedroom.) He wished me good night and began to move toward the door.

"Just one last thing, Gray," I said, as he opened it.

"Yes, Colonel Julyan?"

"This is important, Gray. Always remember, if you should need to talk this over, and if I should happen to be unavailable—if I should be having a rest, say, or taking a nap, something of that kind—you can't do better than talk to Ellie. She has a good heart and a sound head on her shoulders."

"I already know that, sir," he quietly replied. "I became aware of that almost as soon as I met her."

I was satisfied with this reply, and the steadfast way in which it was made. In that moment, the last of my reservations fell away. I forgave him everything that had caused me doubts: his occasional evasiveness, his unfortunate dryness of tone, his unilateral tendencies—even that grammar school.

"Over to you now," I said.

When he had left, I settled myself back on my pillows, with loyal Barker at my bedside, and the sound of the sea just audible. I fell into a doze. In an instant, I was back in the Manderley woods, and coming toward me through the trees, in her white dress, wearing that little blue enamel butterfly brooch, was Rebecca.

2

Gray

APRIL 13, 1951

TEN

I<small>T'S ONE O'CLOCK IN THE MORNING; THE WIND HAS VEERED</small> round to the southwest, which means rain, and it's gusting. I came back too late to light a fire, so the cottage is freezing. I'm sitting here in three sweaters, with a glass of the black-market malt whisky I bought in London. Colonel Julyan and Ellie finally took me to Manderley on my first official visit this afternoon—with disastrous results. In view of what's happened, I can't leave Kerrith now; I'll have to rearrange my schedule—and I won't be able to meet Jack Favell in London until next week, Monday at the earliest.

It was past eleven when I finally left The Pines; I felt anxious and restless, so I went for a long solitary walk upriver from Kerrith toward Pelynt, before coming all the way back here again. I hoped that might have some calming effect—or at least put the day's events in perspective. There's no sign of that happening. I've tried looking at this from every possible point of view. I'd like to believe Ellie when she says that this could have happened at any time, the doctor had warned her. I'd like to believe that, as she claims, the Colonel's stroke was caused by a quarrel she had with him; but I don't. I am responsible.

I've been pressing him too hard with my questions recently—I should have had the sense to draw back. And I made a selfish error in going down to the boathouse cove this afternoon; I wanted to inspect it in daylight—it never occurred to me that he'd attempt to follow. Until he talked to me tonight, I hadn't understood how much that place means to him. This is just one example of the maddening way he *witholds* information: He'd never told me how much time Rebecca spent there in the months before her death, and he'd never explained that, in his view, it was her last place of refuge. I wish I'd known that months ago. In the light of what the Colonel told me and showed me today, I'll have to rethink everything.

Even so, I should have foreseen how upset he'd be. I know how protective he is of Rebecca. It was blind stupidity on my part not to see that I should go down there only if he had sanctioned it—and to go there as I did, without permission from him, was in his eyes a kind of sacrilege.

I hadn't even reached the boathouse when I heard Ellie calling. I've never approached the cove from that route before. The path is very overgrown, and there's been landslip in several places. I was walking toward the boathouse when I heard Ellie's shouts, looked up, and saw him collapse. She reached her father first and she was distraught—I'm sure she thought he was dead. For a moment, I feared the same; then I realized that he was breathing, but very shallowly. I knew it was a stroke at once. His lips were blue, and there was slight paralysis on the left side; I saw it in the facial muscles first, then, when he started to come round, his speech was slurred. His right hand was functioning—he gripped my arm with astonishing strength, as if he'd never let go of it—but his left arm and hand were completely slack.

I had to make a decision and make it fast: Which was worse, to leave him with Ellie and go for help (Ellie would not leave his side), or try to move him? Manderley is isolated. The nearest house with a telephone that Ellie knew of was a cottage off the Four Turnings road once lived in by the Carminowe family—but that was a good three miles away. Then there would have been more delays while we waited for assistance. I was afraid that, if we did this, the Colonel might die in Ellie's arms, and she'd be left alone there by the sea with him. I wanted to spare her that; I decided to risk moving him.

I had to carry him—and there was no difficulty in that. He's a tall man (he stoops now, but would once have been my own height), and in the old photographs Ellie has shown me I can see that he was once strongly built; he's now painfully thin—he layers himself in tweeds, so I'd never realized exactly how thin, until I lifted him. He's a man of formidable presence and formidable will, but he is pitifully frail. I could lift him as easily as a grown child or a woman.

We managed to get him back to the car, and into the rear seat; I sat beside him, still afraid he might die before we could get him back to The Pines—and Ellie wouldn't hear of taking him anywhere else. The nearest hospital is even farther away than Kerrith, but that wasn't the reason: "I'm taking him home," she said. "That's where he'll want to be, and that's where I'm taking him."

I knew she was right, so I didn't argue. I sat next to the Colonel, who was lying back, with his eyes closed; his dog, Barker, was in the front, resting his head on the seat behind him, and I swear that on the entire journey that extraordinary dog never once took his eyes off his master.

Ellie is a good—and a fast—driver. We sped back up that endless winding drive—and then something curious happened. As soon as we were on the road again, the old man seemed to revive. First, his right hand stole out, and grasped my arm; then, gradually, the color came back into his face and he opened his eyes and looked around him. I could see he was trying to speak, and I tried to quieten him, to tell him to rest. I don't know whether he heard or understood me.

I looked at his bright blue eyes, and I thought of these past months, and the games of cat and mouse he's played with me. I thought of all the times when I've been infuriated and exasperated by him, when I've gone away cursing him for his tetchiness, his wiliness, and his recalcitrance.

None of it mattered. Not one jot. Did I care, in that moment, that he was one of the most difficult, prejudiced, manipulative old buggers I'd ever encountered? No, I didn't. I *liked* him. In that moment, I more than liked him. I wanted him to live—and the sudden intensity of that wish took me by surprise. I never had a father (Nicky claims that's why I'm not just a bastard, but, as he cheerfully puts it, "a cold-blooded bastard"), but in that moment I think I knew how it felt to be a son. I felt a rush of emotion so conflicting and so unexpected that I had to look away—and, desperately ill though he was, I think the old man *knew*. He started pulling at my arm and I finally made out what he was saying. He was calling me by his dead son's name: "Thank you," he said. "Thank you, Jonathan."

(BRIEF PAUSE HERE; ONE OF THE SHUTTERS HAD COME loose in the wind; I had to get up and fasten it.) I'll continue. There was one last scene to be played out before I left The Pines, and, re-examining it now, in retrospect, I'm certain Colonel Julyan had planned it. He'd pretended to believe that diagnosis of a "faint" for Ellie's sake, but I'm sure he knew it was nonsense. He knew, just as surely as if the doctor had told him, that the next forty-eight hours were critical, and he might not survive the night. And ill as he was, he was determined, *determined*, not to sleep until he'd spoken to me. Come what may, he was not going to let me leave that house until the ritual he had in mind was effected.

The doctor had given him enough medication to "fell an ox," as he put it. It had no effect whatsoever—far from being felled, the Colonel carried on as if he'd swallowed a handful of pep pills. Ellie and I managed to get him into bed, whereupon the Colonel, whose power of speech was improving by the second, ordered her out of the room. Ellie hesitated; the doctor had said that it was imperative to avoid the least agitation. Since nothing agitates the Colonel quite as much as not getting his own way, Ellie didn't hesitate very long. She left us.

"Sit there, Gray," said the Colonel, pointing to a chair. "Sit there and listen."

I sat. The curtains had been left a little drawn back, as he likes. The window was a fraction ajar. The ancient gas fire was lit, and was faintly sputtering. Barker, a dog midway between a bear and a sheep, a sort of brown ambulatory hearth rug, was sitting at my feet, regarding me soulfully. Through the crack in the window, I could just hear the sound of the sea, whispering, whispering. Out there in the dark, across the bay, lay Manderley, and a mile or so beyond it, the small gray Saxon church where Rebecca lies buried. I knew the Colonel had loved her once—I think I knew that very, very early. I could see it there in his eyes, almost from our first conversation. I'm certain that love was unexpressed and unrequited—and all the more powerful for that. The emotions we never admit to, never confess, are, as I've learned to my own cost, always the most powerful, and sometimes the most enduring.

I looked at the old man, who might or might not survive the night. He was wearing striped flannel pyjamas; his white hair was standing up in a tufty aureole; his nose—of which he is vain, it is a "Julyan nose," and in his view it is "hawklike"—was jutting at me. His thick brows were drawn together in a frown, and those bright, sharp blue eyes of his were fixed on mine. He was impressive, absurd, and poignant. I wondered what was coming: revelation at last, or more of his crafty, careful mix of truth, evasion, and mendacity?

It was some while before he spoke, and as I waited I had a vision of myself at some point in the future, still waiting for this exasperating old man to decide he trusted me. Survive the night? This man has unnatural resilience and willpower. I had a sudden image of the wily old bird hanging on for another two decades, and *still* keeping me in suspense. I eyed him with a certain amusement, with the respect of one adversary for another, and with affection—a deep affection. Then, to my great surprise, the Colonel began speaking.

Some of what he said was wild, and irrational—I didn't believe for a moment that he had actually seen anyone inside that boathouse, for instance, though he insisted he had, and blamed that for his "faint." But, as he continued, his voice becoming stronger, and his diction miraculously clearer, I began to see where this conversation was leading. I'd been outflanked again. The crafty old soldier had nipped around my defenses and cut off my retreat; he had made me like him, he had made me surrender—and I know he sensed that.

Apparently, he had also decided he liked me. Apparently, I had passed the "tests" he had set me that day (these tests, I suspect, involved my table manners at lunch, as well as my conduct while at "Castle Perilous," or Manderley). Apparently he believed I'd saved his life—he certainly said so, which gave him the opportunity for more shameless emotional blackmail. For all these reasons, he went on—and it was the more urgent in that he might "turn up his toes at any moment"—the time had come for us to make a solemn *pact*. We were to unite our forces. No more fencing around. He'd talk, in other words, if I did.

I might have known there would be conditions. But that was all right; much of what I know I was happy to tell him—and I'd have done so long ago, had he ever asked me. Obviously it would have been difficult had his questions become more personal: I wouldn't have welcomed cross-examination on the subject of Mr. Terence Gray's past, or "Auntie May," and so on. Fortunately, there were no questions of that kind. We stayed firmly on the subject of Manderley, Rebecca, and the de Winters.

We didn't talk for that long. I was anxious not to agitate him, and I knew he should sleep—but I also knew that he would not rest, he would *refuse* to rest, until this matter was settled.

After about twenty minutes, I rose to leave. I told him that I would put off my visit to London and my interview with Favell for three or four days—until I was certain he was on the mend. I'm not sure he took in this suggestion, or even heard it. He was struggling to sit up in bed again, Barker was circling back and forth anxiously, and I found that—before I left—there was one last element to this ritual: Would I fetch that key on his chest of drawers, and the black note-book he'd asked Ellie to bring up, which was lying next to it?

I did so, and I was astonished. All day the Colonel had been concerned about a package in a brown envelope he'd received that morning; it had been sent anonymously, I now discovered. This notebook had been inside it, and this notebook had been Rebecca's. For the first time, I was holding in my hands something that had belonged to her. After all these months of searching, the emotion I felt was very strong—I was struggling to conceal it. My hands were unsteady. On the first page, there was a photograph of her as a child, wearing a strange costume. On the last page (I could see the marks where it had been pasted in, but it had come loose) was a picture postcard of Manderley. This was the notebook's alpha and omega. Apart from its title page, the notebook was empty.

The title page contained just two words: *Rebecca's Tale*, written in what the Colonel was sure was her hand. The child in the photograph was approximately eight or nine, but the handwriting was that of someone older—a girl of about twelve, I'd have said, but that was guesswork. The final "e" of the word "Tale" curled all the way down the page in a childish punning flourish.

Had she intended, as a child, to write a story, maybe her life story?

If so, she'd abandoned the attempt, for the rest of the book was empty; I went through it carefully, in case there was anything the Colonel had missed; but, no, all the other pages were blank. I thought of the scene in *Twelfth Night*, when Orsino asks Viola-Cesario what happened to the woman whose story she's been telling him and Viola replies, "A blank, my lord. She never told her love . . ." I forget the rest of the quotation.

A blank, my lord. To hold this in my hand—to be given so much, and so little simultaneously: it was deeply frustrating. I kept turning the pages, telling myself there *must* be something, a single word, a note—but there was nothing. The child's photograph looked as if it had been taken professionally, and, even this young, the eyes of the child were unmistakable—I'd have known them anywhere. The postcard, in sepia, had nothing written on it, and no printed information beyond the identification of the house, and the name of the photographer, with a studio address in Plymouth. It may be possible, armed with this information, to date the card more precisely; meanwhile, I could date both pictures roughly: 1907 to 1915, I'd have said. Rebecca as a child—and Manderley. My mind began racing—did that mean, could it possibly mean, that Rebecca had known Manderley long before she went there as Maxim's wife? Did it mean that her connection with that house began far earlier than I, or anyone else, had suspected?

I wasn't allowed to take this evidence away. The Colonel would not be parted from it. I persuaded him to let me keep the picture postcard, and it's here on my desk, but I had to give the notebook back, which I did with the greatest reluctance. Then the key—and it was the famous key to the Manderley gates, about which he is so secretive—was pressed into my hands. It was mine now.

I don't, of course, need this key. There are routes into Manderley other than those gates, and, unbeknownst to the Colonel, I've been taking advantage of them for some while. But I was deeply touched, all the same. That was when I began to understand the true nature of this ritual. The Colonel may choose to present himself as a stereotypic bluff old military buffer, but I saw through this disguise months ago: Arthur Lancelot Julyan is a romantic. You can see that straight away if you look at his bookshelves. He's never shaken off the influence of his favorite Malory, and now, drawing himself up, fixing me with a stern eye, the old soldier, the old knight at arms, sent me off to complete the quest he'd left unfinished. Now I must discover the truth—I had to provide at last the answer to the question that, as he finally admitted, had troubled him so long: *Who are you, Rebecca?*

Was he consciously echoing Malory's *Le Morte d'Arthur*, in which the quest for the grail passes from Lancelot to his son, Galahad? I've been re-reading Malory, in an effort to understand the Colonel better—and I thought it was possible. That touched me—and saddened me. Galahad was conspicuously pure—which rules me out for the role. The Colonel bears more resemblance to Don Quixote than he does to Lancelot. And as for the quest . . . had it never occurred to Colonel Julyan that he might well prefer never to hear the "truth" about Rebecca?

He believes in "his" Rebecca; tonight he seemed certain that he knew most of her story (that I doubt), and that if we managed to discover "the few scraps" of information still eluding him, they would exonerate her. Any new information we obtained would give the lie, finally, to those in this neighborhood who claim that she was manipulative, faithless, and unprincipled. But will that be the case? I was by no means as sure as the Colonel seemed to be. But then I can be objective, and the Colonel cannot. I felt anxious for him. The last thing I would ever want to do is bring him information that hurt him.

I said nothing of this, obviously. There were a thousand questions I wanted to ask him, but they would have to wait until he was stronger. The Colonel, seeming to tire at last, settled himself for sleep. Barker curled up by his bedside. I went downstairs and talked to Ellie for several hours; we ate supper together.

Afterward, I went for that long walk, turning all these things over in my mind. I was excited by what the Colonel had shown me, anxious for him, and deeply troubled. I begin to see that it isn't possible, as I'd believed, simply to come to a place, make one's inquiries, and leave. Day by day, I get drawn closer; it is becoming harder and harder to be an impartial observer and investigator. I have made friends here, which I never intended to do. To deceive an interviewee, a provider of information, is not particularly pleasant, though I've found I can do it without great difficulty. But to deceive and misrepresent myself to people I have come to care about, to the Colonel above all, but also to Ellie and the Briggs sisters, all of whom have shown me great kindness, that is despicable. I dislike the process, and myself, accordingly.

(ANOTHER PAUSE; IT'S NOW RAINING HEAVILY AND THE wind has strengthened; that damn shutter is still loose. I'll have to fix it properly in the morning.) I'm tired. I'll take myself off to bed, and worry about this tomorrow. Meanwhile I must *think*. What are the implications of the two photographs in the notebook I saw? Who could have sent it? Is it feasible that there is another Rebecca notebook, as the Colonel claimed to me tonight? Could it conceivably still exist? And, if it does, how do I get my hands on it?

There is a great deal I must do: I have innumerable personal letters to write, since unfortunately I can't put my own life on hold to quite the degree I'd hoped. As regards my task here, I *must* track down that Danvers woman, though it's proving very difficult—I'm hoping Favell will know where she is. I need to talk to Frith again: I still want to ask him about Lionel de Winter's womanizing, and his death. I must write again to Frank Crawley, who is being politely but firmly uncooperative, and I need someone to check out those Brittany details for me. I wonder if Nicky would be a good choice? He's in Paris now, so it would be easy for him to go down there, and it's the kind of exploit he might like.

Meanwhile, as I'll have to be here for the next few days, I must make use of the time. Apart from Frith, I might have another go at the Briggs sisters (I've got them to the point where they're eating out of my hands), and also James Tabb, the former boat builder who converted *Je Reviens* for Rebecca. Tabb, unlike the Briggs sisters, *isn't* tamed yet—the man will not be persuaded to talk to me.

And then there's my promise to the Colonel: Maybe I'll walk over to Manderley and take a look at that boathouse some time. But I'd better be discreet. One of the chief difficulties here, as I'm beginning to understand, is that one is always *watched*. I've never been in a place so well stocked with binoculars. Every boat, every cottage, every walker comes equipped with them. Under the pretext of watching boats or birds, even little old ladies become the most shameless spies—no wonder the Kerrith bush-telegraph is the most effective I've ever encountered.

I don't want my activities to attract attention. So, if I do go over to the boathouse, I'd better choose my time carefully. Sunday morning would be good—around dawn, preferably.

ELEVEN

I SET THE ALARM FOR FIVE A.M., BUT WOKE AT FOUR-thirty—I've been sleeping badly. As washing facilities at my cottage are primitive, I go for a quick dip most mornings. Today I decided to swim out to the Kerrith point before setting off for Manderley; it isn't far, and I thought it might clear my head of the dreams I'd had, though it was still dark and the water was scarcely inviting.

The sea was black, flat calm, and icy. Depending on the state of the tide, the currents here can be dangerous—there's a strong undertow, especially if you venture out toward the Manderley headland. Even on the Kerrith side of my cove, the tidal pull can be very strong, but I'd timed the swim well and had no difficulties. I went only as far as the buoy that marks the entrance to the harbor. I hauled myself up onto the flat rocks at the end of the point, and rested there for a few minutes. I had a clear view of the narrow tongue of land where The Pines is situated; there wasn't a light to be seen in Kerrith, but, silhouetted against the lightening sky, I could see the eccentric turreted Victorian romance that is the Colonel's house, and a light *was* burning there. I knew it wasn't the Colonel's room, so it must have been Ellie's.

So she must be wakeful, even though the Colonel, confounding the doctor, seems stronger by the day. I've been calling in every morning to check on his welfare, and although he's still too weak for long conversations, he's already begun directing operations. He enjoys ordering me about to such a degree that I feel he's certain to make a full recovery. It seems tactful not to say this.

I watched Ellie's window for a short while, to see if the light would be extinguished. It wasn't. I wondered if she was reading, and, if so, what—Ellie is a bit of a mystery. Then I eased myself off the rocks and slipped back into the dark still water. The tide was on the turn; I could feel the ebb pull commencing; I swam back to my cove, and returned shivering to my cottage. It felt several degrees colder than the water.

There's no bath here beyond a tin contraption stored in the shed, which you're supposed to place in front of the fire: I thought this had a certain quaint charm, until I discovered how many kettles of hot water it took to quarter-fill it. There's no washbasin, either, so I wash and shave in the sink in the ill-lit, wood-lice-infested scullery. There's a feather mattress, which is permanently damp, and I'm cooking on a paraffin stove—which is fine since I can't cook anyway. In short, the cottage is picturesque, and, like most picturesque cottages, has draw-backs. But there are many compensations. I like the silence and the isolation. I like the ceaseless changes of the sea, which I can watch from the windows, as I always did at May's house. And I like to stand, as I did today, and watch the first thin dawn light slowly reveal the woods of the Manderley headland opposite.

I pulled on some warm clothes and walking boots. I stowed this journal and my papers in the usual hiding place, and then set off. I wanted to take a closer look at that boathouse, in view of what Colonel Julyan told me the other night, but I wasn't expecting to make any discoveries. I certainly didn't expect any evidence of the Colonel's "watcher at the window," and so—as I can now see—I was ill prepared for the surprises that awaited me.

I took the coast path that leads directly up from this cove to the headland. The sun was beginning to rise, the sky was opalescent, and in the quietness of the very early morning, it was astonishingly beau-tiful. This path, overgrown, extremely steep, and dangerous in places, seems to be rarely used. As always, so far, I met and saw no one.

Great clumps of pink sea thrift were in flower on the cliff edges to my left; on my right, on the landward side, the banks were rich with primroses, cowslips, and a little vetch that I must ask the Colonel, or Ellie, to identify. The drop was vertiginous in places—straight down to the rocks and the churning water. There have been landslips here, too—the cliffs are unstable—and at some points the path disappears completely. The first time I made one of my moonlit expeditions this way, I had several near disasters, when the path disappeared without warning, or I stepped onto what felt like solid ground, only to have it crumble away beneath me.

But I'm familiar with the route now, and it was much easier in daylight. As the sun strengthened and I gained height, I could look back toward the bright pygmy cottages of Kerrith and see the whole town laid out, clustering around its central church and steeple. Looking westward, I was dazzled by the great glittering expanse of the ocean. I felt sure it was too early for anyone to have their binoculars trained in this direction; the only sign of activity was one fishing boat, turquoise and scarlet, chugging out to sea from Kerrith harbor. It's unusual for the boats to go out on a Sunday—the Sabbath is still observed rigorously here, just as it is in my part of Scotland. I drew back into the shelter of the banks and raised my own glasses; there was no answering flash from the fishing boat's deck. I could see its skipper in the wheelhouse, blessedly unconcerned with me, smoking a pipe, his gaze on the horizon.

Finally, I reached the familiar outcrop of gorse where the coast path now gives out completely. From here, it was once possible to walk around the point and on down to the coves below Manderley— I've checked the old maps of the region, and the route can be seen clearly. But the cliffs are constantly eroding, and there was a rockfall about ten years ago, so that approach has become virtually impassable; I'd like to attempt it sometime—it would be an exhilarating climb—but I wouldn't risk attempting it without ropes and proper equipment. As it is, you're forced to cut inland, following an almost nonexistent path parallel to the estate walls, which finally emerges after miles of mud, brambles, and nettles, on the Four Turnings road. But there is a place about half a mile back from the cliffs where you can get over those estate walls without great difficulty. It has the advantage of being invisible (even to binoculars) from Kerrith.

I used this route, and made my now familiar way through the woods. It was cool in the half shade; the first bluebells were just breaking into flower; the still air smelled of leaf mold and spring. By moonlight or at dawn I find this the loveliest and most haunting part of Manderley. A wood pigeon murmured from the branches; a robin caroled and proclaimed his territory. I saw a dog fox, out hunting early: a glimpse of russet; I halted. He lifted his head, sniffing the air, then, with no sign of alarm, slipped away through the undergrowth and left me.

I could willingly have stayed here a long while. The local people claim these woods are malevolent and haunted, but I've never felt that. When I first came to Kerrith, my state of mind was troubled; I still couldn't come to terms with Julia's death and Nicky's grief, or with the guilt I felt during those last months of her illness. To be in Kerrith, to have embarked on this search after years of delay and avoidance, created its own turmoil, too—but I think the beauty and solitude here have helped to effect a cure. Something or someone (the Colonel, perhaps) is beginning to restore me to a more normal state, anyway; equilibrium and hope are returning, and I can sense it.

I came out of the woods above the so-called Happy Valley where a few of the swathes of species of azaleas that Rebecca de Winter planted still survive, though most were choked by nettles and bindweed long ago. I could smell the azaleas' sweet lingering perfume in the air as I reached the rough grass above the cove, and began negotiating the overgrown path that leads down to it. The dark shape of Manderley itself was now behind me; I stopped halfway down the path, shielding my eyes with my hand; the light was strengthening, and the sea was dazzling. I scanned the water, and eventually made out the dark line that marks the ridge of rocks running across the bay. This ridge is clearly marked on all the marine charts, and I wanted to look at it carefully. I sat down on a rock and trained my binoculars on it.

There are many mysteries in Rebecca's life, as I've been discovering—and the circumstances of her death are equally puzzling. This rock ridge is at the heart of the puzzles surrounding her death. Were it not for its existence, Rebecca's boat and her body might never have been discovered. It was pure chance. Over a year had passed since the disappearance of Rebecca and her converted Breton fishing vessel, *Je Reviens*. It was believed she had gone sailing at night, and foundered at sea—and that her boat would never be recovered. Then, in the second summer after her disappearance, in heavy seas and thick mist, a German merchant vessel strayed into this bay. It foundered on that very ridge of rock I was now inspecting through my binoculars.

The crew was taken off; a salvage vessel was brought in, and a diver was sent down to inspect the German ship's hull for damage. He happened on the sunken shape of a sailboat, which proved to be *Je Reviens*. It was just clear of that ridge, lying on sand, and apparently undamaged; it was the diver, looking in through the porthole, who saw the body lying in the cabin. It was Rebecca—and, despite her having been underwater for so long, she was quickly identified by the two rings, a wedding ring and an eternity ring, that were found on her finger—although the body was heavily decomposed, these remained. Her hands had been clenched, apparently.

It was fifteen months since Rebecca had disappeared. And during those months, two things had happened that interested me very much: First, Maxim de Winter had identified another woman's body washed ashore much farther up the coast as that of his late wife (mistakenly, as it turned out); and, secondly, less than a year after her death, he had remarried.

As de Winter's defenders locally have been quick to tell me, his identification of this body was made only a few months after Rebecca's disappearance, at a time when he was under great strain, mourning his wife, and on the edge of a breakdown. In such circumstances, they say, mistakes happen. At the time they were deeply concerned for him—and greatly relieved when he subsequently decided to leave Manderley for a while and travel abroad, retracing the route he and his beloved wife had taken on their honeymoon. An affecting story. I might be more inclined to accept it, had de Winter not then found a new wife for himself with such alacrity.

To remarry less than twelve months after your young wife's sudden and tragic death would raise eyebrows even now. Twenty years ago, it was a flagrant breach of convention. Did Maxim de Winter *want* to cause talk? If so, he certainly succeeded. Or didn't he care? Was he so in love with that "sad little ghost of a second wife" of his (as the Briggs sisters describe her) that he was prepared to flout convention? Possibly, for he married in haste, only weeks after first meeting her at a hotel in Monte Carlo.

I find this difficult to understand. De Winter was then forty-two—twice the age of his wife-to-be. He wasn't some impulsive young man—he was six years older than I am. Surely he could have seen that to remarry so precipitately and bring his new wife back here would make her position very difficult. He might be indifferent as to his own reputation—but I felt that, if he truly loved his new wife, he would have wanted to protect her from the least hint of scandal.

What would it have cost him to wait a few months more, and then bring her to Manderley in less invidious circumstances? If I'd been in that situation, I'd have acted differently—or I hope that I would. On the other hand, maybe I wouldn't. When in love, who does act sensibly? I've been in that state once, I still haven't recovered, and I'm not anxious to experience that chaos again. Can I say I conducted myself well, or even rationally? No, I can't—the very opposite.

I frowned at the sea. Puzzling—every aspect of this story was puzzling, and Maxim de Winter's behavior most of all. Some people here claim that he never loved his first wife, that he came to hate her—but, if so, why go on that strange pilgrimage after her death, retracing the route of their honeymoon? Other people claim that he *did* love Rebecca, that he was obsessed with her—but could that be true, when he mourned her less than a year before remarrying? And if he *killed* her—as most journalists who've written about the case believe—why then behave with such ineptitude? Why identify the wrong body, even have it laid in the de Winter crypt, and then, just when he had everyone's sympathy, forfeit that sympathy and cause an instant outbreak of rumors by remarrying?

If, as his accusers believe, he *was* guilty of Rebecca's death, then remarrying so swiftly was just about the stupidest thing de Winter could have done . . . though not, perhaps, quite as stupid as leaving her body in her boat, and scuttling that boat so close to shore, within view of Manderley. I've studied the plans of the house: I calculate that from the upper floor of the west wing where he and Rebecca had their rooms, he could have seen this stretch of water clearly. From those windows, he would be looking at the place where his wife's body lay. . . . So perhaps it's significant that, as Frith told me, he moved his rooms to the other side of the house when he remarried.

I stared at the dark line of the submerged reef. I could just see the paler water close by it, where Rebecca's boat was found, where the sand below made the sea azure. I was certain in my own mind that she *had* been killed, and, for want of any other candidate, felt her husband was probably the murderer; I think this is what Colonel Julyan also believes in his heart of hearts. But why risk sinking her boat so close to shore? At the mouth of this bay, the seabed shelves deeply. *Je Reviens* could have lain there, fathoms down, with very little risk of discovery. Had the killer panicked—or had he subconsciously *wanted* Rebecca's boat to be discovered? If it was de Winter who killed his wife, his subsequent actions seemed designed to draw attention to himself, and to awake suspicions. It was as if he were saying, Yes, I'm guilty, I killed her, arrest me. . . .

Questions, questions. Sitting there above the cove, I felt that I'd answer them only when I understood Rebecca herself, when I knew more about her. But that was proving peculiarly difficult. By accident or design, Rebecca had left behind virtually no evidence of her existence. It was as if the slate had been wiped clean. The thought of that made me suddenly impatient. I put the binoculars away, rose, and continued on down the steep path to the cove. I began walking across the sand and shingle, making for the boathouse.

I was thinking about the progress I've made—and the lack of it. My search hasn't been helped by the fact that all the recent de Winter family papers were destroyed in the Manderley fire—but that fire can't explain the extraordinary absence of all the usual official records. I located Rebecca's death certificate very quickly, that was straightforward; but, to my astonishment, I still can't lay my hands on either her marriage or her birth certificate. Each time I've thought I had some new lead, it's taken me up a blind alley; I still don't even know her maiden name. This failure to locate the obvious documents that would give me a starting point is making me suspicious. In my weaker moments—and this morning was one of them—I've begun to believe that this covering of the tracks was intentional, that inquiries such as mine were intended to be thwarted.

I continued on down to the shingle and began to walk toward the boathouse. This small square building, with its thick walls and tiny windows, summed up in a way all the contradictions about Rebecca that I've been battling to resolve since I came here. To the Colonel, and those of his persuasion, this was the refuge of a beautiful and unhappy woman in her last months on this earth. To Rebecca's detractors, it was a place of assignation where her lover (or lovers) was taken, a place that witnessed acts of shameless degradation— even perversity. . . . The idea of "perversity," of course, gets the Kerrith gossips wonderfully excited.

To the defenders, it's the place where she resolved to die rather than linger on for months with a painful and debilitating illness. To the detractors, it's the place where she met her comeuppance. And, as far as they're concerned, when a lovely woman stoops to folly, murder is fully justified. "After all," as one of them said to me, and without shame, too, "carrying on the way she did. She was asking for it, wasn't she?"

For several reasons—not least I have a brain—I don't accept that kind of argument. But then my views on what constitutes morality (or perversity, come to that) are not widely shared in places such as Kerrith. So I keep quiet. It's difficult enough to get reliable information, without alienating everybody. So I'm that "nice Mr. Gray"— and a very useful cipher he is, I thought, as I approached the boathouse. I came to an abrupt halt. A sweet and familiar scent stopped me in my tracks. Perhaps I'm not as immune to the stories of Manderley hauntings as I should like; perhaps I was discovering that an obsessive interest in a person now dead is a form of haunting anyway. Whichever the reason, I recoiled sharply.

In front of the boathouse door was a small paved area of thick Cornish granite. Lying in the center of these flagstones was a wreath—at least, I think it was intended as a wreath, but it was of a curious kind, not the monstrosity associated with funerals; more the garland once used to bind the brows of poets, heroes, or generals. It was not a wreath of bay, however. It had been fashioned from the branches of those azaleas once planted in such abundance in the Happy Valley.

These azaleas, as the Briggs sisters, both impassioned gardeners, had explained to me, were remarkable for the delicacy of their habit and their fragrance. According to the sisters, Rebecca had always worn a particular scent, which smelled very like those flowers; they associated it with her to such a degree, Elinor said, that they could not pass one of these shrubs without thinking of her. I'd noticed this perfuming of the air when I brushed past the few surviving plants in the Happy Valley. The flowers, small and of a pale yellow color indeed had a scent that was fresh and sweet. It was the scent of these flowers that first stopped me in my tracks. I smelled them a second before I saw them.

The thin branches had been carefully wound together to form the garland. I crouched down to touch the flowers; as soon as they were moved, the scent intensified. The branches had been laid in shade; there was no sign of wilting, but by midday these flagstones would be in full sun. Had the garland been placed here yesterday it would be shrivelled by now. So, someone had laid it here much more recently, at the earliest the previous evening, or during the night—or even this very morning.

It was now seven—I'd been sitting staring at that ridge for longer than I'd realized. For the past hour this cove had been in full view; I'd seen no one. Who would come here, to this particular place, with that particular token of remembrance? Someone who had loved her, surely. Someone who still thought of her when she'd been dead twenty years. Who could that be?

I felt a prickling unease. Straightening up, that unease at once intensified. I saw that the lock on the boathouse door—a flimsy affair of hasp and padlock—had been broken. The door had swollen with damp, but two pulls and it was open.

Someone had been in here, too. Peering into the gloom inside, letting my eyes grow accustomed to the half-light, I saw that there were footmarks on the dust of the floor, and the two windows had been screened off with sacking. I crossed to the landward window and pulled the material aside. So the Colonel hadn't been hallucinating after all. Someone *had* been here, perhaps on the very day we'd come to Manderley. Had I been seen, approaching the cove? Had someone heard my footsteps on the shingle? On both windows, the sacking was dry and new. Like the strange wreath outside, it had been placed there recently.

I looked around me with growing astonishment. I'd expected the place to be empty, but now there was more light, I could see that the furniture Colonel Julyan had described was still here; it had been stacked either side, as if to give clear passage down the center of the space, but several items were recognizable. I could see the deal table and the sofa bed he had spoken of, its metal frame flaking with rust. On top of it was a pile of moldering boxes; the whole place stank of damp, and the walls were green with it, but—unbelievably, after twenty years—some of Rebecca's belongings were still in situ.

I felt a sudden excitement. I thought, *No one ever cleared this place out*. It wasn't cleared after Rebecca's death, or even after the fire at Manderley. It was left untouched. Maxim de Winter just walked away, went abroad; the servants left—no one thought of this place, and no one touched it.

Was that possible? I knew that it *was* possible. The abrupt manner of de Winter's departure from Manderley was the one aspect of this story on which everyone I consulted was unanimous. When the fire that would destroy the house started, he and his second wife were returning from London, where they'd seen the doctor who provided the evidence of Rebecca's final illness. They drove through the night, and first saw the blaze from six miles away in the early hours of the following morning. It lit up the western horizon. By then the fire, fanned by the wind from the sea, had spread from the west wing to engulf the entire building, and the roar of the flames was audible, according to newspaper accounts, from as far away as Kerrith. By the time the de Winters reached Manderley itself, the house was beyond saving.

I could imagine how devastating a blow that must have been. De Winter's ancestors had lived here since the Conquest; generations of his family had altered the house, added to the house, demolished parts of it, rebuilt it, been born, married, and died in it. Now it was gone—and de Winter seems to have found that insupportable. He stayed for just two days, dealing only with the most essential formalities. Then he and his wife left for Europe, where they remained for many years; his estate manager, Frank Crawley, was left to make all the other final arrangements. Then he, too, departed, and the land agents took over.

"So I never paid my last respects to Mr. de Winter," Frith had said to me. "After all those years I'd been with the family. That came hard, that did. Fourteen years old, I was, when I first came to Manderley. I remember the day Mr. de Winter was born, I remember his mother and his father—and I thought he'd come to see me before he left. Not thanks—I didn't expect thanks, not when I'd only been doing my duties. But I thought he'd say good-bye. He was punctilious, Mr. de Winter. Of course, he was very distressed. I have to remember that, and he was generous—I had no complaints there, I was well provided for, all the servants were. After I heard he'd left— it was Mr. Crawley told me—I thought maybe he'd write. But he never did. Broke his heart to lose Manderley. Couldn't bear to be reminded of the old place. . . . I expect it was that—don't you think, sir?"

What did I think? I thought Frith's explanation was partly true. I also thought that, as the Colonel had hinted, there might be other reasons for Maxim's long and punitive self-exile. But that wasn't my concern now. The point was, he had left in haste; the handover to those land agents had been made in haste. I had read the details in the estate papers. Frank Crawley's letters had survived. All his arrangements for the paying off of staff, the future maintenance of the tenant farms, and so on, had been meticulous. But meticulous Frank Crawley had made one oversight: He had forgotten this place, forgotten Rebecca's boathouse.

I could feel my excitement rising. I knew it was absurd, but I couldn't prevent it. At one time, the notebook the Colonel described to me had been here, *and Rebecca had been writing in it*. What if Rebecca kept it here those last months—and what if it were *still* here, amidst all this damp moldering rubbish?

I looked. Of course I looked. I went through every damn thing in that place. I went through the boxes. I checked every last container and cupboard. I checked under and in and behind and above. I looked everywhere once, and when I still wasn't satisfied, I looked everywhere again. Behind this room, I discovered there was a further, smaller, area, where sailing equipment must have been stored. I blundered around in there, too, lifting up rotting canvas, shoving a broken oar to one side, rooting around in old coils of wet rotting rope, and scrabbling through thick clinging cobwebs. Nothing. I found nothing.

Well, that's not strictly true. I found evidence of past use, just as the Colonel described. There was a scrap of an old plaid rug, a filthy pillow spilling feathers. There were some grimy cups and glasses. There was a collection of books, stuck together and stained brown with damp. There were some torn, near illegible marine charts. I found two of the model boats intact, and the fragments of others. In a tin, I found some tea that had formed a thick hard black cake. I found a broken pen, and, plunging my hand into one of the boxes, a pink pulpy substance that I finally realized might once have been a blotting pad. I found a rusty biscuit tin; it was heavy and my heart leaped—a perfect storage place, I thought, in a damp boathouse. I cut my hand forcing it open, and all it contained was more old books, one of them that history of Manderley and Kerrith written by the Colonel's grandfather. I stood there, sucking the blood on my hand, breathing hard, and I gradually came to my senses.

I was ashamed at the greed of my search. I was a fool. It wasn't here; the notebook was not here—and, for all I knew, the damn thing never had been. I only had the Colonel's word that it had ever existed.

Meanwhile, I wasn't using my brain. I wasn't thinking clearly. This boathouse wasn't some time capsule, untouched since Rebecca's lifetime. According to Colonel Julyan, poor simpleminded Ben Carminowe had haunted this beach when she was alive, and after her death continued to return here, sometimes dossing down in the storage area behind me. More recently, anyone could have used it who had a mind to do so; the building wasn't secure, but it was hidden away, it was private. I wondered, did lovers use it now? Was it a convenient and private trysting place? Possibly, though if so it was a very damp and uninviting one. Yet someone had undoubtedly been here, and recently, too. Someone had left that wreath. Someone had been inside this building, and had bothered to screen the windows. Could they have been searching for something, as I was? Why? Who?

I was no more likely to discover the answer to those questions, I realized, than I was to discover that notebook. I tidied up. I put back into the boxes all the objects I'd taken out. I pushed the furniture back into place. I went outside into the sun and the fresh air, and pushed the swollen door shut again. I left the wreath where it was, and, filthy from head to foot, furious with myself for pursuing a will-o'-the-wisp in that stupid undisciplined way, I made for the cliff path.

Unbelievably, I'd been in that boathouse for over two hours. It was now well past nine o'clock. It would take me nearly an hour to walk back, and, once on the coast path, I'd be in full view of any watcher in Kerrith. I had to clean myself up, change my clothes, and turn myself back into Terence Gray again.

"Nice Mr. Gray" was expected at The Pines, and then at the Briggs sisters' cottage for Sunday lunch. I hated nice Mr. Gray in that moment; the last thing I wanted to do was change myself back into him. Mr. Gray had further interrogations in mind—and, irrationally, I blamed him for my own behavior in the boathouse. I'd behaved like some tomb robber. I was heartily sick of Mr. Gray, and myself; I couldn't wait to get out of Kerrith, and go back to King's—or London.

I could give all this up, I thought to myself as I mounted the steep path. I don't have to do this. I do it of my own free will. I can stop; I can abandon the entire search any time I want. I'm never likely to discover the truth about Rebecca—and what is the truth, anyway? Not a fixed thing, in my experience—never a fixed thing. The truth fluctuates, it shifts; look at it from this window and it takes one shape; look at it from another, and it's altered. *Who are you, Rebecca?* What a hopeless question that was. Colonel Julyan had known her well for five years, so had the Briggs sisters, so had Frith—and if they couldn't answer it, what chance did I have?

I paused at the top of the path. The sun shone down hotly on my head. I looked down at the cove, and then back toward the cool of the woods. I wouldn't give up. I couldn't give up. It mattered too much to me.

I turned toward the trees, and, as I did so, there was a flash, a little burst of light on the periphery of my vision. I stopped, and looked out across the water. In the mouth of the bay, the fishing boat I'd seen earlier was at anchor. I moved back into the shelter of the trees, and then raised my glasses. But whatever I'd seen, it had not been the flash of binoculars, I was almost sure. There was no one on the boat deck, and as before the skipper was in the wheelhouse, with his back to me, and his eyes—I assumed—on the far horizon.

I walked home, cleaned myself up, and, before I left for The Pines, completed the letter I've postponed writing to Nicky. I suggested he might like to make a quick foray to Brittany, and do some research there for me. A simple task for someone of his abilities; my French is reasonably good, but Nicky is bilingual. I worded the letter carefully—I didn't want him to suspect my real reason for writing. He doesn't know what I'm up to, and would find this quest of mine worrying if he did know—but then his background and circumstances are so very different from my own that he's never understood this side of my character.

"You know who you are," I said to him once—it was at Cambridge, in my room at King's, I think. Or we may have been walking on the Backs. Not that it matters. "You know who you are, Nicky, and I don't. That's the difference between us."

"One of the differences," he replied quietly. "But not the main one."

I posted the letter on my way to The Pines. It wouldn't be collected until the following day, but I didn't want to risk changing my mind and not sending it. I don't have time to go trailing around Brittany. I need Nicky's help. I never find it easy to ask anyone for help, but on this occasion I felt the better for doing so.

TWELVE

I SET OFF FOR THE PINES FEELING DISPIRITED; MY LACK OF success at the boathouse made me acutely aware of the obstacles I'm encountering in my search for Rebecca. I had to remind myself that I *had* made advances, even if they weren't the kind of rapid advances I'd hoped for.

Walking up the hill to the Colonel's house, I told myself that I must learn to break this slavish dependence I have on *facts*—I've spent too many years in libraries, too many years working from documents, and I'm still too hedged in by my own disciplines and training. My instinct is still to approach these inquiries as if they were part of my academic work, or a chapter in my next book. But the historian's approach doesn't entirely work here. It may be appropriate when I'm writing about people that have been dead and buried for over four centuries, but it can be counterproductive now I'm dealing with more recent events and living witnesses—knowing how to handle *them* can be very tricky indeed. I may know how to read documents, but I'm less good at reading people, I've realized.

I'm now learning, I hope, how to *look* and how to *listen*. Very often it isn't *what* someone told me, but the *way* they told me that is the most revealing. No doubt I'd be less vulnerable to these bouts of pessimism if I had someone to talk to, someone I could discuss all this with over a drink at the end of the day. If a Cambridge friend were here, or May were still alive, I probably wouldn't get as downcast as I sometimes do. But they aren't, and there's no one in Kerrith I can confide in, so occasionally I feel lonely and cut off here.

It isn't that I mind being alone. I learned to value privacy very quickly at the orphanage. If you spend all day every day being herded, if every act is a public one, witnessed and jeered at, if you go to sleep being taunted and wake to more taunts, then solitude is a luxury. It always has been for me; it probably always will be, and if I'm denied it too long I start to crave it. That's one of the legacies of the orphanage years—Nicky would say one of the scars. I don't like that term; it's predictable. Besides, scars indicate healing, and they're harmless.

But there's a vast difference between being alone and being lonely—there's an ocean between those two states, as I'm discovering. I'm not the child I was, thank God, and I'm no longer the sullen suspicious young man I was when I first went up to King's. I now need friends, and can even admit that to myself. In fact, I've made such progress that Nicky says I'm approaching normality—though there's still room for improvement, he tells me. He says I can now talk to people as if they were people and not robots, which is an advance. A few more years and, with luck, I'll be emotionally "housetrained," as he charmingly puts it.

I thought of Nicky's comments as I finally reached The Pines. Maybe I'd have progressed further and faster with Colonel Julyan had I been more open with him—though there was a limit, obviously, to how open I could be. I decided to make an effort today. I'm fond of the old man, and I was looking forward to seeing him. He'd promised to start going through all those boxes and files of his in search of letters he wanted to show me.

I wasn't sure whether this "archive" (as the Colonel's now begun to call it) contained anything of use, or decades of irrelevant rubbish. I was hopeful, though. I'd been given glimpses of its contents, enough to feel that there might well be some gems, especially if the Colonel can locate the folders he claims he's mislaid, which contain "Notes from Rebecca" and "Letters from Maxim."

Even though we've made our pact and I am now "co-opted," I'm not allowed, of course, to search through any of this material myself.

The Colonel has to do so, and in conditions of some secrecy—so I suspect he might want to vet the contents of anything he finds before showing it to me. He is beginning to trust me, though, so perhaps today I'd make a breakthrough, I thought. My spirits rose; they were dashed almost as soon as I entered the house. The Colonel was nowhere to be seen, and Ellie met me with the news that he'd worn himself out looking through all his boxes and files the previous day; this morning he'd been very fretful. Taking me through into the kitchen, she told me she'd packed him off to bed, where he was now sleeping peacefully.

I was concerned, and genuinely sorry to hear he'd been upset by his activities, but my face fell. I wasn't able to hide my disappointment. Ellie, who misses very little, saw it at once; it may have hurt her, but if so, she covered it up quickly.

"Don't look quite so miserable," she said with a smile. "I know it's my father you want to see, but it won't hurt you to talk to me for five minutes. I'll make some coffee and we can sit outside—it's such a lovely day. No, please don't rush off—I haven't had a chance to speak to you alone since the day we went to Manderley, and there's something I want to tell you."

She made the coffee; I was instructed to fetch cups and a tray. The kitchen at The Pines is a pleasant room; it looks as if it hasn't been altered in years, and I'm sure hasn't changed since Ellie was a child. I could imagine a time when Ellie had sat here with her brother and elder sister—and I suppose that made me like the room even more. Never having had one in the usual sense, I'm sentimental about families. On the table was a pile of the Sunday newspapers, and a book that Ellie had evidently been reading before I arrived. I wanted to see what it was, but I couldn't read the title without moving the papers; I had to wait until she had her back to me. I'm not sure what I was expecting: one of those women's novels about marriage and domesticity, perhaps; or, given her aunt Rose's influence, Austen maybe, or the Brontës. It proved to be Camus, *The Outsider*. I hid it under the newspaper again.

We went out into the garden, past the palm and the monkey puzzle, and down to the terrace at the far end. The church bells were ringing for morning service; a light breeze from the water made the rigging of the yachts anchored below us reverberate with a strange rhythmic humming. The view over the harbor, with the boats moving lazily at anchor and the ferry churning the water as it departed from the pier, was ceaselessly interesting and calming. In harbors, time stretches; and of all the ones I know well, including the tiny and remote one that May and Edwin's house overlooked, I like Kerrith the best. I associate it with the first true freedom and happiness of my childhood.

Ellie stretched like a cat in the sun, then sat down on the wall, hugging her knees, and watching the water. I tried to decide if she'd changed in the months since I first met her, or if I was only now learning how to look at her. For a long time, I think, I couldn't see beyond the fact that she was the Colonel's daughter; it certainly took a while for me to notice she's pretty—in fact very attractive, in a boyish gamine way. She's very slim; today, her soft brown hair was tied carelessly back from her face; she was wearing a short-sleeved blouse and narrow trousers; she'd kicked off her shoes, and I noticed her feet, like her arms and her face, were tanned gold. The light was dazzling. Ellie pulled out a pair of dark glasses and put them on. At once she looked different again—and I realized how much I depend on reading her eyes. Ellie has remarkable eyes, of a clear hazel. They're exceptionally candid—and, now they were hidden behind those smoky lenses, I was thrown. I felt I had no idea who she was, or how to go about talking to her.

She may have sensed this, because she took charge. Trying to put me at my ease, I suspect, she began telling me about her father and his progress. I was thinking how little I knew about her. The Briggs sisters had told me that as a child Ellie was exceptionally clever, that she took after her aunt Rose, that she'd won a scholarship to Cambridge, and would have gone there to study literature at Girton, but her mother became ill, so she gave it up and stayed here to nurse her. Now she was nursing her father. I wondered if she ever fretted, if she regretted sacrificing her life in this way. I thought not. There's nothing bitter about Ellie. She's generous, smart, loyal, and observant—with flashes of intelligence that took me by surprise at first. Would I have regarded Ellie differently had she gone to Cambridge and taken a degree? I knew I would—and that made me ashamed. Now I knew her better, I was beginning to see that I might have underestimated Ellie.

"I want to say something to you," she began, after we'd been sitting there in the sun for a while. "It's about my father, and, no, it's not about his health, or not directly. I want to ask you not to judge him."

That took me by surprise. If Ellie knew me better she'd realize I'm in no position to judge anyone. "Why should you think I would?" I said.

"You might. People here have. Journalists have. And my father's suffered accordingly. He's learned to live with that—but he likes you. How you think of him matters to him—not that he'd ever admit that. He's proud, as you've probably seen. I'm sure he'd never defend himself. So I want to do it for him."

"Ellie—you don't need to do that."

"Yes, I do. I want you to understand. People here accuse my father of a cover-up. I know they'll have told you this. I know you'll have read all the articles, those damn stupid books. They say Rebecca's death was never investigated properly, that more could have been done—I don't know what, and neither do they, but that doesn't stop them. They talk and write such rubbish—some people even claim my father invented all that evidence about Rebecca's having cancer and being mortally ill. Well, he didn't. They'd never have traced that London doctor if it hadn't been for my father. And Rebecca *was* dying—I hope you're in no doubt about that? Dr. Baker sent written confirmation. I've seen the letters."

"I've never doubted that, Ellie." I hesitated; I knew how defensive of her father she was, and this was difficult territory. I could see that the Colonel's hands had been tied. Even so, he did not believe himself blameless. Should I risk pushing Ellie on this point? I decided I would. "I've asked your father several times," I said, "but there's still something I'm not clear about. What did your father think at the time? What did he believe in his heart, Ellie?"

Ellie gave me a look that might have been scornful or amused—I couldn't tell because of those dark glasses. With a restless gesture, she swung her legs off the wall, and produced a packet of cigarettes from her pocket. I'd never seen her smoke before—but then I've scarcely talked to her without her father being present. "In his heart?" she said now, lighting her cigarette. She gave me a small glance that I was almost sure *was* amused. "Well, it's always difficult to read people's hearts, of course.... But he *knew*—of course he knew. Not at the very beginning. I'm sure he believed in the accident at sea at first. He had no suspicions when that first woman's body was found and Maxim identified it as Rebecca's. He pitied Maxim then—everyone did."

She paused. "It was later that everything changed, when Maxim went abroad and he remarried. That caused such a scandal. My mother was appalled, and people like the Briggs sisters—they were bewildered, I think. You see, they'd all believed Maxim loved Rebecca, that he adored her. And then, when she wasn't cold in her grave—that's the way Elinor Briggs put it—he came back from France with a child bride. It was like *Hamlet*—you know the line in *Hamlet*?"

" 'The funeral baked meats did coldly furnish forth the marriage tables'?"

"Exactly. My father tried to defend Maxim. I know he was shocked, too, because he's old school; conventions matter to him. But he was loyal to Maxim, and he was very short with people who criticized him. . . . I'll tell you when his doubts began: It was when Rebecca's boat was found. My father was there when they raised it. They went down to the boathouse cove at dawn—and that's why he's avoided that place ever since. It haunts him. They took *Je Reviens* to that little deserted creek, the one near James Tabb's old boatyard. That creek silts up at low tide, and it was disused even then; no one ever goes there—do you know it?"

"I've passed it."

"They wanted somewhere quiet, and private. A fine and private place . . ." Ellie looked away toward the water; the smoke of her cigarette curled. "My father was there as magistrate; Maxim was present, of course, and our local doctor, Dr. Phillips. The harbormaster was there and a police inspector. . . . It was all very official. You have to remember that, at that point, everyone believed that Rebecca's body had *already* been found, so no one knew whose body this was; they didn't even know if it was a man or a woman. When the body was finally brought ashore, and they came to identify it, Maxim tried to touch Rebecca's rings—she was still wearing them. My father didn't tell me that until years afterward, but I know it was then that he started to have doubts. He saw something in Maxim's eyes, maybe. Then, after the inquest, he was deeply uneasy. . . ."

"Because of Tabb's evidence? Because the boat had been deliberately scuttled?"

"Well, obviously," she replied, her tone cool. "That inquest was a farce. The coroner must have been a fool. But it wasn't just that—it was something less tangible. Has my father ever talked to you about Rebecca's burial service?"

I shook my head. This subject, as I'd learned, was verboten for Colonel Julyan.

"Maxim and he quarrelled about it," she went on. "Maxim insisted on Rebecca's being buried in the de Winter crypt, and my father knew Rebecca hadn't wanted that. But Maxim wouldn't listen. He insisted it all had to be done quickly, immediately after the inquest."

"What about the other woman—the woman whose body he'd misidentified? She was already buried there."

"I know. Her coffin had to be removed. I think that was done during the inquest. Frank Crawley probably made the arrangements—he usually did. I know there were police present. They spirited her away, at a time when they knew there'd be no danger of publicity because all the journalists were at the coroner's court. I don't know what happened to her then. Nobody was interested in her, poor woman." There was a pause; when I didn't speak, she turned away, frowning, her gaze resting on the water below us. "I can understand the secrecy up to a point," she went on. "You've read the newspaper coverage. My father loathed publicity of that kind, and it was anathema to Maxim. So I see why those arrangements had to be made in that surreptitious way—but when it came to Rebecca's burial, why did that have to be such a shabby hasty affair? She'd been Maxim's *wife*; there were people here who loved and admired her—and yet she was buried like a pauper, or a criminal."

"That caused comment presumably?"

"It caused *offense*," Ellie said sharply. "No one in Kerrith even knew the funeral was happening, and we only did because my father was attending it. I can remember that night so well: My brother was away at school, but the rest of us were here; my mother was very distressed, and so was my sister, Lily—Lily worshipped Rebecca. She'd come home—she lived in London then—because she wanted to go to Rebecca's funeral. And then she couldn't, because there *wasn't* a funeral as such, just this horrible, hasty, guilty interment. When my father came back that night, his face was white—ashen. I'd never seen him look like that. He wouldn't speak to any of us. He went into his study and shut the door on us.

"I'm certain my father believed Maxim was guilty then. But he's never discussed it with me. He won't talk to anyone about what happened that night in the crypt—and he doesn't like talking about what happened later the same night at Manderley, either. If he does, he's always reticent, or nearly always. He leaves out key details—he's good at that, as no doubt you've noticed. . . ." She hesitated, and glanced at me. "I hope you forgive him for that. He loved Rebecca very dearly, you see. And he's an old-fashioned man, so he'll move heaven and earth to suppress any information he thinks reflects badly on her."

I could hear the appeal, and I was touched. "There's no question of forgiveness," I began. "I understand that. I respect it. I won't say it doesn't infuriate me when he dodges my questions. But you have to admire the turn of speed—"

"I thought you might say that," she said, interrupting me, her tone dry. "I can see you might admire the way he evades questions. You're quite dexterous at that yourself. Maybe you've picked up some tips from him. More coffee?"

She had removed the dark glasses as she spoke; she smiled, and in a demure way, with no further comment, refilled my cup. Until she began speaking again, I had the unpleasant sensation that I'd given the wrong answer, or she suspected me of insincerity. Ellie could be disconcerting, as I was beginning to realize.

I think I must have said the right thing, however, for she then moved on to the whole issue of what had happened at Manderley on the night of Rebecca's funeral—and she gave me some very interesting information, describing events that Colonel Julyan has resolutely avoided from day one.

Within an hour or so of the interment, no more, Colonel Julyan had been called back to Manderley. There—and I'd had no inkling of this—he'd been confronted by Maxim, the second Mrs. de Winter, the ubiquitous Frank Crawley, and a very drunken Jack Favell. Favell had several bombshells to drop. First, he produced a note from Rebecca that he had *not* offered as evidence at the inquest earlier that day, although he had attended it. This note had been hand delivered to the porter at his block of flats by Rebecca, shortly before she left London for the last time. Second—and without the least sign of shame and embarrassment, apparently—he'd announced that not only had he and Rebecca been lovers, she had been about to leave her husband for him, and would have done so, had she not died. I stared at Ellie.

"You're sure about this?"

"Absolutely sure. At one time, my father would never have discussed what happened that night. But he's changed since his heart attack. Since you began asking your questions, too. He talks to me now much more openly." She hesitated. "Maybe you haven't realized quite how much it preys on his mind."

"But, I don't understand—why was your father there? Why did Maxim ask him to go over to Manderley? He can't have wanted your father to witness a scene like that, surely?"

Ellie gave me a quick glance that might have been approval; I couldn't tell, because she'd replaced the dark glasses. She gave a shrug. "Oh, I agree," she replied. "But Maxim had a plausible reason. Favell had turned up at Manderley, none too sober, and tried to use Rebecca's note as a way of extorting money, you see. Favell always was after money—you'll discover just what a vile man he is when you meet him tomorrow. It is tomorrow you're seeing him, isn't it?" She paused. "Make sure you ask him about that note. It must have been the last thing she ever wrote, and—this is the intriguing part—in the note, Rebecca said she had something she urgently needed to tell Favell. She asked him to meet her at Manderley, at her boathouse that same night. . . . Which seems a rather strange request if you're intending to drive back there, go out in your boat, and commit suicide."

"It certainly does. Did Favell do as she asked?"

"No, apparently not. I don't know why; you'll have to ask him. But the point is, that note cast doubt on the suicide verdict—presumably that's why Favell thought he could make money out of it. He assumed the last thing Maxim would want was that verdict's being overturned, or any further investigations. And I suspect he was right about that. Even so, Maxim called his bluff. That's when my father was asked over there—as magistrate rather than friend—and Favell was invited to put his evidence and his accusations to him."

"He produced the note? Your father read it?"

"Oh, certainly. Then Favell blustered and boasted—made all the claims about himself and Rebecca. And accused Maxim of killing her. Claimed Maxim was insane with jealousy—gave him a motive, in other words." She paused. "I gather it became very ugly. My father couldn't believe that Maxim was allowing this man to say these things about Rebecca, in what had been her home, and within hours of that terrible funeral. It got worse, too. Mrs. Danvers was called in, to confirm that Rebecca had been unfaithful. Can you imagine my father's reaction to that? A servant being cross-questioned about Rebecca's loyalty as a wife? He was appalled. But he could see this had to be investigated. That's why he suggested they look into Rebecca's final movements. If they knew what she'd done that last day in London, he thought they might discover what she'd wanted to tell Favell so urgently. Mrs. Danvers produced Rebecca's diary—"

"Mrs. Danvers?" I said sharply. "Why on earth would the house-keeper have Rebecca's diary?"

"I don't know—I've never thought about it." Ellie frowned. "It wasn't a journal kind of diary, I'm sure. Just an appointments book. Mrs. Danvers kept everything after Rebecca died—her room, her clothes, nothing was altered. I remember Maxim's sister, Beatrice, telling my mother that. But then Mrs. Danvers worshipped Rebecca. I think she'd looked after her as a child at one point. Surely my father told you that?"

"Yes. He mentioned it. Even so, a diary, her personal papers—it seems odd—never mind. Go on, Ellie."

"Well, they looked at the diary entries for the last day of her life. And that's when they discovered the appointment with that consultant. My father insisted they go to see him. . . . You see, he was a woman's specialist. A gynecologist."

I stared at her dark glasses; a scene the Colonel had never described to me, a scene that I'd heard of only at third- or fourth-hand, disentangled itself from the veils of gossip, and began to take on a new shape. I'd been looking at these events with hindsight, I realized, from the wrong end of the telescope. Viewed in the sequence they actually happened, they took on new shape. Revelations of infidelity; an appointment with a gynecologist . . .

"Rebecca and Maxim had been married five years," Ellie went on.

"There had been no children. There was no heir—and there had been speculation about that locally. So, when my father discovered she'd consulted a London doctor, not her local doctor; when he heard the man was a women's specialist . . . you can imagine what he thought."

"He thought Rebecca had been expecting a child?"

"Yes. He did. And, if that proved to be the case, then obviously everything was altered. The suicide verdict would inevitably be over-turned. But Rebecca's boat hadn't sunk by accident. It was scuttled. So that left only one alternative. I think my father could see the hangman's noose tightening around Maxim's neck as they drove to London. . . ." She paused. "But it wasn't just that—do you under-stand? There were other implications, too, very serious ones."

"I see. I see." I stood up, and walked across to the edge of the ter-race; I looked at the yachts swaying at anchor. Why had Colonel Julyan never told me this? It would have meant that, driving to Lon-don, he must have been considering the possibility that Maxim de Winter had killed not only his wife, but also her unborn child. If so, it raised a terrible question: Could Maxim have killed Rebecca believing her to be pregnant? I couldn't begin to answer that, and neither, I suppose, could the Colonel, but the images it conjured up in my mind were dark and terrible ones. Where had it happened? On the shore—no, not on the shore, and not on her boat either. In the boathouse, in the place I'd been standing this morning. Of that I felt suddenly, and irrationally, certain.

The scene was very sharp in my mind, and I could feel my attitude to Maxim de Winter hardening. I've been trying to fight that inclina-tion ever since—I was conjuring the scene out of the air, and I had no proof. But I still can't dislodge it.

I listened to the few remaining details of Ellie's story with less attention—they were already familiar to me. Had Rebecca suspected how ill she was, I wondered, or had the news come as a complete sur-prise to her?

"My father spent that night in London," Ellie was saying, and I realized I'd scarcely heard her for the last few minutes. "He was ter-ribly overwrought. He'd spent the whole day trying to conceal his thoughts. He went to stay with Rose, at her house in St. John's Wood. I expect he wanted to talk it over with her. . . ." She paused.

The dark glasses turned in my direction. "Rose had a house in London then. In fact, she still has. She's there now. She's working on a new book. She's on sabbatical from Cambridge, did my father tell you?"

I dragged myself back to the present with some difficulty. "No," I said. "No. He's been steering me away from Rose. He likes to pretend she's a recluse in the Fens. Of course, I did know that was misleading. In academic circles, your aunt is very well known. She—" I stopped myself.

"Ah, yes," Ellie said, her tone dry. "You were an undergraduate at Cambridge, weren't you? I'd forgotten that."

I don't think she *had* forgotten it—not at all. I changed the subject quickly. I was furious with myself for making that slip, and I didn't want to get drawn on the issue of Cambridge, past or present. We talked for a little while longer, about her father, the predicament in which he'd then found himself, and his decision to draw a line under the whole affair.

"If that inquest had been held in Scotland," I said, "there could have been a 'not proven' verdict. It's a pity that option doesn't exist in England."

"Isn't it?" Ellie replied. "Why *does* Scotland have a different legal system? I wish I knew Scotland better—I've never been there, and neither has my father. So we're very ignorant. Unless I looked at a map, I wouldn't know the difference between Perth and Peebles."

Her tone was innocent. Was she fishing, or teasing me? I couldn't tell then, and I still can't. I looked at my watch, and discovered that punctual Terence Gray was about to be late for Sunday lunch with the Briggs sisters.

We began to walk back toward the house, and I suddenly found I was reluctant to leave. I wished I didn't have that lunch with two elderly women, fond though I am of them; I've been spending so much time talking to people twice my own age that I'd almost forgotten how it felt to talk to someone of my own generation. I was realizing that I should have talked to Ellie about all this much earlier; I should have asked her about Rebecca. Ellie was observant, and with her I didn't have to fight my way through interminable evasions and circumlocutions.

"How old were you when you first came back to The Pines?" I

asked as we rounded the house, making for the side gate that leads directly out to the lane.

"I was six." Ellie plucked at a clump of herbs and began rubbing a leaf between her fingers. "I'd never lived in England. I'd grown up in the Far East—first Malaya, then Singapore." She gave me a sidelong amused glance. "That won't interest you, I know. So, as I'm sure you're wondering, I was six when I first met Rebecca, and eleven when she died. I can't claim to have known her—I was too young—but I used to see her all the time. She came here, and we went to Manderley often. All that endless entertaining! I went to some of the garden parties—and my mother used to describe the grown-up ones. Troops of people coming down from London all the time—everyone from ambassadors to artists. I think my mother found it intimidating; it made her feel shabby, a bit of a bumpkin—which wasn't the case. Anyway, I met Rebecca frequently—"

"And?"

"And I was a very watchful little girl. I used to watch her all the time. She fascinated me."

"Tell me why."

"At first, because she was beautiful. People always say that, I know. They all talk about her beauty and her wit and her charm—and they're such bankrupt words. They're anodyne and approximate. They don't give you the least idea what she was like. They make her sound empty-headed and frivolous. The society beauty. The society hostess—that's another word I hate." She gave an impatient gesture. "As if Rebecca thought about nothing but parties. That's so misleading. If I remember her now, she's where she was happiest—on her boat, or walking in the woods, or with her dogs. Alone, usually, which is odd. I remember her *alone*. . . ." She hesitated. "But you can't *not* mention how she looked. I'd never seen anyone that beautiful before—and I haven't since. She had the most extraordinary eyes—unforgettable eyes. She was bewitching. She captivated you—that's how it felt. And I was a little girl. Imagine what it was like for men. They'd stare and stare—and Rebecca would be talking away, and half the time, I don't think they even heard her. That irritated her. And bored her."

"She didn't like to be admired? Most women do."

"Do they?" The dark glasses tilted in my direction. "Well, then, she wasn't like most women."

It was a reprimand, lightly made, but sharp nonetheless: I colored. As I've said, Ellie can be disconcerting. " 'At first,' you said." I went on. "What did you mean by that?"

"I meant that her beauty blinded you—for a long time I simply couldn't see beyond it. When I finally did, I was still fascinated." She frowned. "Partly because I could see how much my father admired her, and I wanted to understand why. I didn't *want* to like her, but I did. She had an unusual way of speaking—very direct. You know how there are things people think, but never say? Well, Rebecca said them, straight out. I don't think it occurred to her how unconventional that was. But then she never cared tuppence for convention. She could be very funny, very quick—and very ruthless if people were pompous or pretentious. And I thought she was sad. Behind all that gaiety and wit—I thought she was sad. Not unhappy—sad. It's not quite the same thing, is it?"

"No. It isn't." I opened the gate. "Sadness is a more permanent condition. Unhappiness is somehow temporary."

Ellie made no comment on this, though I think she understood. There was a silence between us; the breeze gusted, stirring up the dust of the lane. "Did you ever discover why she might be sad?" I said finally, and regretted the question at once. Perhaps I shouldn't have harped on Rebecca quite so much. I do tend to use people as conduits for information, and sometimes they resent it. Looking at Ellie then, I had a vague but strong sense of a missed opportunity.

"No. No, I didn't." Ellie looked at her watch. "I told you, I was too young. Lily knew her much better. Lily was in London by then, studying at the Slade. She wanted to be a painter—well, I think she wanted to get away from Kerrith as much as anything. The golf club, the tennis club, the regatta—Lily couldn't wait to escape. She shared a house with some artists in Chelsea, in Tite Street, by the river, just a few doors away from the flat Rebecca kept in London. They had friends in common—painters, writers, actors. But of course, Lily's dead now."

There was another silence. There were suddenly many questions I wanted to ask Ellie, and not all of them concerned Rebecca. I hesitated. "One thing before I go: Did your father show you that notebook he was sent?"

"*Rebecca's Tale*? Yes, he did." She closed the gate and latched it. Her tone altered and became brisk. "Look, I really must go back to the house—"

"Just tell me one thing. You remember the postcard, the one of Manderley? I want to follow that up. There's someone I know in London who might help with it—it suggests a great many possibilities, that card. . . ."

"Perhaps." Her tone was now cool. "I wouldn't jump to conclusions. Anyone could have glued that card in that notebook at any time, including the person that sent it to my father."

"I don't jump to conclusions. And I know that. But the glue marks were old and—Ellie, did you ever hear it suggested that Rebecca might have come from this part of the world? Or that she came here as a child?"

"As you did, you mean?" The dark glasses tilted. "No. I didn't."

I was now sure that I had offended her in some way. Even so, I pressed on. "Did you ever hear where she *did* come from? Was anything like that ever discussed, that you remember? Her background? Who her parents were?"

"Never. And you couldn't ask. She hated questions, especially personal ones. I expect you can understand that. Now, I have to go. Call in this evening, if you'd like to see Daddy. I know he'd be pleased to see you."

She lifted her hand, then turned, and ran back toward the house. I was now sure that I'd upset her. It occurred to me that I'd said nothing of my visit to the boathouse, or the azalea garland, and I regretted that. Ellie had just given me a better description of Rebecca than anyone else had. I might have profited from Ellie's reactions, I realized.

I set off in the hot sun down the steep hill to the Briggs's cottage. I thought about that azalea wreath, and who might have placed it there. I thought of the rumored lovers, of possible male candidates. Then I thought about Ellie, and that book on the kitchen table; then I found I'd walked half a mile without noticing, and I was at the gate to the sisters' cottage. I walked up to the front door, which was instantly opened. Jocelyn and Elinor Briggs emerged, with little cries of welcome.

"Dear Mr. Gray—how nice. . . . Come in, come in. You've been at The Pines? You look rather anxious. How was Arthur? And dear Ellie?"

"We're just back from church—such a lovely service! And the rector is joining us for lunch. . . . Rector—this is Mr. Gray, whom we've been telling you about. . . . Yes, our new neighbor, our local historian! Now, if you'll forgive me, I must just check on something in the kitchen. Jocelyn, dear, look after them!"

"Of course! Mr. Gray, Rector, let me give you a glass of our bargain sherry."

I tensed. The rector, unsuspecting, said a glass of sherry would be delightful. I could see that there was no way of avoiding either the sherry or Terence Gray, so I took the glass, and let Gray's gray mantle fall upon me.

THIRTEEN

THE BRIGGS SISTERS WERE ANXIOUS TO DISCUSS THE church service that morning. The text for the day had been: Cast thy bread upon the waters for thou shalt find it after many days. Both Jocelyn and Elinor were very fond of this text; they thought it was a very *deep* text, which repaid thought, and they were full of praise for the sermon the rector had preached on it.

I could remember that text only too well from my childhood; at the orphanage we were dragged off to the chapel three times on a Sunday, and the idea of casting bread anywhere was never too well received. But then we "orphans" were literal minded and always hungry. I said nothing about that, and the rector said nothing about my absence from church, so I knew he'd been primed. Terence Gray, thanks to the influence of "Auntie May," is a strict Presbyterian—and the nearest Presbyterian church is a convenient three hundred miles away.

The rector, who has only recently been appointed and has lived here only a few more months than I have, seemed amiable. He said he'd heard of my interest in churches, and that one of these days I must let him take me around the Manderley church. There were some fine medieval brasses on the de Winter tombs in the nave; there was a remarkable view from the bell tower, and the crypt repaid exploration. It was fascinating from an architectural point of view, and much earlier than the main church building. Terence Gray said politely that he would like that very much.

At that point there was a crisis in the kitchen (there had been several already, but this was obviously a more major one), and with little cries both the Briggs sisters deserted us. The rector took a sip and his eyes met mine over the rim of his sherry glass. "Good grief," he said. "What *is* this?" I explained it was black market, and suggested paraffin. The rector felt Jeyes Fluid was much nearer the mark. "Jeyes Fluid—and *syrup*," he added. "Wherever did the good sisters get it?"

"Dear Colonel Julyan found it for us," said Elinor, emerging pink and flustered from the kitchen, and catching only the end of his remark. "He bought it from Robert Lane, I believe—Robert used to be a footman at Manderley. He and his wife run a most unsavoury public house over at Tregarron. Mrs. Lane is a Manack by birth—and all the Manacks have been smugglers from time immemorial. We were a little doubtful. It may be illicit, and we didn't want Customs and Excise knocking on the door—but the Colonel insisted, so we have a whole case to drink up! Let me pour you another glass, Rector."

Not quite the version I'd been given by Colonel Julyan, I noted. I managed to evade another glass, and tales of smuggling, as fabled in the past and rumored in the present, kept both Briggs sisters going until we were at table and the difficult business of carving the roast chicken (the rector) and handing vegetables (me) had been completed.

Finally, the sisters stopped fluttering and agitating, and at last we all sat down in their tiny cottage dining room. The Briggses' entire cottage would fit into one of the cavernous rooms at The Pines. It's like a very small and exquisite dollhouse, painted white inside and out, and perched above Kerrith harbor. The sisters moved here about twenty-five years ago, but they grew up at St. Winnow House, a Queen Anne palace of a place now converted into a nursing home for the elderly—the very house where I was due to see Frith later the same afternoon.

Their father, Sir Joshua Briggs, was a shipping magnate, I believe, and not from this part of the world originally; but their mother, Evangeline, a famous beauty, was born a Grenville and their aunt

Virginia was Maxim de Winter's mother. After their parents' deaths, unsuspected debts and inheritance taxes took their toll; the sisters found themselves having to live in reduced circumstances.

This cottage, on which they were granted a long lease by the de Winter estate—thanks to Rebecca's intervention, apparently—was offered them in the nick of time, at a point when they'd been resigned to leaving the district. Unable to bear parting with all their family belongings when they came here, they brought as much as possible with them—as a result, the dining room, which is ten feet by eight, if that, has to accommodate a Georgian mahogany table and chairs, a huge Georgian sideboard, and a sarcophagus of a wine cooler. There are innumerable pictures, including a full-length portrait in oils of the young Evangeline Grenville, two small pastels of her sisters Virginia and Isolda, and several vast Victorian seascapes, now very dark and discolored, which conceal ships in them somewhere. I am very fond of the cottage and the room and the sisters—but you have to be careful not to bang knees under that table, and it's necessary to pretend (as it is at The Pines) that there's an invisible cook, and probably some invisible maids, in the kitchen.

Neither of the Briggs sisters can cook, of course. They were not brought up to cook, they were brought up to marry. I suspect Elinor, who is the elder, the sharper, and the taller, had her eye on Arthur Julyan when she was about eighteen. Jocelyn, the plumper, prettier, and more naive of the two, had a fiancé killed in the trenches. Now both sisters garden (their garden is as exquisite as their house, no mournful monkey puzzles here) and devote themselves to good works; they have shown me endless kindness. Their memories of Manderley go back as far as the Colonel's do, and—like his—can be unreliable.

We stayed on neutral subjects while we ate the chicken and the very overcooked vegetables. The pudding was a curious lumpy affair, with jam in it, and over this lumpy pudding, in which there was an occasional currant, I managed to turn the conversation back to Manderley. We meandered around in the sisters' memories; they talked at length about Rebecca's celebrated fancy-dress balls, and the various disguises people chose to wear to them. I was interested in this question of disguises. Apparently, Maxim de Winter always refused to wear costume, and went in evening dress; Colonel Julyan, who was very afraid of being made to look a fool, wore the same costume every year. He always went as Oliver Cromwell, Lord Protector. Given his devotion to Rebecca, that struck me as appropriate. Over the years, the sisters' disguises had included Cleopatra and the Queen of Sheba; on one memorable occasion, at the ball held the year before Rebecca's death, Elinor had gone as Medusa, and Jocelyn as Nell Gwynn, complete with oranges.

I said I wished I'd seen that—which I certainly did. I asked them if they could remember Rebecca's costumes. To my surprise—both sisters can be very vague, and untangling their stories is like untangling a yard of knitting—they could.

"Oh, yes, I remember them *very* well," cried Jocelyn. "Let me see—there were four balls altogether. At the first, she came as a French aristocrat on his way to the guillotine; she looked quite astonishing. Then, another year—I think it was the third—she came as an Elizabethan page, well, a young gallant really. She looked just like one of those beautiful young men in a Hilliard miniature. I told her, 'Rebecca, if Shakespeare were here now, he'd write you a sonnet. . . .' Then, let me see, at the second, what did she wear at the second, Elinor?"

"Jocelyn, you're getting it all wrong. She was supposed to be that girl-boy in *Twelfth Night*, or was it one of the princes in *Richard III*? I forget—something Shakespearian anyway. At the second . . . wasn't it something Greek? Medea? No. Iphigenia? I can't remember exactly, but she wore a toga."

"A chiton, dear. Togas are Roman."

"I stand corrected. A chiton. With a wreath of flowers in her hair."

I hadn't been paying great attention. Suddenly I was. "A wreath of flowers? What kind of flowers, Miss Briggs, can you remember?"

"Gracious me—yes, I can! She had such glorious hair—this was before she cut it. It was *roses*, because the balls were always held in June. Her dress was white, and her hair was so dark, almost black, and there were these wine-red roses, with the most heavenly scent."

"And then at the *last* of the balls, the year before she died," Jocelyn put in, "she came as Caroline de Winter. And we said—didn't we, Elinor?—she'd never looked lovelier, but she was getting too thin. We didn't know about her illness then, of course—no one did. We wondered if she'd been dieting."

"*You* wondered, dear. That's because you were always banting in those days. But Rebecca was as slim as a wand, always."

"No hips to speak of. I always envied that. Hips can be a terrible misfortune."

"Anyway, dear, you're right—she *was* becoming too thin. And we both remarked on it. Even so, the costume was a great success. Quite stunning! She'd had it copied from the famous Raeburn portrait at Manderley. It used to hang in the gallery at the head of the main staircase. Every detail was exact—the likeness was extraordinary. Unfortunately, Maxim wasn't too pleased by her choice. I'm sure she hadn't warned him."

"Not too pleased! Elinor, dear, he was in a temper all evening. When I remarked to him how lovely Rebecca looked, he snapped my head off. I'm afraid dear Maxim could be a little moody."

"Well, Caroline de Winter was a great beauty, and of course she was an ancestor of Maxim's, so it was appropriate in many ways. But dear Rebecca did like to shock—and it was a rather daring choice, perhaps."

"Daring?" prompted the rector. I didn't need to prompt; I knew the story of Caroline de Winter. I could already see why this choice of costume was "daring"—and very interesting.

"Oh, Caroline was notorious, and so was her brother Ralph de Winter," Jocelyn said eagerly, but with a small glance at her sister. "She went on to make a good match—to some Whig politician, wasn't it, Elinor? But her brother took his own life, of course, and *before* Caroline's marriage there were tremendous scandals, really the most shocking stories about the two of them."

"We certainly don't want to dwell on *them*," Elinor put in swiftly. "I can't remember all the details, and Jocelyn can't either. The person to ask is Arthur Julyan—he is *tremendously* good on all those old tales."

Indeed he is, and in the early months of our acquaintance the Colonel had told me this racy story: The famous Raeburn portrait had been commissioned by Caroline de Winter's brother Ralph, a celebrated rake. The white dress his then unmarried sister wore in it had been designed to disguise the scandalous alteration in her figure, for wicked Caroline—so the story went—had been generous with her favours to her brother from an early age. Latterly, she had been equally generous to a handsome young groom at the Manderley stables. "How, sir, shall I paint your sister?" Raeburn is said to have asked. But as to the answer given him, tradition divides: "As the strumpet and whore she is, sir. So let her go down to the yard and be painted with the brood mares," goes the first version. "As my dearest love and my damnation, sir," goes the second, more provocative version.

A surprising choice of costume, then, on Rebecca's part; it was typical of the Colonel, I noted, to have told me the ancient part of this story, but not its modern corollary. I looked at the Briggs sisters, interested to see how they would extricate themselves, since to have given these details at their table was unthinkable. Jocelyn was less willing to relinquish the story, I saw, than Elinor.

"In any case," Elinor was saying, "those old tales are all twaddle."

"Oh, Elinor, you know you don't believe that," Jocelyn said, in an obstinate way. "Beatrice *always* said that Caroline de Winter brought bad luck. And she was right. Rebecca wore that costume, and then she died, God rest her. And the *second* Mrs. de Winter chose the *very same costume* for the one and only fancy-dress ball she gave at Manderley. We didn't attend that ball, did we, Elinor?"

"We did not. Others did—people who were more forgiving than we were."

"But we heard all about it—Beatrice told us! Such a calamity! The dress was to be a surprise, apparently, so of course no one knew, and no one was able to warn Mrs. de Winter. When she came downstairs . . . well, for one terrible moment everyone thought she was Rebecca's ghost. Maxim went as white as a sheet—Mrs. de Winter had to change and wear an ordinary frock. She was in floods of tears, Beatrice said. Maxim had been rather cruel about it, I understand, and, at one point, she was refusing to come downstairs at all."

"That girl lacked spine," Elinor put in. "Mousy hair, no dress sense, and no backbone."

"And then look what happened! She chose that costume, and there was more disaster! Rebecca's boat was discovered, and then there was the inquest, and then Manderley burned to the ground. It made us very uneasy. There was a disturbance in the spirit world and I could sense it. I felt someone was trying to *contact* us from the other side. I felt sure there was a *message*. . . . I wanted to consult my Ouija board, but Elinor wouldn't let me."

"Jocelyn had a Ouija board phase," Elinor said, in a very firm tone. "She also had a Tarot card phase. Both phases are now over. It is very unwise to meddle with such things, as I'm sure you'll agree, Rector."

"I do agree," said the rector. "Unwise—and dangerous."

After that, Jocelyn was chastened, and Elinor changed the subject firmly. I had to wait until we had all returned to the sisters' drawing room for the warm water that passes for coffee in Kerrith before I could raise the issue of Manderley again. This time, I was helped by the sisters, who had turned the conversation to the question of weddings— a topic of which they are exceedingly fond, and which they never discuss without numerous little nods and smiles in my direction.

The rector, to my relief, took the subject out of their hands, and began to discuss the baptisms, marriages, and funerals at which he had recently officiated. He was probably going to decide I was a monomaniac, but I didn't care; I steered us toward one wedding in particular—the extremely mysterious wedding of Rebecca to Maxim de Winter. Had the sisters attended it, I asked. (I'd asked them this about ten times before, but somehow they'd always veered off the subject.)

"Oh, didn't we explain?" said Jocelyn. "We missed the great event, didn't we, Elinor? It wasn't long after our dear Mama had died. We were in a sad state, with St. Winnow's having to be sold, and there was that cook—do you remember her, dear? She *kept* giving warning. It was a very trying time. . . . So we decided to visit our cousins in Kenya. We went on safari, and we saw lions."

"We stayed with those friends in Happy Valley!"

"We did. We were away four months, maybe five, I forget. So we missed all the excitements at Manderley! By the time we returned— and we called at once, of course—dear Maxim and Rebecca were already married. We told her all about our trip; that's why she gave *her* valley its name. Happy Valley! So charming! How lovely she was—do you remember, Elinor?—that first day we met her. Some people found her disconcerting, but we never did, did we dear?"

"Disconcerting? Certainly not. It was just that she had this very direct way of speaking, and that was unusual then."

A direct way of speaking? I sighed. I could have done with that there and then—but, as I'm beginning to learn from long conversations with elderly people, directness is rare. And it's a mistake to press too hard, or to show the least sign of impatience. Then they clam up completely.

The Briggs sisters were not alone in missing this famous wedding. Colonel Julyan had also missed it; he was still in Singapore on his last Army posting at the time. So far, although I'd tried all the obvious candidates, I hadn't found a single person who had attended it. Nor—and this was odder still—could I trace any newspaper coverage of it, beyond its de facto announcement in *The Times*. And that puzzled me greatly, for it took place at a time when society weddings attracted crowds, full reports, and photographs.

I asked the Briggs (as I've asked others) whether, having missed the great event, they had ever seen any wedding photographs at Manderley. This put both sisters in a flurry: They had; they hadn't; they thought they might; no, now they considered it, they probably didn't—but Rebecca had described her dress with its twenty-foot train, so they felt as if they *had* seen it. I made one last-ditch attempt, though the rector was getting very restive. I asked if they could remember where the wedding had taken place. "Someone told me it wasn't in London," I said, and this was true. I could name umpteen places where the marriage *hadn't* happened.

"Oh, no, definitely not London," said Elinor. "If it had been there, our Wyckham cousins would have gone, wouldn't they, Jocelyn? And they didn't go, either, though they weren't away, and dear Maxim would certainly have asked them. Let me think—it seems absurd not to know, but it was so long ago! Her people would have arranged it, of course—but were her parents alive?"

"Rebecca's? I don't think they were, dear."

"It was in the winter, I feel sure of that, because I remember our dates in Kenya. So it was rather an odd time of year for a wedding. I always think a June bride is such a lovely idea. . . . February? March?"

"Abroad!" Jocelyn cried, making me jump. "I'm sure it was abroad, dear—Italy, perhaps? Somewhere remote and romantic. . . . Didn't someone mention canals, Elinor? Venice?"

"No, no—they're weren't *married* in Venice, they went there on their honeymoon, I'm almost sure. They went to France first—did dear Rebecca have family in France? You know, I rather think she did. I'm sure I recall some chateau's being mentioned. And I'm almost certain they went on to Monte Carlo, which Maxim took against for some reason, and then Venice. I do remember Rebecca's telling me about gondolas."

"Ah, gondolas," said Jocelyn with a sigh. "Do you know, I've *always* wanted to ride in a gondola. I've always wanted to go to Venice and I never have."

"I understand it can be very unsanitary," said Elinor in a final way. "You're much better off here, dear."

I could have tried one more time, I suppose. I could have asked about the "family in France," but I'd missed my chance, and I could see the rector was chafing. I gave up. I fielded a few questions about Scotland, and when I glimpsed the glint of sectarianism in the rector's eyes, so I knew that if I stayed I'd be grilled on Presbyterianism, I rose to leave.

Both sisters saw me out, and in their tiny hall, hemmed in by ancestral oils, they exchanged glances. Becoming a little pink, they told me I must be sure to call on them as soon as I returned from London. "We're planning a dinner," Jocelyn cried. "A *small* dinner," corrected Elinor, "with dear Arthur, if he's well enough. And Ellie, of course. . . ." The sisters exchanged meaningful smiles.

"I shall look forward to it," I said. "I'll come and see you as soon as I get back. And I'll bring you some chocolates from London."

"Dear Mr. Gray! Chocolates! We wouldn't hear of it!"

"Violet creams," I said. "You have my word on it."

Ellie had told me about their weakness for violet creams. Violet creams, along with malt whisky, drinkable sherry, coffee beans, and most of the other necessaries for a civilized life, are unobtainable in Kerrith. Both sisters blushed crimson. If I'd discovered they had a weakness for lacy camiknickers, they couldn't have been more embarrassed.

From the sisters' house, which, like Colonel Julyan's, is on the eastern side of Kerrith, I set off to walk upriver. St. Winnow's Nursing Home for the Elderly is about a mile beyond the town, on a beautiful bend of the Kerr, and close to the tiny fishing village of Pelynt.

It was a pleasant walk, the narrow road winding along the riverside. The fine weather had brought people down to the water; I was passed by several yachts and skiffs, out practicing for the Kerrith regatta, a great event on the local calendar. I passed the dark narrow creek, accessible only at flood tide, which Ellie had described, the creek where Rebecca's boat was taken, and her body finally identified. I came to a halt at the boat builders' yard once owned by James Tabb, the man who had adapted Rebecca's Breton boat for her.

It was Tabb who, giving evidence at her inquest, had revealed that Rebecca's boat, *Je Reviens*, had been deliberately scuttled. It was he who had insisted on inspecting it, and he who found that the sea-cocks had been opened, and holes had been driven into its bottom boards. His evidence caused a sensation at the time, as the newspaper accounts make clear, but his honesty seems to have caused him problems afterward. In the atmosphere of gossip and rumor that attended the inquest, James Tabb lost custom—or so the Briggs sisters, great champions of his, have told me. He went bankrupt a few years later. His family had been boat builders here for four generations: Now, the yard was derelict.

Tabb is still refusing to speak to me, and looking up at the faded letters on the side of the building, JAMES TABB & SON, BOAT BUILD-ERS, I could understand why. The son named on the sign was killed during the D-day landings. James Tabb now runs a small garage on the outskirts of Kerrith, and ekes out a living as a mechanic. I could see that he might be embittered, that the subject of the de Winters, and Rebecca's death, was not one that he'd discuss willingly.

Tabb's former premises were fine, honest, foursquare buildings, impossible to date, but probably centuries old. I thought of the loving and highly skilled work that would once have kept men employed here—and I felt melancholy. I remembered that long, punning, coiling tail the young Rebecca had drawn on the final "e" of her "Tale."

Twenty years after her death, her story was not over. Rebecca's tale continued. A great house lay in ruins; her husband was dead—and died a broken man, or so people have told me. Her friend, Arthur Julyan, gave up his seat on the Bench, and endured years of vilifica-tion. Frith sits in a wheelchair, and mourns a lost world. And James Tabb, a man on the very periphery of Rebecca's story, even he has been affected. He lost his yard and lost his livelihood—and, to me, that loss, after generations of skill and labor, weighed as heavily in the scales as the destruction of Manderley.

Standing there by that boatyard, I tried to tell myself that this story and its repercussions were almost done, that I was here just in time to see the tail end of them. Another few years and all those who knew Rebecca, all those whose lives had been altered or affected by her, would be gone.

But was that the case? I doubted it, even as I thought it. I could see its aftereffects in Ellie. Once her father had retreated to The Pines, cutting himself off from his malicious accusers in Kerrith, she was forced to share his isolation; they see few people now, apart from the Briggs sisters, so Ellie, a young, intelligent, pretty woman, is imprisoned by the events of twenty years ago every bit as much as her father is. She would no doubt deny that analysis fiercely, but I wondered sometimes if she longed to be rescued from the fortress her father constructed—and who might do the rescuing. And what about the second Mrs. de Winter, Maxim's widow? She was still a comparatively young woman; I doubted she would feel that the story was over yet. She went to live in Canada after her husband's death, but she must have taken the story with her; she was part of its continuation. Nor was I exempt myself. I never intended to be that involved—I meant to come to Kerrith for three months at most, find out what I wanted to find out, what I *needed* to find out, and then leave it behind me.

After six months, I was still here. And I was more deeply involved, more caught up in this, than ever. Sometimes I felt as if I had always been part of this story, hidden away in its recesses. And sometimes I felt I was willfully writing myself into it—and that idea disturbed me.

I walked on rapidly, and took the lane that led up to the higher ground where St. Winnow's was situated. I walked up to the house through the well-kept gardens. As I had expected on such a warm day, Frith was outside on the sheltered terrace in his wheelchair; from there, he had a perfect view down the river and out to sea. In the far distance, as he had reminded me at regular intervals during my last visit, was Manderley.

I checked that I'd brought the copy of Lionel de Winter's death certificate with me, though I knew I had, and then joined him on the terrace. I was sure he had very little idea of who I was, but that didn't appear to bother him at all. He remembered me from my previous visit and seemed pleased to see me.

FOURTEEN

Before I met Frith, he had been described to me by the Colonel in unflattering terms: He was ninety-five at least; he was senile; he was a martinet, a nosy-parker, a fusspot, a terrorizer of maids, an old fool, and a wily operator with an eye for the main chance. "One minute he was the boot boy, the next he was butler," said the Colonel. "Draw your own conclusions."

Frith was never a boot boy, and the rest of the Colonel's description was similarly inaccurate—with the possible exception of that eye to the main chance. Frith was very far from senile; he was born in 1867 (I checked) and was now eighty-four, though he claimed ninety. His father had been in service elsewhere in the West Country, and Frith had gone to Manderley as a boy; before becoming butler in 1915, he had worked his way up the chain of command, serving time as a footman, and as Lionel de Winter's valet. He was exceedingly well informed about the de Winter family, and prided himself on his unique knowledge of their history. As he liked to hint to me, his was the *inside* story.

He was a shrewd, small man, much shrunken, I think, from his former stature. He had a head of neat white hair, and poorly fitting false teeth that were a constant source of distress to him. In the very distant past he might once have had a keen eye for pretty girls—

certainly he was very jealous of the nurses' attentions, preferring the younger ones. I had the impression that this taste had been kept firmly in check. Frith had never courted or married, had no children. Why would he have wanted to marry, he'd said to me scornfully. Why would he have wanted a family of his own? He *had* a family: the de Winter family.

His de Winter pension pays his bills here, but he receives no visitors, or so the young red-haired nurse who was Frith's favorite had told me. And he is mindful of his status, even now. This afternoon—and I gather this is his usual practice—he had seated himself at a distance from the other nursing home patients. At one end of the terrace was a group of women, several of whom were knitting; toward the other end was a group of male patients, clustered around a wireless set, listening to a concert. Frith had segregated himself from both groups, and was occupying pride of place on the terrace, shaded by a canvas awning. From there he could watch the boats on the river below, and look out beyond Kerrith to the hazy shape of the Manderley headland. He has cataracts on both eyes, however, so his vision is dimmed, and I feel sure he cannot see it.

He had had a good lunch, and a little sleep after lunch, and now he was ready to talk about old times again, which he liked to do. "It brings it all back," he said, clasping my hands in his, and urging me into the chair next to him. "Things I haven't thought of, not in years, I see them again, as sharp as I see you now, sir. Mr. Lionel as a young man—and his wife, poor Mrs. Lionel—a Grenville, she was, Virginia Grenville, sister to Miss Evangeline and Miss Isolda, God rest them. Ah, things were different in those days. One afternoon off a month I had. And work! These nurses complain about the work—I tell them, you don't know you're born. You should try cleaning the plate at Manderley, I say. I'd be down in the silver room for days at a time, knives, forks, spoons, place settings for fifty. And then all the big pieces, and if you left so much as a smidgen of the silver powder in one tiny little crevice—well, you knew you were in trouble then."

He gave a wheezing sigh. "And when I got to waiting on table—one tiny mark on my gloves and I was for it. Mrs. de Winter the elder—Mr. Lionel's mother, that was—she had eyes in the back of her head, she had. Nothing went on in that house that she didn't know about. Mr. Lionel, he'd be up to his tricks, and he'd take me on one side, and slip me the wink, and say, 'Just between you and me, eh, Frith? Make sure the old girl doesn't get to hear about it.' . . . But she always did. And sometimes she minded, and sometimes she didn't. You never knew with her. And if Mr. Lionel went too far—*which* he did, and many a time, too—he'd go to her. And she'd take care of all the arrangements. . . ."

I was listening intently—particularly to those last remarks. This was the difficulty. With Frith, as with the Briggs sisters, it was hopeless to chivy or overdirect. I had to wait. I had to listen to a million details about his methods of polishing silver or cleaning livery or storing claret, until Frith finally meandered in a direction that interested me.

On my last visit, I'd tried to direct Frith toward more recent events at Manderley, but had met with little success. He had virtually no memory of the second Mrs. de Winter—he seemed to have erased her brief time at the house almost completely. On the subject of Rebecca de Winter he refused to be drawn, telling me only that she had taken both Maxim and his grandmother by storm, which had surprised him because he'd expected resistance on the grandmother's part to any bride selected by Maxim.

"Beauty, brains, and breeding," he said, giving me a sidelong look. "That's what she had, according to the old lady. She was set on the match from the day she met Miss Rebecca. Mr. Maxim was in love, bowled over—but, even so, his grandmother influenced him, I'll wager. He was that much in awe of her; she'd raised him, sir, you see, his poor mother dying as she did when he was just three years old, poor mite."

Beyond this, Frith had refused to go. He had nothing more to say on the subject of Maxim's first wife, he insisted. He couldn't remember; he wouldn't be prompted. He preferred to go back to a much earlier period. As with many elderly people, his most vivid memories were those of his own youth; Frith was at his happiest, and most voluble, when discussing Lionel de Winter.

Today, I, too, wanted to discuss Maxim's father—and I wanted to do so even more since that suggestive conversation over lunch at the Briggs sisters. Why had Rebecca selected that costume for the last fancy-dress ball she gave, and why had her husband reacted to it with such anger? This was an avenue I wanted to explore—and Frith had just given me an opening. I was extremely interested in the occasions when Lionel de Winter had "gone too far"; I was equally interested in the "arrangements" his mother had then made on his behalf. I allowed Frith to meander a little more around the subject of Lionel's amatory exploits (and they're still famous in this neighborhood); then I tried roping him in.

"Frith," I said, "why don't you tell me about the Carminowes?"

To my relief, Frith didn't balk or divert; he was off and away at once. "Well, John Carminowe, he was one of the keepers, sir," he began. "And his father before him. A nice little cottage, they had, off the Four Turnings road. I had my eye on that for a time, for my retirement. Would have suited me down to the ground, that place would."

"And Mrs. Carminowe, Frith?"

"Came as a maid, first. I remember her well. A lovely girl, she was—tall, strong, a good worker, I'll say that for her. She had beautiful hair, and a way with her. . . . John Carminowe took one look, and he was smitten. So they started walking out, and then they married— she wasn't more than sixteen. And then there were babies, three strapping boys to begin with, and then a gap, and then two more. And the two youngest, they were a sore trial, they were. There was a little girl, and there was Ben Carminowe and he was born a half-wit. Broke his mother's heart, he did. All his brothers came to work at the house, in the stables or the gardens—there was work for all in those days. And Ben, he'd follow them and hang around. And the family, they didn't like that. He wasn't a pretty sight, poor child, and he was a peeper. He'd creep up to the doors, or they'd catch him listening at windows, and he *wouldn't* stay away from the old boathouse down on the shore. Mr. Lionel couldn't abide the sight of him. He'd fly into a rage—he said if he saw him there one more time, he'd take a horse-whip to him. And he might have done, too. Mr. Lionel had a temper you wouldn't believe."

I would believe. I thought I could understand Lionel de Winter's mood swings and tempers. I had evidence concerning them in my pocket.

"Why couldn't Lionel abide Ben?" I said. "Was it just his appearance, Frith—or was it more than that?"

"Might have been more. . . ." To my surprise, the old man began to chuckle, then wheeze. "I told you—turned heads, Mrs. Carminowe

did. Even after she was widowed. Black hair, black eyes, black dress—
she wasn't thirty when John died. Could have married again, I always
reckoned. Could have taken her pick in Kerrith, but she never did.
And the de Winters looked after her like one of their own. She kept
that cottage until the day she died, Mr. Lionel saw to that, and his
mother did, too, after he'd gone. . . . Sarah, her name was. Sarah
Carminowe. Buried over in the churchyard by Manderley, she is."

I already knew that. I'd been to Sarah Carminowe's grave, and her
husband's. I'd seen, in the estate papers, just how well the de Winter
family had looked after her. After the death of her husband, and then
of her three older boys in the first world war, she remained in that
cottage, with her only daughter and her simple-minded son. Other
tenants in her situation were moved out to make way for more pro-
ductive workers. Not Sarah Carminowe. She was still housed and
still being paid a "pension" during Maxim de Winter's day, by which
time she was in her fifties and her husband had been dead two
decades. The de Winters protected her and her two last children:
Ben was sent to the county asylum only after her death, and that was
several years after Maxim de Winter left the country. Ben was now
also dead. I didn't know what had happened to the daughter.

I looked at Frith, who was regarding me in a somewhat sly sidelong way; he fumbled with the rug around his knees, and I tucked it
in for him. I had taken a close interest in Sarah Carminowe and the
exceptional charity shown her; I'd found it was useful to compare the
important dates in her life to the key dates in that of the de Winter
family. She had married at age sixteen in 1893, three years after
Maxim de Winter was born. Her first three children—those strapping boys—were born over the next five years. There was then a gap;
her last two children, the little girl and Ben, were born in 1905 and
1906 respectively. The surname they bore, Carminowe, was presumably discretionary, since her husband died in 1904. Someone had
consoled the pretty widow.

"Tell me about Sarah's two youngest children, Frith," I said. "Who
was their father? It wasn't John Carminowe, was it?"

There was a silence. Frith continued to look at me under his
brows; I knew he knew the answer, I could sense it—but it was
impossible to predict which would win, the desire to talk or the habit
of discretion.

"Sickly," Frith said, after that long pause. "They were both sickly, the boy and the girl. He had fits—an idiot from birth, he was—and the girl, she had her wits all right, but she wasn't right—never. Couldn't keep her food down, people said. Never grew, never thrived like normal children. She was this thin little scrap of a thing, with these dark blue eyes. Ben had blue eyes too, but lighter. . . ."

"Frith." I decided to risk pushing much harder. "Both Ben and the girl were born after John Carminowe died. The little girl ten months after he died, and Ben two years after. John Carminowe couldn't have fathered them. So who did? Was it Lionel? Is that why the de Winter family looked after them?" I paused. "Is that why the children were sickly, Frith?"

"By-blows," said Frith, so suddenly he startled me. "By-blows, that's what they were. That's what Mrs. de Winter the elder used to say. We take care of them, Frith, she'd say to me. And we don't talk about it. Mr. Lionel had a way with him. He was a handsome man. Women liked him—not just down here, oh, no. Up in London, too, abroad even; he had a string of them. And he was always generous. We kept a little book—when I was his manservant, this was. I'd write down their birthdays in it, and when there was one coming up, I'd remind him. And we'd send to one of the London stores, and get something sent round. A trinket. A nice pair of gloves. He was thoughtful that way. Liked actresses." Frith began to chuckle again. "A terrible weakness, he had, for actresses. Bold, I expect. He liked that. And his wife, poor Mrs. Lionel . . . well, you wouldn't describe her as bold. Not by a long chalk. A lady, she was."

I looked away. In the distance, the sea crested and turned. The red-haired nurse was moving along the terrace, pushing a trolley with a tea urn and little sandwiches and cakes. Once the tea reached Frith, I knew my chances with him were over. I tried another line of questioning, and I tried to keep it gentle.

"Frith," I said, "Lionel de Winter was ill, wasn't he? Ill for a long time, years before he died. Will you tell me about that?"

"His legs." Frith gave a wheezy sigh. "His legs, he had this trouble with his legs. On his thighs first, these dark red marks. Then ulcers. And they wouldn't heal, no matter what we tried, they wouldn't. We bathed them and we bandaged them—but no, they got worse. Mrs. Lionel was dead by then, and Mr. Maxim, he was only a little boy and he couldn't understand. He missed his mother—she was always hugging him and sitting him on her lap, she doted on that boy, poor creature—and, once she was gone, he was starved of all that. Well, he had to learn—boys do—but even when he was six or seven, if he saw his father, he'd run to him, see, and clasp him round the legs, and beg to be lifted up—and that made his father angry. He'd say the boy was soft, and he'd been spoiled. He'd shout at him, and it got so Mr. Maxim was afraid of his father. But Mr. Lionel didn't mean to be hard on him, sir. He wasn't a bad man. It's just he was in all that pain and it was so bad some days he could scarcely walk. He didn't like anyone to know that, and he wouldn't have it talked about, and he couldn't get up to London. . . ."

Frith fell into one of the musing, muttering states that punctuated his stories. Eventually, when he seemed to have forgotten I was there, I prompted again.

"But the ulcers on the legs—they healed eventually, Frith, am I right?"

"You are, sir." He brightened. "After a year or two—they cleared up, just like that. And then Mr. Lionel was back to his old ways, up to London every month or so, cock of the walk—you forget pain, sir, that's the thing. You can't remember it. When my arthritis plays up . . ."

"So, when did he next become ill, Frith—can you remember?" I looked over at the red-haired nurse in her cap and starched white uniform; she was serving tea to the female patients at the other end of the terrace. At best, I had five minutes.

"Oh, a long while after. When Mr. Maxim was about twelve, it would have been, sir. The boy was slow at his lessons, and it was the summer the old rector used to tutor him, Colonel Julyan's grandfather, that was—a fine man. Mr. Maxim was very fond of him. That's when Mr. Lionel's headaches started. And his teeth, he had terrible trouble with his teeth, sir. They'd given him this ointment to rub on his gums, and there was mercury in it. It made his teeth go black—and it got so bad, it made him difficult. Very difficult. After that . . . well, he went from bad to worse. Even with me—some days, he'd be quiet as a lamb, and others he'd start up, fly off the handle, for no reason at all."

Frith fumbled with his rug, and turned his faded eyes back toward the sea. If his cataracts obscured his view of Manderley, he saw it with his mind's eye, I was sure of that—and what he was now watching was beginning to distress him.

"Sometimes he'd improve," he went on. "Months at a time. 'I'm right as rain, Frith,' he used to say to me. But the headaches always came back—and there were other symptoms, too—and I think they frightened him. As time went by he got very unpredictable, sir. It got so you'd never know what he might do. His mother wasn't having that. She didn't want talk. There'd be ladies to tea—and in he'd come, quite normal, and then he'd *say* something. . . ."

Frith gave a shake of the head. "Something had to be done, sir—so Mrs. de Winter called a doctor in from London, and we gave him the injections after that, and they kept him quiet. It was morphine, sir, for the pain, and it eased him at first—but then it gave him night-mares, such terrible dreams, he'd scream with fear, sometimes. He never left his room, sir, not for the last four years. I had the key—and I wouldn't allow talk below stairs. Never. Mrs. de Winter depended on me, she knew she could. She had a will of iron, she did. It came near to breaking her, but you'd never have known it. She never gave way, not for a second, not even in front of me—and then it got to the end, and she took me on one side, and she said there was one last thing I could do for Mr. Lionel. So I witnessed his will, sir, the day he died. I witnessed it along with Colonel Julyan—Captain, he was, then. And I was butler after that, which was all I'd ever wanted."

The last of the female patients had been served. The red-haired nurse and her trolley were now coming toward us. I could hear the clatter of cups—and so could Frith. There were a few last questions I had to ask; I was interested in this will, made in 1915. I leaned forward.

"Frith, why was that will made so late? Lionel was seriously ill, and had been for years. Surely he must have made a will before that?"

"He had, sir. That was the problem. He'd made it . . . oh, nine or ten years before, in one of his good periods. Went to a lot of trouble about it, too, swore me to secrecy. His mother didn't know about it. And when she finally found out, not long before he died, oh, there was trouble then! She wouldn't rest till he changed it. I never did dis-cover who told her about that will. I never said a word about it, so it was a mystery, that was. . . . Is that the tea coming now, sir?"

"No—not yet. It'll be here soon," I said. The red-haired nurse had paused to speak to an older woman, wearing a Sister's uniform. I leaned forward again and lowered my voice. "Frith, why didn't Lionel's mother approve of that will? Had he made bequests she disapproved of? Why was a new one necessary?"

"I don't remember." Frith was suddenly becoming fretful. He fumbled with his rug. "It was a long time ago. It was during the war—the Great War—Mr. Maxim was serving in France, and he might have been killed any day. Captain Julyan was in uniform, on leave. . . . I didn't like to look at Mr. Lionel—not then. 'He's being eaten away'— that's what the nurse said. And the nurses wouldn't stay, they couldn't stomach it. Where's the tea? I want my tea. It's Sunday today. They always make sponge cake on Sundays—it's my favorite."

The Sister was departing. The red-haired nurse turned in our direction. One last effort—and it seemed wise not to mention Lionel de Winter directly.

"Frith, you remember you were telling me about Sarah Carminowe's two last children? What became of the daughter? Ben lived on, didn't he—but what happened to the little girl? Lucy, that was her name. I found her baptism entry in the church register. What happened to Lucy Carminowe?"

"She died. They *all* died. They're all dead now." Frith's voice rose on a querulous note, and I knew I'd gone too far and pushed too hard and I'd frightened him. "They're all dead. They're all gone. I'm the only one left. And I want my tea now—nurse, nurse, I want some sponge cake." He tried to turn in his chair and look for her; then he looked at me, angry and flushed and confused. "Who are you?" he said, his voice rising on a high thin note. "Why am I talking to you? I don't know you. I've never seen you before. . . . Nurse, nurse, tell him to leave me alone. . . ."

"Now, now, Mr. Frith . . ." The little nurse arrived and bent over his chair. She patted his hand, and then, straightening up, made faces at me. They meant I should leave—but I'd known I'd have to leave anyway. I stood up and said good-bye to Frith, though I don't think he was even aware of me by then.

"What a state you do get yourself into," the nurse was saying as I walked away. "Look at you, working yourself up over nothing, when the nice gentleman's come to see you specially! Now, Mr. Frith, here's your sponge cake. . . ."

I walked down from the covered terrace into the grounds, and when I was out of sight beyond the great banks of shrub roses for which St. Winnow's is famous, I took Lionel de Winter's death certificate out of my pocket and re-examined it.

When Frith spoke, I could see Manderley as it had been. It rose up before my eyes with a vividness I knew could be deceptive. I felt I could see Lionel and his mother—but could I? No, I couldn't rely on such images; I preferred to rely on documents—especially documents like the one I was holding. This was evidence, and it was incontrovertible.

Lionel de Winter had died in June 1915; cause of death was General Paralysis of the Insane. Or, to give it its modern name: syphilis.

Whether or not he was aware of it, Frith had just given me a description of that disease's stages—primary, secondary, and tertiary. And the implications of Lionel's illness were considerable. Syphilis is a cruel and virulent disease: If it affects a man, it can infect a wife or a mistress—and children.

It was too early to call in at The Pines yet, and, besides, I needed to be alone, and I needed to think. Not for the first time since I came here, I cursed my lack of transport. I'd felt Terence Gray wouldn't own a car, so did not bring mine, and now I regretted that. If I'd had a car, I could have gone over to the Manderley church now, and looked again at the Carminowe gravestones. Not that I really needed to do so—I could remember them perfectly well: John Carminowe and his wife Sarah lay in a quiet section of the churchyard, under the branches of a yew, overlooking the sea. Their three elder sons did not lie next to them. Those strapping boys had been buried in some corner of a foreign field, and their names, along with those of some thirty of their contemporaries, were on the war memorial in Kerrith. They had died aged seventeen, eighteen, and twenty. I pitied their mother, living on at that cottage with her two last children. Sarah Carminowe must have looked ahead and made provision for her son, for Ben, frequenter of Manderley, had been laid beside her. I had found no gravestone for Lucy Carminowe—and no record of her death, either.

I began to walk slowly down the lane to the riverside; instead of turning toward Kerrith, I gave in to impulse and turned the other way, toward Pelynt and the fisherman's cottage May and Edwin rented the year we came here. It is set apart from the rest of the tiny village, right next to the water. It is still let, rather than lived in all year, I think; I found it empty, the interior shutters closed, and the small garden neglected. I sat on the steps by the house for a while in the late afternoon sun, throwing stones idly at the water and trying to make them skip, as I did as a boy. I was angry with myself. I was falling into the most obvious of traps, the trap any apprentice historian learns to avoid: In the absence of sufficient facts, I was trying to make those facts I did have fit my own hypothesis.

It was possible, but not certain, that Lionel de Winter had fathered Sarah Carminowe's last two children—and the way in which Frith had spoken certainly encouraged that view. That would have meant that Maxim de Winter had at least one half-brother and -sister, possibly more, given his father's philandering. Had Maxim known, or at any point suspected, that a boy treated as a village idiot might be a blood relation? That would have been a terrible realization for any young man—especially since there was the possibility that Ben Carminowe's mental defects might be a result of Lionel de Winter's illness. Maxim himself had almost certainly been born before the onset of his father's disease, or so I calculated. But if he knew what killed his father, and I could see no way in which he could have escaped that knowledge, he might not have felt certain of that himself. Even if he were perfectly healthy, would it not cast a shadow over him, would he not feel tainted?

And Ben Carminowe's sister—why was I so haunted by this sister, especially these last few days? I knew the answer to that: It was because of that notebook sent to the Colonel, with the postcard of Manderley inside it. It was because it suggested a link between Rebecca as a child and the de Winter family—and I had gone chasing after that tenuous suggestion with the desperation born of months of fruitless inquiries into Rebecca's background and antecedents.

It was utterly stupid. It was equally stupid to be influenced by the conversation at lunch concerning costumes and legendary eighteenth-century incest. I was looking for a connection that didn't exist; the dates, the ages—none of it corresponded. According to her death certificate, Rebecca de Winter died in 1931, at the age of thirty. She must then have been born in either 1900 or 1901, on the cusp of this blighted century. Lucy Carminowe was born in 1905. There was not the least resemblance between the poor sick child Frith had spoken of and Rebecca as a woman. Lucy Carminowe, sad little ghost that she was, had probably died in infancy—and if I went back through the records and the church registers one more time, no doubt I would eventually find her. If I didn't, then possibly, like me, she had been adopted. In which case, as I know only too well, any tracing procedures would be very difficult, if not impossible.

Not only was I losing my capacity to be objective; I was losing my capacity to think rationally. I was being affected by the half-truths, the quarter-truths, the endless rumors, legends, and fabrications that pass for history in a place like Kerrith. What I needed was a rest from the place, and a dose of London, I told myself. Well, I would get it tomorrow. I hurled the last of my stones as far as it would go out into the river, and watched the ripples circle.

I turned to look at the cottage where May, Edwin, and I stayed that first summer. I minded desperately about my birth in those days: A boy at the orphanage had told me my father could be any man with five shillings in his pocket, that my mother only had me after the gin and the knitting needle failed her. I believed him—and there's probably one part of me, even to this day, that still does, even though he had no more knowledge of my parentage than his own, as I can see now. "That is a wicked lie," May said, one night when I confessed this story, in the little room under the eaves that was my bedroom when we stayed here. "A *wicked* lie. Why, she wept when she had to give you up, the matron told me. Whoever your poor mother was, she loved you—just as I do."

I now know this was not true, either. May had had no such conversation with the matron at the home, and the matron concerned had never met my mother. Even so, there's a part of me that believes that story of May's, too. I stood looking up at the small window under the eaves; I thought that with this legacy, peculiar to children in my situation, I was ill suited to this particular investigation. No wonder I ran after the story of Ben and Lucy Carminowe; no wonder I started to leap to conclusions and chase shadows: It's in my blood. I have made myself an historian, but on my birth certificate there is a blank and the word "unknown" in the space where a father's name and a

mother's should be written. "A blank, my lord": I have the illegitimate child's fatal weakness—a longing to discover identity and lineage, in myself and in others.

I turned away from the cottage, and walked at a swift pace back to
Kerrith. I called in at The Pines, as Ellie had suggested. Colonel
Julyan, much restored from his restful day, was in good spirits, but I
was not; I think he sensed something was wrong, for his manner was
kind, and he did not cross-examine me.

I sat in his study for a while with him and his gentle dog. Barker, so
sensitive to his master's moods, now seems to be attuning himself to
mine. He sat his great rump down on my foot, and licked my hand
occasionally. He is not the most sweet smelling of dogs, but I felt
consoled by him. We talked about Jack Favell for a while—Colonel
Julyan said he wanted to prepare me. Then he listened to my edited
account of my day; I wasn't ready to discuss what Frith had told me,
but I did tell him about the boathouse and the azalea wreath I had
found there.

This seemed to perplex him very much, and he kept returning to
the subject. He had assumed that the person he'd glimpsed at the
boathouse was the same person that had sent him the notebook, but
he was now forced to reject that idea. "Favell could well have sent the
notebook," he said, shaking his head. "I can see him doing that, anything to stir up trouble or cause distress, even after twenty years. But
Favell would never leave that wreath there. An azalea garland?
Never."

We could both see that Favell was one of the few people who
might have laid hands on the notebook—he could have been given it
by Rebecca herself or by Mrs. Danvers, Colonel Julyan thought.
Since Favell had claimed to be more than a cousin as far as Rebecca
was concerned, I felt he might be responsible for the wreath, too; it
was the kind of gesture a lover might make—always supposing he
and Rebecca *had* been lovers. I couldn't understand why the Colonel
rejected that idea so firmly. He wouldn't elaborate.

"Wait until you meet him, Gray," he said. "Then you'll see. But
I'm telling you, it's an impossibility."

Even then, the old man continued to fret, and eventually Ellie was
called in to "consult," as the Colonel put it—and this surprised me. I
had never seen him inclined to consult Ellie previously. The story

was repeated; Ellie listened quietly and thoughtfully. At last she was called upon to adjudicate: Could Jack Favell have left that garland at Rebecca's boathouse?

"Absolutely not," said Ellie.

That settled the matter, as far as Colonel Julyan was concerned. He looked proudly at Ellie, and then at me. I was still mystified. As I understood it, Ellie had met Jack Favell precisely once, aged eleven, at a Manderley garden party that Favell had "infiltrated," as her father put it. Did this provide grounds for an answer that had been given without hesitation? My instinct told me Ellie believed Favell had not sent the notebook, either.

I wasn't in a mood to trust my own instincts, however. Both Ellie and her father pressed me to stay to supper, but I refused. I wanted to write up my account of the day while its details were fresh in my mind—and besides, I knew I'd be poor company. I rose to leave, and was presented with a curious fait accompli. The Colonel said he'd been worrying (I'd seen no sign of it) about my journey tomorrow. Which train was I catching? How did I propose to get to the station? The bus? The buses were slow and unreliable. Fortunately, tomorrow was Monday, and on Monday the Julyans' charwoman came up to The Pines from Kerrith: Ellie was therefore free and was going to drive me to the station.

I think Ellie was as surprised at this development as I was, but the Colonel would brook no arguments—and those buses *are* slow. Slightly puzzled, I thanked him, patted his dog, and left. Ellie showed me to the door, and I stepped out into a beautiful violet dusk, with a thin sea mist rising.

"I'll pick you up at seven," Ellie said. She lingered in the doorway; I lingered in the driveway. For a moment, I saw her as I'd done earlier that day, as a girl in a fairy tale, a *princesse lointaine* imprisoned in an enchanted and impenetrable castle, under guard, and awaiting rescue. I glanced up at the extravagant turrets of The Pines; in the distance came the hushed expectant sound of the waves. I knew I was being fanciful, yet I felt strangely reluctant to leave. I had the same sensation that I'd had this morning—that there was something I might say or she might say. It drifted away in the mist, and I couldn't grasp it.

"That azalea garland . . ." Ellie said after an interval. "There's one possibility none of us mentioned. A *woman* might have left it. Had that thought not occurred to you?"

It hadn't. And I think Ellie knew that. She lifted her hand, and then slipped back into the shadowy hall. I walked home slowly.

In retrospect, I think this suggestion is unlikely, but, even so, the fact that I hadn't considered it annoyed me. I've discovered enough blind spots in the course of the day; I don't need to discover any others. If May were here, no doubt she'd give me a lecture on female insights and female intuition—and that I can well do without.

It's very late. I shall go and pack, not that I need to take much with me. No more Gray suits, thank God. My own clothes await me in London.

FIFTEEN

THE TRAIN FROM LANYON WAS ON TIME, BUT THE JOURNEY was interminable, and uncomfortable. The nonsmoking carriages were all full, and I ended up in one infested with pipe smokers, wailing babies, and a woman who munched cheese and pickle sandwiches most of the way to London. I'd left without breakfast, and by Exeter I was starving but I couldn't risk the dining car because that abomination, Marjorie Lane, a woman I cannot stand, was on the train. I was hoping she hadn't spotted me at the station, and I was praying she hadn't seen Ellie and me in the Lanyon waiting room. At Paddington, when we finally arrived six hours later, I skulked behind a porter, only to bump into Kerrith's most assiduous gossipmonger in the queue at the taxi rank. She was dressed to kill in a black suit, black high-heeled shoes, black gloves, and a regrettable hat with a regrettable veil, and a deeply regrettable scarlet feather.

"Mr. Gray!" she cried. "I *thought* it was you at Lanyon! I did wave—but you and Ellie were so deep in conversation. . . . Well! I must say you're *full* of surprises. Quite the dark horse! I'm just up for a day or two to do some shopping. Shall we share a cab? Which way are you heading?"

I'm sure she'd have been delighted to know, and I had no intention of telling her. "Potter's Bar," I said, and shot off to the Underground.

Only two stops to Baker Street, then a short walk through Regent's Park. Within twenty minutes I was here, in my familiar room with its familiar view along the curve of the Nash terrace and out across the park. The cherry trees were in bloom, and the grass was strewn with petals. *Rus in urbe.* The first time Nicky brought me here to meet his parents, I thought this was one of the most beautiful houses I'd ever seen; that was before the war, and circumstances have greatly changed since then, but I still think so, and my heart lifted as I approached it. Despite everything that has happened, my memories of the Osmonds' house, unlike Nicky's, are happy ones.

Mrs. Henderson was here to greet me and seemed pleased to see me; the family scarcely uses the place now, and I imagine she gets lonely. She had gone to a great deal of trouble, as she always does. The bed had been made up in the little attic room that for years now she's spoken of as "my" room; despite my protests, she'd laundered the shirts I used when I was last here, and eyed the shirt I was wearing with a critical eye. It didn't meet the Henderson standards, I could tell—but then I'd ironed it, so that wasn't surprising.

I was taken on my usual tour of the house, and shown the latest wonder: Nicky's father has provided her with a television. He's always been keen on gadgetry, and apparently thought it would be company for her. It stands in the corner of her sitting room, a big beast in a shiny mahogany cabinet. The screen is quite large, about eight inches across. Mrs. Henderson gave me a demonstration; it took a while to warm up, like a wireless set, then these ghosts came flickering out of the dark—it was strange, like watching a dream or a memory.

She had made sandwiches for me. I was allowed to eat in the kitchen, which is a privilege I've had to fight for, and she sat with me, bringing me up to date. She's heard from Nicky more recently than I have, and thinks he will stay another three months in Paris at least. His mother is on some cruise ship in the Caribbean—with the latest man, I suspect, though Mrs. Henderson did not say so. His father still shows no signs of recovering from Julia's death, although it's over a year now. I'm fond of Sir Archie and had hoped I might see him on this visit, but Mrs. Henderson said he rarely leaves the Oxfordshire house, and although he has been promising her to come to London, he never does. "He never thought of Julia as a daughter-in-law," she said. "To him, she was the daughter he always wanted." She paused, and then added, looking at me, "Poor man. He can't relinquish her, you see. Even now."

Neither can Nicky, which is why he's likely to stay in Paris a great deal longer than three months. Both Mrs. Henderson and I knew that; neither of us said so.

I stayed talking to her for about half an hour, but began to feel increasingly restless. I was due to meet Jack Favell at 6:30 at Favell Johnston Ltd.'s car showrooms in Mayfair. The arrangement was that we would go for a drink at what he described as one of his "local watering holes," and then—if I passed muster—he might allow me to take him out to dinner.

I'd traced Favell without difficulty—he is in the London telephone directory, and has a flat in a mansion block in Maida Vale—but it was not easy to persuade him to see me. My first letter, sent to his flat, was not answered, and, when I telephoned, there was never a reply. I sent a second letter to the Mayfair car showroom, and, after a delay of several weeks, a follow-up note finally produced a noncommittal answer. Favell stalled; he wouldn't rule out a meeting, but he wouldn't commit to one either. Then, just when I was beginning to believe he'd continue to stall indefinitely, he telephoned me out of the blue, proposing we meet—and meet soon.

This call came last Wednesday morning, on the day the Colonel took me to Manderley, and I still don't know what provoked Favell's change of heart. I think he was intrigued (I've discovered that's a powerful weapon when persuading people to talk), but I suspect he's hard up and may have scented money, too. I can't be sure what it was that finally tipped the scales in my favor, but I do know that a meeting he's avoided for months is now, for some reason, urgent. When I had to postpone it, his reaction was one of annoyance.

I'd already booked a table at a French restaurant in Soho where the wine and the food were good. That was as far as I was prepared to go. I had no intention of bribing him, so, if Favell refused to talk, I'd have to find some way of persuading him. Meanwhile, the prospect of the meeting was putting me on edge; I didn't want to spend the next two and a half hours kicking my heels, so I called Simon Lang, who now works for London's leading dealer in books and manuscripts. After deflecting numerous questions about King's, and where I was now, and what I was up to, and why hadn't anyone set eyes on me for the last six months, et cetera, I was finally given the advice I'd hoped for.

"There's a chap in Compass Yard," he said. "Just off the Charing Cross Road—you know it? Francis Browne—with an 'e,' he's very fussy about that. Mention my name. He deals in that sort of stuff. Rooms of it. Cataloged by subject and place. He's your best bet. Why the sudden interest in rubbish like that? Not exactly your period, is it? You're not going to tell me, I suppose? No. Ah, well, I might have known. Say 'hello' to Nicky from me. Oh, by the way, we sold a copy of one of your books the other day. Let me think, which was it? The one on Walsingham? No, the Sidneys. What a tome! A first edition, mint. So mint I had the teeniest suspicion it hadn't been read. Terribly learned, dear. What a mole you are, burrowing away. We got quite a nice price for it, too. What was the print run, d'you know?"

"About a hundred and fifty," I said ruefully. "Most went to libraries."

Simon laughed. "That explains it. Rarity value, dear, you can't beat it."

I rang off, took a taxi, and twenty minutes later found myself outside Francis Browne's premises. His shop was next to a gaping bombsite; it looked dirty, disreputable, and unpromising. I hesitated, foreseeing a wasted journey, then went in holding the *Rebecca's Tale* picture postcard of Manderley.

Francis Browne was on the premises; he looked even more disreputable than his shop. He was a tall, thin man, with a camp, mournful demeanour, a silvery beard, a pinstripe suit that had seen better days, and a dubious regimental tie with soup stains on it. He had shifty eyes, and in a shifty way, as if unsure whether I were a punter or a policeman, he kept lowering his voice and telling me that he had "more specialized items" for his "discerning collectors," and I was "very welcome to go through to the back room" if I couldn't find the exact type of postcard I needed. I looked around me with disbelief. I couldn't understand why anyone would want to buy this stuff, let alone collect it.

I wasn't searching for any type of card, but, if I had been, I'm sure that sooner or later I would have found it. The shop was quite large, but it was almost impossible to move in it. It bristled with cards; there were thousands upon thousands. The four walls were stacked floor to ceiling with boxes of cards; there were boxes underfoot, boxes on trestles. I could see hundreds of handwritten labels. On the table in front of me were Aviation—Early; Aviation—Mid.; Locomotives; Religious—Churches A–C; Lochs—Various; Theatrical—Assorted; and Views—Midlands & Essex Marshes. On a shelf to my right was a bulging box with the simple label, Saucy.

It took time to convince Francis Browne that I hadn't come to buy, and that I wanted advice. Simon Lang's name proved completely useless—rather as I'd feared. "Him? Mr. Hoity-toity? Well, I'm not speaking to *him*, dear boy. Tell him to put *that* in his pipe and smoke it. . . . Oh, very well, if I must, let me have a look at it. Ah—Manderley. I have a batch of those somewhere. West Country, where are you? I think I put it out, someone was looking through it only the other day. Let me see, Pixies—no. Potteries—no. What's the photographer's name again? Ah, John Stevenson. Of course—know *his* work well. Some of my topographical collectors are very fond of his stuff—it's excellent quality. I've a separate entry for him, somewhere. . . . Let me see. Let me see. . . ."

It took an age. Francis Browne dived and delved among boxes; he consulted ledgers; he rejected ledgers. Dust rose in the air; dust settled. It was the purest chance—I had to divert myself somehow, and when I couldn't stand the disorder and dust any longer, I started flicking through those boxes on the table in front of me. I looked at the Lochs—Various, several of which I knew well and instantly recognized. I looked at Churches, A–C, most of which proved to be Victorian monstrosities; then, having no interest in Locomotives or Aviation or the Essex Marshes, I began to flick through Theatrical—Assorted.

As its label implied, the contents of this box was a hotchpotch; all the cards were in black-and-white, and most were old; no filing system that I could understand was being used: Cole Porter was next to Lillie Langtry, Ivor Novello came before Sarah Bernhardt; Henry Irving was cheek by jowl with Noël Coward. There were famous names in famous parts, but crammed in with them was a great crowd of the forgotten and the anonymous: bosomy Edwardian beauties, moustached men in absurd costumes, clowns and killers, endless lovers striking attitudes.

Shakespeare was well represented; there was a young Gielgud as Richard II, and Donald Wolfit as King Lear; I looked at a Victorian *Hamlet* at the Lyceum, and an Edwardian *Hamlet* at the Birmingham Alhambra. Old theatrical knights—I'd never heard of most of them—addressed their troops before Agincourt, or wooed Juliet on her balcony; they embraced their wives, or stifled their wives, or handed their murderous wives a set of bloodied daggers. Browne was still rifling his boxes, and to pass the time I set myself the task of guessing the plays from the sets and the costumes. I was doing well, on my tenth card, when I found her.

Othello, A Midsummer Night's Dream, Richard III . . . I stopped and looked more closely. Was it her? Was it possible? I was looking at a photograph of one of those unknown theatrical knights, Sir Frank McKendrick. He was got up as Richard III, with a fearsome hump, painted eyebrows, and murderous black-rimmed eyes. Next to him, adopting a swaggering stance and flourishing a diminutive dagger, was one of the two princes in the Tower—or so I assumed. I looked closely at that prince, who was being played by a girl—that didn't surprise me; this picture was dated "1909" on the back, and I knew girls often played such parts at that time. The prince had very dark hair, arresting eyes—and a marked resemblance to the winged child in the notebook sent to the Colonel.

I took it out of the box, moved to the door, and held it up in the light. The resemblance immediately seemed less striking. I went back to the box, and started thumbing through it very fast. When I'd first seen the picture of the winged girl, the Colonel remarked that she seemed to be wearing a *costume*. Like him, I'd assumed it was some form of childish fancy dress—but what if it was a theatrical costume, a fairy's costume, for instance? Suddenly I remembered that conversation with the Briggs sisters: the costume balls at Manderley, the costumes Rebecca had chosen. *Jocelyn, you're getting it all wrong—it was something Shakespearian.*

I found the card for *A Midsummer Night's Dream*. There were Oberon and Titania, but no fairies that in any way resembled her.

"Found it!" Francis Browne said, emerging from a pile of ledgers. "I knew I had it. The John Stevenson Studio, Plymouth—specialized in topographical work in the West Country area. Village scenes, beauty spots—and mansions. Made a bit of a name for himself with mansions, did Mr. Stevenson. Early souvenirs, dear boy. Let's see— John Stevenson: Started up the studio in the summer of 1913, closed it down in January 1915—he volunteered, I imagine. Reopened in 1920, and moved into color quite early. So that dates your card for you: It's definitely not postwar, so it's between summer 1913 and the end of 1914. It's quite a rarity. I'll take it off your hands, if you like. I've scores of postcards of Manderley from the 1920s, all the same, taken from a painting—very dreary. But I've never seen one this early. No? Oh, well—anything else I can do you for while you're here?"

"I'd like to buy this." I handed him the *Richard III* card. "Anything you can tell me about that?"

"Sweet, isn't it?" Francis Browne looked at it admiringly. "Don't you just love that hump, dear? They were troopers in those days, terrible old hams, of course—but I've a bit of a weakness for hams, myself. Let me see—ah, the immortal Sir Frank McKendrick. Touring company, dear—never made it to the West End, but did very well in the provinces. Wopsel on his last gasp, really. Repertoire of Shakespeare, Shakespeare, and Shakespeare. Sir Frank was still playing Romeo when he was in his fifties—you have to admire them, don't you? Floreat 1870 to around 1914—the war again, you see. No one remembers him now, of course, but he was well known in his day. Roused the galleries, dear boy. You'll find him in all the obvious directories. What? The girl? Is it a girl? Oh, so it is. I haven't a clue, I'm afraid. And McKendrick's a bit of a rarity—that's the only two I have left, the *Richard* and the *Dream*, so I'm afraid the price is a bit stiff: half a crown the pair, as it's you, and you're a friend of Mr. Hoity-toity...."

By THE TIME I'D PAID THIS EXTORTIONATE PRICE AND finally escaped Francis Browne's shop, it was 5:15: too late for a book shop search, and too late for libraries. Sir Frank McKendrick would have to wait until tomorrow—and that was probably just as well, I decided. Every time I looked at that faded photograph of a doomed prince, the likeness to the child in the notebook decreased. Besides, with luck, and good steering, Jack Favell should provide quick and clear answers to my questions about Rebecca's background and origins; there was no need to chase hares, and my tendency to chase hares was beginning to alarm me.

I returned to Regent's Park, bathed, and changed into one of my Cambridge suits. I took a cab, asked the driver to drop me in Park Lane, and then walked to Favell's premises from there. As I walked, I went over Favell's details in my mind, the details I'd discovered, and those provided last night by Colonel Julyan.

Favell was older than his cousin—always supposing Rebecca *was* his cousin—and was now in his mid-fifties. I had been unable to trace any birth certificate for him either, but I knew his age from newspaper reports: Favell had had a very checkered career. As a young man, he had been drummed out of the Royal Navy; he was subsequently involved in several dubious business transactions; not long after the inquest into Rebecca's death, he had gone down on charges of fraud, false accounting, and operating a gambling club without a gaming license. He had served three years in Strangeways.

He had then disappeared from view, and I could find no trace of his activities until his company took a lease on these premises, some three years ago. The firm of Favell Johnston Ltd., in which he claimed to me he was a partner and codirector, was listed at Companies House, but had filed no annual accounts. Several telephone calls to their showrooms had failed to locate his codirector, Johnston; I suspected he didn't exist, or was very much a sleeping partner. The premises the car showroom occupied were expensive; the overheads in Mayfair must have been high, and I doubted the firm was prospering. On my last visit to London I'd walked past the showrooms, and, as I approached the windows now, I noticed that not one of the cars I'd seen then had been sold in the interim. Petrol is no longer rationed, but I felt the market for this kind of classic car, beautiful, but expensive to buy and expensive to run, must still be limited.

I paused just short of the entrance. In the window was a British racing-green Jaguar, a glorious Bentley, and an early Hispano Suiza. I thought of Colonel Julyan's descriptions of this man—as a blackmailer, a drunkard, and a sponger. I thought of Ellie's remarks about him, and of the interesting comments Colonel Julyan had made last night—but I bore in mind the advice he is always giving me: Beware the biased witness. On the subject of Favell, I suspect there are few witnesses more biased than Arthur Lancelot Julyan.

According to the Colonel, Favell had initially shown no interest in discovering the truth about his cousin's death; not a peep had been heard from him until after the inquest when, as Ellie had told me, Favell had turned up at Manderley, and produced that note left at his apartment building by Rebecca on the last afternoon of her life. It was headed with the address of her own London flat by the river. "And you can work out exactly when it was written," the Colonel added, with a sharp glance at me. "The consultation with Dr. Baker was at two P.M.—and, according to him, it was brief. The porter at Favell's apartment block told him she'd left the note there—Favell was out—shortly before three P.M. That means Rebecca must have seen the doctor, returned briefly to her own flat to write the note, left it at Favell's apartment block, and then left London at once for Manderley. It was a six-hour drive then—and that's at speed—and she was definitely back at Manderley by nine that evening."

I was listening intently. There was no question, as Ellie had said, of the importance of this note—yet the man I was about to see had concealed its existence from the inquest jury. Instead (and Colonel Julyan left me in no doubt about this) Favell had tried to use it as a means of extorting money from Maxim de Winter. Whereupon, as Ellie had said, the Colonel had been called in—and his take on what then happened interested me.

"By the time I arrived at Manderley, Favell was already drunk," Colonel Julyan said. "His manner was obnoxious. He started waving that damn note under my nose and making the most lurid claims. He said that he and Rebecca had been having an affair, that she'd been going to leave her husband, and run off to Paris with him, and that Maxim had killed her in a jealous rage.

"Well, let me tell you, I took all that with a fistful of salt. For a start, that note proved nothing. It was short and it was curt. Rebecca asked Favell to drive down to Manderley, and meet her that same night at the boathouse. She wrote that she 'had something to tell him.' I'll admit that sounds underhand, but Rebecca couldn't meet him openly at Manderley. Maxim had banned him from the house months before. It didn't sound like the note a woman who was planning to kill herself would write—but it didn't sound like a note to a lover, either. It was notably lacking in any sign of affection. It was a summons, and its tone was cold. Yes—*peremptory* would be the word for it."

The Colonel paused, then gave me a sharp blue-eyed glance. "You see, I think Favell *knew* that note didn't provide sufficient grounds for reopening the investigation, let alone overturning the inquest verdict of suicide. If he wanted his accusations to be taken seriously, he *had* to provide Maxim with a motive for murder. Suggesting Rebecca was unfaithful provided a very effective motive. Favell isn't stupid. You'd do well to bear that in mind when you meet him."

I'd asked the Colonel, whose face was troubled, whether he had believed these claims of an affair. It took some nerve to do it, and, a few weeks ago, he'd have sent me away with a flea in my ear if I'd risked it. He's more open with me now, but even so his answer was hesitant. Eventually he said that he had never believed that Rebecca was going to leave her husband for her cousin; that, he felt, was an improvisation, designed to strengthen Favell's case, and made up on the spur of the moment. As to whether there had been infidelities, he had reluctantly come to believe that Rebecca had sought "consola-tion" outside her marriage, he said—but it did not follow that her lover was Favell, despite his claims.

"I refer you back to Rebecca's note," he said. "That note is crucial. Rebecca would never have written in that way to someone she loved, I'm certain of it. So why did she write it? Why did she want Favell at that boathouse that night? Was she intending to tell him about her illness? Why drag him all the way down to Manderley to do that? She could have waited and told him in London. No, there's *another* reason for that note. Find out what it was, and you might get some-where—and that's my final word on the subject."

I was interested in this suggestion; this account was franker than any I'd previously been given, but it remained circumspect, I felt. I could hear the dislike of Favell that lay behind it. I could understand why the Colonel, given his own devotion to Rebecca, would wish to scotch the idea that Favell could be her lover; but that did not mean he was correct. I remembered how partisan Colonel Julyan was, how deeply misleading his description of Frith had been. Perhaps the same would prove true of Jack Favell. After all, whatever his failings, and however reprehensible his methods, there was a strong possibility that, in accusing Maxim of murder, Favell had been accurate. Resolving to keep an open mind, I walked up to the showroom doors and caught sight of Rebecca's cousin for the first time.

He was inspecting his reflection in the Jaguar's window and adjusting the Windsor knot on his tie. As soon as he saw me, he came forward to greet me with considerable bonhomie: a tall man, good-looking, but with something weak and petulant about the mouth; fair haired, blue eyed, looking ten years younger than his age at first glance, and ten years older when I inspected him more closely. He was wearing an old but well-tailored Prince of Wales check suit, a shirt with frayed cuffs, a flashy gold wristwatch, and brown suede shoes that would have given Colonel Julyan an apoplexy.

I learned two things about Jack Favell very quickly. He "could do with a drink," he said—and I didn't doubt that condition was semi-permanent. And his idea of a "local watering hole" was the bar at the Dorchester.

SIXTEEN

I<small>T WAS STILL RELATIVELY EARLY, AND THERE WERE FEW</small> people in the bar. There was a group of American businessmen at one table; at another, two women in smart New Look dresses were discussing the spoils of a recent shopping expedition: "Such a joy not to have those wretched *coupons* any more," said one as we passed. A pianist in a dinner jacket was playing a tinkling selection of show tunes. I loathe such places; Favell led the way past the Art Deco tables and chairs, paused to admire himself in a mirror, and approached the bar as if he owned it.

"Walter not on tonight?" he said to the barman. The barman, looking unimpressed, remarked that Walter hadn't worked there for the last six months. Favell looked irritated. His tone became blustering: "Well, he served me two nights ago, so I'm surprised to hear that. I come here all the time—maybe you're new. What will it be, Gray? A scotch, I expect. Barman, a scotch for my Scotch friend, and a single malt for me—make it a large one. Glenfiddich. Very well, Glenmorangie then. . . . No ice for you, old boy? I'll have ice. Soda? No? Put that away, this is on me—I wouldn't hear of it. Oh, if you insist. Cheers, old chap. Where shall we park ourselves?"

I suggested we park ourselves as far as possible from the pianist. Favell had just committed several cardinal sins: I can't stand being called "Scotch," a word that ought to be confined to the drink; I can't stand southerners who put ice in ordinary blended whisky, let alone a single malt; adding soda to mispronounced Glenmorangie didn't improve things. Favell's wallet, I noticed, had been flashed briefly and repocketed swiftly. It didn't surprise me, in what turned out to be the course of a long evening, that this was the wallet's one and only sighting.

We sat down in a far corner of the room, Favell selecting the chair opposite a looking glass. He smoothed back his hair, fingered his signet ring, downed half his drink in a single swallow, and looked at me narrowly. I noticed the slight tremor in his hands, and wondered whether it was a symptom of drink or nervousness: both, I decided. He was certainly ill at ease, and was probably one of those men who manifest that state by belligerence. As an opening tactic—and I wasn't to understand why until much later that evening—he pressed me hard on the contacts I'd made with him.

Had I sent him just the one letter? I explained I'd sent two, and had written to his place of work only when I received no reply from the mansion flat address. For some reason, this seemed to put his mind at rest. In an evasive way, he said he wasn't living at the flat any more; he didn't volunteer any information as to where he was now living, and I didn't press him. After a couple more swallows of whisky, which seemed to steady him, he drew out a heavy crested silver case, lit a cigarette, blew smoke in my face, and, watching me closely, came to the point: "So, canter this past me again," he said. "What's your angle exactly?"

I'd prepared for this. From the first, I'd felt sure that Terence Gray, earnest young librarian, was unlikely to cut any ice with Favell, useful though he's been to me in Kerrith. So I'd killed off that Mr. Gray, and invented a new one, with a journalistic background, and an interest in crime stories—especially ones involving a possible miscarriage of justice, or unsolved murder. I was pretty sure Favell had talked—circumspectly—to journalists before. I now dangled the possibility of newspaper features, maybe even a book, another account of the "Manderley Mystery." This story had all the right elements, I suggested: a beautiful woman; a famous house; a jealous husband; a mysterious death; rumors of scandal and love affairs . . .

"Only one problem," I said. "Enough has been written about this,

God knows, but as far as Rebecca's concerned, there's a marked shortage of material."

Favell had been listening closely. A glint came into his pale blue eyes. "Might be a bit of money in it, then?" he said. "Something in it for you, old boy?"

"Possibly," I said. "But that's a long way down the road yet. What I need is *background*. I need new material. I've checked out the de Winters—fine. But Rebecca? There's very little information. I need to know who she was, where she came from, how she came to marry de Winter—what she was *like*. That's where you could help. You knew her as a child, I hear. And I've been told you remained close, that you were one of the few people who understood her."

Favell's pale eyes rested on my face. He was indeed by no means stupid, I thought; I'd have to be careful not to overdo the flattery. He was still in the process of assessing me; I saw his gaze take in my suit, my shirt, and my cufflinks. I could sense the cogs of his mind turning over. His glass was already empty.

"Of course, there is Mrs. Danvers," he said in a meditative way, his gaze never leaving my face. "The housekeeper at Manderley. She was close to Rebecca from her childhood onward. You know about Danny? Hear anything about her when you were sniffing around in Kerrith?"

"I haven't tracked her down yet. In any case, I wanted to talk to you first. She may be able to help, but she must be old now, and she's a woman. I'd rather hear a man's view—especially if the man concerned was close to Rebecca."

"You could be right there. And I was closer than most. An intimate, you could say." Favell winked and then laughed. "Cigarette, old boy?"

"I don't, I'm afraid. Kicked the habit during the war."

"Had a good war, did you? What outfit were you in?"

"The RAF. Never made it beyond Flight Lieutenant. Nothing glamorous—pen pushing and square bashing mostly. Let me get you another drink."

Not a good idea to say I'd spent the war in Military Intelligence, I felt sure. And the RAF seemed safe; Favell, given his age, would have escaped call-up. He was perhaps a man who liked an opportunity to patronize others. This misinformation certainly seemed to incline him in my favor.

"Lowly Flight Lieutenant, eh?" He laughed. "Ah, well, we can't all be heroes. I wangled a nice little billet—Ministry of Supply. Lots of opportunities there. And then I had a lot of Yank friends. So I could lay my hands on whatever I needed. . . . I had a good war. Best years of my life, I think sometimes."

I was making some progress, I thought—and the second drink helped. Favell remained watchful, but he warmed up considerably. I let him talk on about the war years, and at first made no attempt to rein him in. Most interviewees, I've discovered, cannot wait to hold forth. They *want* to talk, and love to claim special insight, even when they possess very little. It helps if you can identify, then exploit, an informant's weakness, his Achilles' heel. Sometimes it's vanity or a taste for self-justification, sometimes it's simply garrulity. What was Favell's? As he talked on, I was watching for an opening.

Favell was a heavy drinker, that was obvious just looking at him— and I was beginning to wonder if he'd been drinking before I met him that evening. I could see he was vain, and he did respond to flattery. But I needed something more, and I finally saw it. It was when I recognized the light of long-buried grievances in his pale eyes that I knew I had my opening. I bought him another whisky—a single. I didn't want him too drunk, and I didn't want him too sober.

I asked him about Rebecca's death and the "cover-up" afterwards. That led to ten minutes of accusations against Max de Winter (as Favell called him) and "that old snob" Colonel Julyan, who had hushed things up for his friend. I had the impression these accusations had been Favell's party piece for years.

"Max killed her," Favell said. "I don't give a damn about that doctor's evidence. I still don't believe it was suicide, and I never bloody well will. All right, Rebecca was ill, she was dying, and that's why she wanted to see me that night, of course. She must have been going to tell me about her illness. . . ." He hesitated, and his manner became evasive. "I never went to Manderley as she asked, you see. Got her note too late. I was out at a party, on the razzle, didn't get back till four in the morning. And it was damn lucky I *didn't* go, as I realized afterward. If Max had found us together, he'd probably have killed me, too. He was being eaten alive by jealousy—he wasn't sane when it came to Rebecca."

Favell then changed the subject, which surprised me. He moved rapidly on to other examples of prejudice against him. Not only did Favell nurse grievances, I discovered, but they went way back—to his father; his teachers at the boarding school he attended in Kenya; his instructors at Dartmouth Naval College; the officers on the ship where he served as a midshipman; the officers superior to him on every other ship he'd ever served on; the officer in charge of the court-martial that led to his leaving the Royal Navy; the so-called friends who'd refused to help him when he was back on civvy street; and the numerous friends who had let him down since. There was no reference to his prison sentence, but then I didn't expect there to be. And there was no sign that his cousin Rebecca was exempt from these charges of neglect and indifference.

I listened very carefully. And I noticed something interesting: the reference to Kenya, of course, but beyond that the striking consistency of his complaints. Favell had a mountainous chip on his shoulder, and the only person in this saga that he *did* exclude from his charges of persecution, snobbery, and neglect was his mother. She had been a "saint"; she had scrimped and saved to pay his school fees in Africa; she'd gone without to raise the money for his passage to England when he was seventeen; she'd had a "miserable" life, with a spendthrift snobbish husband, who looked down on her and abused her both verbally and physically throughout Favell's childhood. All her love and hope and expectation had been lavished on her son— and that son now felt he had failed her.

"I never made it up to her," Favell said, and his eyes watered. "I left Kenya early in 1915, and I never saw her again. I used to write—not as often as I should have done, but I'm not much of a letter writer. I tried to hide it from her, how much I loathed the Navy, that bloody farce of a court-martial—but she found out. Some so-called friend wrote and told her. If I'd gone back to Kenya then, I could have explained, I could always talk her round. But I hung about in the Far East. You could live well there for next to nothing in those days. So I wasn't with her when she died: 1928. Worst year of my life. That's when I cut my losses and came back to England—which wasn't the smartest move I've ever made, I can tell you. And that's when I remet Rebecca."

Drawing on another cigarette, he began to explain what had happened when he returned to England. What did he discover? Why, the little cousin that he hadn't set eyes on or heard from in years was mistress of Manderley, and was married to the very rich Max de Winter.

"Well, when I found that out I cheered up, old boy, I can tell you," he said. "I made a few inquiries. Rebecca and I had lost touch; it must have been a good ten years since I last saw her, and I hadn't written for seven at least—not one of nature's correspondents, as I told you. But Rebecca was always damn fond of me. We'd been very close for a couple of years when we were young, and, not to put too fine a point on it, when I found I was a bit short of the readies, I thought she'd be sure to come through. Had my eye on a nice little flat in Cadogan Square; so I spruced myself up, and hightailed it down to Manders. Didn't get the warmest of welcomes, old boy. Met the husband—a cold fish if ever there was one. Met Rebecca—and there was quite a change there, I can tell you. But would she help cousin Jack? No. Couldn't put me up because the house was full for the weekend. Couldn't help out on the financial front. Said she didn't have any money of her own—said it to my face, when just one of her rings would have paid for that flat, *with* some change left over."

He paused, his face clouding, as if he had just remembered some detail that worried him. He stubbed out one cigarette, and lit another. I asked him if anything was wrong.

"No. Just thought of something, that's all. Not important. Where was I? Ah, yes—trying to get my little cousin to help me through a rough patch. And getting turned down. Not very pleasant. Got told a few home truths, old boy. She had a cutting tongue, Rebecca."

He hesitated. "Don't get me wrong, I didn't hold it against her. A couple of months later, when I really *was* in Queer Street, she came through for me—on her terms, of course. She was like that. She bought a car through me; I did a few car deals for friends, even back then. This was a real beauty, a Bentley, went like the wind, and Rebecca paid way over the odds for it. She knew perfectly well she was paying through the nose, you could never put one over on her, but that was her way of helping me out. Maybe she thought it would hurt my pride less, doing it indirectly like that. It's possible—she could be good like that, Rebecca."

He paused, then laughed. "On the other hand, she might have thought she was buying me off. She didn't want me at Manderley, you see. I'd wangled a few more invitations. Knew some of her London friends, her more *bohemian* friends." He gave me a small glance. "Gate-crashed a few parties. And that didn't suit my little cousin at all. No ifs and buts about it—she didn't want me there."

"Why do you think that was?" I asked. I could well see why Rebecca might not want this cousin at her smart parties. Favell had a different explanation.

"Knew her too well, old boy," he said, "Knew her of old, didn't I? Rebecca couldn't hide things from me. I'd heard all the stories—love at first sight, how happy they were, the ideal couple, still on their honeymoon after nearly three years of marriage . . . Well, she couldn't fool me. I knew within ten minutes of walking into that house she wasn't happy, and neither was he. I *knew*, as soon as I saw them together—there was something badly wrong. Right at the core."

He paused, frowning into the middle distance. Again I had the impression that he was scarcely aware of me, that he was locked back in his own memories. After an interval, he seemed to snap back into the present; he gave a shrug.

"Not sure I ever got to the bottom of that, old boy. A little mystery there, I think. But I'll tell you one thing for free. It was a fake, their marriage. A fake from start to finish. What's that term the French use? A *marriage blanc*, that's it. They weren't sleeping together. No sex—and I'd have laid money on it."

I didn't say anything, but I may have raised my eyebrows or given some other indication of disbelief because Favell showed immediate signs of irritation. As I was beginning to learn, he disliked the least hint of contradiction.

"Fine. Don't believe me, it's no skin off my nose, old chum. But I'm telling you I'm right. Oh, I don't doubt he *had* slept with her—and before they were married, knowing Rebecca. I don't doubt he still *wanted* to sleep with her. I could see that in his face every time he looked at her—it was naked. That man was dying inside, and I wasn't surprised. That's the effect Rebecca had on men, and it started way back, when she was still in her teens. She could break your heart with one glance when she was fourteen years old, and didn't she know it! She was born a tease, she was bloody shameless—lapped up admiration, led you on, and then slapped you down. . . . I looked at Max, and it was like looking in the mirror. I knew how it felt to be on the receiving end, you see—"

He broke off abruptly. "So I had *plenty* in common with Max," he went on, after a pause. "And I once made the mistake of telling him that. Shouldn't have done, I suppose—family loyalty and all that. But Rebecca's attitude was narking me, to be perfectly frank, and I'd had a few drinks too many probably, so I put it to him straight. . . . Wasn't news to him, as it turned out; in fact, I was surprised how much he knew, because Rebecca was always secretive. Anyway, the long and short of it was, I got myself banned from Manderley. Thrown out on my ear, old boy. Still no point in dwelling on all that now. Any chance of another drink? I'm feeling a bit low. Been a bloody awful week for me, as a matter of fact. One thing after another—problems with my lease, blasted accountant on my back, thought I'd sold that Jag, then I hadn't. . . . I could do with another scotch."

I'd seen something in his face then, something in his eyes. There was an evasion. I would have liked to know just what information he had given de Winter, and whether it was true or false; I was absolutely certain he wouldn't tell me.

I persuaded him to fill in a few details—the names of some of those more "bohemian" friends, for instance, and what he'd heard about the first meeting between Rebecca and Maxim. He was informative on the first, vague and nonspecific on the second. I suggested that rather than having another drink there, we go on to the restaurant in Soho. When I mentioned its name, he seemed to forget the proviso he had made on the telephone. "Good idea," he said. "Might buck me up a bit. I could do with a night on the town. Spot of decent food. I don't get out and about as much as I did. Little lady in my life cracking the whip—you know how that feels, I expect? You married, Gray?"

"No. I'm not." I rose; with one last reluctant glance toward the bar, Favell pushed his chair back.

"Ever have been?" he continued, as we walked out to the lobby. "No? Me neither. Hang on to the liberty as long as one can, that's what I say. But sooner or later, the ultimatums start—don't you find that? Usually, I see the warning signals, I'm off, but this time it's been a bit tricky. Never mix business and pleasure, eh? I should have thought of that sooner, but the lease on the showroom came up, and

I was a bit short, and my little Susie was flush at the time, so, there you are. In up to my neck, *not* so easy to extricate myself."

"You mean your partner—Johnston—that's a woman?" We came out into Park Lane and stood on the pavement, waiting for a taxi.

"Got it in one." Favell winked. "Sleeping partner in more than one sense. All fine to begin with, but women change, don't you find? I meet this girl, cute as a button, pretty little blonde, sweet as pie. Common as they come, but good natured—or so I thought—and with a *very* nice little nest egg. Just been left several thou' by some sugar daddy. Looking for investment opportunities was how she put it, eager to help me out—and then what happens? Hard as nails, old boy. Wants the ring on the finger. Starts dictating terms. Well, I wasn't having that." His face clouded. "The hell with her—I'm well shot of her in any case."

A taxi drew alongside and we climbed into it. I gave the driver directions; Favell slumped back in the seat beside me. His mood seemed to change again, and the man-to-man bravado deserted him. As we turned east, he stared out of the windows at the streets; dusk was falling.

I had numerous leads, but it seemed best to avoid pressing him before we reached the restaurant, so I kept silent. Favell surfaced from his brooding state once or twice to ask a few questions; he asked me about my "visits" to Kerrith, and whether I'd seen Manderley itself, and whether it "had fallen down yet," but my brief answers scarcely seemed to penetrate. He seemed surprised to hear that Colonel Julyan was still alive.

"Thought he'd have kicked the bucket years ago. I cooked *his* goose good and proper," he said, gazing at the passing cars. "Didn't see why he should cover up for his friend and get off scot-free. Didn't like his attitude, old boy. Bloody snob. So, I spread the word, I had the odd contact in Kerrith. I heard he'd resigned from the Bench—I knew my job was done then. Haven't set foot in that part of the world since Rebecca's inquest, of course. Couldn't face it, frankly. Stayed in touch with a few people for a couple of years. Robert Lane, used to be a footman at Manderley—good sport, old Robert, liked a drink, liked redheads; have you come across him? But I lost touch, lost interest. Then there was the war—you know how it is, old boy."

I did; more important, I believed him. I saw now what the Colonel and Ellie had meant last night: I could not believe this man would have left that azalea garland at the boathouse; I was pretty certain he'd had nothing to do with the notebook, either. Favell, I judged, was motivated almost exclusively by self-interest: Where was the advantage to him in sending Colonel Julyan that anonymous offering? Nor could I see how Favell would have obtained it, in view of the information he'd given me. That left one other obvious candidate, the person who, as Ellie had told me, had been in possession of Rebecca's appointments book after her death. I waited awhile, then raised the question of Mrs. Danvers.

Favell evinced little interest, and I had the impression his thoughts were elsewhere. "Danny? Haven't laid eyes on her in . . . what? Eight years? Nine? Haven't a clue where she is. Don't care, to be honest with you. Rebecca could always handle her—but Danny's a weird woman. Obsessional. Tightfisted, too. Never any help to me, only ever saw me because she wanted to talk about Rebecca all the time. Rebecca this. Rebecca bloody that. She never understood about Rebecca and me. I got sick of it in the end. I mean, why make the effort? Life's too short. She was back in London last I heard. Could have died in the blitz. Could have died of old age. Could have died of bitterness—she was well on the way the last time I saw her. Look at that. . . ."

We were approaching Piccadilly Circus by a side-street route; Favell was gesturing along a terrace of fine early-nineteenth-century houses, in the middle of which was a bomb site. It was boarded up, but you could see broken walls, sprouting weeds. A fireplace hung over air; the bricks still retained patches of plaster, and—extraordinarily, after all these years—thin obstinate strips of wallpaper.

"Why don't they clear the place up? Why don't they rebuild?" Favell glowered out of the window. "Six years—and you'd think the war ended yesterday. Look at it! There's London for you, there's England. You win a bloody war and, six years later, you can't buy decent food, and you can't get decent clothes, a bottle of scotch costs a fortune—and no one knows how to have fun any more. Look at it, like a bloody morgue. You see that place there, that bomb site? That used to be a restaurant. One of the best. French food. French wine. French waiters—I loved that place. La Pomme d'Or, it was called. It was the first London restaurant anyone ever took me to. I was straight off the boat from Mombasa, and green as they come. Seventeen years old. Jack Devlin met me off the Southampton train and he brought me there, gave me anything I wanted—oysters, champagne, brandy; I was sick as a dog afterward. I couldn't believe how beautiful it was: the white tablecloths, and the candles, and the silver glittering. That's the first time I saw Rebecca. Sitting at that table. I can't remember how old she was then—fourteen, maybe. She looked twelve, and I couldn't take my eyes off her. She never said a word, not a single word, all evening. A black dress, I remember that. That's it, a black dress, because she was in mourning for her mother. A black dress, and this white skin, and these huge dark eyes. . . . Christ. Tell that driver to get a move on, will you?"

The cab lurched forward across an intersection. Favell slumped back in his seat again. I tensed; I hardly dared speak in case he balked, or shied away from what he'd just told me. I waited until we were turning into Piccadilly Circus, with the Eros fountain ahead of us.

"Jack Devlin?" I said, watching him.

Favell gave me an irritable glance, as if I were being very slow. "Jack Devlin. My uncle. My mother named me after him—he was her favorite brother."

I waited. I'd waited six months for this, so I felt I could wait a little more. We turned left. The restaurant was now in sight; the lights of Soho glittered, and Favell seemed to rouse himself. He gave me a sharp glance, then smiled.

"Oh, I *see*," he said. "You mean you didn't know? Jack Devlin was Rebecca's father. At least, he was married to her mother at one time. So *maybe* he was her father—but it wouldn't do to jump to conclusions, would it, old boy?"

No, indeed. We climbed out of the cab. I knew there was no danger of Favell's wallet's reappearing, so I paid off the driver.

SEVENTEEN

I HAD CHOSEN THE RESTAURANT WITH CARE. I COULDN'T risk any of the places I used to frequent with Nicky and Julia, where I might be recognized; I wanted to avoid anywhere too noisy and fashionable, where Favell might be distracted. Chez Vincent, unchanged since I first went there before the war, seemed a good choice. It was a small, unpretentious place of the kind all too rare in London; it served excellent food, and had a good wine list. The tables, each plainly set with immaculate linen cloths, were divided from each other by high wooden banquettes, which created the perfect conditions for private conversations. On a Monday night, it was not crowded; we were shown to a quiet table; Favell's first reaction, I could tell, was not favorable.

"Bit of a hole in the corner place, isn't it, old boy?" he said. "Still, I hear the food's good. Mind if I have an aperitif? Tell the boy I'll have a *fine a l'eau.*"

I asked the waiter for this; Favell examined the menu. His brandy was brought swiftly; by the time he had ordered the most elaborate and expensive items on the list, and had lit another cigarette, he seemed to decide the place might suit him after all. Surfacing from his former preoccupied and gloomy state, he remarked that it wasn't exactly the Savoy Grill, but sometimes these little places could be surprisingly good. He turned his pale eyes toward me and gave me a long assessing stare.

"So where d'you want me to start, old boy?" he said. "Rebecca's father? Her putative father? I can tell you a few stories about *him*. I think Jack Devlin had a few doubts about his paternity, to put it mildly. But he kept quiet about them. Didn't want to hurt Rebecca, I expect. He adored her, you see. Never laid eyes on her till her mother died—but once he did . . . well, nothing was too good for her. She could wind him around her little finger."

For the first time that evening, I felt a little uneasy. There was an odd, brooding quality to that stare of Favell's. Perhaps he was now leading up to some suggestion of payment for information; if so, I'd deal with it when it came. Meanwhile, I'd already begun to see that Favell disliked interruptions, so I decided to let him tell this his way. I could always backtrack later. Favell took a deep swallow of brandy, and, with every sign of enjoyment, launched himself.

"Jack Devlin was quite a character—'Black Jack' Devlin, people called him. He was a buccaneer, always ready to chance his arm, a bit of a desperado. I take after him in that respect . . . I've always been a risk taker. Of course, he was luckier than I've been. He *really* had the luck of the Irish—and it made him a fortune. As for charm, Jack Devlin could charm the birds out of the trees. When I first met him, he was in his late thirties—and he was one of the handsomest men I've ever laid eyes on. Flamboyant. Wasn't a gentleman, and didn't pretend to be. Six feet tall, black hair, blue eyes. He was a one-off. Had a taste for the gee-gees, and what he didn't know about horses wasn't worth knowing.

"Jack Devlin could drink any man under the table," he continued, lighting another cigarette. "He was a gambler—that's how he got his nickname, apart from his looks—and it wasn't too smart an idea to play cards with him, I can tell you. And if you were a woman—watch out. Not that they ever did, old boy. Jack was only too successful in *that* department. It wasn't just his looks, he was polite to women, considerate. He was a hell-raiser, but there was this dreamy gentle side to him, and women liked that. And he never lost his brogue—he had this soft Cork accent, and when he told you a story you'd be spellbound. He could talk like an angel, Jack Devlin."

I considered this Irishman, this Celtic charmer, this riverboat gambler with a taste for the gee-gees: I thought that, as the Colonel might have put it, a fistful of salt was in order—but then I hadn't expected Favell to be the most accurate of witnesses. I tried steering Favell toward some *facts*, and, eased by the *fine a l'eau*, he began to give me some.

Jack Devlin, he said, was the youngest of a family of eight children, brought up in Cork. His father had built up a "nice little business." Beginning with a small haberdashery store, he had ended up owning the largest and most fashionable ladies' outfitters in the city, specializing in the import of the finest French silks and brocades. Both Devlin's parents had considerable business acumen, were good Catholics, and deeply pious. Of the five children who survived into adulthood, three went into the family firm; the two youngest, the beauties of the family, struck out on their own. The daughter, Brigid, Favell's mother, married up into the Anglo-Irish gentry, and the youngest child, Jack Devlin himself, left Ireland, made a disastrous marriage, and kicked over the traces.

Favell was clearly sensitive about this background, and, as I'd noticed before, unease made him belligerent. "So, the Devlin grandparents were in trade," he said as the waiter brought our first courses: I was having fish, Favell a rich concoction involving cream, mushrooms, and pastry. "I don't apologize for that—why should I? I don't know about you, old boy, but I've no patience with all those old snobberies. People looking down their nose at you, just because your grandfather earned an honest wage. My father was like that. Max de Winter was like that. Bloody snobs, the pair of them. You'd think the war would have put paid to all that—but it hasn't. Well, I've no time for it myself. I've got a soft spot for the underdog, always been a bit of a socialist in my own quiet way. . . ."

The socialist who'd described his girlfriend to me as "common" took a swallow of the white wine I'd ordered, and settled down to explain yet another grievance.

"My father thought he was so bloody grand," he continued. "He was a second son, never stopped boasting about the ancestral home, all his bloody Favell connections—well, the ancestral home was some vast ruin, and what money there was went to his elder brother. When Pa discovered he couldn't make ends meet despite his old school tie and his connections, he was more than ready to marry a draper's

daughter, especially when there was a generous marriage settlement—
which he got through inside three years, incidentally. He dragged my
poor mother out to Kenya because you could get land for next to
nothing. Tried to ingratiate himself with the smart set, wrote to his
old school pals, thought he'd make a go of it with a coffee plantation—
and what did he end up as? A bloody pathetic little shipping clerk in
a Nairobi office. Give me Jack Devlin every time. He never gave a
damn what anyone thought of him. *And* he made a fortune, several
times over. Of course, that really got up my father's nose. Liked to
say that if he earned a pittance, at least he earned it honestly."

"The implication being that Jack Devlin didn't? Was that true?
How did your uncle make his money?"

Favell gave me a sidelong glance, then smiled. "In South Africa,
eventually. And he may well have sailed a bit close to the wind; I told
you, he was a born risk taker. But that's jumping the gun a bit. He
started out in the family firm to begin with. He worked for his father
for a year or two, went to France, found new suppliers for the silks
and the ribbons. Lived it up in Paris, I gather. . . ."

Favell paused to mop up the last of his food in a greedy way, as if
he hadn't eaten a square meal in days. I considered this information.
From the first, my instinct had been that there was a French connection somewhere.

"Did he meet Rebecca's mother in France?" I asked.

"What makes you think so, old boy?"

"It occurred to me Rebecca could have had French connections.
Someone mentioned to me that she might have had family in France.
She chose to sail in a converted Breton fishing vessel, when she could
easily have had a boat made for her locally. Her boat had a French
name: *Je Reviens*. Also, there's no record of Rebecca's birth certificate.
So, like you, she could have been born abroad."

"Well, well, so you have done a bit of sleuthing." Favell smiled,
and lit another cigarette. "I was beginning to wonder. Come up with
anything else, old boy?"

"Quite a few things." I thought of the McKendrick postcard and
decided to take a gamble. If my suggestion was wrong, it didn't matter. It still might provoke a revelation from Favell. "For instance, I
think she had theater connections as a child," I said. "I think her
mother was an actress."

Favell raised his eyebrows, then laughed. "Not bad at all. How did you find that out? Rebecca kept *very* quiet on the mother question. Max probably knew, and I think that old Tartar of a grandmother of his knew as well—she didn't miss a trick, in my opinion. But I don't think they'd have been too keen on advertising the fact at Manderley, do you? Might have raised eyebrows among the county set down there. I mean—an actress! One step up from a loose woman in their eyes. They were still living in another era—probably still are. Even Max was a terrible old Victorian in some ways. Strait-laced. Full of inhibitions. Besides, there was the question of his father, Lionel. *He* never had any inhibitions about actresses, I hear. A regular stage door Johnny. He'd been dead for years, but his reputation lived on. You couldn't spend five minutes in Kerrith without hearing about *his* exploits. So, Rebecca kept very quiet about dear Mama's profession. Wouldn't have gone down too well at her grander parties. Ah—food. And a Bordeaux. Pushing the boat out a bit, aren't you, old boy? No complaints, mind you."

There was a pause while the waiters served us our main course. Favell refilled his wine glass, and then returned to his story, picking up its threads where he had left off. There was no sign of any reluctance to talk—that came later.

"So—where was I? Paris, that's it. Jack Devlin was based in Paris but he traveled a lot, visiting suppliers in France, but also Italy and England—and on one of those trips he met the fair Isabel. My mother used to say he met her on the Monday, married her on the Tuesday, and left her on the Wednesday—he didn't hang around, Jack Devlin, that was the point. He was a young man, twenty-four, something like that, and he fell in love at first sight—one look. And I think that's true, because he told me so, and he always said that to Rebecca, years later. Anyway, he married the fair Isabel at some little French country church, and he sent my mother a telegram and he was over the moon—and then something went wrong. Six months later there was another telegram: The fair Isabel was still in France, I think. But Jack certainly wasn't. He'd left his wife; he was cutting his losses, making a new start, and he'd sailed for South Africa."

He gave me a pale glance. "And don't *ask*—I can see the questions ticking over. Well, I can't answer them. You have to remember, this is going back a long way. It must have been 1900, because he left before

Rebecca was born, and she was born that November. I was three then, so all of this is hearsay, from my mother. She always said Jack had his heart broken; he certainly never divorced and he never remarried. But I didn't even *meet* Uncle Jack for another fourteen years. I didn't even know he had a child until I came to England, and I don't think my mother knew, either . . . There's always the possibility it was news to Uncle Jack, too. That idea crossed my mind more than once, I can tell you."

Favell was right: There were umpteen questions I wanted to ask, but I decided to wait. He began eating with gusto, and, as he ate, began to fill me in on Jack Devlin's subsequent career in South Africa. The details he gave me were colorful and, I suspected, apocryphal.

After some years of struggle, Jack Devlin, it seemed, had finally found his metier: It was mining, and he came into the mining business by accident. "He met some old panhandler in a bar in Jo'burg," Favell said with a smile. "At least, that's the way he told it. The old man was a standing joke, but he liked a drink, and a game of cards, so they played poker. Jack won. He won the man's horse and his gun; by then the old boy had nothing left but the clothes he stood up in and the title he'd staked out on this little patch of ground in the Modderfontein area, which the man swore had gold in it.

"They opened another bottle of schnapps, and they played one more time. The man had a good hand, but Jack Devlin held all four aces. So Jack won a pair of worn-out pants and a worn-out shirt and a little bit of land everyone said was worthless. Then they shook hands, and Jack let the old boy keep his clothes and his horse, but he took the gun and the title to that land—and it made his fortune." Favell laughed. "There was gold in them thar hills. And that's how Jack got rich. Or so he said. And it might have been true; he kept the revolver—or *a* revolver. It used to hang on the wall over his desk in the house he bought in Berkshire. It was his lucky gun, he said. And until he came back to England, Jack's luck always held. . . ." He paused. "Something wrong, old boy?"

"No, nothing," I replied.

"Don't believe me, eh?" Favell had seen me react, and he misinterpreted my reaction; he gave me a mocking glance. "I don't blame you. But the point is, that's the kind of man Jack was—and, the way he used to tell it, I could see him doing it. If it wasn't true—who cares? It comes down to the same thing in the end: He went into mining, and he invested in mines—not just gold, diamonds, too—and he made money, big money. I don't say it was all aboveboard, and there may have been more to it than met the eye; in fact, later on, Rebecca used to tease him and say he made his fortune in armaments." Favell smiled. "*Maxim* guns, maybe—who knows? Maybe that's why Rebecca called her husband 'Max'—no one else called him that, except me, of course. I followed suit. I could see it irritated the hell out of him. . . . Rescue that bottle, will you? None for you? I'll finish it up, then. No point in wasting it. Where's the gents, old boy? Downstairs? I won't be a second."

Favell rose to his feet. I considered the word "Berkshire," which had come curling out of his story, and had hit me the harder for being unexpected. I must persuade him back in that direction, I decided. And when he returned, I tried to do just that. But it was then, just when I most wanted facts, that my difficulties began.

Until that moment, Favell had seemed perfectly willing, even eager, to talk. He certainly enjoyed his Jack Devlin stories, and I thought they were probably a regular part of his repertoire. When he returned to the table, I could sense his mood had changed. I noticed he looked pale, and his manner was irritable. He slumped down into the seat next to me, and waved the menu away.

"Eaten too much, I think," he said. "Rich food. Not used to it, old boy—not these days, that's the trouble. Order another *fine* for me, will you, there's a good chap. That always settles my stomach."

I ordered the *fine*, though I thought he'd have been better off without it, and some coffee for myself. I waited for Favell to revive a little, and then tried some questions. I wanted to move him on to the moment when, aged seventeen, he came to England for the first time—and met Rebecca. I wanted him to tell me about the house in Berkshire. But it was at this very point, when his story, Rebecca's, and her father's intersected for the first time, that he became recalcitrant. At first, I had to coax every answer out of him.

"Jack Devlin came back to England in 1914—the summer the war broke out," he said. "I don't know why he left Africa. He'd had enough of it maybe. He'd made his pile; he was still a young man, in his prime, not yet forty. And no, I don't bloody well know exactly when Rebecca's mother died. She was young, and it was sudden, and it wasn't long before I came to England in 1915—I told you, Rebecca was still wearing mourning when I first met her. Beyond that, I don't know a damn thing about her mother. I wasn't interested in her mother. I never met the woman. I was interested in Rebecca."

"I'm wondering if Jack Devlin came back to Europe *because* Rebecca's mother was ill or had died. How did he make contact with Rebecca, *why* did he make contact?"

"Danny wrote to him, I think, and told him Isabel was ill. She traced him, and wrote to him. Danny was always in the picture, from way back. She was in service; she was in service her whole bloody life, and I think she'd worked for some family Rebecca's mother knew. Danny was devoted to the mother *and* Rebecca, and it's no good asking me the details, because, in the first place, I don't *know*, and in the second, I don't bloody well *care*. All I know is Jack Devlin came home and he bought this damn great house, stockbroker style, vulgar as they come, on the edge of the Berkshire Downs, and he went into horses in a big way. Built these vast stables, hired a trainer. Wanted to breed a Derby winner—not that he ever did. And by the time I arrived, they'd all been there a few months. Danny was looking after Rebecca for Jack Devlin, running his house, making herself indispensable—in like Flynn, was our Danny. And she was a pretty weird woman, even then. Never married. The 'Mrs.' was a courtesy title. Housekeepers were always called Mrs. Something then—God knows why."

He frowned, and took a swallow of the brandy. "Greenways," he went on, gazing off into the middle distance. "That's what it was called, the house: Greenways. Near a village called Hampton something. Not far from Lambourn. . . . Ever been to that part of the world, old boy?"

"No—but I know of it. I had an aunt who grew up in the Lambourn area."

"Pretty place. I wonder if the house is still there? I've thought of going back to take a look at it once or twice. Lovely setting. You could walk right out of the grounds, and up onto the Downs. I used to watch Rebecca ride there. She was a brilliant rider. Absolutely without fear. And at fifteen she looked pretty damn amazing in a riding habit, with a whip in her hand, I can tell you. . . ."

He left the remark hanging in the air, and glancing back at me, smiled. The next question had to be asked, and he'd just given me a cue, so I asked it. "You spoke of a couple of years when you and Rebecca were close. When was that exactly? When you first came to England?"

"Did I say that? Well, yes, then—I suppose . . ." He hesitated, and when he continued speaking, his tone had altered; from being suggestive, it became defensive. "Look—I was just a *boy*, all right? I was different then; I hadn't had any bloody setbacks, for a start. So I was full of plans—optimism. I wanted to go into the Navy; I'd always wanted to serve in the Navy. My mother had stuffed my head with a whole lot of bloody nonsense about the Senior Service. So I was mad keen to train—couldn't wait to captain a ship and kill Germans. . . . That's how naive I was. It was exciting, planning it all. Rebecca and I used to lark around—practicing semaphore, learning Morse code— we just had *fun*. She was like a little sister to me—she looked up to me, couldn't wait to see me in uniform. I was a hero to her. She was a funny little kid in some ways. Very droll. But we clicked. We laughed at the same things. We just got on together."

"And then?" I prompted.

"And then Uncle Jack pulled a few strings, got me into Dartmouth. While I was training, it wasn't too bad; I could get back to Greenways and see her. But Dartmouth was a damn snobby place: I didn't get on with the other officer cadets, I didn't like the discipline—and Rebecca couldn't understand that, which was pretty rich, coming from her. So I lost a bit of the old luster. Had one or two rows with Uncle Jack—he thought I was a bad influence on her. Then, I was sent on my first tour of duty, and that was a bloody disaster. I hated it from day one. It was wartime, I could never get leave. . . ."

He paused; a familiar aggrieved note had entered his voice. "And when I finally *did* get home, Rebecca didn't exactly overdo the sympathy. She wasn't a little kid any more, she was growing up fast; she was beautiful, and she knew it. Uncle Jack spoiled her. He was going to make her into a fine lady—he'd set his heart on that. She'd sweep in, in these amazing dresses, with her long black hair, and she was—

scornful, always putting me down. It riled me. So we had a bit of a falling-out. Nothing serious. But I saw her less after that. She'd been telling tales out of school, I think." He looked away. "Queered my pitch with Uncle Jack. Fed him a pack of lies. Which didn't endear her to me. But I got over it."

I could sense evasiveness again. I thought there was more to this sequence of events than Favell was prepared to say. I tried pressing him, but got nowhere; he was becoming surly. Eventually, I was forced to change tack.

"Did she ever talk to you about her childhood, about her life with her mother?"

"A few times. I wasn't that interested."

"Was her mother French? Did Rebecca spend time in France as a child? When did they come to England?"

"I don't think her mother was French, she was just staying in France when Devlin met her—that was the impression I got. I think they came back to England when Rebecca was small—five, six? Beyond that, haven't a clue, old boy."

"Did her mother act under the name Devlin? Isabel Devlin?"

"Might have done. I really couldn't say. She wasn't exactly Sarah Bernhardt, you know. She was very, very pretty—and I suspect very, very untalented. Rebecca wouldn't hear a word against her. Adored her. Put up this little shrine to her in her bedroom at Greenways: a little triptych of photographs. Mama as a walk-on. Mama in some two-line role. Oh, and Mama's big moment. You know what Mama's big moment was? Playing Desdemona to some old ham's Othello in some second-rate dump of a theater, on some third-rate tour.

"Jesus—" He stubbed out his cigarette in an irritable way. "It was pathetic. Rebecca put flowers in front of those pictures every night—lit a candle and said her prayers in front of them, I expect. She was very childish, in some ways, Rebecca, when I first knew her. But then she'd never been to school; Mama gave her lessons, and, frankly, I don't think Mama was too well qualified. Very much the gentle-woman, Mama, despite being an actress. She could play the piano, and sew, I gather, and that's about it. So, Rebecca was a funny little thing then—knew yards of Shakespeare by heart, knew those bloody plays backward—but she couldn't multiply or divide, she could scarcely add two and two. Didn't know the simplest things: no geography, no history—not until Uncle Jack started shipping the governesses in, anyway, and Rebecca gave *them* a hard time. She was very willful. Spoke French, of course, and spoke it like a native—and she was a brilliant mimic. She could do any accent, any voice, she only had to hear it once, and she had it off pat. All those years in the wings, I imagine. . . .

"Of course, Uncle Jack loved all that, and he encouraged her. He was turning her into a bloody performing monkey in my opinion— not that anyone ever asked me. We'd sit down after dinner, and it would be 'Becka, won't you recite a bit of a play, now, for your old father?' Old? I told you: He wasn't forty. And she'd be on her feet, before you could blink; we had hours of the bloody stuff. I've never liked Shakespeare—can't see the point of him, myself. Half the time you can't understand a word he's on about. But Uncle Jack didn't think so, oh, no. Especially when his precious Becka was giving the recitation. She made him read some bloody stupid play—what's that one where the dead wife comes back as a statue, and the king's reunited with his daughter?"

"The Winter's Tale."

"That's it. Well, that was his favorite. 'My long-lost daughter'— that's what he started calling her. That's how he used to introduce her to people. 'This is Becka—my long-lost daughter. My own little . . . ' What's the girl's name in that play?"

"Perdita."

"Perdita. That's it. 'My own little Perdita.' I used to cringe—he could be a sentimental fool, now that I think about it."

"Did it embarrass her, when he spoke in that way?"

"Embarrass her? Some chance! You couldn't embarrass Rebecca. She never gave a tuppenny damn what anyone thought of her. And she'd never hear a word of criticism against her father. She loved him, the same way she loved her mother. I told you: She was very childish in some ways. She'd cling to an idea, or a person, or a place; she'd attach herself to them—and then nothing would shift her."

"So, she and her father were very close. Did they remain close? Was he still alive when she married?"

"What?" Favell gave me a blank stare. "No. Of course he wasn't. I told you—"

"I don't think you did, actually."

"Then I'll tell you now. He died young. When I came to England, he had six years left, poor devil. Got thrown by one of his horses, some great black brute of a thing, out on one of the gallops. It was 1921—Danny sent a telegraph to the ship I was on, and those bastards wouldn't give me compassionate leave. So, I never even went to his funeral. . . ." He turned his brooding gaze to the wall, then tossed back the dregs of his brandy.

"Never went back to Greenways. Cut my losses. There wasn't any money anyway. Not a bean—can you believe that? In debt, up to the eyeballs—he'd lost money on investments, on those bloody horses, he was in hock to the banks, the Jews, you name it. It was all a sham—that blasted house, the stables, the horses, Rebecca's clothes, a house full of servants and hangers-on—and the whole damn lot was on credit. That was a bloody shock. I mean, I didn't expect him to die, and I told you I wasn't in his good books at the time. . . ."

He paused, looking away. "You see, I'd assumed . . . I'd thought I could expect a nice little legacy. I knew Rebecca would get the lion's share, he was besotted with her, but I thought there'd be something coming my way, enough to buy me out of the bloody Navy anyway. But there wasn't. Sweet F.A. I didn't get a penny—and neither did Rebecca. That's when we had our little falling-out. I wrote to her, asked if the creditors were letting her keep her jewelry—some perfectly bloody harmless inquiry of that kind. And she wasn't too nice about it, old boy. Called me some pretty vile things. She always had a vicious tongue. So, that was that. End of a lovely friendship. No contact for seven years, and don't ask me what she was doing then, because I haven't a clue. Then, I come back to England, and there she is—at Manderley. And we know what happened *then*, don't we?"

He broke off, fiddling with his cigarette case. His expression had become preoccupied. I could see he was following some train of thought, and I wondered if he felt ill. He was very drawn, and beginning to sweat a little.

"What was Rebecca *like* . . . that's what you said earlier, wasn't it?" he went on. "I'll tell you what she was like: She was *dangerous*. Oh, you'll meet plenty of people who'll say she was kind, and beautiful, and charming, and witty. But I knew her better than most, and I'm telling you: It was a bad idea to cross her. If you did, she paid you back. Sooner or later. And the way she did it was clever. . . ."

He gave a frown. "Strange, isn't it? You start talking about the past, and you think you've understood it, and then you suddenly see: Maybe it *wasn't* the way you thought at the time, maybe there's a *different* explanation. That note she sent me the day she died, for instance. I've been thinking about that all evening, and I'm just beginning to see . . ."

"What about the note?"

"I told you, if Max had caught me with her at the boathouse he'd have killed me, too. There's no doubt in my mind about that. He wasn't too stable by then, and he hated my guts. Rebecca knew that. So, think about it: Supposing she *meant* him to kill me? What if she was setting me up? That way, we all three of us end up dead. Rebecca escapes months of illness, cousin Jack gets his comeuppance, and Max goes to the gallows. Very neat. And she could have pulled it off, too. . . .

"Don't you see?" He turned his brooding gaze back to me. "It was pure chance I got the note so late, that I didn't go down to Manderley. It was pure chance that Danny had kept Rebecca's diary, so we found out about that doctor in London—and Rebecca didn't *want* us to trace the doctor, I see that now. She'd covered her tracks; she hadn't told anyone she was ill, not even Danny. You bet she didn't want that doctor traced: His evidence saved Max's neck. . . . What a bloody joke. She had it in for *both* of us—and I've never once thought of that possibility until now; it's taken me twenty years to see something so damn obvious. . . ."

The suggestion seemed unlikely to me; I suspected the drink was now affecting him. But I could see his mind inching its way through these possibilities, and I could see he believed them. Oddly, he spoke without bitterness. His tone was ironic, pitched somewhere between admiration and amusement.

"That presupposes Rebecca wanted you dead," I said, trying to keep the skepticism out of my voice. "Have you any reason to believe she did?"

"One or two. Now I look back." Favell gave me a quick evasive glance. "I told you—it wasn't a good idea to cross her. She was vengeful."

"Had you crossed her? In what way? I thought you were lovers."

"That's what they say in Kerrith, is it, old boy?"

"I gather it's what *you* said. In front of several witnesses, three of whom are still alive. Frank Crawley, for instance. Colonel Julyan. The second Mrs. de Winter. At Manderley, on the night of your cousin's funeral."

That remark, and the tone in which I made it, was unwise, and I saw that instantly. Favell turned his pale blue eyes in my direction; he gave me a narrow considering look. "Well, you know all about it already then, don't you, old boy? No point in my explaining, even if I felt inclined to do so—which I don't. Not just at this moment." He pushed back his chair, and tossed down his napkin. "Why don't you get the bill? I've had enough of this place, quite frankly. Why don't we go on somewhere else? I know a club just round the corner where we can get a nightcap. We could continue our little chat there. What say you?"

I didn't welcome this suggestion, and I tried to block it, but Favell merely smiled. He could sense he had the upper hand now, and he was enjoying it. "Up to you, old boy," he said. "You can push off, if you prefer. But if you want to continue our little conversation, we'll do it on my territory. Besides, I've sung for my supper now, and— fair's fair—it's my turn. You see, I've got the feeling you've been holding out on me. That's my instinct. More to you than meets the eye, I think. Could be wrong, of course, but before I say anything else, there's something important I need to ask you. . . ."

It was the last thing I wanted to do, but Favell could be obstinate. Nothing would persuade him to remain in the restaurant: It was either consent to the club or say good-bye to him. I paid the bill, and we went out into the Soho street.

Favell's manner was making me uneasy. I wondered what he knew, or thought he knew, about me. I told myself he knew nothing, that he was simply building up to the question of payment. I was wrong—as I shortly discovered.

EIGHTEEN

FAVELL'S CLUB WAS NOT "AROUND THE CORNER," AS HE claimed; nor was it along the street, or up the alleyway where Favell insisted we look for it. Eventually we found a basement with a flickering pitchfork sign that said RED DEVIL. "Found it," said Favell. "I knew the damn place was around here somewhere."

He plunged down the steep steps, brushed past a notice that said MEMBERS ONLY, was stopped in his tracks by a thickset man in an ill-fitting dinner jacket, and was eventually admitted after I'd handed over a five-pound note. We entered a small dark room, with a pianist and a brunette in a gold lamé dress who was crooning a Sinatra song into a microphone. The air was thick with cigarette smoke; the place smelled of nicotine, desperation, and alcohol. All the patrons were male, the "hostesses" who served us were predatory, and the only drink available was champagne—at three times the normal price, naturally.

I was rapidly losing patience. I don't like clip joints. I'd had enough of Favell's cat-and-mouse games, and I knew that if one of the hostesses joined us—Favell seemed keen on that idea at first—I'd get nothing out of him for the rest of the evening. Favell sat opposite me, looking morose and resentful. He was drinking the champagne steadily, and he was building up to something, I could sense it. With little to lose at that point, I abandoned tact. I pressed him on the remarks he'd made at the end of our meal. He refused, in a sullen way, to elaborate. I asked him a whole series of other questions. Having received no useful answers to any of them, I changed tack. Thinking of the notebook and that picture postcard, I finally asked him whether, to his knowledge, Rebecca had ever known, or visited, Manderley in her childhood.

I knew it was a question too far, but I didn't care. Favell, who had been growing increasingly irascible, lost his temper.

"No, I *don't* know," he said. "What *is* this? What's your game, old chum? Some reporter you are. Let me tell you, I've known a few journalists in my time—got pretty pally with them on occasions, when it suited me—and I've never met one like you. I smelled a rat when you first wrote, and I smelled a rat as soon as I laid eyes on you. Fine: I thought I might as well get a decent dinner out of it, but now I have, let's lay our cards on the table. You've been trying to lead me up the garden path, old pal. You've been lying to me. Claim you've written twice and that's it? I don't think so. You want to know why I agreed to see you? I agreed because you sent me this. Arrived last Wednesday, brown envelope—about this big. No covering letter, nothing to warn me."

I stared at him. I'd been about to leave; I'd already pushed back my chair. Favell had taken a small envelope, a tiny envelope, from his inside jacket pocket.

"This was inside the large envelope. I hadn't a clue what it was until I opened it up and nearly died of shock. That's your idea of a joke, is it, after twenty years? Well, it's not funny. It's bloody hurtful. Whatever you think, I'm not all bad—in my way, I was damn fond of Rebecca."

He tipped the little envelope into his hand, then held it out to me. Lying in his palm was a small ring, made for a narrow finger; an eternity ring; a little circlet of diamonds.

"That was Rebecca's ring. I'd know it anywhere. She always wore it; I never saw it off her finger. She wore it as a child, and she wore it as a woman. And that ring was on her finger when they brought her body up; it was how they identified her. By that ring. I always thought—I assumed—I thought that bastard buried her with it. Max arranged that funeral, and he didn't ask me to be there, he didn't even tell me about it, though I was her only blood relative, and I'd been sitting in that bloody coroner's court that same day, not ten feet away from him. But I thought even he would have left Rebecca this. That's what she'd have wanted, and he must have known that. But no, it was taken off her finger, and after twenty years you sent it to me, didn't you? Why? What's your connection with Rebecca? Who are you? And where did you get hold of it?"

I stared at the ring, which I wanted to touch. Then I looked at Favell, and saw that he was as troubled as I was. Whatever he'd been, and whatever he was, I had no right to judge him. However ambivalent his feelings toward her, there was a part of Favell that had cared for Rebecca—and I could see it in his eyes now.

I told him he was wrong. I said nothing about the notebook sent to the Colonel in similar circumstances on the same day, but, apart from that omission and one other, I told him the truth: I said I'd read about that ring in the inquest reports, but I hadn't sent it to him, and I had no idea who had. I gave him my word on it.

I think he believed me, but the denial seemed to increase his anxiety. He gave me a bewildered look, then tipped the ring back into the envelope, and replaced it in his pocket. He drained the last of the champagne in his glass and rose unsteadily to his feet. He looked so dazed that I thought he was about to pass out.

"I'm sure there's an explanation for this." I reached for his arm to steady him. "You'd better sit down. If you think about it, there's any number of people who could have removed that ring—the undertakers or the pathologist or the police. There's probably a reason why it's been sent to you. Maybe . . ."

I wasn't convincing Favell—I wasn't convincing myself. Favell was swaying on his feet; he now looked desperately ill. "I know why it was sent," he said thickly. "I know who sent it. Christ, she's remorseless. . . ."

I tried to persuade him into a chair, but he shook me off. He stared around him, peering into the corners of the room. He passed his hands across his face. "Jesus. Christ," he said. "What a hellhole. What a hopeless miserable pit. That damned monkey on the door. And those girls—just take a look at those girls. Death's heads, the whole lot of them. What am I doing here? What in Christ's name happened to my life? Get me out of here, will you?"

He fumbled his way past me to the door. He lurched up the steps and into the street. Perhaps the alcohol had just kicked in, perhaps he'd been drunker than I'd realized in the restaurant. He seemed very drunk now, unsteady on his feet, his face white and ghastly in the street light. I realized that he almost certainly had been drinking before he met me, that all the alcohol he'd tipped down his throat since had been a constant topping-up process, his way of keeping his particular demons at bay. Maybe the whole evening had been a part of that process.

"Here," he said, clutching at my arm and fumbling in his pocket as I reached his side. "Here—you can bloody take this. I don't want it; I wish I'd never set eyes on it. Take it with you to Kerrith next time you go. Throw it in the sea. Sell it—I don't bloody care what you do with it. I'm not keeping it. . . ."

He pulled out the small envelope with the ring and tried to press it into my hand. I tried to argue with him, but he wouldn't listen.

"I don't bloody *want* it. I don't want it anywhere near me; my luck's bad enough already. Either you take it or it goes down this drain, right now." He pushed me hard in the chest and leaned over the grating in the gutter, envelope in hand, his face white and fixed. I knew that if I didn't take it, he'd do exactly as he threatened, so I took the envelope from him. Favell straightened, staggered back a few paces, and looked wildly up and down the street.

"Look, just get me a cab, will you?" he said. "I've had a shock, I'm not well anyway—I *knew* it was a mistake to talk to you."

There was a taxi coming along the street then, and I hailed it. I offered to go with him, but he refused. In the end, I had to give in. It occurred to me that wherever he was heading, he preferred me not to see it. When the cab was out of sight, I looked at the ring. It glittered in the light from the street lamps; it was exceptionally tiny. I knew I couldn't keep it, much though I wanted to do so; once Favell was sober, he'd want it back anyway. I decided to return it to him at the car showroom some time tomorrow.

I SET OFF TO WALK BACK TO REGENT'S PARK. I HOPED THE night air would clear my head and lift my spirits, but it didn't. It was just after eleven when I reached the house. Mrs. Henderson was about to go to bed; she said no one had called for me. That depressed me further. I had given Ellie the number here, in case there should be any emergency with her father; there could be no other reason for her to call, yet I wished she had. I'd have liked to talk to her. I'd have liked to talk to *someone*.

I made myself some coffee and sat with it in the kitchen. I felt confused and restless: Too much had happened too fast. I listened again to Favell's accusations against Rebecca. Could she really have intended him to die? I saw a young girl in a black dress in a restaurant, sitting silently at a table, not speaking all evening. I saw a little shrine of photographs to her dead mother. I saw a house called Greenways, in a Berkshire village whose name Favell couldn't remember exactly. Near Lambourn; Hampton something, he had said. The village was Hampton Ferrars—and why was I so sure of that? Because I knew of that village already: My adoptive mother, May, grew up there.

I couldn't yet see inside that house, or see what might have happened there, but something had, and I could sense it tucked away in the convolutions of Favell's stories. I looked at the occupants of Greenways: I saw two cousins, and a youthful, handsome, and doting father. I took out the little eternity ring that Rebecca had worn as a child and worn as a woman. Eternity rings are not worn by children or unmarried women. Who had given her that ring, and what had it meant to her? Why had Favell felt it brought bad luck? I was missing something, I could feel it. I had been missing something all evening, but, no matter how carefully I went back over the sequence of events, I couldn't place it. Yet I felt a definite unease, a sense of trouble impending.

I decided to go up to my room and begin writing up this account of my day. I went out into the hall, and was about to go upstairs when the telephone on the table right next to me began ringing. It startled me badly. I was suddenly seized by a certainty that the caller must be Ellie. Ellie was calling, it was almost midnight—and that meant something was wrong. I snatched up the receiver.

A woman's voice said: "Is that Tom Galbraith?"

"Yes, speaking," I replied. I was agitated, and spoke without thinking.

There was a pause, a buzzing and a hissing, then the line went dead. I stood there, filled with a sudden superstitious fear. Then I came to my senses. The dead can make their presence felt in many ways, but placing telephone calls is not one of them.

I've been thinking about that call ever since. The woman was definitely not Ellie. I did not recognize her voice, yet very few people have this number, and even fewer would have known I might be here. But whoever placed that call had good timing. On an evening when I'd never felt less sure of who I was, someone had wanted to confirm my identity.

IT WAS VERY LATE WHEN I FINISHED WRITING MY ACCOUNT of the meeting with Favell, but the evening's events had left me restless, and I had difficulty sleeping. I dreamed I was walking through the Manderley woods, and, just ahead of me, moving swiftly and silently through the trees, was a woman I knew to be Rebecca. I kept calling her name and trying to catch up with her, but I never succeeded. She was always just out of reach; once, when I despaired, she turned to me and held up her hand with its diamond eternity ring and then beckoned. When I finally woke, found it was light, and dragged myself out of bed, it was six in the morning. I felt exhausted and miserable. I was as close, then, as I've ever been to extricating myself from this search, and abandoning it.

Mrs. Henderson was still not up—and I was glad of that. I didn't want to speak to her, or to anyone. I made myself some coffee and took it outside into the paved garden behind the house; I sat there in the soft morning light, under the cherry tree that Julia and Nicky planted to mark their marriage. Its branches were bowed with blossoms; at the least breath of air, the petals scattered like wedding confetti.

I told myself I had to decide: give up—or go on. Whatever I decided, I had to be honest with myself, and I had to abandon the pretence that this search of mine was objective. It was *never* objective. I always believed in my heart that there was a connection between Rebecca and myself, even if such evidence as I had was inconclusive. Why, then, when the conversation with Favell last night suggested that a link *did* exist, did I back away from it? It was because I could hear the secrets inside Favell's stories, and they made me fearful.

I knew I could no longer shy away from this, so I sat there under that marriage tree, and I went back down the corridor of my past, opening all its locked doors—including the one that is the most securely bolted of all, the door I slammed years ago on all those painful questions about my parentage. I opened the orphanage door, and the adoption door, and I opened the door marked "Pelynt." I looked at the summer I spent there with Edwin and May Galbraith, when I was eleven years old and newly adopted. I watched the weeks of that first holiday—and I watched myself as I was then, a little animal, resentful, afraid, tormented by fears and suspicions. I'd known I was damaged goods. I'd known it could only be a matter of days before I was packed up like a broken toy, and returned, with indignant complaints, to the place that had supplied me.

If I was rude, sullen, and unresponsive, would that do it? What if I wet the bed? Or swore? Or stole from May's purse? When Edwin discovered how stupid I was, or May found out how I lied, would that be when they decided to return me or exchange me? Would it be this week or next? Like a maltreated dog, I fawned and cringed, and then bit: I was determined to provoke the action I most feared—but then the only response I'd ever learned to provoke from adults was punishment, and punishment was preferable to indifference.

These tactics had never failed me before, but they did now. No matter how hard I tried, May never shouted at me, and Edwin never hit me. Once, when I lifted my arm to shield my face from the expected blow that never came, I saw that, for the first time, I had succeeded in shocking him.

May and Edwin taught me about "tomorrow." I'd never understood how that word could be full of promise until they took me to Pelynt. Under their tutelage, I began to discover that "tomorrow" meant something one could look forward to—and there were more sources of pleasure than I'd ever believed possible. It was pleasurable to go to the beach, to take out a boat, or to pack a picnic; it was pleasurable to be read to; to explore a castle or a church, to look at plants or birds and identify them. I can see now that Edwin and May were desperate to find something to which I responded; when they saw that I liked stories, though I read atrociously, and I liked places where the past could be felt, they encouraged me. In this way they began to tame me, but I knew it couldn't last. I waited, and one morning—I must open that door now—May said she would take me over to the Saxon church at Manderley. She would show me how to do brass rubbings.

This proposal was unusual. Edwin was not joining us, for one thing; for another, May's bright tone of voice could not disguise a certain tension. I was suspicious at once. I looked at their smiling faces and smelled treachery. I refused to go, and when they both insisted, I saw through their plan. They weren't going to take me back to the orphanage and exchange me—they were going to whisk me off to some strange place, and abandon me.

"You're going to leave me there, aren't you?" I said to May as we wound our way up the hill from Pelynt in her little Ford motorcar. "You're going to take me there, and lose me, and then jump back in the car and bloody leave me."

"Oh, Tom, how can you think that?" May said, with a sigh. "Of course I'm not going to do that. Why would I do something that made us both miserable?"

"Wouldn't make *me* miserable." I said. "I couldn't care less. Bugger it. Good riddance to bad rubbish, I say . . ."

"Sorry to disappoint you," May replied. "You won't get rid of me that easily."

"Boring. Stupid boring church. Stupid boring brasses." I kicked the bag at my feet, which May had carefully packed with the special paper and black waxes. "Don't want to go. Don't want to be with you. Grumpy old bitch. I'm sick of you. I'm *bloody* sick of you."

"Give it a chance," May said quietly. "Give *me* a chance, Tom."

I looked at her, struck by her tone, and I saw that she was crying.

That silenced me. I stared at the road ahead and bit my nails. I had a sense of terrible power and a certain knowledge that I had just mis-used it. I could misuse it some more, it would be the easiest thing in the world. I could make May *really* weep. I could make her suffer—or I could stop. The choice was mine. I stared at the choice all the way along that road. I had the power to hurt, I'd never possessed it before, it made me muddled and afraid—and that is why, even before I met May's friend, I remember every detail of that morning.

When we reached the tiny church, it was deserted. May and I walked among the graves, in brilliant sunshine. I spelled out some of the names cut into the tombstones, scratching at the lichen: BELOVED

WIFE OF . . . ; DEAREST MOTHER TO . . . ; HUSBAND OF . . . ; FATHER OF . . . ; even then, I liked to trace the relationships I'd never experienced. May and I walked down to the river; the tide was high, and the water was fast flowing. I tossed a stick into the eddies and imagined it traveling all the way to the sea at Kerrith, all the way across the Atlantic. If I could hurt May, I wondered, did that mean she cared for me?

Then May took me into the cool, dimly lit interior of the church. It wasn't much of a place, I thought in my ignorance. I glowered at the plain whitewashed walls, and the great thick pillars. The altar cloth was blue and gold. The dead were under my feet. I knelt down by the brass effigy of a de Winter knight, and glared at him. He was in full armor and helmeted, so I couldn't see his whole face. His gauntleted hands were crossed on his chest; his feet rested on a small dog with a curly tail, and his inscription, on a banner above his head, was in Latin. I couldn't read Latin. May, who could, said his name was Gilles de Winter, and he died on his return from the Crusades in 1148. His wife, Marguerite, who had born him ten children, four of whom survived, lay next to him.

May showed me what to do. She showed me how to fix the paper in place with tape; she showed me how to rub the black wax back and forth. I snatched the wax rudely out of her hand, and, with a sigh, May said she'd walk in the churchyard for a while, and leave me to it. I saw her look at her watch, and I knew she was hiding something. This was the moment when she'd drive off and leave me.

See if I care, I said to myself. I scratched away with the stupid wax. I listened to the sound of the oak door closing, my heart beating very fast and a sick dread rising in my stomach. I listened for the sound of the car's engine. The minutes passed; I thought maybe May hadn't been lying after all. I wanted to go and see if she was still in the churchyard, but I was bitter with pride, and I felt I'd rather die than let her see I was anxious.

I rubbed away with the wax; a pair of armoured feet began to emerge, Gilles began to emerge. I stared at him. He was there, of course, all the time, under the paper, and I knew that. Yet I felt I made him. I conjured him up. There was his helmet and his gloved hands, and his little dog with a curly tail and a lively eye. If I listened very hard, I felt I'd hear that little dog bark at me across the centuries.

I grew absorbed in my task. I had almost forgotten about May, and, when I heard the creak of the church door, I assumed she was returning. Then I heard a footstep, too light and too swift for May. I sat back on my heels and looked up. A stranger had come to a halt a few feet away. She was tall and slender. She was gripping the side of one of the oak pews, and looking down at me.

"It's Tom, isn't it? How quick you are!" she said. "Why, you've almost finished—and you've done it beautifully. I just met May in the churchyard, and she told me I'd find you here. I'm a friend of hers. How do you do, Tom?" She came closer, bent down and held out her hand to me. "I'm Rebecca."

I looked at her warily, and then, with reluctance, took the hand she held out to me. I was suspicious of everything then—but especially of strangers. The woman looked closely at me, and I inspected her in return. I saw her eyes rest on my hair and my face; her hair, long and worn loose, parted on one side, was as dark as my own. I thought she had the strangest eyes I'd ever seen. In the dim light of the church, I couldn't decide if they were a very dark blue or a very dark green or a very dark violet. I decided they were sea-colored.

She was wearing boating clothes: a loose striped cotton sweater, white trousers, and rope-soled shoes. Her hand felt cool in mine, and her clasp was strong, but as she drew back from me, I saw that she was trembling slightly. I thought it very curious that she should be as nervous as I was.

She sat down next to me on the cold floor of the nave and, after a pause, I went on with my brass rubbing. I bent my head over the paper, and refused to look up. I knew that in a minute, just as all adults did, she'd start talking, she'd start asking questions. I waited, feeling for the ridges and crevices, rubbing back and forth with my wax. She said nothing.

After a while, her proximity and her silence began to unnerve me. I looked up at her, to find that she was still watching me with her sea-colored eyes. I wondered if I were imagining her, or if she might be magic; she could be a river nymph, I thought—Edwin and May had given me a book with pictures of gods and goddesses; they'd been reading me stories about creatures who sprang from the waves, or from trees and breezes. They had strange names that I couldn't spell, but was learning to pronounce. A zephyr. A nereid. A dryad. I tried closing my eyes, in case that would make her vanish, and, when that didn't work, I thought I'd answer the questions before she asked them.

"I live in Scotland now. I'm here on holiday," I said, rubbing away at the brass plate. I gave her a quick glance. "I used to live in an orphanage. I'm adopted."

"I know that," she replied, and then added: "May told me."

"I'm eleven. That's old to be adopted. It's unusual. Most people want babies."

"I know that, too."

"I have two names. My orphanage name and my new one."

I stole another look, to check her reaction. May said all this information should make me proud; it meant I was loved and chosen—but I wasn't too sure I believed that.

"That's excellent," said the woman in an easy way. "Everyone should change names from time to time, don't you think? You have to find a name that fits—and once you do, you can keep it forever. Does 'Tom' feel as if it fits yet?"

I considered this; it had never occurred to me that you could try names on, like a pair of gloves. "It might do," I said cautiously.

"I think it suits you," she said. "It's a handsome name. And for Sunday-best, you can always be 'Thomas.' "

I turned this over in my mind; I think I smiled, because she responded, and her face lit in the most extraordinary way. She leaned forward, and touched my face with her fingertips, and such was the spell she'd begun to cast over me that I didn't flinch or shy away, but let her hand rest there while she looked at me.

"Do you live here?" I asked when she finally drew back.

She laughed. "What, here in the church? No. Not yet, anyway."

She made a face. I saw her gaze fall to my hands. My nails were chewed, and the cuticles were torn where I gnawed at them. I made a fist of my hands, so she couldn't see them, and the blood rushed up my neck and into my face.

"I used to bite my nails," she said in a practical tone. "My hands looked horrible—much much worse than that. My mother said I was a little cannibal. She went to the chemist and bought something called bitter aloes. It was supposed to taste so vile that you gave up biting them. Well, that didn't work! I was so angry, I chewed them all the more."

I looked down at her hands. She had long thin tanned hands, with perfect unblemished nails, cut short. On her left hand she was wearing two rings, one of which glittered like sunlight on water.

"I'll tell you what to do," she went on, in a conversational way, as if we were exactly the same age, and had known one another forever. "If you want to go on biting them, do—and the hell with what anyone thinks. But if you don't, and you want to stop, just use your willpower. If you will something strongly enough, you can move mountains. You can do anything."

I looked at her carefully. I was impressed by the word "hell," especially in a church. No one had ever mentioned willpower to me before; at the orphanage it was faith that was supposed to move mountains, and the emphasis was on prayer. I'd spent a lot of time praying. I'd prayed to be adopted for at least seven years—but maybe I hadn't been praying after all; maybe I'd been *willing*.

"Anything at all?" I asked warily.

"Absolutely anything," she said. "For instance: I was very small as a child, I never seemed to grow and I wanted to be tall, so I willed it. And I grew six inches in six months. Just like a plant in a pot. It was easy."

"Could you will yourself to read better, if you wanted? For instance?"

"Simple. Just snap your fingers, and do it."

I frowned; this was encouraging, but I felt there was something missing here, possibly God. I glanced over my shoulder at the blue and gold altar table. I looked at Gilles and his little dog. I looked at her, and I saw that she wasn't as confident as she sounded; maybe she'd believed that once, but perhaps the willpower wasn't working too well for her now. There were doubts, way back in her eyes—a tide of doubt and sadness was welling up in them. I scowled at her and made a sneering face, and gestured at Gilles de Winter.

"What about him? I'll bet you can't will *him* back. He's dead, he is."

"No, no, you're wrong." She gave a sigh, and ignored my rudeness. "You *can* will the dead back. But you have to be careful, Tom. They don't always manifest themselves in quite the way you expected. So on the whole it's better to let them rest . . . or whatever it is that they do down there."

She spoke seriously, her sea-colored eyes fixed on my face. It suddenly felt very cold in that church, and I shivered. I thought of all the dead down there under our feet; I think she thought of them, too, for her face contracted. Then the church clock chimed the hour, and the spell was broken, and May's strange friend sprang to her feet. She held out her hand to me for the second time.

"I'm very glad to have met you, Tom," she said. "Tell May to bring you to see me one day. I live at Manderley—May knows where it is. It's just near here. We could go out in my boat. It's the prettiest boat, very strong and safe—would you like that?"

I would have liked that, and I passed on this invitation to May almost immediately. But May, who seemed pleased to "run into" her former friend, as she put it, was vague about the suggestion. We stood in the sunlight in the graveyard, watching a gleaming car disappearing fast up the lane; I stole out my hand, and took May's. I'd decided I didn't want to hurt her. I'd decided to *will* her to love me— and it seemed to work, for her face took on a soft, crumpled look, and she put her arms around me and hugged me. "When can we go and see your friend and go out in her boat?" I asked on the way home, and I kept on asking. "Oh, one of these days," May would answer— but then she always seemed to forget, though I often reminded her.

Somehow there was never time, or we were doing something else—and I could sense that wasn't the truth. I discovered a little. I found out that the woman with sea-colored eyes was newly married to someone called Maxim de Winter, a descendent of the very same Gilles whose effigy I'd copied; that May had first met her as a girl, when May was twenty and she was fifteen and they lived near one another in Berkshire.

Beyond this, May would not be drawn; one day Edwin took me aside and explained that my questions made May anxious; they made her feel I preferred her friend, he said, and that hurt May. "Give her time, Tom," he said. "We're still getting to know one another, and May wants to make you happy."

I cared for May, so after that I dropped the subject. Our holiday ended, we returned home to Scotland; we never visited Pelynt or Kerrith again, and I never again met, or heard from, Rebecca. For a long while, though, her fascination endured, and I often thought of her. I discovered May's strange friend had been right in her advice: I *was* able to stop biting my nails; I *was* able to read better; I *was* able to be less stupid. But there are limits to willpower, of course. One day, there Rebecca's picture was, on the front page of a newspaper. That boat of hers had not been so safe after all; it had disappeared at sea; it was gone, and she was gone with it.

Time passed. When her body was finally found, and I read the newspaper reports of her inquest, I saw the verdict was suicide. A last act of will, and the end of the story, I decided. Now I would never know who she was and why she had wanted to meet me that day—and by then I was very sure that encounter was willed, that May had been coerced, and Rebecca determined to meet me.

I put the matter out of my mind, and for years thought of the episode only rarely; but the story was not yet over, nor was my own involvement in it. Edwin Galbraith, a good and kind man, died when I was still at school. May, to whom I owe so much, died two years ago, of a heart attack. When her house in Scotland was finally sold last year I had to go through all her belongings. I found among her papers a letter that she might have destroyed had she not died suddenly and unexpectedly. I've been carrying it about with me ever since; sitting in the garden in London this morning, I opened it again, and re-read it. The address was 12C Tite Street, London SW3; the date was 1926, and—as I now know—the letter must have been written shortly after Rebecca's marriage, and some months before that one occasion on which she met me.

She wrote:

My dear May,
I was glad to see you yesterday—and very sad to hear of your predicament. Not to be able to bear a child is such a hard fate for a woman. But you can still have a child and look after him and love him. You must adopt one—I'm sure Edwin will agree if you ask him.

As it happens, I know of a little boy who needs a family. He is in an orphanage near London at present, and a very barbaric place it is. He was moved on there from some foundlings' home—in the country, I believe. According to when the children were placed there, they christened them. This little boy was part of the "T" contingent, so they called him "Terence." His intake all had surnames taken from colors; there was a "Brown" and a "Black" and a "White" and a "Green"; Terence's surname is "Gray." I think Galbraith would suit him much better.

I think you should go there and rescue him. I would rescue him myself, but Max might not welcome the idea, and you would certainly make a much wiser and better parent than I would.

I knew his mother once, poor woman—she is dead now—and I've only recently discovered that her son is alive. She would bless you, I know, and so would I, if you took care of him. You will make him a good mother, and I'm sure Edwin will make the best of fathers.

Telephone me as soon as you receive this, and I will tell you where to find him.

Rebecca

Every time I've read this letter, I've put a different interpretation on it. When I first read it, I felt a painful certainty that I had found my mother at last. Later, I told myself that I had at best found my mother's friend—and that was no help to me, for the friend was dead now. Then I discovered that, in this predicament, I can believe everything and anything—and, such is my need, I can believe in any number of opposing ideas simultaneously. So my mother is Rebecca and is not Rebecca. She is her friend; she is that woman failed by the gin and the knitting needle; she has a hundred faces—and I cannot rest until I find the one face that is hers, and the one name that fits her.

But, today, sitting under that tree, with the petals falling on the page as I read that letter, I saw another face looking over my mother's shoulder—the features were indistinct but I knew it was the face of my father. I was born in 1915, and my birthdate is approximate; it was calculated by the orphanage authorities, or so I was always told. But it cannot be more than a few weeks out at most; that means that if I were Rebecca's child, she would have still been a child herself when she had me—she would have been only fourteen, living at a house called Greenways, with a cousin I'd detested on sight, and a father who had doted on her.

So did I want to go on? Was I sure I wanted to go on?

I folded up the note and replaced it in my pocket. I heard the traffic of the city for the first time that morning. I *had* to go on, I knew that in my heart. There were numerous arguments against that course of action; I could see that this Pandora's box might be better left unopened. Even so, I had to discover the truth—and, besides, how could I give up now, when I knew that, at last, I was getting closer?

NINETEEN

REACHING THIS DECISION GAVE ME A NEW SENSE OF PUR-
pose. I went back into the house to decide on my route for the
remaining hours I had in London. I was booked on the evening train,
which would get me to Lanyon just after midnight, but I had the rest
of the day to follow up my new leads. I tried calling Favell, but
received no answer from either number. Presumably he was lying
low, nursing a hangover.

I sat down in Sir Archie's study and borrowed his desk, with its
view out over Regent's Park. Nicky's father is retired now, but he was
a distinguished civil servant, a man of neat habits, with an orderly
mind—and his desk was exceptionally neat. Its only adornment was a
wedding photograph of Nicky and Julia, with myself as best man,
standing just off to the side, and looking away from the camera. I
didn't want to be reminded of Julia's beauty or Nicky's happiness that
day, and I certainly didn't want to be reminded of my own feelings on
that occasion. I turned the photograph away from me, and spread out
my journals, notebooks, and newspaper cuttings.

The person I most wanted to speak to now was Mrs. Danvers, the
woman whose knowledge of Rebecca went further back than Jack
Favell's, the woman who had remained close to her throughout her
marriage; I'd been banking on Favell's knowing her whereabouts.

Since he couldn't help, and on the whole I believed him when he claimed he'd lost touch with her, I still had no way of finding her— though it wasn't for want of trying. Thinking she might still be employed as a housekeeper, or as a companion perhaps, I'd approached every single one of the large domestic service agencies, and most of the smaller ones. I'd tried questioning all the former Manderley servants still living in the Kerrith area, and I'd obtained no clues as to her whereabouts.

A concretion of myths and stories had attached themselves to her, as they had to the de Winters and Rebecca: A number of those who had worked under her or alongside her, including Frith, felt she was in some way connected to the fire that destroyed Manderley. They stopped short of accusations of arson, but they felt she was *involved*; on one point, they all agreed—no one had laid eyes on her, or heard of her, since the night of the fire. She had packed up her belongings that day, they said, announced she was leaving for good—and vanished.

As I unpicked this story piece by piece, I came across Mrs. Danvers again and again. Mrs. Danvers was the obvious route back into Rebecca's childhood. If any links did exist between Rebecca and Manderley before her marriage, then Mrs. Danvers would be the person who knew of them. If Favell could be believed, Mrs. Danvers had been involved in the key transition period of Rebecca's life, when her mother died and she went to live with her father at Greenways. Might she not therefore have information about me, too? Someone had deposited me as a baby at an orphanage in 1915, and had done so, if Rebecca's letter to May was to be believed, without Rebecca's knowledge.

Failing Mrs. Danvers, who was there to consult? I would have to go back to my only other strong lead, to Sir Frank McKendrick and that touring company of his. There was a strong possibility that the "old ham" Favell had spoken of last night was McKendrick, and that the photograph of her mother as Desdemona that Rebecca had placed on her "shrine" featured a McKendrick touring production. Find the mother and find the child, I told myself.

I called the information desk at the St. James's Library, one of the best libraries in London, and my favourite workplace in the city. I was in luck. McKendrick had written an autobiography. It wasn't out on loan, I would find it in the stacks, and its title, the librarian said, sounding amused, was appropriately Shakespearean: *Taken at the Flood*.

It took me a moment to place the quotation. Brutus to Cassius, in *Julius Caesar*. I was by no means sure that there *was* a tide in the affairs of men, which, taken at the flood, leads on to fortune—but I felt encouraged. I tried calling Favell again, without success, then called The Pines to check on Colonel Julyan's welfare. Ellie answered, and I spoke to her for some while before I left for the library.

In passing, I asked her about that mysterious call I'd received last night. Ellie confirmed that, as I'd expected, she had given this number to no one.

"Why do you ask?"

"Someone called yesterday, and didn't leave a message. . . ."

I hesitated. Ellie had been addressing me by Gray's name, and that made me feel shabby. There were deceptions here, and I knew I couldn't let them continue much longer. There was a moment when I almost confessed. I just stopped myself in time. If any confession were to be made, it had to be made face-to-face, and not on the telephone.

Ellie said that her father had been feeling tired the previous day, but seemed stronger this morning. Tomorrow, at the doctor's suggestion, he was going over to the county hospital for some tests—but they were routine, she assured me. She would be with him at the hospital for most of the day, but would call me at my cottage tomorrow evening. Meanwhile, her father would be glad to hear I was coming back tonight; he was missing me, she said with some emphasis.

I thought this unlikely; I hesitated, then replied that I was missing him, too. This seemed to please Ellie; I heard the sudden lift in her voice—and her mood affected mine. I left for the library feeling purposeful, and considerably happier.

By 10:15, I was going through the card catalog in search of Sir Frank's autobiography, and by 10:20 I was in the stacks, searching the shelves for it.

The St. James's Library is an old building, and its geography is confusing. The theatrical history section proved to be in a remote wing, on one of the upper stories, reached by a whole series of staircases, anterooms, and narrow passageways. Like certain other parts of the library, this section was ill-lit, cramped, and somewhat sinister. I was hemmed in by the stacks, which were only a few feet apart, and which ran in serried ranks across the width of the area. There were no windows; both the ceiling and the floor were constructed of iron gratings, so I could sense other searchers in the sections below and above me.

I moved between the narrow stacks, pulling the light cords, illuminating first this, then that section of shelves. Sir Frank McKendrick's autobiography was not in its assigned place, and I assumed that the book had been put back on the wrong shelf by another browser; sometimes this happened. I began checking; along the books, spine by spine. I drew out a couple of general histories of the Edwardian stage, and Shakespearean touring companies, but their references to McKendrick told me little more than Francis Browne had already indicated. No mention of his Othello, and no details about other actors in his company. I felt a sense of angry frustration. That book *must* be here. A shifting sighing sound came up through the grating on the floor. Footsteps tapped on a metal staircase around the corner. Someone unseen moved between the stacks farther up the room. A door closed in a distant part of the building.

I went back along the relevent shelves three times. The book wasn't there. I was about to return to the main hall and consult the librarian; I turned back toward the stairs and passed a dark corner where there was a small reading desk, little more than a shelf, really, to be used for reference rather than serious reading. I'd passed that little desk earlier, and was almost sure it had been bare; now there was a book on it. Picking it up, I found it was the missing autobiography.

It fell open at one particular place, and a sweet familiar scent rose up from the page. I started, and almost dropped it. Pressed between the leaves of the book was a sprig of azalea—the same azalea I had seen woven into a garland at Rebecca's boathouse. It was browned and crumpled, but the perfume was still strong. This was not an old specimen, pressed and dried; it could not have been in the book very long. I swung round and looked back along the stacks. Someone had been there earlier, I'd heard movement. The stacks were now empty.

I sat down at the desk, switched on the reading light, removed the azalea sprig carefully, and looked at the page it had served to mark.

On the right, there was a photograph of Sir Frank McKendrick, wearing an exotic costume. His face was blacked up, and he was bending over a bed; on the bed, her long fair hair tumbling over the pillow that would be used to stifle her, was a pretty young woman, mouth rounded in an O of pleading despair. The caption read: *Theatre Royal, Plymouth, September 1914. My three hundredth appearance as the Moor. My Desdemona was Miss Isabel Devlin. "A fine histrionic display in which Sir Frank surpassed himself,"* was the verdict of the *Plymouth Courier.*

Looking at the paragraphs opposite, I saw that someone had marked them with a faint pencil line. I began reading at the top of the page:

My hopes ran high for our regular three-week season in Plymouth, where we have always enjoyed lively and loyal audiences. We were to present our repertoire of nine plays, with my three hundredth performance as Othello being given on the first Saturday evening. As my dear wife was indisposed, the part of Desdemona was undertaken by a younger actress, Miss Isabel Devlin, who had been an adornment to our company for years and whose elevation to more testing roles was a well-deserved one. Miss Devlin was always of an original cast of mind, and she contributed some intriguing notions to our rehearsals, most of which I was, alas, forced to overrule; with Shakespeare's plays, as I have always maintained, the tried-and-true traditions are ignored at one's peril.

Miss Devlin looked charming, and sang the "Willow Song" with the sweetest of voices; her scenes with myself, and with Cassio (played by Mr. Orlando Stephens on this occasion; he was shortly to leave our company), were most tender and affecting. On the first night, I remember, I felt her Desdemona's death stuggles were too desperate, and this caused some consternation, the more so as my wig fixings were unreliable. I had a discreet word with her about this afterward, and advised her against this tendency to "milk" the moment. I persuaded her that her belief that Desdemona might "fight back" was mistaken. Desdemona is a gentle and passive creature, and the attention of the audience as the terrible murder occurs must, I reminded her, be fixed upon the husband.

Miss Devlin took my advice to heart, and her performance improved thereafter. The critics were kind, though, as my wife had cause to point out, Miss Devlin's voice lacked strength, and she had perhaps not mastered the art of projection inborn in the greatest thespians. Despite these birth pangs, and teething troubles, however, the production was little short of a triumph. My own performance was greeted with many plaudits, and the traditional presentation of wreaths from my admirers. Had it not been for the recent advent of war, I feel sure more seats would have been sold, and our takings would have been more remunerative.

As a postscript, and by way of tribute, I should add that, sadly, Desdemona was Miss Devlin's last role with our company—indeed her last on any stage. My wife, whose opinion of her abilities had always been lower than my own, had concerns as to Miss Devlin's health, which had never been strong. When her condition did not improve, it was felt we should dispense with her services. Not long afterward, we heard that she had died, in the most tragic of circumstances. She was in her prime of beauty, with the prettiest golden hair; "April was in her eyes," if I may misquote; she was a "lass unparallel'd," and a lady to her fingertips, with great delicacy of mind and demeanor. My wife and I could not attend her funeral, but I grieved for her.

I should add that Miss Devlin's daughter was also at this time a member of our little "band of brothers" and showed a precocious ability for the Bard. She was a most unusual and wicked Puck to my Oberon at a very early age, and was of great use to us in boys' roles. I remember her as a swaggering but subtle young princeling to my Richard III, and her pitiful death as Macduff's son in the Scottish play brought tears to many an eye. She might have had a future on the boards, I always felt, though my wife doubted she had the necessary discipline and temperament; but we heard no more of her after her dear mother died.

Once our triumphant season in Plymouth was over, we moved on to Bristol, but the financial difficulties I have mentioned earlier continued to cause us problems, so we feared we might have to disband. I stared defeat in the face on several occasions, but soldiered on. My wife and I . . .

I skipped to the end of the page, then flicked back and forward through the chapters. I checked the very unscholarly and erratic

index and found a list of company members. This was the only reference to Isabel Devlin, and her daughter was not identified by name.
Even so, there was no doubt in my mind that I had found Rebecca—
and so had someone else, of course.

I looked at the sprig of azalea blossom; I turned to the front page
of the book, where the dates when it had been on loan were recorded.
There was clearly little demand for Sir Frank's windy reminiscences.
Taken at the Flood had languished on the shelves. Someone had consulted it, and recently too, but for the last three years no one had borrowed it.

I sat at the small desk, with my head in my hands, trying to puzzle
this out. Someone had sent a notebook of Rebecca's to Colonel
Julyan; on the same day, someone had sent Jack Favell her ring;
someone had been at her boathouse—and perhaps at Manderley, too,
I realized, thinking of that boarded-up window that had been broken
into. Someone had left that azalea garland by the shore; someone had
consulted this book—and recently someone had been looking
through Francis Browne's postcards of Manderley, too, I now
remembered.

Whoever this person was, he or she seemed intent on leaving a
trail. Who could have had access to Rebecca's belongings? Who
might now be in the grip of some unbalanced, half-demented obsession . . . apart from myself, of course, I thought ruefully. It had to be
someone who had been very close to Rebecca, surely, someone who
had known her as a child. I could now see that Ellie had been right,
and the likeliest candidate was a woman. It seemed that, yet again, I
was up against Mrs. Danvers, the elusive, unfindable Mrs. Danvers. If
she had sent that first notebook, and if there was at least one other, as
the Colonel believed, then the likelihood was that she was in possession of it. But *was* she unfindable? This was a trail, and trails are
meant to be followed.

Where, then, did the trail lead? Where should I go next? Greenways? I would have liked to go there, though I doubted I'd find anything more interesting than a house long since occupied by others. If
not Greenways, where else? What other place had associations with
Rebecca?

I sat there puzzling over this for another five minutes, before the
answer came to me—yet it was obvious, it had been staring me in the

face all morning. I drew out the letter Rebecca had written to May all those years before, the letter that had altered the whole course of my life. 12C Tite Street—the flat Rebecca had kept in London, by the river. I had been there before, several times, on previous visits; although there was at least one other occupied flat in the building, no one was ever in. Maybe now was the time to return there.

I FOUND A TAXI IN ST. JAMES'S SQUARE, AND ON MY WAY to Chelsea re-read Sir Frank's account of Rebecca and her mother; some of his wording struck me as odd—but at least I had now narrowed down the dates, and they corresponded closely, I noticed, to the dates Francis Browne had given me for the Manderley postcard.

In September 1914, Rebecca and her mother had been in Plymouth, which happens to be the nearest large city to Kerrith and Manderley, and, nowadays, by car, about an hour or so away from it. Sometime "early in 1915" (or so he claimed; I had not been able to pin it down more precisely than that) Jack Favell arrived in England from Kenya, and Rebecca had been in mourning. Therefore, in the space of one winter, of some six or at most seven months, there had been great change: Rebecca's mother had died, Mrs. Danvers had taken charge of her, and Rebecca herself had gone to live with her father at Greenways.

What had caused her mother's death, I wondered. Sir Frank's account suggested a legacy of ill health; perhaps Isabel Devlin had died of some then-lethal wasting disease, tuberculosis, for instance. It should be easy enough to establish the precise date and cause of death; provided "Devlin" was the only name Rebecca's mother used, I should now be able to find her death certificate in the records at Somerset House quite quickly. If I didn't have time to do it myself today, I could always get a friend like Simon Lang to do it for me.

Meanwhile, given the timing, I felt sure that Isabel's state of health *did* explain the return of Jack Devlin from Africa. I wondered if Favell was correct, and it was Mrs. Danvers who had traced Devlin. Certainly Mrs. Danvers was involved somehow in these events, but it was not necessarily she who had contacted him. If Devlin had never divorced his wife, perhaps they had remained in touch with each other after they parted. And as to why they had parted—well, there I had no evidence beyond Favell's insinuations, and the suggestive "six months" he claimed they had lived together. Were they merely incompatible, or had Devlin discovered something so unacceptable about his wife that he walked out on her? That she was having an affair with another man, or that she was expecting another man's child when he married her, for instance?

The taxi had come to a halt on the corner of Tite Street and the Embankment. I paid it off, and walked slowly up the street toward the tall resplendent redbrick Dutch-gabled house where Rebecca had had an apartment. It was at the southern end of the road, not far from where Whistler had once had his studios. When they were first built, many of these houses had been lived in by artists, and, like several of the others, Rebecca's house had, on its upper floors, a huge arched studio window. I looked up at it now, from the pavement on the opposite side.

The sun glanced against the glass; from that window it would have been possible to see the Thames. Rebecca had chosen to live less than two minutes' walk from the river, I noted; and it occurred to me, thinking of Favell's strange accusations the previous night, that if she had decided to end her life after being told the nature of her illness, she had no need to drive all the way back to Manderley. The means of death lay at the end of her street; she would have been able to see the dangerous waters of the Thames from her own window.

I crossed the road to the house, and examined the doorbells for the flats, as I had done before. Twelve A was the basement; it was shuttered up, and appeared uninhabited. Twelve B seemed to be the ground floor, and 12C the upper floors. None of the bells had names on them.

Without any great hope of reply, I pressed the bell for 12C and waited. I had asked Ellie about this flat when she drove me to Lanyon station—and that was yesterday morning, I realized, though it felt like a month ago. She was sure that Rebecca had had the flat for some years before her marriage, and that she used it only occasionally after her wedding, though Colonel Julyan said Rebecca was there more often in the last six months of her life.

I pressed the bell again. I had asked Ellie what happened to the flat after Rebecca died. She said her sister Lily had continued to live close by for years, and she couldn't recall any mention of the flat's being relet. "Maybe Rebecca passed the lease on to someone else," she said.

"Someone else must have moved in. Someone must have packed up Rebecca's things." Who would have done that? I asked, though I knew the answer before she spoke the name: Mrs. Danvers.

Always Mrs. Danvers. I pressed the bell again, and this time I kept my finger on it. It jangled in the depths of the house—and suddenly, at last, I heard a response. A door banged; footsteps approached; I tensed. The front door was flung back to reveal a young woman of about twenty-five. She was dressed in artistic black from head to foot—and she was not in a good temper.

"Look, do you *mind*," she said. "What a racket! You can stand there ringing that bell all day, and you won't get an answer. . . ."

She paused, and looked at me closely. A curious change came over her; she smiled, blushed, apologized for "biting my head off," explained she lived in 12B, on the ground floor and proceeded to take a warm interest in my predicament. When she discovered I wanted to know about Flat 12C and its occupant, the flirtatiousness diminished, and her manner became nervous.

"Oh, my God," she said. "Do you know anything about her? You'd better come in. It's quite a story. Would you like some coffee?"

She drew me into a large hall, with a black-and-white flagstoned floor; a wide, curving handsome staircase led up from it. She looked at the stairs, raised her finger to her lips, and led me into her flat. Maybe I have an honest face; maybe she was trusting; maybe she was glad of male protection (that possibility did cross my mind, certainly when she began on her tale). Whatever her motives, two minutes later I was in her sitting room.

Her name was Selina Fox-Hamilton, I discovered. She had lived in the ground-floor flat for just over a year and intended to move out at the first opportunity. She worked in an art gallery in Cork Street, and was only at home that day because she had a hangover. She sat me down on a sagging sofa, introduced me to her three cats, and started talking. She explained that she wasn't of a nervous disposition, and didn't believe in ghosts, never had, but she'd changed her mind since moving into this house. I wanted to know about the flat upstairs? Was it empty? Not exactly, she replied, with a small shiver. The flat *was* let—but its tenant was peculiar. Very.

"Okay," she said, sitting down opposite me and lighting a cigarette. "This is how it is. First of all, I move in, and I'm really pleased, because the rent's rock-bottom low, and it's a lovely house and a nice flat, and the cats like it. The agents told me the basement flat was empty, and they said there was a woman living upstairs, but she was rarely there, so she wouldn't bother me. That was fine by me—and then I began to notice . . . just little things at first, but they were odd. There'd be lights on when I came home late from a party—but I'd never hear anyone, and I never saw anyone go in or out. And who-ever lived there, or stayed there—she never got any mail. Not once. I've never seen a single letter for that flat, and you've got to admit that's pretty peculiar.

"So, I started asking around," she went on. "There's some artists just up the street who've lived here forever, and they told me the whole story. The flat upstairs used to belong to this woman, and she was very beautiful and very young when she died. She died in myste-rious circumstances about twenty years ago. She drowned—and some people said she killed herself, and some people said she was murdered by her husband. She lived in this beautiful house, in the West Country, and the house burned down on the day after her funeral.

"Anyway, they told me this story, and then they said, *Have you seen her?* Well, you can imagine, that made me nervous. I hadn't seen her, I hadn't seen anyone—but they had. Or they claimed they had, and recently, too. One of them said he saw her, standing by the river and looking down at the water, just at the end of this street. Another one had seen her coming out of the front door one evening. And one of the women said, *Have you heard her moving the furniture yet?* Because, apparently, that's what happens, in the middle of the night—and that's why the agents can't get anyone to stay in this flat very long, and that's why the rent's so exceptionally low. It's been going on ever since her funeral, ever since the night of the fire, they said. That's twenty years! I'm the seventh person to live here since the war, they told me."

Selina looked at me, round-eyed. I asked her if she'd believed these stories.

"Well, I couldn't see why they'd make them up. But I never saw anyone, and I never heard anything, so, after a while—I'd been here about three months then—I put it out of my mind. Then, I began to notice . . . my cats started behaving strangely. They hide—

sometimes they won't come out into the hall, and nothing will persuade them to go anywhere near that staircase. Then, one night, it started. The noises. And it was just the way they'd described—horrible dragging noises, as if something heavy were being lugged across the floor. It went on and on. And always very late—two, maybe three, or four in the morning."

"Can you remember when this started?"

"I *know* when it started. On April twelfth last year—I wrote it down in my diary."

April twelfth was the anniversary of Rebecca's death. I thought it was better not to tell Selina that. She lit another cigarette and continued with her story. The noises had continued for over a week, then they had stopped. Months of silence ensued; Selina told herself the "hauntings" were over. Then, on one occasion, and only one, there was an encounter: It was last November and she had returned home in the afternoon earlier than she normally did. It was approaching winter, so it was already dark, and there was a thick fog, a clammy pea-souper of a fog that had been hanging over London all week. She let herself into the house, reached for the light switch in the hall, and then saw a figure on the stairway.

"I could only just see her," she said. "The porch light was on, and I had the door wide open, and the fog was drifting in, but there was a little light, a *band* of light shining across that staircase. I saw her move through it. She sort of *glided* through it. I was so startled, I made this gasping noise. Then I found the light switch, and the hall light came on, and she'd gone." She paused. "I don't think it was a ghost—not really. But at the time I was very frightened. I said, 'Who is that?' or 'What are you doing?' or something. She didn't answer. Then I heard the door close. That was it. I've never seen her since. And I don't want to, either."

This was not, however, Selina's final encounter with the female tenant upstairs. There were two more, both indirect and both peculiar.

Some months after the vision on the stairs, the furniture-moving noises began again. This time, they were so frequent, and so prolonged, that Selina decided to take action. One morning, very early, when she'd had virtually no sleep, she braved the stairs and knocked on the door of 12C. She was certain the woman was in the flat; the noises had finally ceased only a few minutes before, and no one had left the house during that time. She was determined to complain, but her knockings and callings produced no response. The door to 12C remained closed—and Selina remained absolutely certain the woman had been there, just the other side of the door. She could hear her breathing.

Finally, and this was less than a month ago, she could stand the noises no longer. When complaints to the managing agents produced no response, she wrote a note—a polite note, she stressed—and went upstairs, and slid it under the door of 12C. Then, she left for work. When she returned that night there was an envelope on her mat, a blank envelope, with nothing written on it, not even her flat number. Inside it was her own note, torn into hundreds of tiny fragments.

"Well, that scared me," she said. "I mean, that's not normal, is it? Since then, I've stayed out of her way, and I can't wait to move out. I *have* to find another flat. I don't want to be alone in a house with a ghost *or* a madwoman."

I asked Selina a few questions. Had she ever learned the tenant's name? No: The agents had refused to give it to her. Could she describe the woman she'd glimpsed on the stairs? She'd been wearing *scent*, Selina said, she noticed it at once, this delicate fresh scent, like spring flowers. She was tall, and she'd been wearing black, and her hair was covered . . . but she'd only glimpsed her for a second. I told Selina that ghosts didn't tear notes into fragments and leave them on people's doormats, though I didn't expect that to console her very much. Then, I asked her if she had an envelope she could let me have, and I went out into the hall. Nothing would persuade Selina to go anywhere near the stairs, so she stayed in her doorway, and I went up alone.

It was a fine staircase, wide, with ornate balustrading. When I came to the heavy black door on the first landing, I listened intently. There was a strange smell on the landing, a very faint burning smell. I took the envelope Selina had supplied and slipped the azalea sprig I'd found at the library inside it. I sealed it. I wrote "Terence Gray" and my address and telephone number in Kerrith on it. I stared at the door, and thought of what Selina had been told: *It's been going on ever since her funeral, ever since the night of the fire.* It was on the night of the Manderley fire that Mrs. Danvers had vanished.

It was a remote chance, but it seemed to be worth taking. I leaned against the door, and in a low voice I said, "Mrs. Danvers? Are you there? I'd like to speak to you. I'd like to speak to you about Rebecca. . . ."

No sound came from beyond the door. I knocked lightly on the panels; there was no response. From the hall below, I heard a stifled sigh from Selina. It echoed up the stairwell, oddly amplified by the acoustics.

"Mrs. Danvers?" I said again—and this time I thought I *did* hear a sound, a soft slithering noise, as if a piece of material, a long skirt or something similar, brushed against a carpet. I might have imagined it. I pushed the envelope under the door; I waited for several minutes, and when there was no response at all, returned to the hallway. Selina and I exchanged telephone numbers, then I extricated myself, not without difficulty, and escaped to the street again.

I walked across the road and stationed myself on the pavement, directly opposite Rebecca's tall studio window. The sun reflected on the glass. If a woman had been standing at the window, I could not have seen her because of the angle of the light; but she could have seen me. I allowed her time to inspect me, always supposing she was there. It was disconcerting, to feel watched, but not to be sure one *was* watched. It made me deeply uneasy.

THIS SENSE OF BEING WATCHED WAS ONE I COULD NOT shake off; it clung to me for the rest of the day, and the remainder of my time in London was inconclusive and frustrating. Selina had given me the names of the artists who had told her that ghost story, and the name and telephone number of the managing agents for the Tite Street house. The agents refused to give me any information whatsoever; the artists were not at home. I wasted time knocking on doors in Tite Street, in search of neighbors who might know something of the occupant of Flat 12C, but all were recent arrivals, and knew nothing. I then wasted even more time at Chelsea Town Hall, going through the electoral register. Whoever lived in apartment 12C was unregistered; Selina was listed, but no other occupant.

By the time I'd completed this dispiriting search, eaten a dispiritingly bad sandwich in a small cafe, and fought my way back down a crowded King's Road to the tube station in Sloane Square, I had only a few hours left in London, and I was more than ready to escape the heat, the traffic, and the exhaust fumes for the clean air and the calm of Kerrith.

I took the tube back into the center of London, and set about more practical tasks. I went to Fortnum and Mason, and bought the Briggs sisters their violet creams, as promised. I went into Hatchards, and bought two books as a present for Colonel Julyan. I saw my own book on Walsingham and his Elizabethan spy network on display; on impulse I bought a copy for Ellie. If I confessed my identity to her and her father, I could give her this; it seemed a reasonable idea at first, but, the instant the purchase was made, I regretted it. This was a book aimed primarily at scholars; it was interesting to me, but it was peppered with footnotes, it was dry and specialized. Was that how I wanted to introduce Tom Galbraith to her? She would find him very dull—but maybe she found him so already.

I had one last task before I could return to Regent's Park, pack my bag, and make my escape. I had to see Jack Favell, return Rebecca's ring and—if he was in a fit state—question him. I walked back up Bond Street, and through into Mayfair. The streets were crowded now; the warmth of the weather created a gaiety, a spring fever, that was palpable. A man and a woman strolled past, hand in hand; a uni-formed nanny pushed a pram, and two girls stopped to peer under its sunshade and smile at the baby. I paused at the corner. I could sense that promise peculiar to cities in spring, its possibilities were in the air, in the glitter of the pavement, in the song of the traffic. Its allure was all around me. I felt very alone, marked out by my isolation, locked in my searches of the past for too long, a man who had lived out his life looking for truth in the small print; a man imprisoned in libraries.

The sensation clung, and I fought it off with difficulty. I walked through to the quieter Mayfair street where Favell's showroom was located, but found to my surprise that it was empty, and locked up. There was a bell, which I rang, but nobody emerged. One of the cars I noticed yesterday, the Bentley, had disappeared; perhaps Favell was out taking a client for a test-drive, I thought. I hung about for half an hour; when there was no sign of his returning, I left. I would call him from Kerrith, and, meanwhile, I would have to keep Rebecca's ring.

As I walked back to Regent's Park, I turned it over and over in my pocket.

At the Osmonds' house, I used my remaining time to write letters and make telephone calls. I wrote again to Frank Crawley, though I expected this letter—the third— would be met with the same polite refusals as the first two. I called Simon Lang, and persuaded him to do a little simple research at Somerset House for me. I called some friends and colleagues at King's, where I'll be returning this autumn. I called my publisher, spoke to my editor, promised to have lunch with him soon, and explained that my new book on Raleigh was taking longer than expected; he's a sanguine man, and did not sound too brokenhearted. I packed, said good-bye to Mrs. Henderson (no one had called for me), and left for the station. I was impatient to be back in Kerrith. I wanted to walk by the sea; I wanted to tell Ellie and her father of the progress I'd made, and I was hoping that, if he'd felt strong enough, the Colonel might also have made some discoveries.

By six, I was at Paddington, and by 6:30 the train was pulling out of London. This time, I had a carriage to myself—the train was not crowded—and I was glad of the solitude. I slung my bag in the rack, scanned the front page of the *Evening Standard* I'd bought at the station, then tossed it aside. I stared out of the window, and watched the suburbs slip by. I listened to the rhythms of the train, and thought myself back into my search. I went over the events of the last two days, what I'd been told—and what I'd not been told: The omissions and the evasions, of course, being as significant as the information.

We were well beyond the city and dusk was falling before I picked up Sir Frank's autobiography again, and in a desultory way, growing increasingly irritated by the circumlocutions of his style, began to read it. The train was in open country, and it was almost dark outside, before I saw what I had missed this morning. It was there on the previous page to the one on which I'd been concentrating; just a passing mention, easy enough to overlook in the ramble of his memories. It came just before his reference to those regular seasons in Plymouth:

As has been our habit for many years, my wife and I, and several members of our company, stayed with Millicent Danvers, who keeps the excellent "St. Agnes" boarding house in Marine Parade overlooking the Plymouth sound. She is widowed now and getting on in years and her daughter (formerly of great help to her) is in service, but the standards we had come to expect had not diminished in the slightest. The cleanliness and order of her household are exemplary—would that it were so in all our "diggings"! We talked over "old times" with great pleasure and begged to be reminded to her daughter, but fortunately she is employed close by, and so was able to attend a performance of *Othello*. Edith Danvers, or "Danny" as we always called her, was always most loyal in her appreciation of our efforts, and had made many friends among our company from her girlhood. She would not have missed our performance for the world, and the killing of Desdemona made her blood run cold, she told us.

Edith Danvers: She had been here in this book, all along. Now at last I understood where she came from; here, perhaps, lay the origins of her connection with Rebecca—and if Edith Danvers had attended that performance of *Othello*, then she *had* been in touch with Rebecca and Isabel Devlin in the months leading up to Isabel's death, I noted. I took Sir Frank's autobiography to the dining car, and read through it as I ate; but this was the sole reference to her. She came flickering out of the past toward me, and then returned to it.

I went back to my carriage and stared out into the night, watching the dark rush past, and my own double, a pale reflection, move against the window. After a while, I closed my eyes; but although I can only have slept an hour or two at most last night, and was twitchy with fatigue, I could not sleep properly now. I fell into awkward and unsettled dozes, states between unconsciousness and waking, in which I half dreamed I was walking up endless stairs, to a black door that was never opened.

I must have slept in the end, I think, because when I surfaced at last, even more tired than before, we were rattling across the Tamar, and rushing toward the dark wild empty landscape that lies between it and Manderley. In an effort to distract myself, I picked up my newspaper.

The item was brief, set down low on the second page. Jack Favell, codirector of the Favell Johnston classic car dealership in Mayfair, I read, had been involved in a car accident in the early hours of the morning. It had occurred at a notorious "black spot" blind bend, between Lambourn, Berkshire, and the village of Hampton Ferrars. The Bentley Favell was driving hit a wall and caught fire on impact. Two witnesses, both stable hands out exercising horses, said the car was being driven very fast, and no attempt was made to brake at the corner. Favell had been killed. Police inquiries were continuing.

The train jerked, slowed, then gathered speed again. I felt shock—and guilt, too. I took out the ring Favell had given me, and looked at it. I thought back over our conversation, and death altered and reshaped it. I heard him describe Greenways again, and walking up onto the downs to watch Rebecca ride there.

Was this death accidental? Or had Favell intended to die—and in circumstances that seemed so deliberately to mirror the death of Maxim de Winter? When these men crashed their cars, had they been seeking Rebecca, or escaping from her? I tried to imagine the hours Favell must have spent between leaving me and driving off early the next morning. Had he sobered up, or had he continued drinking, still trying to keep his demons at bay? He must have been far more desperate than I had understood, I realized, and I should have listened better, watched more closely. I looked at Rebecca's ring—that unlucky ring, he had claimed—and I thought of the time I myself had seen it on her hand. I felt death brush past, very close; its sea-colored eyes looked at me. *Do you live here? What, here in the church? No. Not yet, anyway.*

The dark rushed past; lights glinted on the horizon; my double moved against the glass. Shortly after midnight, the brakes screeched, and the train slowed; at half past midnight, we pulled into Lanyon station. One taxi was on duty, and I persuaded the driver to take me across the moors and back to my cottage. I stood outside it, watching his lights disappear into the distance. There was no moon, the tide was high and the water black, whispering against the shingle. The wind was strengthening, and it was beginning to rain. I stood for a moment looking out across the sea toward Manderley.

I let myself into the cottage and lit the oil lamp; the flame guttered. Those ghosts that had felt close all day felt close to me still, as if they had followed me here, and were moving about the room, settling themselves in the corners. I took out Rebecca's ring and turned it over in my hands, watching it catch the light. I found myself wondering if Favell had been right, and the ring was unlucky. I told myself I did not believe in ill luck of that kind, or ghosts, for that matter. The wind sighed, and that loose shutter at the back of the house rattled.

Tomorrow I would continue my searches, and follow up those leads I had; but, without further assistance from Favell, and with Mrs. Danvers proving still elusive, I could not see how I could progress much further, unless Colonel Julyan found some new information in that "archive" of his, and that prospect seemed increasingly unlikely. Meanwhile, I could not put my own life and work on hold forever; my temporary job at the county records office ceased, to all intents and purposes, two weeks ago; I was due to collect the last of my things from my office there tomorrow. I didn't regret that—it meant I had more free hours at my disposal—but it did mean that I no longer had a pretext for being in Kerrith. There would come a time, I recognized, when I might have to abandon this search of mine, and accept that the past had swallowed Rebecca up, that she was now in a region of the lost, in an underworld where I could not reach her.

I could feel a familiar melancholy creeping up on me, as stealthily as the mist from the sea. I listened to the murmur of the waves on the shore and the rain on the roof. Then, under and behind the wind, I thought I heard something else, first the sound of footsteps on the shingle, then the rattling noise made when the front gate is unlatched. I turned out the lamp, waited until my eyes grew accustomed to the dark again, then moved quietly to the porch outside. The lights of a ship moved on the horizon; the sea sighed and shifted on the shingle.

I peered out into the darkness; the rain was falling heavily now, and I could see little. The gate swung too and fro in the wind; possibly it was the wind that had unlatched it, though that had never happened before. I walked quietly down the path and refastened it. I looked toward the shore; something pale moved against the rocks, and fear tightened around my heart like a fist. The thought flashed through my mind—*she's come back for her ring*.

Then I regained control. Telling myself it was a trick of the light, I returned to the cottage.

TWENTY

I CALLED ELLIE THIS MORNING BEFORE SHE LEFT WITH HER father for the hospital and I left for the county library. I was looking forward to speaking to her, but our conversation was brief, with none of the ease of yesterday. Ellie sounded anxious, but insisted there was no cause for concern; if she sounded odd, she said, it was just that she was rushing to get her father ready, he was being difficult (he hates hospitals, apparently), and she had slept badly.

I had slept badly, too, pursued by Manderley dreams for most of the night. I had no inkling then of the revelations that were to come today; my mood remained despondent. The rain was still pouring down, the sky was overcast, and the wind from the west had strengthened overnight. The sea, so calm for the past week, had an angry swollen look, crashing and booming against the rocks where I had glimpsed, or imagined, that pale shape yesterday.

Jeremy Bodinnick, the archivist with whom I've been working these past six months, picked me up in his small car as he usually does. He lives in a cottage close to the Briggs sisters, has worked at the county records office for forty years, and is a rotund, kindly, confirmed bachelor. Usually, he's the most cheerful of men, but this morning, he, too, was melancholy.

"A sad day, Terence," he said, as I settled myself in the passenger seat. "A very sad day. I shall miss working with you. The library won't feel the same without you. All that work cataloging the de Winter estate papers, your help with those exhibitions . . . invaluable! If only the council could see their way to funding a permanent position—but of course, they won't. They're philistines, you know, every last man jack of them. Don't understand the importance of local records, no interest in history, cut my budgets to the bone, I told them . . ."

This was a familiar recitative. For years, Mr. Bodinnick has been fighting a heroic campaign against the funding misers at the county council; he likes to dwell on his cunning ploys to outwit them, his frequent defeats, and occasional victories. Hiring me counted as a victory, I think (he certainly viewed it as such), though the salary for an assistant was forthcoming only because the gift of the de Winter estate papers had been made conditional on their being cataloged.

I was hired on a six-month contract to help with this cataloging, and to assist Mr. Bodinnick with the exhibitions he planned for the archive, of which there have been two so far, on the traditional local industries of tin mining and china-clay production. Both exhibitions were well researched and well arranged, but since the library is a well-kept secret, they attracted at most a score of visitors. Mr. Bodinnick immediately began planning a third spectacular, this time on the equally traditional and ancient local industries of wrecking and smuggling—and I think believed that by such stealthy means he might be able to prolong my employment indefinitely.

The penny-pinchers at the council saw through this ruse. My employment was extended by two weeks, then terminated—and it has hit Mr. Bodinnick hard to be thwarted. His grievances against the council kept him going the whole way to Lanyon, but, once we were in the library, he confessed his more immediate worries. How was I now going to manage financially? He took off his spectacles, and began polishing them hard, always a sign of acute anxiety. Looking at me kindly and shortsightedly, he admitted that someone had told him I was thinking of buying the cottage I was currently renting.

I wondered who this informant was. Marjorie Lane? The Briggs sisters? Colonel Julyan? The butcher, the baker, the chemist, the milkman? I stared gloomily out of the window at the rain-swept streets. The suspects included every member of the Kerrith local history society, all their cousins, aunts, grandmothers, and acquaintances. In other words, all those residents in a ten-mile radius possessed of those useful accoutrements—long noses, binoculars, and clairvoyance.

Not only was I about to become a permanent resident, it seems, I was also thinking of "settling down," a process that means only one thing in these parts. This prospect made Mr. Bodinnick even more anxious, since "settling down" involved responsibilities. He was sure I'd manage to provide for myself, but providing for "dependants" was a more serious matter, he said, working up a great shine on the spectacles. When I refused to be drawn he gave a sigh. I think he felt that he was painting too pessimistic a portrait of the married state, because he at once began singing its praises.

He himself had never "settled down," he said, but of course the condition had much to recommend it. Polishing hard, he dwelt on the domestic joys he himself had never experienced, the slippers by the fire, the dinner in the oven, the constant calming presence of a soulmate . . . When Mr. Bodinnick diverted to the illustrious history of the Julyan family, I saw my bride's face clear. I tried to hint that Ellie and I were just friends, but of course he didn't believe me. I said nothing more; I lacked the energy and the inclination to disillusion him.

In the end, I managed to assure him I'd survive financially, by reminding him of that useful "Aunt May" legacy. This isn't a complete lie, and seemed to set his mind at rest. I was then spared further questions. Mr. Bodinnick had begun opening his mail, and amongst it was a letter from the Canadian solicitors acting on behalf of the second Mrs. de Winter. This successfully distracted him. Mr. Bodinnick was very pleased to receive it; he felt the letter was gracious: "Oh, dear me, yes. Very gracious. A charming gesture, Terence," he said, and handed it across to me:

Dear sir:
We understand the cataloging of the de Winter estate papers is now complete. Our client, Mrs. de Winter, asks us to express her appreciation for this work, and trusts that these records will form a useful addition to your archive.

Yours faithfully,

The letter was signed by one of the partners in the Toronto firm that had handled this transaction from start to finish. The tone did not strike me as especially gracious. I filed it away with the other letters from these solicitors, all of which were similarly meager.

At the very beginning of this search, I had written to Mrs. de Winter via this firm of legal guard dogs, to ask for her assistance. After a month's delay I had received a two-line note from them: Mrs. de Winter, they informed me crisply, had nothing to communicate on this matter. They would be obliged if I did not write again. This reply hadn't surprised me. I suspected that Maxim's second wife might well know the truth about Rebecca's death, but, since her late husband was almost certainly involved in that death, I hadn't expected her to help me willingly. Perhaps I should have written again, I thought as I replaced the file. I hadn't been able to bring myself to do so. The realization that I wasn't unscrupulous enough for this kind of work depressed me further.

I finished packing up my few belongings, and at Mr. Bodinnick's request looked through some of the photographs he was assembling for his next exhibition. I listened to his tales about current smuggling activities, though I was preoccupied, and paid little attention until, warming to his theme, he confided that the most successful local smugglers at present were rumored to be that ex-Manderley footman, Robert Lane, and his wife, the former Nancy Manack, whose family had been active in the trade for generations.

Had I noticed the Manack fishing boat? he asked. I couldn't miss it; it was painted scarlet and turquoise, and its skipper was one of Nancy's five brothers. People said that Customs and Excise was currently making life very hard for the Manacks. There had been a series of raids, and it was now difficult for them to find the deserted coves and storage places they needed. . . . Mr. Bodinnick gave a sigh. I think he regretted this interference with a time-honored local industry.

It had occurred to me before that the boathouse at Manderley, even the ruins of the house itself, might have their uses in this regard—though those wishing to store cases of poisonous sherry or other contraband were unlikely to leave azalea garlands outside their improvised warehouses. I stored this information away for future reference, and before I left asked Mr. Bodinnick's assistance on another matter. Could he help me discover the name of the present residents of a house in Marine Parade, Plymouth?

Mr. Bodinnick loves problems of this kind, and he roused himself immediately. He started ferreting away among maps, gazetteers, and street directories. In the end, it took him just one telephone call to a colleague and old friend at the Plymouth archives to get an answer: The street no longer existed. Like much of the city, Marine Parade and the St. Agnes boarding house with it had been bombed into the ground by the Luftwaffe.

I'D BEEN EXPECTING A NEGATIVE ANSWER OF SOME KIND. There had been, I suppose, an outside chance that Mrs. Danvers had retired to live in her parents' former home, just as there had been an outside chance that she might have gone into hiding in Tite Street. My outside chances were getting me nowhere.

It was still raining hard. I walked through the market square at Lanyon to the bus stop, cursing yet again my decision to leave my car in Cambridge. I consulted the timetable, an excellent work of fiction, in my experience. In theory, there was a bus to Kerrith due in twenty minutes time. This could well mean that it had already left twenty minutes earlier. The bus stop was opposite the coroner's court where the inquest into Rebecca's death had been held. I stood there with the rain dripping down my neck thinking my way through the reports I'd read of that inquest, in particular the part played in them by the second Mrs. de Winter.

The proceedings had been straightforward until James Tabb had insisted on giving the evidence that Rebecca's boat, *Je Reviens*, had been tampered with. It was shortly after that, when Maxim de Winter had been recalled to the stand, and the questioning was taking a difficult turn from his point of view, that his second wife had caused a well-timed diversion: She had fainted. It was the timing of that faint, so convenient for her husband, that made me think the second Mrs. de Winter might be complicit in her husband's guilt. Had she been an accessory after the fact, or the shy innocent described to me by most Kerrith residents?

Given the cold response from those Canadian solicitors, I was as unlikely to discover the truth about her as I was to discover the truth about Rebecca, I told myself. I stared along the street in the direction the bus might come; it was some while before I noticed that an elderly woman was waving to me. It proved to be Jocelyn Briggs, who had been driven into Lanyon by a friend to buy a hat, she said, and who—to judge from the number of parcels and bags she was carrying—had succumbed to a number of other temptations. "Oh, Mr. Gray," she cried, "you're getting soaked! Are you all right? You look dreadfully down in the mouth! What a miserable day! I was just going to have a cup of coffee; won't you join me? Then we can give you a lift back to Kerrith."

I was about to refuse—then I discovered that the person providing the lift was James Tabb. I accepted immediately. Jocelyn led me along the street to a tea shop famous in the area, called the Blue Kettle. I think I was the first man to set foot in it for several decades, and my arrival with Jocelyn Briggs on my arm caused a great buzz among the other women, all of a similar age to Jocelyn, who, seeing their interest, became very pink and fluttery.

The front room was full, so we were shown to a quiet and secluded place in an annex at the back. We were seated at a table with a lace cloth, by a window with lace curtains; the china had pink rosebuds on it; in the background there was the constant lulling hum of quiet gossipy conversations. We were brought scones and homemade biscuits by an ancient waitress with a white cap and a white starched frilly apron—and it was in this unlikely setting, this temple of femininity, where I felt deeply foreign, an alien, that Jocelyn Briggs gave me the information that changed everything.

I had never encountered either of the Briggs sisters alone before. I discovered that Jocelyn was much more inclined to talk when her sterner sister was not there to curb her. Of the two, she perhaps has the softer heart; I had always found her warm and sympathetic. Today, I noticed another quality in her, or perhaps responded to it because my spirits were low: She was motherly. With deft movements she poured out coffee, and plied me with scones and questions. Her gentle and faded blue eyes rested on my face. "Now tell me, my dear," she said, "what's worrying you? You look so sad and preoccupied; are you anxious about the Colonel, perhaps? Or dear Ellie? I'm sure dear Arthur will be fine—such willpower, you know. And Ellie tells us these tests are quite routine. . . ."

She hesitated, and I felt she was less than convinced by that explanation. "So sad," she went on, in her vague gentle way. "Ellie has been a pillar of strength. She is spirited—she was quite a tearaway at one time, you know—but she is selfless. And her father can make things very hard for her—I expect you've seen that. He worries about her future, of course, and so do we. What will happen when dear Arthur dies? We have to be realistic; it will happen sooner or later, as it does for us all. . . ."

She gave a little sigh, and a shake of the head. "You see, if anything should happen to Arthur, what will poor Ellie do? That great house—she can't possibly go on living there alone, even if she could afford to. So, The Pines will end up being sold, and they'll build bungalows there, I expect. I said to Elinor, I hope, dear, that I never live to see it. . . ." She paused, then patted my hand. "Still, let us hope that's a long way in the future. Tell me about your visit to London—was that what was worrying you, perhaps? Wasn't it successful?"

I hesitated, and then for some reason—perhaps influenced by the gentleness of her sympathy, or my liking for her, or the strangely confidential, female nature of our surroundings—I told her. I spoke more openly than I had ever done about the nature of my search, the degree to which it had taken over my life, and the frustration I felt at being able to get thus far and no further. I didn't tell her everything, but I conveyed more than I said, as I came to realize. Jocelyn listened intently, her eyes resting on my face, and never once interrupted me.

When my stumbling, awkward explanation finally came to an end, she gave a sigh. "I understand," she said. "Elinor and I always knew that this meant a great deal to you. It's such a hard task, isn't it, resurrecting the dead, trying to see them and comprehend them? Elinor and I have learned that with members of our own family—but then families do hide the truth about people, and do it very efficiently. They invent myths and legends, and one hears them as a child, and believes them, and then later in life . . . Still, never mind that now."

She looked away, and I wondered which member of her family she was considering. Resurrecting the dead—was that the task I was engaged upon?

"You see, even if you were to find Mrs. Danvers," she continued, "I'm not sure how much help she would be to you. It's true, she might have kept some of dear Rebecca's things. But she was always a strange woman, you know—I always said to Elinor that I found her *vampiric*. She never really had a life of her own; she drew all her energy from Rebecca. She never wanted to talk about anyone or anything else—and when she did talk about Rebecca, there was this peculiar excited quality, almost as if she were intoxicated. It was the only time she ever showed the least animation—but then Edith Danvers was odd even as a girl. . . ."

She left the sentence hanging. I stared at her; neither she nor her sister had ever given me the slightest indication that they had known Mrs. Danvers prior to her arrival at Manderley as Rebecca's housekeeper. "As a girl?" I prompted.

"Oh yes. She started in service with us. She worked for my mother, as one of the parlor maids, when Elinor and I were girls and we lived at St. Winnow's. . . ." She paused. "She stayed only a few months—Mama found her unsatisfactory, and the other staff didn't take to her. Of course, she was young then, only fifteen or sixteen, not much older than Elinor—I think she came to us on trial. It was a favor on Mama's part, really. She was fond of Edith Danvers's mother."

"She knew her mother? Millicent Danvers?"

"Oh, very well. Millicent was in service for years; she only took on that boardinghouse after she married, and she married comparatively late in life. Before that, she was senior nursemaid with my mother's family. She looked after Mama as a child. . . . Mama was the eldest of the three Grenville sisters, if you recall. There was Evangeline, my mother; poor Virginia, who married Lionel de Winter, and died young; and the baby of the family, Isolda. They were regarded as beauties—they were famous in this neighborhood. There was a Sargent portrait of them, you know—it was nicknamed *The Three Graces*, and it used to hang at Manderley. Maxim loved it so, because it was the only portrait of his mother. Rebecca cherished it, too, I remember—but it was destroyed in the fire, alas. . . .

"So sad . . ." She gave a small shake of the head. "Anyway, Millicent brought the three sisters up, and my mother was devoted to her. They remained in touch after Millicent married and Mama always took an interest in her affairs. That's why she agreed to take Edith on—but it wasn't a success, as I say. She was very proud and sharp and difficult. Another cup of coffee, Mr. Gray? Won't you have a biscuit? You've eaten nothing, and they're so delicious."

She gave me an artless look. I did not think for a moment that these revelations were artless. "Miss Briggs," I said, "why have you never told me this before?"

"Well, you never asked about Mrs. Danvers," she replied gently. "You never really explained the nature of your search—and Elinor and I don't like to intrude. So, until today, I hadn't understood exactly how much it mattered to you, or *why* it mattered, perhaps. Somehow I see things much more clearly now. It's not a great help in any case. It doesn't help you trace Mrs. Danvers. . . ."

She paused. "One thing I *did* want to add, though," she continued. "If you should succeed in finding her, don't take everything she says as gospel, will you? I may be wrong, but I never felt she understood Rebecca. To hear her talk, Rebecca was invincible—and rather cruel, I always thought, the kind of woman who would never let anyone or anything stand in her way. I'm not sure how true that was. Rebecca was intensely determined, of course, had the most extraordinary willpower, but I always thought that cost her dear. There were sadnesses in her life, I suspect. She never discussed them, ever. But you could sense they were there. . . ."

She raised her faded gentle eyes to hold my gaze. "In fact, I always wondered if she knew she was unable to bear children—or if that came as a terrible revelation to her at the end, when she saw that doctor in London. . . ."

I became very still. The information came to me from nowhere, and I was totally unprepared for it. I tried to disguise my reaction, but it's hard to disguise intense shock. I stared at Jocelyn Briggs, and I saw sympathy flood her gaze.

"Ah, you didn't know—I thought so," she said quietly. "I always imagined Arthur would have explained, but I see he didn't. You see, poor Rebecca could never have had children. Nothing to do with the disease that was killing her. There was . . . well, there was some gynecological problem, a malformation of the womb, I believe. So, even if she hadn't contracted the cancer, even if she had lived, she could never have borne a child. She saw that London doctor twice, you know. There was a week's interval between the appointments. At the first, tests were done and X rays taken. When she went back, seven days later, he told her she was mortally ill, and that she could never have conceived. We'll never know now, I suppose, whether she already knew, or suspected it, poor woman." She hesitated. "You should understand—there's no question about this. If you ask him, I'm sure Arthur will show you the letters of confirmation that doctor wrote. I know I can be vague, but for once I'm not muddling the details. There's no possibility of error, I'm afraid. Elinor and I have seen the doctor's letters."

Her color had risen. I think it was very difficult for her to discuss this with a man, and she had to force herself to do so. There could be only one reason why she had chosen to speak out so frankly, and to do so now: She had seen through me. She knew I was adopted; today, I had dropped my guard; she had seen that poor edifice of hope and supposition that I had built up—and she had seen the necessity of dismantling it. It was done with the utmost tact and gentleness, and I was unable to hide the pain it caused me.

I saw my own distress reflect in her face; I'm not sure what I did—the moment is a blur. I think I stood up and began on some apology. All I could focus on was the importance of escape. Jocelyn's eyes filled with regret and anxiety.

"Oh, Mr. Gray—Terence—please wait. Don't go. Perhaps I shouldn't have spoken. I just felt that I must make things clear, because I could see what you believed—oh, dear, what have I done? Elinor will be furious with me. You see, you *do* look like Rebecca, that's what's so strange. Other people may not see the resemblance, even Elinor can't, but I remarked on it the first day I met you. Your eyes are very like hers, and . . . when I saw you at the bus stop today, and you looked so sad, the resemblance was very strong, terribly strong, but it can't be. . . . I felt you should know that. It's not possible."

I can't remember what I said, or what excuse I used. I think I invented some forgotten appointment, some lame pretext that would not have fooled Jocelyn or anyone else for one second. She had the kindness and good sense not to argue. "Of course, of course," she said, rising to her feet. "But, please—won't you come and see Elinor and me this evening—or tomorrow? I'll explain to her what I've done, but I think we must talk—oh, I'm so sorry. Please forgive me. . . ."

She took my hand. There was an awkward moment of semi-embrace, and I saw she was close to tears. I broke away from her and blundered my way past the tables in the next room, conscious of the stares from the other customers. I hurried out into the rain and walked away fast, blind to the direction I was taking, hating myself for my own obstinate stupidity. I tried to tell myself there might be some mistake—but I knew there wasn't. I'd seen the certainty in Jocelyn's eyes. I'd never realized how passionately I'd believed Rebecca was my mother until the moment when I was forced to recognize she could not be.

Lanyon was invisible. I walked through the marketplace and on; I only noticed the Kerrith bus when it almost knocked me down. I boarded it, and sat with my face turned to the window. Against the dark skies beyond, the pale shifting outline of my other self moved on the glass. I have no memory of the return journey. Back at my cottage, I paused by the sea, watching the waves rush in, black with kelp, tossing ashore all the weed and detritus stirred up from the ocean bed by a storm far out in the Atlantic.

The salt in the air stung my skin and eyes. I turned back to the house, intent on putting a closed door between me and the rest of the world. The key snagged in the lock. As I opened the door, and the wind tugged at it, the telephone began ringing.

It was Simon Lang, in jubilant and loquacious form, fresh from his visit to Somerset House, and reporting back on the question of Isabel Devlin.

He had found her death certificate quite quickly, he said; the whole process had been fascinating. It was extraordinary—all those millions of details of births, marriages, and deaths, there for the retrieving. He'd felt ancestor inquiries coming on, he said; if he'd had time, he'd have started looking up his grandparents and his great-grandparents. . . .

"Get on with it, Simon, for God's sake."

"All right, all right. What's the matter with you? There's no need to bite my head off. I'm doing you a favor here, I might remind you. Now, Tom, have you a pen handy?"

I picked up a pen and a notebook, and scribbled.

Isabel Honor Devlin had died on February 6, 1915, at the age of forty-two; her death was recorded in the Registration District of Lambourn, Berkshire. She had died at a house called Greenways, in the village of Hampton Ferrars. The person identified as the "informant" of her death was Edith Danvers, housekeeper. Isabel's "rank or profession" was given as wife to Jack Sheridan Devlin, Gentleman—no mention of her having been an actress, I noted. But it was the cause of death, as certified by a Lambourn doctor, that was so arresting to me. Isabel Devlin had not died of a wasting disease such as tuberculosis. Now I could understand why Sir Frank McKendrick had described her final months in the coded terms he did. It was complications, specifically septicemia, following on childbirth that had killed her.

"And before you ask, the baby seems to have survived," Simon Lang continued. "I was getting quite caught up in it all by then. No death certificate for any infant with the surname 'Devlin' in that area in 1915 or 1916—I checked. So I got onto the Registrar's office in Lambourn. Still no luck. No deaths of *any* newborns there in a nine-month period either side of Isabel's death."

"Did you ask them to cross-check with 'Births'?"

"Of course I did. I have a good brain, if you recall. Perhaps not quite as good as some, dear, but perfectly serviceable. I had them check all births registered in Lambourn in the December, January, *and* February—and they must have been an infertile lot there, because there weren't that many. Not one Devlin. Hullo—this is odd, I thought to myself. The disappearing baby. So I persuaded them to check again. I was about to give up—and then, Tom, breakthrough! I think I found him."

"Him?"

"Male child. Date of birth given as February 1, 1915, in other words five days before Isabel died, which is about right, given the septicemia, I reckon. Registered as an illegitimate birth, father unknown, mother unknown, two days *after* Isabel's death, on February 8. Given the name 'Terence Gray' and registered by some official from the Lambourn and District Foundling Hospital. Someone dumped the baby, do you see? Which rather suggests that Isabel had been up to something, and the baby's father *wasn't* Jack Devlin, Gentleman, et cetera. I think it has to be Isabel's baby, though. It was the only birth in that district in the right period that isn't legitimately accounted for. I've requested copies of both certificates, and I'll send them on to you. Now—tell me I've done well."

I told him he had done well. I got rid of him, hung up, and stared at the dark sea beyond the window.

Now Rebecca's intervention in my life made sense; my resemblance to her, which no one had ever remarked on until today, made sense. I reached for Sir Frank McKendrick's book and read his comments again feverishly; I tried to remember everything Favell had told me. What did I know of Isabel Devlin? She was Rebecca's mother. She had married her husband in France, and been abandoned by him; she had become an actress; she had believed Desdemona might fight back when Othello murdered her. She had sung her "Willow Song" with a sweet voice, but did not know how to project to an audience. She had the "prettiest golden hair." To the sentimental Sir Frank, she was a "lass unparallel'd"—and she had died in a botched childbirth at the beginning of a vicious war, leaving a daughter to make a sad little shrine to her memory.

I found these scraps unbearable. They suggested much; they told me too little. I didn't want to be indoors for a second longer. I went out into the air and the rain and the crash of the surf on the shore, and began walking to the little church by Manderley. There I had met Isabel's daughter, and there the daughter who was my sister or half-sister was buried.

THE CHURCHYARD WAS DESERTED. I WALKED BETWEEN THE wet tombstones, and down to the river where I stood with May all those years ago; the water was in full spate, brown with mud, rushing for the ocean. I looked at the Carminowe graves again, the plain granite memorials to black-eyed, black-gowned Sarah Carminowe, and her poor son, Ben; but I could no longer see where the Carminowes fitted into Rebecca's tale. They were a sad coda to it, I told myself, ghosts at the story's periphery. The rain swirled and beat on the stones. I turned back to the church itself, pushing back the heavy oak door, and entering a place unchanged since my childhood—a place where twenty-five years was as nothing in the slow quiet passing of the centuries. The altar cloth was still blue and gold; the dead still lay under my feet. I felt they were expecting me.

I edged between the oak pews, and when I looked down at Gilles de Winter's pale, glittering effigy, I was a child again. All the protections I've built up fell away. I touched the cold little dog at his feet, then looked up at a pair of sea-colored eyes. I thought of all the things I could have said to Rebecca that day if I'd known who she was and I said them now in my mind, when it was twenty-five years too late for her to hear me.

She'd promised me that willpower worked, so I tried to will my sister back from the dead. I didn't care that she had once warned me against this very activity. I wanted her, and, wherever she was, in whatever dim and remote part of her underworld, I meant to have her back. This time she was not going to slip away from me, like some latter-day Eurydice. I said her name in my mind, and I felt something start to stir in the church. Its cold still air became charged. I could feel the crackle of its electricity. I could sense disquiet all around me, and I knew Rebecca was close; her shadow burned me. I rose to my feet and left the church. I looked around the deserted graveyard. The rain was blinding, but I felt she was just out of sight, just ahead of me. I set off on the narrow steep path that led to Manderley.

I was drenched, and there was one small part of my mind that knew these actions weren't sane—but I beat it down, and the farther I walked, and the harder the rain fell, the more that part of me was silenced. I leaned against the wind, and wiped the rain out of my eyes. I turned into the Manderley woods, fighting my way through wet undergrowth. I lingered by the dark rainswept shape of the ruined house; I stood above the cove; I looked at her boathouse and the threatening swell of the bay beyond it. I could smell gorse blossom and salt; there was not a ship to be seen, the sea was wide and empty. I took a step forward, felt the ground start to give way under my feet, and with a lurch of adrenaline, stepped back from the edge. I watched the waves roll in against the shore. The ache of my childhood began to loosen its grip. Gulls wheeled above the waves. I looked at the detritus of the tide line, the slick black mounds of kelp, and something—or someone—stilled my mind: I became calmer.

I turned back to the woods and the familiar cliff path that led toward Kerrith. I began the final slippery descent to my cove. The thin gray light was failing; on my right hand, low over the sea, a full pale moon was already rising. Then I halted, peering through the rain. A woman was standing in front of my cottage. She had her back toward me; she was tall and slender; I saw her unlatch the gate, and move toward the door. I knew instantly that it was Rebecca. I began running. It's a measure of how disturbed I still was, I suppose, that even when I saw the familiar car parked just beyond my house, its presence didn't register. I reached the gate, and fumbled with the latch. I moved toward the steps like a sleepwalker. The woman turned, and I saw that it was Ellie.

I startled her as much as she startled me. She gave an exclamation, swung around, and stared at me, at my drenched hair and my sodden clothes. "Oh, you frightened me," she said. "I couldn't hear your footsteps because of the wind. You're soaked—I didn't recognize you—may I come in? I can't stay . . ."

I fumbled with the lock on the door, fumbled with the matches and the lamp. Ellie stood stiffly in the doorway; she didn't look at me.

"Something's wrong," I said as the light flared up. "Ellie, what's happened—is your father all right?"

"I think so, I hope so—they still haven't finished their tests. They kept us hanging around all morning, and now they say . . . they say there's signs of arrhythmia, I think that's the word. So they're going to keep him in overnight. I came back to The Pines to get his things, pyjamas and things, then I'm going back to the hospital. They're letting me stay there. I insisted. I told them, I won't leave. I have to be there. They said that wasn't routine. If they use the word 'routine' once more, I'll . . . I don't know what I'll do. Shout. Throw something . . ."

She bent her head and made a small sound. Her voice had been almost as usual, and it took me a moment to realize that she was crying.

"Ellie, don't, don't . . ." I approached her, and when she didn't look up, I put my arms around her. "I'll come with you. Let me come with you—"

"No. I want to be alone with him." She pushed me away. "Call me tomorrow. We should be home by late morning. I'll talk to you then. And, meanwhile, I came here for a reason. I have something to give you. . . ." She reached in under the wet folds of her mackintosh, and drew out a brown envelope. It was identical in every respect to the one containing that first notebook of Rebecca's.

"This arrived for my father this morning, just as we were leaving. He didn't see it. I don't want him to know it's arrived. It's making him ill, all this—raking over the past, worrying and worrying about things he did or didn't do twenty years ago." She pushed back her wet scarf, then thrust the envelope at me. "Here, you have it. You'll want to read it as much as he does. Just don't tell him you have it. Don't mention it—not until he's stronger."

"Read it?" I said.

I think she heard the hope in my voice; her face contracted. "Yes. Read. It's a proper document this time," she said, her tone sharpening. "Right up your street. That's what you do, after all, isn't it? Read documents. Piece together the past. And then write books about it."

There was a silence. She had twisted away from me so I couldn't see her face. I said, "Ellie? You know? How long have you known?"

"Oh, for God's sake—do you think I'm an idiot? If you want to tell lies efficiently, don't mix them up with the truth. It's much better to lie from beginning to end, and be done with it. . . . At least, I think so." She half opened the door, and looked at the rain. It was sheeting down; it made a curtain of transparency. "Why tell the truth about which university you went to, which Cambridge college—you *know* my aunt Rose is a don there. You must have known how easy that information was to check."

"Maybe I thought no one would care enough to check," I said, turning away. "Why should they?"

"*I* cared. I wanted to know who you were. I like to know who my so-called friends are. When they're taking up hours and hours of my father's time, I'm especially keen to know. I waited for weeks. I kept thinking, He'll tell us in the end. He'll explain all this. I drove you to Lanyon that day—I thought you'd tell me then. When you didn't, when you got on that train and you never said a word, I called Rose. I asked her to make some checks. I described you; that helped. You're quite memorable, you know, quite distinctive. And it couldn't have been easier. The Provost of King's is a very old friend of Rose's. It took her precisely two telephone calls."

"Ah, I understand." I turned back to look at her. "One to her friend the Provost, and one to me in London. That was Rose, wasn't it? Making assurance doubly sure. I thought you said you hadn't given out that number."

"I lied. Why shouldn't I lie? You had. You made my father like you. You made him trust you. And all the time, you've been deceiving him and deceiving me. It's so underhanded—I don't understand it. Using a false name . . ."

"It isn't a false name. Not exactly." I hesitated. "Ellie, let me come with you now. Let me talk to you. I can explain. I want to explain—I nearly did when we spoke on the telephone yesterday."

"That's easy to say. Yesterday? How convenient. Well, I haven't time for explanations. I must go. I must get back to the hospital—and, besides, I know you'll be anxious to open that envelope."

"Don't go yet. I bought this for you yesterday." I turned back to my desk and picked up my book on Walsingham. I gave it to Ellie. She looked at it in silence, her head bent, her face hidden.

"You bought this for me? Yesterday? You're not lying?"

"I'm not lying, Ellie."

She lifted her head then, and I watched her face change. The beautiful candid eyes rested on mine; a drop of rain from her wet hair ran down her temple.

"Why yesterday? Why not before?"

"No particular reason. I suppose I'd had enough of lies and evasions. You don't have to read it. You're bound to be bored by it. It's very dry. Full of footnotes . . ."

"Oh, I'm not afraid of footnotes," she said.

We looked at each other. A sudden warmth came into her eyes, she began to smile, turned away, turned back, and then, in a quick, impulsive way, reached up and kissed me. "You taste of salt," she said, drawing back. "You've been walking by the sea. You're soaking wet, Mr. Gray, Mr. Galbraith—Tom—whatever I should call you."

I began to say something and reached for her hand, but she slipped from my grasp, and turned to the door. "This cottage is so cold—you'll freeze to death if you're not careful." She gave me a wry glance. "Take my advice: Put on some dry clothes. Light a fire—and *then* begin reading."

I stood on the steps and watched her run down the path. By the time she reached the gate, the rain made her insubstantial: It turned her back into a ghost. I watched her leave. I thought about that unexpected kiss, then resolved not to think about it. I went back into my cottage, picked up the envelope Ellie had given me, and examined it. The handwriting was identical to that on the first parcel the Colonel had been sent. This package had arrived exactly a week after the first, I realized. I could see Ellie had checked the contents; the envelope had been opened.

I drew out another black notebook, identical to the first. My hands were unsteady. I undid the leather ties; no photograph this time, but these pages had been written in. I looked at the black ink, at the distinctive sloping hand, with the strongly marked capitals. The pages smelled faintly of salt; there were marks on them, as if they had been stained with tears, or sea water.

I made myself close the notebook again, then I took Ellie's advice. The cottage was damp and icy cold, and it felt colder without Ellie's presence. I changed into dry clothes and lit a fire. I drew the curtains on the rain and the wind, turned up the lamp, and sat down at my desk. The flames of the fire flickered; they crackled and flared green as they burned up the salts in the driftwood. Who had sent this, and why? Which of the many possible Rebeccas would I find in these pages?

I thought of the story the Colonel had told me, of his encounter with Rebecca in that boathouse of hers, shortly before her death. Was this the notebook in which she had been writing then? Was this the account of her life that she had told him she'd begun writing for her children? If that memory of the Colonel's was accurate, I realized, then I had the answer to the question Jocelyn Briggs had raised that morning: Rebecca could *not* have known she was infertile.

I thought of the boathouse as he'd described it to me, with its red rug, its bright driftwood fire, its little carved boats, its atmosphere of childlike refuge and seclusion. I thought of the way in which Rebecca had intervened in my life, altering it forever: I've never doubted what would have become of me, had she not rescued me from the ignorance and anguish of my childhood.

I could hear the sound of the sea rattling on the shingle. With a troubled mind, I opened the black cover and began reading.

3

Rebecca

APRIL 1931

TWENTY-ONE

Such a cold, fierce, glittering day—a magnificent sea, green as glass bottles, surf grinding shells to powder on the beach, a high blue bare sky. Such exhilaration. I thought of you today, I thought of you all day, my darling.

Max was away—the cat was away—so I was free, and early this morning I escaped from them all. Breakfast in the mausoleum first, mirrored eggs, and kidneys seeping blood in silver dishes, Frith creaking his way in and out—I can't keep food down in the mornings. Just a little coffee and dry toast, then I went to the usual room, sat at my usual desk, and arranged my life: lists, letters, menus, appointments. I'm efficient, dearest—my future's an alphabet, I file it in pigeonholes. By ten, Jasper and I were walking in the woods; the first azaleas were coming out; we had only the gulls for company.

We came down to the shore. I threw sticks for Jasper; he chased them into the waves, then came back and shook himself, and out from of his fur flew richness—a spray of diamonds as big as hailstones, bright as the ones on my wedding finger. I'll bring you here one day, my love: I'll show you the secrets of this bay, the rock with the blue-mauve mussels, like mermaids' fingernails; the place where I gather my driftwood; the ledge where the white fulmar lays its one white egg every April, and the pools that are deep enough to drown in.

I looked in the pools today, and saw your reflection. The seaweed was your hair, your tight-shut eyes were cockleshells; your hand, opening, closing, was a starfish. The tide rocked you, the sea sang to you, your bones grew as strong as coral; you were as quick as a fish, as perfect as the ripples in the sand. *Move*, my dearest. Hurry up and be born. I want to hold you in my arms, and show you Manderley. All this will be yours, one day.

I'VE NEVER KNOWN SUCH A PLACE FOR GHOSTS AS THIS. Could you sense them today? I could. I think ghosts have an affinity for the sea; maybe it's the sound it makes, the sighings and washings and whisperings, the tides of departures and returnings. Today, my mother was here, dancing in bare feet at the edge of the water, tossing back her hair, which truly was gold, a deep dark gold, rippling down to her waist when she unpinned it. And my father was here, too. He was out there by the rocks, watching and brooding, so tall and dark in his black clothes, with his eyes shadowed. They're both in my blood, the fair and the dark—and they're in yours, too, my dear one.

We can be our own ghosts, too, we can haunt ourselves—did you know that? So some of the other Rebeccas were here, too. The imperious one never comes down to the shore—she stays up there, wrapped in her silks and her furs. She was born one day at a house called St. Agnes, and I've nourished her ever since. I can call her up when I need her. But sometimes she springs up of her own free will—and then she alarms me. You have to be careful with her, and you wouldn't want to cross her, for all her charms. She's got knives in her eyes, fire at her fingertips, serpentine ways, and an unquenchable thirst for blood—Madame Medea, I call her.

She was up there today, dreaming revenge I expect, revenge being meat and drink to her. And that girl was with her, the girl who used to be me, the girl who looked at Manderley and knew she'd come home at last.

I looked at that drab girl, and I remembered how it was that time I first came here: I ran out of the house in search of the sea. It was a glaring bright day; the sea was lucid and implacable. I thought, *This place is mine by right. Whatever it takes—I shall have it.* I was so small then, it was before I taught myself to grow; I was small and thin, and I bit my nails; I was thirteen, nearly fourteen, but I looked about ten—not attractive! My mother was somewhere else, and she was dying—getting ready to die—though no one had told me. My father was just a name then—he hadn't sailed into my life yet—so I was all alone, neither pretty nor clever nor powerful, just a drab child with a headful of plays, standing up there by the path on a hot autumn day, wanting something so hard it hurt my heart and took my breath away.

Then Max came up the path from this cove. I'd heard of him, but it was the first time I'd seen him. He was off to the trenches, off to fight in the war; he was leaving that day and he was wearing his uniform. His father was dying in the tower room back there; the house was at sixes and sevens, the maids scurrying about, Max's grandmother firing orders and questions in all directions. "There'll be a shortage of men," she said. "How am I supposed to run a house without menservants?" The sun glinted on Max's buttons and buckles; his boots shone like chestnuts. A revolver in a holster. Brown eyes and a handsome face. The son and heir. The sun and air. I looked at him, and I thought, Aha!

My love, I have so much to tell you.

THOSE GHOSTS ANGERED ME A LITTLE, ESPECIALLY THAT girl, because I know what became of her. Also, in truth, I'd begun to feel desperately tired and sick—I do sometimes now. It takes great energy to grow a baby—all those nerves and sinews and bones rooting inside me. So I came in here to my sea house, and I've been lying here, watching the light fade, willing you to stretch, or flex your starfish fingers or kick; I wish you would. It's four months, and you're so still it makes me anxious.

I tried to eat a little because I can see I'm too thin, and that can't be good for you. I must feed you! I managed not to be sick; I kept down some tea, and a dry biscuit, and I felt better then. I lit the fire, and now the driftwood is burning brightly; the salt makes the flames spurt blue and green and sulphur yellow. It's high tide, and the spray from the sea is licking against the west window. I've drawn the curtains and lit the lamp, and it's cozy and warm here for you. There's a red rag rug on the floor, and some boats I've made for you; my guardian, Jasper, is asleep by the fire. The walls are four feet thick.

We could be in the eye of a storm here, and survive safely. I feel better now, alone and content. Everything I can possibly need is inside this room—or inside me, my darling one.

I shall go and see a doctor in London in a few days. I should have gone before, but I was superstitious. I kept telling myself it was too good to be true; if I arranged to see a doctor, I'd start bleeding again. So I waited out the months, and now I don't need any doctor to confirm your existence, I can sense you under my heart—but I want to be sure you grow well and strongly. This afternoon a strange blue melancholia came seeping up from the sea; it crept into my bones, and I kept thinking of my own mother, who died giving birth to that little half-brother of mine. I met him once in the church here—a nervous boy, eyes the twin of mine, and a way of holding his head and tilting his chin that was exactly my mother's. She never knew her baby, and he never knew her. I felt suddenly cold. Suppose that happened to us?

I'm strong and healthy—I've never known what it was to feel ill until these last few months—but even so, mothers aren't immortal. The gods—and sometimes the husbands—can be jealous of their joy, so they snuff them out on a whim. They silence us. No point in lying—it happens all the time, my dearest.

I don't want you to grow up without me to protect you. I won't let you be told lies about me by people who neither loved nor understood me. I want you to know who I am; I want you to know where to find me. I promise you this: I'm as tenacious as Old Hamlet's ghost, with his whispers of revenge. If you should ever need me, you'll find me at Manderley, and I'll ignore cock crows—I shan't be confined to the hours between midnight and dawn, I assure you!

I swear: Walk by the sea and you'll feel me. Stand at the windows and you'll see me. Listen in the corridors, at the turn of the stairs, and it's my heartbeat you'll hear. My blood and bones put the beauty back in that house. I made it for my mother, for me, and for you. Whenever you're there, I'll be close. Meanwhile, just in case those jealous gods do get up to their tricks, this is who I am, my love: This is your inheritance, and this is our story.

I WAS BORN IN A HOUSE BY THE SEA, NOT A GREAT PALACE of a place like Manderley, but a gray foursquare house set down by a rocky shore so close to the sea that you could hear it singing all day and all night, a Lorelei's lullaby.

The first thing I remember is lamplight in a square room, and my mother Isolda holding me, rocking me back and forth, while the sea sang to me. The second thing I remember is escaping from my mother, and crawling across the sand toward the water—it was alive, and I wanted to be inside it. I reached out to a green glassy wave, and just as it broke over my head, my mother caught me by the heels and pulled me clear of it.

She taught me the words *la mer* and *ma mère*, and to my ears they sounded identical. So for a long time I believed I had *two* mothers, Maman and the sea. Both mothers were beautiful and powerful and both would always watch over me. Do I still believe this? Maybe.

Our house was in Brittany. It was near the church and half a mile from the crumbling chateau where my mother's third cousins lived. The village was called St. Croigne Dulac; it was a tiny fishing village, but there were many romantic tales about it, and some people said it was the village where Sir Lancelot's father had had his palace— Lancelot's father, you know, was a king in Brittany. Maman used to say we were in a *far countrey*—but Brittany isn't remote, or not from here, anyway. When my boat, *Je Reviens*, was brought here from St. Croigne, it was only two days' sail. Stand and look southwest from the cliffs by Manderley, and you can see my birthplace. You have to look the other side of the horizon, but that's easy enough, I have the technique—I'll teach you, one day.

We lived there in seclusion, my mother and I, until I was seven years old. I loved our house and St. Croigne with a passion—that place lodged in my heart, and I dream of it constantly. When I do, it's always summer, and the dawn light wakes me, and I feel nothing but joy and expectation at the long day ahead of me. I'm free to do whatever I like. My mother preferred to rest and dream her days away; she'd write letters or read books; sometimes she would give me lessons—she taught me to read, we read poems together—and sometimes she would play the piano—we had a piano that Maman had shipped over from England. It was too big for our salon, and it suffered from the damp sea air and once it made her cry, because it needed tuning, and there was no one for miles around who knew how to cure it.

All summer long, I went without shoes. I'd have a bowl of café au lait and bread in the kitchen with my friend Marie-Hélène, who cooked for us, and then I'd run out of the house and straight onto the shore. I could swim like a fish; I could catch shrimp in the rock pools; I could play with the village children. On Sundays I went to Mass; I knew the Stations of the Cross, and Maman gave me a rosary made of coral, but I didn't believe in God any more than Maman did, and, once, when I went to visit the priest, an old man who was a good friend of mine, he laughed when I said I wanted to make my first communion so I could have a bride's veil and a frilly white dress, as the older girls did. He shook his head and smiled and said I was *une vraie petite païenne*—a true little pagan.

I used to watch the fishermen bring in their catch, great baskets of violet mackerel, huge crabs with watchful black eyes, and mysterious sea-blue lobsters with trembling antennas. Marie-Hélène taught me how to scale a fish and gut it—we fed the guts to the gulls, great long loops of fishy intestines. She taught me how to plunge the lobsters into a vat of boiling water; we bearded mussels; we cooked cockles and razor clams, which you prepare just by pouring the boiling water over them; you kill them by scalding them—and I learned that food was a pleasure and an art, but it necessitated death and it was violent. Some of the recipes Marie-Hélène taught me we still use at Manderley, and Max's English friends say, Oh, Rebecca, how delicious, how original, where did you find such a brilliant cook? And I smile and say, Oh, Mrs. Danvers oversees all that, she supervises the kitchens—which she does, but it was I who taught her, years ago, when we were living at a place I'll tell you about, called Greenways. And sometimes, if I want to tease Max—because he's always afraid I'll confess my past, and it amuses me to keep him on tenterhooks—I say, Oh, I have friends in France, or cousins in France, and it's one of their family recipes. . . .

We did have those cousins of Maman's after all, and once a week we paid them a duty visit. They owned the house we lived in, and Maman used to say, with a toss of her gold hair and a wicked blue glint in her eyes, that we must never forget we were beholden to them. They had taken her in when she left England, and it was thanks to them we had a roof over our heads: "Best behavior now, Becka," she would say. "No fidgeting when Luc-Gerard starts on his stories."

What a bore cousin Luc was! I suppose he wasn't that old—forty-five, maybe—but to me he was ancient and desiccated, living in that decaying house with five dogs and his mother, the Countess, who always wore black, and was deeply religious. Six courses for lunch, old Sèvres plates, and, whenever a roast chicken was served, they brought in its poor brain, white, the size of a pea, on a special saucer because that was a special delicacy, reserved for the master of the household; cousin Luc would swallow the cerebellum down and smack his lips and start on those tedious stories, while his mother patronized mine and dispensed her charity like very thin soup, and explained to Maman for the millionth time how sad and difficult Maman's situation was, and how she had discussed it with the priest and how she prayed constantly for Maman's deliverance and welfare.

What a hypocrite she was. We only had one problem that I could see, and that was lack of money. And that *delighted* the old Countess. Our being hard up kept her going all week; half her pep and verve came from thinking up new ways in which her "*chère* Isolde" could practice little economies. "No more silk dresses for me," Maman would say when we left. "What an old beast she is. No more dresses, no more ribbons, no more books, and I'd better stop curling my hair, don't you think, Becka? I'm going to have to be as plain and dull and sour as she is, if I ever want to get to heaven."

But she wasn't always so defiant. Sometimes, when the check from England didn't arrive (and I never understood who sent those checks; Maman said it was her eldest sister, Evangeline, but I wasn't always sure I believed her), there would be a crisis. Maman would come into the kitchen and sigh. She'd tell Marie-Hélène there must be cutbacks: "Perhaps if we didn't always have a soup," she would say in a vague way, in her halting French. "Or fruit. Must we always have fruit, Marie-Hélène? I'm sure it's very expensive."

Marie-Hélène would raise her eyes to the heavens—and ignore her, of course. If Maman had but known it, the fruit was a gift from Marie-Hélène's father, and not to have a soup course would have been a grave affront to Marie-Hélène's ideas of proper household economy. So the soup would continue to be served, and the melons would arrive, and the cream and the black cherries and the brown farm eggs and the barnacled lobsters that sang as they died in their vat . . . and the color would mount in Maman's cheeks, and she would make a face, and forget about the cutbacks until the next check arrived and saved us.

The next check—or the next present, for we received presents, too, and quite regularly. Someone knew that Maman loved pretty things, that she had a fatal weakness for what she called "frivolities." That someone knew Maman's taste very well. A tiny pair of gloves of mauve suede would arrive, or silk ribbons embroidered with roses; once a pair of gray kid boots with pearl buttons was sent—so pretty and charming, and fitting Maman exactly.

They sent a paisley shawl, and an embroidered petticoat; they sent a handkerchief, such a tiny exquisite scrap of a thing, almost all lace, with the word "Isolda" stitched in white across its corner. They sent silk flowers to trim a hat; they sent a cunning gold locket with a secret fastening, and a lock of hair craftily coiled and plaited inside it—and they sent letters, too, with an English stamp, which Maman kept locked away in her little traveling desk, and which she sighed over sometimes. Once, just once, they sent a photograph of a great gaunt gray beautiful house, and Maman showed me that, and said it was called Manderley. I loved that house from the first second I saw it. All those secretive windows; it was my palace of dreams. I made up stories about it and filled it with heroines. The photograph made my mother sad; she would take it out and look at it. Her other sister, Virginia, had once been the mistress of that house—but poor Virginia was dead now. "We're exiles, Becka, you and me," Maman would say. "I've been banished, darling. That's the plain truth of it."

I took no notice. I knew the mood would pass—and if we were exiles, so what? We'd been exiled to heaven, in my opinion. A female heaven, too, with no tedious self-important men like cousin Luc to interfere. Just myself, and my beautiful mother, and Marie-Hélène, and Marie-Hélène's cousin and daughter, who came to clean, and to wash and scrub and iron, who hung the sheets on the line to bleach in the sun, and who stared, awestruck, at the lace and embroidery and the monogram "I.D." stitched on Maman's nightdresses and underwear.

We women worshipped the House—I learned that very early. The house was a home, certainly, but it was also a temple. How I loved all its rituals! They were strictly observed: Marie-Hélène was a *religieuse* in this respect; she had the highest standards, and she'd tolerate no deviations. Certain days were sacrosanct: Thursday for the market; Friday for the fish; Monday for the washing; Sunday for the Mass. Incense and butter churns, hymns and quilting, psalms and pastry making. Down on our knees: Whether we were scrubbing or praying, it was holy. *Nous sommes dévotes*, Marie-Hélène would say, polishing and panting, proud of our industry: *Tu comprends, ma petite, il faut le faire pieusement.* . . .

I can see and hear it still, I can tell it like the beads of a rosary. The irons set to warm on the range for the ruchings on Maman's blouses, the blue bags of starch, the crack of sheets in the wind, the scouring of the kitchen table, the wax melted down with turpentine to polish the furniture, the windows rubbed with scrim until they glinted, the necessity for airing the feather mattresses, the huge square pillows, and the counterpanes. The wood that needed to be stacked and stored; the floors that needed to be scrubbed; the sin in a speck of dust—this was Marie-Hélène's religion and I learned it at her knee. Even now, my darling, it rules me.

I never saw that there was a missing element, a prop that should have been there, but wasn't; not until I was nearly seven, and at the beach one day, one of the older village boys, a tall thin boy who used to follow me and stare, a boy who didn't know that Maman was *la veuve jeune et tragique*, threw a stone at me, and jeered and said, *Where's your father, little girl, where's your father?*

I told him my father was dead. I told him what Maman had told me, that my father's ship went down on the way to South Africa. I said my father was lying on the seabed by the Cape, being washed by the green-glass waves of the Atlantic. His eyes were pearl and his bones were coral, I told him, for Maman read me Shakespeare, even then, before I ever acted, before we turned into gypsies and joined Sir Frank McKendrick's company.

How the boy laughed at that. He pulled my hair and kissed me on the mouth, and tore my dress. He said I was wicked and proud and my eyes tormented him; he said I'd go to hell where there was a special pit they kept for bastards. I bit his hand so the blood flowed. He hit me then, right across the face, so hard I saw stars. I fell down on the sand. He lay on top of me on my black dress; he put a hand on my neck so I couldn't breathe, then he fumbled and wriggled.

When it was over, he wept, and told me I was sinful, and begged my forgiveness. It was the first time I learned what fools men are, so tempted and so abject. I hated that boy, with his stares and his sighs and his hand on my neck, trying to subdue me. If I'd been strong enough, I'd have struck him down there and then—but he was twice my age and twice my size, so I scratched his face and I cursed him. Another Rebecca sprang to life in me. I told him he was damned for sure, and my dead father would rise up one of these days from the seabed and claim him.

He slunk away, and avoided me after that, and three months later he drowned in his father's fishing boat. He fell overboard in a storm, and died entangled in a fishing net. I gave thanks to my dead Devlin father, who gave me my black hair my mother said, and who'd been so quick to avenge me. But there was talk in the village, I think, trouble at any rate; they were very superstitious, and some people told Marie-Hélène I had the evil eye. Cousin Luc raved and reproached, the Countess despaired of us, and Maman grew sad and preoccupied.

Not long after that, we came back to England. It might have been because of the boy and the gossip; it might have been because the checks and the pretty presents had stopped arriving. There was a crisis, certainly—and Maman wouldn't explain. She was proud, and she hated to be questioned. "What do we care, Becka?" she said to me, hugging me hard, two bright flags of color in her cheeks. "We'll manage. I still have friends. I won't be hidden away any longer, it's insulting. We'll go back and I'll show you England—you'll see, we'll conquer, my darling!"

I told Max this story once—or some of it. Max had predictable ideas about weddings, but I meant to be married in *my* place, so I made him come back with me to St. Croigne Dulac. I thought, we'll be married in the small gray church by the sea. The old priest who called me a little pagan will marry us. Marie-Hélène can cook the wedding feast; tedious cousin Luc can propose a toast— and it's one in the eye for that harridan of a mother of his, the Countess.

These scenes were so clear in my mind, but I hadn't learned how to plan then. Two seconds in the place—what a fool I'd been—it all started unraveling. The priest was dead; the Countess was dead;

Marie-Hélène was widowed and had moved away; cousin Luc was a mad ranting recluse; and officialdom made all these stupid difficulties—I wasn't a proper Catholic, Max was a dreary Protestant, the church was out of the question, it was the *mairie* or nothing.

I was angry, of course—but I didn't really care. All ceremonies are meaningless. I'd have had a voodoo wedding, and it wouldn't have worried me one scrap, but Max—ah, Max was very different. He dared a little, but not enough—and at St. Croigne Dulac he began doubting.

I took him to the village; I introduced him to the fishermen, and to Marie-Hélène's family. I think they'd forgotten about the evil eye, for they opened their hearts to us—and what did Max do? He flinched, he drew back; he was feline and finicky and fastidious. Max can speak German; I speak French: There's the difference between us in a nutshell, my dearest. A terrible Aryan Englishness settled upon him like a cloak, and all those gentlemen ancestors of his rose up to reprimand him. What was he doing here, was he being rash, was he making a mistake he'd come to regret—was there time to get out of it?

Max loves wildness, you see; it tempts him—but if it comes too close, it terrifies him. Back to the cricket scores, then, and tea at 4:30, rules and regulations, worship at the altar of convention—I've no patience with it, it suffocates me. But there was a risk here, and I could see that. We made the arrangements at the *mairie*, but Max did so reluctantly. *Darling, what will people think?* he said. *Darling, why don't we go back to England? We could have the wedding at Manderley. No one need find that odd, your parents are dead, after all. My grandmother will arrange everything. Wouldn't you prefer a church, and a beautiful dress? Darling, don't be rash, think a little—you know my position, you know what's expected of me.* Such concern in his eyes! I suddenly saw the truth: Any delay and he might panic, walk away from the whole thing, and jilt me; he might desert me, the way my mother did, my father did. Well, I couldn't have that; he'd sworn he loved me—and I know he did. I loved Manderley with all my heart, so I had to act quickly.

I took Max down to the beach one dusky afternoon; it was the day before our appointment at the *mairie*, and Max was still objecting. I decided I'd show him who I was, I was quite desperate to show him who I was—wedding nerves, maybe. So I showed him my world, that dangerous sea, the looking-glass pools, the bone-white sand, my avenging father, my golden-haired mother who danced by the waves, the mauve gloves, the locket, the Religion of the House, and the piano that wouldn't play a Mozart sonata because its strings needed tuning.

I think he understood. I think he did. He said I was his dearest love—I'm sure he said that. He looked at me with those sad dark eyes of his; he forgot the February cold; he called me his Lady from the Sea, and when the sea mist drifted in, he caught me close, stroked the sealskin fur I was wrapped in, and kissed me. We'd go to the *mairie* tomorrow just as I wanted, he said. We were already man and wife in every important sense, and he understood now why I wanted to be married here, why it mattered to me. *Whatever you ask of me, I will do*, he said. *That is true now, darling, and it always will be until the day I die. Take my hand—Rebecca, I swear it to you.*

I took his hand, the waves washed the shore, and then—oh, what a mistake!—up came the memory. I told him about that boy. I explained how he jeered, and the wicked things he said; I told Max how I bit his hand; I showed him the place where I saw stars and the boy knocked me down; I told him about the stains on my skirt and the fish-stink smell and how the boy prayed, panted, and wriggled.

I tried to make him understand—but he didn't. His expression began to change. First I saw doubts, then that hideous fastidious distaste, and then—right at the very back of his eyes—a reluctant excitement, slowly deepening. You know what? His expression was the very *same* as that boy's—it was identical! That shocked me to the heart—and I will never, ever, forgive him.

He rallied, of course. He drew on those gentlemanly reserves of his, and he came riding to my rescue years too late, when I didn't need rescuing anyway. All the wormy conventions of his class came wriggling to the surface. He said it was a terrible thing to happen to a child; it was disgusting, repellent, and he so admired me for having the courage to tell him. I despised him for such banalities. I think he thought I was ashamed—which was quite wrong. Why should I be ashamed? But I let that pass. He put his arms around me, and said I'd always be safe from now on, because he'd be there to protect me. Well, that was wrong, too—I'm a thousand times tougher than Max is, and I can protect myself perfectly well. Watch out if you cross me; that boy died, didn't he?

I told him that—but he didn't believe me, of course. He kissed my eyes, then my mouth; if it hadn't been so cold, I think he'd have lain down there on the sand with me. He took me back to our little hotel instead, and came into my room, and pushed me back on the bed; he was trembling. Again and again: I could see that boy haunting him. He was desperate to exorcise him—but he also wanted, very strange this, to *be* him.

Such pleasure; we were drunk with it. All Max's courage returned; we rolled out of damp sheets, and pulled on our clothes, and went to the *mairie* with two witnesses off the street; we were married by ten in the morning. My underclothes were soaked with the seepings of our lovemaking; the white hothouse roses in my bouquet had sharp thorns and they cut my hand; Max licked off the blood, then we drank red wine at the hotel, and went back to bed and the sea pounded all night, and Max wasn't so fastidious then—not by any means. *No one need ever know*, Max said, exultant, the next morning. *If they ask about the wedding, we'll lie. It will be our secret, my darling.*

Yes, it will, I replied. I was exultant, too. I wrapped the damp sheet around me, and tossed back my hair. I said, *This is my wedding dress. It had a twenty-foot train. We had six bridesmaids, and two pageboys. The choir sang like angels. The reception at the chateau was held by candlelight. When we cut our white cake, the knife glinted. My cousin proposed the toast, and Max made an elegant speech, in perfect French. He said—*

I stopped. Max had become very still; he was watching me intently. *You said the wedding would be our secret—you said we should lie*, I began, and leaned forward to kiss him. I was wearing two rings, my new wedding band and my eternity diamonds—that may have angered him. Max turned aside. *I know—but I hadn't realized just how well you can lie*, he replied and he gave me a strange pale look. *None of that happened, yet you make me see it.*

Trouble: I could smell it at once. I suppose I knew that questions were inevitable now the doubts had been sown. Had I told him the whole truth? Had I told him *everything*? Who else, apart from the boy at the beach? When, where, and how often . . . ? Believe me, dearest, such questions are a terrible error in a marriage or a love affair. It's a bad idea to ask them—and it's a very bad idea indeed to answer them, let alone truthfully. Intense jealousy is not a sane state of mind; after the questions come the accusations—and, in Max's case, I didn't have to wait very long, just three days and a long journey into our honeymoon. An interrogation on a cliff top somewhere near Monte Carlo, a wedding-cake white hotel, a suicidal *grand corniche*, questions that had been brewing, fermenting—and, three hundred feet down, a sea even this rich coast couldn't tame, churning.

Truth and lies are twins. Death and desire live back to back—I've always known that, but for Max the discovery was agony. I looked at his white face, I measured the anguish in his eyes, and I knew that there'd be no way back from this edge. *Push me over*, I thought—and he was tempted, my darling.

What a mystery men's minds are. How does their logic work? Why do they invert everything? Why do they start off with some crazed impossible idea, and then rail because the world—or, in my case, the woman—fails to fit it?

I'm sure I was circumspect in the answers I gave Max. I told him about some of the lovers—I was twenty-five, after all, and my sins in that respect didn't seem too heinous. Max wasn't a virgin, so why should I be? But I didn't explain who Maman was. I always called her "Isabel"; I gave her her death-certificate name. I was very careful indeed on the father question (no point in overturning the boat, and, although there are question marks, I think black-haired Devlin certainly was my father, anyway). I censored my stories of Greenways and cousin Jack severely. I was angry, of course, so a few revelations may have slipped past my guard—but nothing important, I'm almost certain. In any case, I might just as well not have bothered, I can see that now. I made my mistake earlier, when I told him about that boy on the beach. *That* was the coup de grâce, definitely. I think our fight to the death began then, my dearest.

Max has never been able to forget that boy, and time has translated him. He's not an enemy or an animal anymore, he's my husband's closest companion, he's his double. When Max speaks of him now—and that boy's still thrown in my face whenever we quarrel—he says he pities him.

Max says it wasn't the boy's fault, it was mine. He says I have bad blood and bad ways, and I led the boy on, I must have done.

I don't deny it now, where's the point? Let Max think what he likes. His accusations make me incandescent. One flick of *that* switch and the high voltage sizzles. But I won't stoop to argue with him. I'd never change his mind anyway, it's made up; as far as my husband's concerned, that poor dead boy is a fellow sufferer. It was my wicked toils he was caught up in, not a fishing net. Even as a child, you see, I was wicked and oversexed and unnatural. The English gentleman agrees with those French peasants: I *do* have the evil eye—and God help any man who comes my way because, in the gospel according to Max, I'm a destroyer. I'm his very own Delilah, and (it goes without saying) his Jezebel.

That boy was the first of my victims, Max says, and my dear husband intends to be the last. Or so I think sometimes, when I see an Othello glint in his eye—and I've been seeing *that* more and more, recently.

A week ago, I caught him oiling his service revolver. Put the mad bitch down, and he'd be doing everyone a favor. I *think* that's what he thinks. He'd like to *silence* me—but if he believes a bullet would achieve that, he's much mistaken.

Whatever Max does, he'll *never* silence me. I'll talk on and on in his head and his heart and his guts, forever and ever. Anyway, he can't kill me now, however much he might yearn to. I'm pregnant.

Pregnant women escape the hangman, no matter how serious their crime, did you know that? They are spared—and Max will spare me. He needs an heir, after all, he's desperate for an heir. So desperate in so many different ways that just occasionally he's tempted out of that monk's bed in his dressing room. He brushes my long black hair; we cling to each other; we think how different it might have been and how different it once was. I do not always hate him and he does not always hate me; we watch that recognition spark in each other's eyes, and when that fire catches, what dry kindling we are, how we burn then, hotter than any furnace, or—

The last time that happened was a year ago. Now my hair is cropped. I have nun's hair now. I lose track of time, sometimes. I think it's because I feel so weary. Or it's that blue melancholy that comes in on the tide, maybe.

I wonder: If I gave Max his heir, if—by hook or by crook—I gave him his heir, what would happen then? Would the knot of our past undo itself?

Probably not. Probably not. Oh, my love, how tired I feel. I'm dizzy and sick with fatigue. I don't want to be silenced, I won't be silenced. I want to talk, and I want the dead to talk through me, but it takes so much willpower.

Maybe I'll sleep for a while, then go on. It's raining. Wait—did I hear something?

I'll have to pause. I'll continue with my story in a while, my sweet. I'll tell you how I learned to act, how I came to be at Manderley, and how I first met Max, the son and heir, in his army uniform.

But just for now, I'm going to close up my little black notebook and hide it away. I'm being spied on again. Someone's coming. Jasper's growling, and I can hear footsteps on the shingle.

Twenty-two

My visitor has left. When I heard the footsteps, I thought it might be husband Max, returning early and hoping to catch me unawares—he's convinced that one of these days his prayers will come true, and he'll catch me in flagrante. Then I thought it might be mad Ben Carminowe, who haunts this beach; Max says he's looking for his little sister, who drowned in one of the rock pools here. Whatever the reason, he will not be driven away, and he stares through the windows at me. I told him, if he spies on me again, I'll have him put in an asylum. He reminds me of the Breton boy on that Breton beach, and I hate him.

It was neither of these: It was Arthur Julyan, my dear Colonel, who comes to my fancy-dress balls as Cromwell, my Lord Protector. He was fighting his conscience on a long coastal walk, and calling in, he said, because he'd seen the light in the window. He is my one true friend in this place—and I was as careful with him as I always am. Today I knew: One tiny gesture, one remark, and he might tip over the edge and confess what he feels for me. I like him too much to risk that—we would both regret a confession of that sort—so I was scrupulous. Despite that bad blood of mine, I have never encouraged him—not one jot, please note! I remain fond of him; he is honorable, lonely, antique, and astute. I regret the pain his feelings cause him.

I suspect that, apart from Max's grandmother, he is the only person in this neighborhood who knows who I am. No one else has made any connection between a thin drab child who visited the area once in 1914 and Max's wife. I've reinvented and transformed myself, so why should they? But I'm almost sure Arthur Julyan recognized me. As a girl, I was introduced to him briefly; over a decade later we remet. He'd just returned from Singapore; I was a bride, three months married. I came running in from the gardens and found him waiting to pay his respects in the shadows of the drawing room at Manderley. I was wearing a white dress and the little blue butterfly brooch Maman gave me. We shook hands. I saw him look at that brooch, and I'm sure, almost sure, that he knew me. If he didn't recognize me, he recognised my talisman.

If so, he has said nothing, to me or to anyone else—and I admire that. I've kept so many secrets to myself for so long, and I've learned that unshakable discretion is the rarest of gifts. One of these days, I'll thank Arthur Julyan for it.

He didn't stay long today, and he didn't miss much. Once he'd gone, I slept for a while, and now I feel stronger. I've locked the door on the wind and the rain, and I'll continue. Here's the rest of your inheritance, my darling.

FOR THE FIRST SEVEN YEARS OF MY LIFE, AS I'VE TOLD you, I never moved from the same place; for the next seven, I never stopped traveling. Those were the years I learned to act—and very useful *those* lessons have been. Up and down the spine of England we went, prop baskets and trains, nine performances a week, then pack up, wave good-bye, and on to the next city on Sundays. "We're no better than gypsies, Becka," Maman would say, and she laughed off her sister Evangeline's shock and disapproval. "I will *not* live on charity," she said. "We need to eat. I told Evangeline, it's *Shakespeare*. I'm not strutting about in some music hall."

Can you imagine, darling, living with those words, those plays, six nights a week, and three matinees—a crash course in murder, adultery, and usurpation, in doubles and doomed love, in witchcraft, white magic, and weddings? We were never in Halifax or Hull; our travels took us way beyond those boundaries. Illyria on Monday;

Tuesday, a wood near Athens; Wednesday, a battlefield; Thursday, a blasted heath; Friday, deaths in Venice; and, on Saturday, my best-beloved place, Caliban's enchanted island, the domain of his mother Sycorax—what an education that was, better than any school or governess, my dearest!

Some nights I'd be on stage myself, because the leader of our company, Sir Frank McKendrick, roped me in to play boys' parts from the beginning. Other nights I'd crouch in the prompt corner, listening to those winged words, learning those winged words. I know tracts of them by heart, yet; they still light up my mind. I hear the meanings behind the meanings under the meanings—what an echo chamber! Max always wants words to be shackled, so "love" means this and "hate" means that. Lock them up in a poor prison of sense and slam the door on them. I don't agree. Words should take you on journeys—and the journey that taught me that began and ended in the same place: Plymouth, in a street called Marine Parade, in a house called St. Agnes.

When we arrived in England for the very first time, Maman's courage faltered. She had been so full of plans and excitement on the journey. "Farewell to my youth," she said when we locked up our foursquare gray house. She looked at the rocky shore, her eyes blazing defiance; but once we'd left St. Malo, something went wrong. Problems, from the instant we crossed the Channel. No one was there to meet us off the boat; we went to the Portsmouth hotel Maman had written to, just as planned, but the letters she'd been expecting weren't there waiting for us.

I'm still not sure who it was she hoped would come to claim us. It might have been her sister, or that admirer who had been so remiss, lately, with the checks and the pretty presents. Whoever it was, we were left in the lurch, and Maman tried to make light of it. "We're like an unclaimed parcel, Becka," she said, looking around the grim little room they'd given us. "But we shan't be downhearted. I shall tell them, we need a fire, and I want supper sent up, and maybe a little wine. It will be cozy in no time, you'll see, darling."

Maman had great charm and style and determination—just as well, in view of what lay in store over the next seven years—so the fire was lit, and the food arrived, and Maman drank two glasses of red wine to give her strength and I drank one glass of wine and water. Then we emptied our purses and counted up our worldly goods—total: seven days, if we economized. "A whole week, Becka—why, we're rich, darling," Maman cried. She put me to bed, but I couldn't sleep. Maman stayed up half the night, pacing the room and fetching out her little traveling desk, reading, and writing letters. We took them to the post in the morning, and waited to be rescued.

It took five days for that rescue to be effected—and when it finally was, our rescuer was not, I think, the person Maman had hoped for. It was eleven in the morning when the visitor arrived, announced by one of the slatternly hotel maids. Maman was asleep—she'd been up half the night again, writing and pacing—so I went down to discover our benefactor. Would it be sister Evangeline, or would it be the admirer? By then, I had a very clear image of *him*: tall, dark, rich, and resolute—maybe with a moustache.

It wasn't the sister, and it wasn't the hero of the suede gloves, either. It was a tall, thin young woman, dressed in black from head to foot, with a black hat jammed on her black hair, and eyes as sharp as the jet on her jacket.

She was waiting in the hall downstairs, standing as still as death. When I approached, and she looked down at me, I thought she was very curious indeed. She was so still and so pale complexioned, but I could feel she was humming with energy, a strange whirring energy, as if her heart ran on clockwork, and the mechanism was rusty or wound up too tightly.

She looked at me, and I looked at her. She was yellow-white as a waxwork, and equally inanimate, but as we examined each other, a change came over her. Faint color beat up from her thin throat to her thin face; she flexed her fingers in her thin cheap gloves; I could just see her ankles under her long narrow skirt, and I saw one of her black stockings had a perfect, meticulous darn in it. The gloves and that darn said: I'm poor. The tight mouth said, I'm proud. And the eyes—what did they say? They had a yearning look, I thought. I could feel tentacles of neediness, reaching out to me, suckering onto me.

When she spoke, her voice was so odd! I didn't understand the messages of English accents then; it was only later that I could see her accent was West Country, painfully and painstakingly overlaid with gentility. She spoke in a flat inharmonious tone, the way the deaf do. What a strange, grating voice. It negotiated a sentence like a minefield. Emotion avoided, but lurking under every word and liable to blow up at any minute. How I longed to mimic it! "Rebecca Devlin. Rebecca Devlin," she said, clasping my hand too tight. "Let me look at you. You poor child. How dark your hair is—I came at once. Will you tell your mama I'm here? Tell her Millicent sent me the instant her letter arrived. Tell her—"

"Who are you?" I said in a haughty way. I didn't like being called a "poor child"—not by anyone.

She might have taken offense at my haughtiness—people did. But her reaction was just the opposite. She gave me a worshipping look, as if she liked to be put in her place. In her black eyes I could see an oil of obsequiousness, a match flare of admiration. Something smouldered in her, then ignited. I've seen that fanatic look a million times since. I loathe it, but I've learned to live with it.

"Just like your mama!" she said. "I see the resemblance now. I am Edith Danvers. My mother had the care of yours when your mama was a child, didn't she explain that?"

I watched her carefully; Maman rarely explained anything, but I was reluctant to say so.

"Your mama will remember me," she went on. "If you'd just tell her: Danny's downstairs. There's a room ready for you both at St. Agnes, and, if your mama would permit me, I'd be only too glad to pack for her."

I went upstairs, woke Maman, and gave her this message. At the name "Danny," she rolled her eyes and made one of her impudent faces. "Oh heavens," she said. "That woman clings like ivy. Her mother's a dear sweet thing—she was my nurse, darling, and I'm devoted to her—but the daughter! Ah, well, beggars can't be choosers. I'd better go down and face her. Toss me my dress, darling—no, not that old thing. Must keep up appearances—I'll wear the silk one."

I laced Maman into her dress and helped her arrange her hair. Seconds later, she looked grand and headstrong and beautiful. What an actress my maman could be! Not onstage, I'm afraid—there, she was always a little stiff and self-conscious; but offstage, she was a marvel—always very quick-witted, so warm and charming, not a sniff of insincerity, you'd have said. She swept downstairs that day like a duchess, and greeted that grim waxwork figure waiting below with

the greatest affection. No one would have known she was less than
pleased to see her; no one could have guessed we were down to our
last guinea. Strange stiff Danny melted in the face of this performance like ice before the sun. Her pale face lit; her eyes grew moist;
she could scarcely speak for the strength of her emotion. So feudal! I
felt quite sorry for her.

"Oh, Miss Isolda," she said. "I can't believe—it's been so long. My
mother says if there's anything we can do . . ."

"Dearest Millicent—I'm so looking forward to seeing her," said
Maman. "*Will* you pack for me, Danny? You do it perfectly, I
remember—and I can't bear the thought of another night in this horrid place."

"Of course, madam," Danny replied, instantly subservient. And
with that brief exchange, the course of our next seven years was
decided.

DANNY BORE US BACK IN TRIUMPH TO ST. AGNES—AND IT
wasn't a church, as I'd imagined it might be, but a very clean, very
organized boardinghouse, everything spruce: "Shipshape and Bristol
fashion," said Millicent.

It was set up high, overlooking Plymouth Sound; you could watch
warships from the window. There were starched antimacassars on
every chair, aspidistras in brass pots in every window, and there was
English food. When we arrived, Millicent Danvers gave us hot
herring roe on toast. She introduced us to her husband, "Mr. D.,"
who was old; he had false teeth, a wing collar, best clothes, and some
mysterious ailment. He was presented, then whisked out of sight.
Daughter Edith poured the tea, and I could see she was ashamed of
the hot herring roe, and her father's false teeth, and her mother's
apron. "Oh, I forgot the serviettes, Edie, dear," her mother said, and
Edith went crimson. "*Napkins*, mother," she said, very sharp. "I'll
fetch them." I ate a small bit of the herring ovaries. I thought, If we
stay here, I'll get as thin as a pin. Maman was very gay and charming
and defiant—but I was beginning to recognize the danger signals
now. I knew there'd be a lapse, and there was. Within a day, once the
initial relief and euphoria had worn off, Maman would rally, then
languish.

Every afternoon for a week, she put on her best dove gray dress, her prettiest hat, and those exquisite mauve suede gloves. She pinched her cheeks to give them color, and tilted the hat over her eyes in the most becoming way; she adjusted her veil and with a determined air she set off on mysterious visits.

Edith Danvers had returned to the house nearby where she was in service, so I stayed with Millicent. She was kind. She told me all about her tenants, two clerks, one traveling salesman, and regular "theatricals." She introduced me to lavender water, and baptized my wrists with two special drops—it smelled like tomcats, I thought. She let me help her in the kitchen; she said all her vegetables were boiled for an hour with a pinch of bicarbonate of soda—that was the secret. I stood on a stool by the sink and swished soap over greasy dishes. I helped sacrifice mountains of poor vegetables daily, and Millicent told me stories. Up out of the dark came shapes: No news on my dark dead Devlin father, alas—Millicent never mentioned *him*—but she fleshed out the ghosts of my English family for me.

Maman was the youngest of three lovely sisters—and the youngest by a long way: She was an *afterthought*, said Millicent mysteriously. The eldest sister, Miss Evangeline, was now Lady Briggs; she lived in a lovely house called St. Winnow's not so very far from here, and she had two charming daughters, Elinor and Jocelyn. Her husband was rich as Croesus. His family wasn't a patch on Evangeline's and my mother's—their branch of the Grenvilles was not well-off, but they could trace their ancestry back to kingdom come, whereas Sir Joshua's background was nothing to write home about, and he was said to be a difficult straitlaced narrow-minded man—but there, he *was* rich, and he'd been handsome when young, and Miss Evangeline had set her heart on him, and, like most Grenville women, she was determined, not to say headstrong.

The second sister, now dead, was the poor dear sweet good Miss Virginia I recognized from Maman's stories. A fine match *she'd* made. She'd married the catch of the neighborhood, the owner of Manderley, Mr. Lionel de Winter, no less—and a merry dance he'd led her, Millicent said, chopping up a carnage of cabbage. Poor Miss Virginia, God rest her, had had two children, first a girl, Beatrice, and then a boy, Maximilian, the son and heir. But she'd never lived to see the son and heir grow up; she'd taken a fever when he was three years old. "Dead in a week!" Millicent said. "So, the grandmother reared him. Miss Virginia never was strong, not even as a child, poor thing. She was nervous—sensitive—I always said as Manderley wouldn't suit her. Great gloomy place, to my mind. Exposed. Too near the sea. You wouldn't want to be up there in a storm, Miss Rebecca, I can tell you."

"I've seen a photograph of Manderley," I said. "Someone sent it to Maman. I think it's beautiful."

Millicent dropped her chopping knife, bent to pick it up. "Yes, well," she said in a flurried way, becoming flushed, "It's a fine place— in its way. Tastes vary."

"Maybe that's where Maman's gone to visit today," I went on, casual as could be. I burned to know where she went, and I knew Maman would never tell me. "Maybe she's gone to call at Manderley; I expect she'd like to do that, when she's been away nearly eight years, don't you think, Millicent?"

Millicent didn't agree. She thought such a visit was very unlikely. After all, Maman's sister was dead now, so the place would have very sad memories for her; she'd give it a very wide berth, Millicent thought, and the more she insisted on this, the less I believed her.

"Did you go to Manderley today, Maman?" I asked, when she finally came home. We were in our St. Agnes bedroom, with its cru- cifix on the wall and a black marble tomb of a chimneypiece. Maman had flung herself down on the bed as soon as she came back; she was lying there now, looking white and exhausted, but when I asked that, she sprang up, and started pacing the room.

"No, I didn't," she said. "Why should I? Who suggested that? Who's been putting ideas in your head? For heaven's sake, Becka, haven't I enough to worry about?"

"No one suggested it. Millicent was telling me about your sister Virginia, that's all, and I wondered—"

"Well, don't," Maman said, very sharply. "Poor Virginia's *dead*. I hate that house. I hate everyone in it. Lionel de Winter, and that ghastly mother of his—she ran roughshod over poor Virginia. And she *never* liked me. She went out of her way to make my life a misery. Old beast! She's an interfering, arrogant old woman. I wouldn't call on her if she were at death's door. She should have died years and years ago—she's been widowed long enough, in all conscience. And I wish to God she *had* died. Everything would have been different, then. Lionel and I were friends once—when I was a girl, and poor Virginia was always so sick, and he had all these worries. We'd be friends still if it wasn't for that mother of his."

"Why would you be friends? You said you hated him."

"We just *might*, that's all. Stop interrogating me, for heaven's sake, Becka. . . . He's ill now, in any case—someone told me. He hasn't been well for months. Oh, what am I going to do? Where are we going to go? We can't stay here; there's hardly any money left. I can't pay Millicent, we're living here on charity, on my own nurse's charity. Evangeline can't help—or won't. She says I should never have come home. My own sister, and she treats me like a pariah. It's insupportable. I don't know which way to turn."

She burst into tears, and, flinging herself down on her bed again, turned her face to the crucifix wall. I began to feel very sick and queer. I'd never seen her like this; I didn't know what to do, but I thought it might help if I knew the truth, so I fetched Maman some tea and some medicine for her headache; then I sat by her side and stroked her hair until she fell asleep. And when I was certain she was asleep, deeply asleep, this is what I did, my darling. I crept across the room, found the tiny silver key I knew she hid in her jewelery box, and unlocked the drawers of her little traveling writing desk.

I took out her secret letters—the admirer's letters, all tied up in that rose-embroidered ribbon. First, he wrote every week, then every fortnight, then every month, then the gaps lengthened. By the time I was four, it was down to one letter a quarter, then once every six months or so. The last letter of all, stained with Maman's salt tears, had been written nearly a year ago.

They weren't very long letters, fortunately, and they were easy to read because Maman's correspondent had big, childish handwriting. I couldn't understand all the words he was using, and some of the things he said he wanted to do sounded strange. They sent little furtive shivers all down my body.

I'll tell you what I discovered, my love. The admirer was Lionel de Winter, her dead sister's husband, my uncle by marriage. He'd been writing to Maman for a long time, since before I was born. He'd been writing to Maman when my Devlin father was alive—months before he set off on that fatal sea voyage. It wasn't right for Lionel to call a married woman his "sweet darling," I thought. If my Devlin father had known about that, he'd have killed him stone dead, I felt sure of it.

I wondered if Maman had noticed how these letters had altered in tone over time, and if it had hurt her. First she was "a sweet darling," then Lionel's "dearest girl," then "dear Isolda." First he was "wild" to see her; then he "wished" he could see her; then, if circumstances changed, he would certainly "try" to see her; meanwhile, he would "help out" whenever he could, and he'd send something pretty—as pretty as she was—to cheer her.

More recently, the letters turned querulous. Lionel had enough nagging to contend with on the home front, he said; didn't his little Isolda know that men hated women who made complaints all the time? It was wearisome. None of this was his fault. Yes, he could see things must be hard for her, and she might sometimes be lonely, but she was better off in a nice comfortable house in France. If she came back to England, there would only be more talk—especially if she turned up with a child in tow. People would get the wrong idea then; they'd leap to the wrong conclusions, he would be compromised, she would be shunned. The notion was insane; would she please forget it immediately?

I stole the last of those letters, to fuel my hate—and just as well I did, because someone (Danny probably) made sure the rest of them were destroyed when my mother died. I know its cheapnesses by heart; here's a specimen. Here's lionhearted, lily-livered Lionel de Winter; here's my husband's father writing to my mother:

Sweetheart, I'm going to be frank: You know I've always been very fond of you, and always will be. You're a dear girl in many ways—but you are headstrong. I've always made the situation perfectly clear; you can't deny that. This entanglement wasn't of my making, you know, Isolda. It's all very well now to say you were just a child, and you fell in love—but if we look back, the betrayals bothered me more than they did you. It was I who had the conscience, dear. Remember that day at the boathouse?

You don't seem to appreciate the difficulties I was laboring under then—a sick, complaining wife, a nagging mother, loneliness, and boredom. I was wretched, dear, so of course I responded to your youth, your gaiety, and sympathy. All men have needs—and when they can't or won't be met in the rightful way, then there's always danger, and the man isn't to blame, in my view.

I've always promised you that I'll take care of things, and I will. Meanwhile, accusations don't help, frankly. You're not "buried alive" as you put it, Isolda—you're living in comfort, as I understand it. It was your family that decided to separate us after Virginia died. It was they who whisked you away to France; Mother and I had nothing to do with that decision—I don't know why you should think we were involved in any way, dear. You then made a hasty and impetuous marriage, which hurt me very much, and which I advised you against, if I recall correctly. It might help if you'd remember that occasionally.

I'm not under any obligation to you, dear, let alone your child, and in view of the attitude of your own family, I feel you should appreciate more the generosity I've shown you as a friend and brother-in-law.

I've told you, Isolda, I haven't been well recently. I've been laid up for months now in considerable pain, and it's made me very depressed in spirits. I've had to make a will—a gloomy process—and insofar as I can, I've made provision for you. It took up days of my time, and it wasn't easy; all of the estate and too damn much of the money is tied up in trusts, but I was determined to do the right thing by you, dear. I think you should be grateful for that, and not nag and threaten, when I'm in no condition to cross the Channel and pay visits, and if you thought for one second, you'd see that.

So, if anything should happen to me, you'll be nicely set up—I haven't forgotten your pretty ways, you see! But for God's sake don't mention this when you write; there are certain persons in this house (you'll know whom I mean) who are more than ready to read private correspondence. In fact, Isolda, I think it might help if you wrote less often. Your letters are very long, sweetheart, and they only increase your anxieties, especially when I can't answer them as swiftly as I might like. I have a thousand and one demands to deal with, you know. The tenants are an ungrateful lot—they never stop complaining. I've had to spend most of this last week at the estate office, sorting out the North Farm, and the Carminowes, for instance—the widow was making difficulties. So I have many calls on my time, dear, and I wish you'd realize that, occasionally.

Now, chin up! Be my smiling girl again. I'm sending some pretty gloves for my naughty little Isolda! Frith will parcel them up and they'll be with you shortly.

How I hated this man, with his cheap words and his cheap promises, his disguised threats and his patronage. All my past turned upside down and inside out. Maybe Maman hadn't been crying over the untuned piano strings, I thought. Maybe she was crying because he'd sent a letter like this. I sniffed the paper; it reeked of fraudulence.

I felt a huge anger stir up under my heart; I wanted to take those trinkets he sent, and rend them and smash them. I wanted to rip the gloves, and grind that locket under my foot. I fetched the locket, and opened its secret clasp, and looked at that lock of cunningly plaited reddish fair hair: Lionel de Winter's hair—I knew that now. I hated his hair, and I hated him; he had lied to my mother and let her down. Well, I didn't intend to let him get away with *that*. I would avenge Maman, and I knew just how to deal with Uncle Lionel.

I stayed as cool as a knife blade. I put the sneaking letters back in their envelopes and back in the writing desk. I replaced the key and the locket, and, when everything was as neat as neat could be, so Maman would never suspect, I summoned up my Devlin father once again, just as I'd done that time in Brittany. I willed his strength into me, and when I was as strong as any man ever was, brimful of anger and hate, I put a curse on Lionel de Winter, his house, and his offspring for all eternity.

It didn't occur to me that I might be cursing myself. I was an ignoramus then, my dearest. I knew about love, but not about sex, et cetera. It was only years later, when my mother confessed some of this to me, that I started to wonder. "I was only sixteen when I had my first admirer," she said. "I was a *child*, Becka, I knew nothing. He was a married man, darling, but I adored him. And he was so *plausible*. He could wind me around his little finger."

A little worm of doubt gnawed away then—but those doubts don't bother me now, and they need never bother you. They vanished, I promise you, the very second my Devlin father came back from the dead and I walked into the Greenways room and saw him. I have his hair and his blood and his Irish luck—so the curse has passed me by, and it will pass you by, too, my love.

But Lionel didn't escape. You'll be pleased to know that he died exactly the way he deserved: slowly, and in agony.

THAT DAY WAS THE DAY MY CHILDHOOD DIED—THAT'S what I think now, looking back. After that, I had to grow up very fast. I had to take the reins from Maman because her grip was slackening. I was afraid that when she made those afternoon visits of hers, she was looking for a handout and a refuge. I was sure she'd have tried Evangeline—and I was right, as I found out later. I was very afraid she might try Manderley, too, if she were desperate enough—and I wasn't having that. Maman had such courage and spirit, and I *refused* to see her pride brought low. So, somehow, somewhere, by some means, we had to acquire, or earn, some money.

How did women earn money? I asked everyone. I asked old Mr. D., who was allowed out more often now that Millicent said I was "part of the family." He'd been a carpenter in the Plymouth naval yards; he used to sit in the St. Agnes garden and whittle little boats for me—just like the boats I've made for you, my dear one. He had capable steady hands, and gentle ways and he was dying of emphysema, but he couldn't help with this problem. He said a man had a trade, but it was different for women—and very different for ladies.

Millicent suggested companions and governesses in a doubtful way, and, one day, when Danny came over to tea, Millicent mentioned that in certain establishments, where they sold dresses, for instance, some of the women serving were really quite genteel. Danny threw down her napkin, and went scarlet. "Don't talk such nonsense, Mother," she said. "Putting ideas like that in the child's head. What are you thinking of?"

Can you imagine what a world that was, a madhouse where a woman lost status by working? Not that it's changed so very much in the years since. Ridiculous! I despise such ideas from the depths of my heart. They're evil. They turn women into slaves or schemers. Years later, when my father died, and I was left with nothing except debts and odious creditors, I went out and *earned*. I didn't give a tuppenny damn what anyone said or thought. I'd have scrubbed floors if need be. But it was different for me. I was brought up by the beaches of Brittany and Marie-Hélène, so I was a practical little savage, and I knew that the Religion of the House could always save me.

Maman's case was different; she had a fatal disadvantage in life. She'd been born and brought up a lady—and that crippled her for good, believe me.

MONEY, MONEY, MONEY. IT WAS ALL I THOUGHT ABOUT for an entire month. Millicent said, Don't you fret, dearie. She said I was doing the work of two maids, chopping all those vegetables, and keeping Mr. D. amused, the way I did—but I knew that wasn't true; she was just being kindly. Money, money, money. I'd go to bed at night and dream of fat purses, full of guineas.

Then one day I came downstairs, and there was salvation, there was our deliverer. *The players had arrived.* There was Sir Frank (he wasn't knighted then, in fact, that came later, but he was born knightly, and was knightly by nature anyway). He was six feet tall, a most gorgeous gentleman; he touched up his gray hair with dye and you could hear him boom "Good morning" from half a mile away. He had a squat fat insect of a wife—how I hated *her*—in a maroon ensemble, with yellow jealous eyes and antennas, quivering.

He was a "Balliol man," as he liked to remind everyone at two-minute intervals. He had been destined for the Church, but the Bard had called; he had served his apprenticeship, straight from Oxford, with the greatest of the great: Henry Irving. "Who are you this morning, Mr. McKendrick?" I used to say, after breakfast. "Today I am Hamlet, Miss Rebecca," he would reply, with a wink and a lordly waft of the hand. Today I am Hamlet, or Brutus, Richard III, or Macbeth. That's how life should be, my love; one should be free as a bird to choose, every morning. Then he would stroll off to rehearse, though he never rehearsed for very long; all his company had been doing these plays since the year dot, so they knew all the parts anyway.

Frank McKendrick had a very soft heart; some people couldn't see beyond the carapace of vanity, but I could. I sensed the soft heart, *and* the weakness for fair ladies, especially fair ladies in distress. He was not without snobbery, too, so the Grenville ancestry went down a treat (Millicent had been gossiping). I spotted all this when he was introduced to Maman: a young and beautiful widow, of good family, fallen on hard times . . . irresistible! He bent over her hand most gallantly; the terrible wife bristled at once, so I knew we'd have to outmaneuver *her*, but I could see the possibilities instantly. I went upstairs and unpacked our books of poetry. Before the week was out, I had Maman reading *The Lady of Shalott* to an appreciative audience in Millicent's front parlor, with the aspidistras and the antimacassars, and the warships passing. One fatal glance at Sir Lancelot, and the Lady began dying:

> *Out flew the web, and floated wide;*
> *The mirror crack'd, from side to side;*
> *"The curse is come upon me," cried*
> *The Lady of Shalott.*

How I love that poem! Maman read it aloud so well, in a sweet harmonious voice; we were all seduced by those rhythms. After that, all I really had to do was explain to Mr. McKendrick that we were experiencing a temporary financial embarrassment—he knew all about *those*—and my work was halfway done. I took him for a morning walk along Marine Parade. I recited some Puck for him; I made it clear that he'd be getting two actors for the price of one, as it were, and I reminded him that he was a lady-in-waiting short. I put my hand in his and told him we'd have to plot, he and I: In the first place, his wife might make difficulties. . . .

"True, alas, all too true," said Mr. McKendrick meditatively.

In the second, Maman would refuse. The stage? She'd never countenance such an idea, not unless she were very skillfully maneuvered into it. But if it was suggested to her that this was just a temporary arrangement; if the lady-in-waiting's dress was pretty, and Maman was warmly encouraged and praised; if it could be implied that she was rescuing Mr. McKendrick and the company, because without her assistance the cast couldn't be complete, and the performance of that play might even have to be cancelled . . .

"Well, well, well," said Mr. McKendrick, coming to a halt and looking down at me from his great height. "I doff my hat to you, young lady." He doffed his hat. "You are a veritable Iago. You are an

infant Richard III. You are a 'notorious Machiavel.' You are filled
with plots and stratagems—and you're not a bad Puck, Missy, either."
He walked on a few paces, mimed indecision, held his hand to his
brow, gave Plymouth Sound an Old Hamlet ghost glare, then turned
back to me with Fortinbrassy resolution. I nearly applauded.

"We have a deal, Missy," he said, shaking me by the hand. "A pact.
Your mama would be a most definite adornment to our little company. She has breeding. She has very pretty ways. I will attend to
Mrs. McKendrick, Missy. You will attend to your mama. We will
divide, to conquer. A week, would you say?"

"Three days," I said, thinking of purses.

"Ah, impetuous youth," replied the splendid man, winking at me.

We were a good team, Frank McKendrick and I. We pulled it off
in two and a half days flat. Maman changed her name to "Isabel," so
as not to shame her family. That first week at the Plymouth Royal, I
played two doomed little boys (doomed boys became my specialty).
Maman played Lady Macbeth's handmaid and understudied virtuous
Hermione, victim of jealousy. At Dunsinane, Maman wore a blue velvet dress, and with her first week's wage she bought me my blue
enamel butterfly brooch, one of my two most sacred possessions—
they'll be yours one day.

There was a racy side to Máman, and I know she took to our new
world like a salmon to the sea—but she'd never admit that to anyone
but me. Years later, when she was making her final appearance as
Desdemona, she was still telling everyone in the company that, of
course, this was only a temporary arrangement.

Better things lay around the corner, she would suggest. They
didn't. Death lay in wait around the corner—but, until the final flurry
that always precedes death, my comfort is that she never knew that.

TWENTY-THREE

I<small>T'S A HEAT WAVE, MY DARLING</small>.

Scarcely a breath of wind, clear skies for almost a week now. I haven't been able to write. Husband Max came back, the house has been filled with guests, and I couldn't escape here once; whenever I had a free hour, and I set off for my sea house, Max would follow me jealously. He's had those white tight moods of his all week—because I went up to London for a day, I think. He hates me to leave and hates me to stay: There's no pleasing him! I went there five days ago to see that doctor at last—but I didn't want to tell Max that, not yet—so he leaped to his usual conclusions. I slept one night in my river flat, quiet as a nun and equally virtuous—but as far as Max is concerned, that flat is my *lair*, and it's a den of iniquity.

The doctor's name was Baker, and he's the best women's quack around, or so people tell me. His rooms are in Bloomsbury, just behind the British Museum. I was eager for my appointment, so I arrived far too early. I went into the museum to pass the time; I walked the marble halls, my high heels tap-tapping and echoing—I thought: Someone's following me! I stared at stone conquerers and painted pharaohs; I lost myself in a wilderness of corridors. I ended up in a death room, hemmed in by white mummies. They remove their hearts, and wrap them up in a parcel at their feet, someone told me once; then they swaddle them in bandages like babies. How patiently they watched me.

I sat in Dr. Baker's waiting room, where the only thing to read was Max's bible, *The Field*. I read the same article ten times, and couldn't take in a word of it.

Into the consulting rooms at last: very grave, with the doctor's pen scratching away, and my heart beating like a bird's—so fast; I was so excited.

I'd called myself "Mrs. Danvers," when I made the appointment—stupid, really, but I had some wild idea that if I used my name, word might get back to Max. Every time Dr. Baker addressed me, I'd glance over my shoulder and expect Danny to be there. I wasn't thinking clearly, my love. I was blurry with joy; I wanted to remember every detail, the tiniest things, because this was my turning point, and this hour was yours. It was momentous for both of us.

It didn't go quite the way I'd expected. I think doctors are cursed with caution anyway, and this one turned out to be caution and gravity personified. Probing, probing: first the questions, then an examination that went on and on. It hurt. Mother of God, spare me from speculums.

He listened to your heartbeat—and I wanted to grab the stethoscope so I could listen, too. "When will my baby move?" I said. "Why am I sick all the time? Why hasn't my baby moved yet?" He looked at a calendar on the wall and balled up his rubber gloves and said in a quiet way that I mustn't be precipitate. In the first place, much depended on the exact date of conception; in the second, just to make absolutely sure, he wanted me to have some X rays.

I refused at first. I'm sure I've read that X rays are dangerous for babies. But he assured me that in this case it could cause no possible harm and then I could come back in a week's time, and he'd be able to answer all my questions.

They put a lead bib round my neck to shield my breasts and aimed a fat one-eyed robot at my belly. "Heavens, Mrs. Danvers, what a lovely slim figure you have," the nurse said, then ducked out of the room while it pumped its rays into me. I asked her how long women went on being sick, and when I could expect to put on weight, and when I'd be able to rest my hands on your curve—I can't wait for the majesty of motherhood. I want to be calm and heavy and *milky*.

She said every woman was different, and when someone was as thin and boyish as I am, why, she could be five months gone and you'd only just begin to see the difference. "Don't you worry about it," she said. I think she understood how anxious and impatient I was; I think she was sorry for me. She had hips perfect for childbearing (unlike mine), so I half wanted to laugh, but she meant well, and I felt so hectic that to me she was a ministering angel.

I gave a tube of red red blood for them to practice their juju on, made an appointment for seven days' time (only two more to wait, now, my darling). Then I went out into the spring streets, with the leaves just beginning to show and the cherry blossom foaming in gardens. I went to a babies' palace of a place in Bond Street, and blew a small fortune on a layette. I bought you nightgowns with ribbons, and a shawl so fine you could pass it through a wedding ring. I bought bonnets and booties, and a silver rattle with coral, and two dozen best terry-towel nappies, just to be practical. It was the best extravagance I've ever known. I was drunk with the joy of it. They packed them up in white boxes; I took them back to my river flat, and gloated over them for a whole afternoon. I wrote down lists of names—I still haven't decided on the right name. I'm giving birth to a *girl-boy*. What do you want to be called? I'll know when I hold you.

Now I'm going to hold fast to what they said, that doctor and that nurse, and not worry about anything. I looked back in my appointments book, and decoded my signs, and I see you might have been conceived a few weeks later than I'd thought, just as Dr. Baker suggested. So that's why you haven't moved yet. I must wait a little while longer and not be impatient.

I'd decided you'd been conceived at my river flat, but I now see it could have been here, in this boathouse—one winter night, when I was at my loneliest. There was a white fat disc of moon, and the sky looked huge and unyielding.

I'm glad it was here. And he was an appropriate man, rougher than the London candidate, a man on the edge of something. He made love to me by the fire in the moonlight. Let's see, what else can I remember? He had dark hair and thoughtful eyes; he was a poet—

and of Irish extraction, as it happens. He isn't important anyway, none of them are. They're just glue, a white measure of usefulness, that's all. And, never fear, there will be no entanglements. *Once*, I say—and I mean it—before I lie down with them.

You should know: He resembled Max to a degree, as they all do, my one-a-month men. I've been careful in that respect, as I've no particular wish to humiliate my husband. You'll have to pass as his child, you see, dearest; I won't tolerate gossip about you or your legitimacy for one instant. Umpteen of Max's ancestors came from the wrong side of the blanket anyway, so who cares? Hybrids invigorate a strain, as any gardener will tell you.

Besides, suppose I were Lionel de Winter's child? I'm certain I'm not, but I wouldn't want you to have a double dose of blue de Winter blood in your veins—and dear fastidious Max would faint at the idea of incest. So, you could argue I'm doing him a favor, by crossbreeding. Besides, this way we avoid my St. Agnes curse—better safe than sorry! And what alternative do I have? It would break most women to endure what I have. I've wedded an iceberg, I've coupled with coldness. If I have splinters of ice in my heart now, I blame the de Winters and their unnatural blue blood for it. It's been an Antarctic, my marriage.

Dearest, I want you to know this: This is my creed: *There is only one true legitimacy, and it's bestowed by love, not male lineage.* I love Manderley and I love you. Everything Manderley now is, I made; I took this place, wedded myself to it, and made it perfect. It was a sepulcher when I came here. It was I who opened the windows and let life in: I will *not* let that count for nothing. Remember, your rights come from the female line. You are *my* rightful heir, and I'll ensure you inherit.

You mustn't think about the centuries of patriarchy and primogeniture, you must forget all those fustian fathers and sons, my darling. Their rule is about to be overthrown. Listen: Can you hear those whispers? It's an insurrection! Revolution's in the air; the women of the house have waited long enough, and now there's an uprising! I've made Manderley *my* domain. I am sovereign here, and every chimney stack, every blade of grass knows it. I claim it on behalf of all the women who labored and bore children here; all the women who sacrificed their names and lost their identities, who were subsumed, who were relegated to a portrait in a gallery, a footnote in a family's history. I claim it for women long dead, and women who have died recently, women who lie in the de Winter crypt, and whose voices speak to me. I claim it for Virginia, and my mother. I claim it for myself, because I am not just a wife, some poor adjunct to a husband. I speak for a long, long line of the dispossessed. I am the one who breeds: I *belong* here.

And I'm armed, too, never fear; I'm ready for any skirmish that's necessary—and a battle or two may well be necessary! I have old injustices in my veins; disrespect and neglect have helped to forge me. My weapons are anger and guile—and no man is going to put his hand on *my* neck and subdue me. Women the weaker sex? I don't think so, my darling!

I'm pure steel now. Honed and polished, bayonet sharp. *Nothing* will stand in my way, I promise you. Last year I decided: If my husband won't give me a child, I'll get one without him. This year I resolved: If my husband tries to thwart me, I'll kill him.

So, husband Max had better be careful. I shall tell him, does he want an heir or doesn't he? Don't mention divorce courts to me, Max, I'll say (not that he would, he's too terrified of scandal and he knows only too well how invincible I'd be in the witness-box). I'd be wary of oiling that gun of yours, too, Max. I'll say, don't you know I keep the gun-room keys on my pretty little chatelaine? Think about it, husband, I'll say, and remember: The ways of death are infinite. A shooting accident? A fall from a cliff? A drowning? Don't expect womanly mercy from *me*, Max, and watch your back, because, come what may, it's *my* child who'll inherit.

A NGER IS A FUEL, MY SWEET—YOU'LL LEARN THAT ONE day. It's pure acetylene, it's ninety-nine percent proof, it's high octane. It is one of my legacies to you, but the energy's very rich; it makes me shake, sometimes.

I'm calmer now. I went for a walk with Jasper to Kerrith. Last week, James Tabb took *Je Reviens* out of dry dock; today I asked him to get her ready for me as quickly as he can. Twenty-four hours, he says—and because he always does what he says (unlike most men), that means I can take you out in my boat tomorrow. Pray the weather holds. We'll take you for your first sail; the tide conditions will be perfect tomorrow night. I'll show you the sea by moonlight.

Meanwhile, all the guests have gone, and today Max is, as usual, at the estate office with Frank Crawley. I passed that building on my way back from Kerrith. I could hear the sound of their voices. I wondered what they were discussing. Acreages? Tenants? Plowing?

I should confess: The wicked Rebecca in me toyed a little with Frank once. I was angry with Max; rejection makes you feel ugly, you know. I woke up one morning all alone in my great Manderley bed; I opened the curtains and listened to the sea and thought—I'll show him. Besides, I was curious to know: Was our estate manager a saint or a eunuch?

Neither, I discovered. But don't worry—he's a poor thing, with the soul of a dullard. It went no further than two schoolboy billets-doux, and a fortnight's sighing. He took himself so seriously that he actually went to Max, confessed his sins, and resigned. What sins? Such conceit! He was reinstated at once, needless to say. I laughed at his presumption—and he's never forgiven me.

Pausing by the estate office today, a sudden idea came to me. I thought, Maybe he and Max *aren't* discussing plowing and fertilizing; maybe they're sitting there in that office and plotting my demise. It wouldn't surprise me. This last year, Max's suspicions have increased, fueled by frustration and my absences, among other things. Love and loathing are such a heady mix that he may well believe he wants me dead, but he's too full of the milk of human kindness to make the best of assassins. He'd need someone to screw his courage to the sticking-place—though I can't imagine Frank Crawley's being much use in that respect; he's far too timid. *I* could make Max kill; I could goad him to murder me easily enough, and I've often been tempted to do so in the past, Bridegroom Death being preferable to the bridegroom I did have.

But supposing I *were* to meet with a convenient accident? Then Max might need someone like Frank to provide him with a cover story. Questions would be asked; my good friend Arthur Julyan is magistrate here, and he'd insist on a thorough investigation, I know it. So Max might need Frank's help to conceal the truth. Could they be planning such a thing now, I wondered.

I moved closer to the windows and tried to hear what they were saying. I couldn't hear a word—and, suddenly, I felt bewildered, dearest. I felt faint. I thought, How did this happen? How did Max and I come to this pass? Who fixed *these* stars? Can't we alter these patterns?

I believed that eventually I'd get used to being hated, you see, but I haven't. Today, the hate stabbed at me. I've tried to make myself strong, but my strength fails me sometimes, even now. My womb hurt. I thought, I've started bleeding again; I'm bleeding internally, all these fibrous placenta bits, and gouts of blood, gushing out of me.

I'm back in my sea house now, my love, on my territory. I'm not bleeding. I imagined the pain. I'm feeling stronger already. Let them plot; I don't care. The brother officers are far too unimaginative and honorable to act anyway—and they certainly won't touch me once I tell them about you. To harm an unborn child would damn a man for all eternity.... I'm carrying a baby; I'm the holiest of holies.

What witchcraft! I bear a charmed life now, my darling.

I<small>T'S COOL IN THE BOATHOUSE, THOUGH IT'S HIGH NOON</small> outside. These thick walls protect us whatever the weather. I've opened the sea window; you can hear the rush of the waves; there's a fresh salt breeze off the water; Jasper is chewing a stick. I have all my inks to hand, a virgin page, and my favorite pen: Today I'm going to wind the film forward seven years; I want to tell you about the summer of crisis.

It was the summer war was declared—one of the hottest summers I ever remember. We'd been inching our way down England's spine, city to city, theater to theater; Sir Frank had been knighted the previous year—but the knighthood wasn't bringing in audiences. He was aging, and some of our best players had left; the words of the plays still echoed to infinity, as they always do, but our performances ... well, they were lackluster, dearest. It was the summer Maman was promoted to proper speaking parts—and the summer takings were so low that we all had to accept reductions in our wages.

By the time we reached Plymouth for our annual visit, the war was a month old, though everyone was still saying it would be over by Christmas. The advance bookings were poor, but Sir Frank was a man of boundless optimism. He insisted we give extra performances of *Henry V*; he thought it would suit the prevailing mood of patriotism. But even the spectacle of Sir Frank urging the outnumbered

English to victory at Agincourt didn't sell seats. "We soldier on," Sir Frank said. "I shall give them my Moor on Saturday night. My three hundredth performance—that'll bring 'em in, you may depend on it, Missy."

I think Sir Frank had a sharp eye for box-office potential, on occasion, despite his naïveté. It hadn't escaped his notice that a grumpy frump of a fifty-year-old wife playing Juliet or Rosalind wasn't exactly a draw; Maman had been playing Princess Katharine of France in *Henry V* for some time now, but that was her biggest role to date, and only given her because she spoke French, a qualification even Lady McKendrick couldn't deny her. For the *Othello*, Sir Frank suddenly decided, beautiful Maman would be promoted to Desdemona. He announced it on the billboards before he told his wife, and, when I saw the expression in her yellow jealous eyes, I knew there'd be trouble. "Indisposed?" I overheard her hiss at our costume mistress. "I may have a sore throat, dear, but it's not *me* who's indisposed. You'll have to let out the green taffeta, Clara, if Mistress High and Mighty's going to wear it."

Maman had been in poor spirits all summer; she was nervy and on edge; she had no appetite—yet it was true, she *was* putting on weight; her Princess Katharine brocade had been let out around the waist and bosom to fit her. She'd been fretful and preoccupied for months; she was quarrelsome with Lady McKendrick; she was very snappy and short with our recent recruit, the handsome hothead Orlando Stephens, who was to play Cassio. She wouldn't confide in me; my body was starting to change, and Maman hated that. She wouldn't share a dressing room with me anymore, and Clara had to help me bind my chest with bandages when I played boys now. "When you put out the Red Flag the first time," Clara said, giving me a kiss, "you come to me. I'll show you what to do, dearie. It can't be long, not the way you're growing."

I didn't know what the Red Flag was, and Maman wouldn't tell me, but I knew red was a danger signal. I hated those bandages. I hated my budding breasts. I wanted to slice them off and be an Amazon. They were like a malignant growth, and I knew, if they grew any more, my princeling days were numbered. No more doomed boys for me—and then what would I do? I loved my doomed boys. I practiced their deaths; I died so *well*—everyone said so.

When Maman learned she was to play Desdemona, her mood changed instantly; overnight, a transformation! Out came the sun, the clouds lifted, Maman's eyes sparkled again and all the courage I loved and admired returned to her. I forgot about my bandages, and all my other petty selfish concerns. I heard her lines again and again; we practiced the "Willow Song" in the blue dusk of Plymouth Sound September evenings. *She has a premonition she's going to die, don't you think, Maman?* I said, and Maman frowned at the sea beyond the St. Agnes windows, and said, *Perhaps, Becka. Maybe, my darling.*

I watched Maman die again and again. She would lie back on Millicent's black horsehair chaise longue. We would imagine the murdering husband, imagine the ways he killed: stifle or strangle? Shakespeare doesn't make it definite; Maman thought *stifle*. "Which is better, Becka?" she'd say. "With my head at this angle, or that one?"

And those strange speeches Desdemona has *after* she's apparently been killed—when the audience thinks she's dead and gone and silenced forever. Those speeches obsessed Maman. She felt she should give a small premonitory flutter of her hand, then rise up very suddenly and speak. It must take them by surprise; it would be a true coup de théâtre. "I shall give a wild cry," she said. "*My* Desdemona won't die quietly—she's always played wrongly, Becka. I *know* she'd fight back. This is a woman who defied her father and ran off with a blackamoor. She isn't some milksop, she's a woman of spirit, and that's why the Moor loves her."

It made me desperately sad. I agreed with everything she said, and I hadn't the heart to tell her. None of this would happen; Sir Frank wouldn't countenance it for a second. He'd elbow Maman into an ignominious, invisible death no matter what she did; he'd interpose his body between her and the audience; he'd clamp the pillow on her mouth midspeech if necessary, and he'd *drown her out*. Maman's low voice didn't carry much beyond the front three rows of the stalls anyway. What hope did she have, with Sir Frank center stage, in the shaft of the limes, going at it with that terrible, magnificent male voice, full throttle?

So I watched her die again and again, and my heart bled. The clock was ticking, ticking on the St. Agnes mantelshelf; she had four months to live and neither of us knew that. A black marble mantel and a black marble tomb. No rehearsals prepare you for what death's actually like, my darling. When that change came to Maman, when she went through that door and it slammed in my face . . . dear God, it was horrible. No miraculous golden words, no tender gestures, just incoherence and ugliness. It happens so *fast*. It turned me to stone; I couldn't move or think. It was Danny who closed her eyes and stroked the sheet over her. *Don't do that*, I said. I said, *Who's that crying, Danny—I can hear a baby crying.* And Danny said, *Hush, hush— there's no baby, what makes you think that? It's you crying, dear—just you sit with her quietly for a while, then I'll take you downstairs. Someone special's waiting to see you.*

I T WAS MY DEAD DEVLIN FATHER, DEAREST, BACK FROM HIS underworld. But I'm ahead of myself. There was an interim—and it's the interim that I promised you we'd step into.

Imagine a murky tunnel; it's four months long. At one end of it is my mother, St. Agnes, and a theater still lit by gas-jets; at the other, my father, and a house too far from the sea, called Greenways. In the background, pulsing away, is a war we're supposed to win by Christmas, but don't. All the women in the company have started knitting, knitting, mufflers for our brave boys at the front, and all the eligible men are talking tactics and recruiting officers.

Maman died wildly, with wild cries, at the *Othello* first night, and I think Sir Frank never forgave her. Danny and I sat side by side in the audience; Danny's clockwork whirred, and she shed tears when Desdemona was silenced. For those tears, I forgive her for much that happened afterward. I held her hand: I was afraid for Maman. I had cramps in my stomach; my head ached and I felt dizzy with nerves. I was bleeding, I discovered in the second interval. Was this the Red Flag? I wiped the blood off and went back to my seat. I wondered if I'd bleed to death, and how long that took. Who'd die first, me or Desdemona?

The following week, it was *Henry IV, Part 1*; Orlando Stephens was playing Hotspur—he was born to play Hotspur, in my opinion. He was a dashing, sweet, hotheaded fool. He had a million ideas a minute, and none of them sensible. Maman and I were in the audience that night; we went backstage afterward to see him, and, still in costume, standing at his dressing room door, Orlando announced he'd joined up that afternoon. Maman went white to the lips, her eyes rolled back in her head, then she fell to the floor in a dead faint. Orlando gave her brandy to drink; I ran to fetch sal volatile. When I came back, she was in his arms, being called his "sweet," being told he'd write every day without fail. A promise Orlando kept for less than two months: *Food for worms, brave Percy.* He died at the first battle of Ypres, that November.

So, what was the meaning of *that* scene, my darling? I was such an ignoramus then; I didn't really know where babies come from. I was still putting clues together, and my understanding was imperfect. But I have the double vision that comes with age now: I have hindsight, second sight—look at the chart and I score a perfect 20/20. Now I'm carrying a child, just as she was, so I ask myself, Was Orlando, younger than my mother by twenty years, the father of the baby I didn't even know she was expecting?

It's possible, but there are other possibilities, too. Sir Frank had always felt a tendresse for Maman, and she *had* been promoted recently. There had been other men, from time to time, who had admired Maman, who liked her "pretty ways," and to whom she responded. Maman *was* headstrong; she was vulnerable to men's interest and flattery; without a second thought, without caring how dangerous it might be, she followed where her heart led her.

I love her for that generosity of spirit, but she was not a good judge of character, and she trusted too easily. Dear Maman! She remained an innocent until the day she died—far more innocent than I was. But then I'd learned my lesson years before on a beach in Brittany. I *always* knew that men were the enemy.

ONCE ORLANDO HAD LEFT THE COMPANY, MAMAN'S strength declined rapidly; she fainted twice in the wings. I knew that my wiles and Sir Frank's gallantry wouldn't protect her from the wife's yellow jealous cat eyes much longer. When the season ended at Plymouth, and the company made ready to move on to Bristol, the crisis came. A shamefaced Sir Frank explained that takings were down yet again, and economies had to be made; bearing in mind my mother's indisposition, and my unfortunate tendency to grow. . . .

"Dear Lady, I fear we must part," he said, shifting from foot to foot in the St. Agnes front parlor. "In view of my indebtedness to you and to Missy here, if you will permit . . ." He reached his hand into his waistcoat pocket.

"I will *not* permit!" Maman cried, those two scarlet flags of color mounting in her cheeks. "Frank, you are a dear good man, but I couldn't."

We were broke, no savings, and I wasn't so scrupulous. I followed Sir Frank out, and bending down from his great height, he kissed me on both cheeks, called me "Missy" one last time, begged me to write, and gave me the waistcoat check. Written with a flourish: Pay to Mrs. Isabel Devlin the sum of ten guineas.

The check bounced, and Sir Frank never answered the letters I sent, but I don't hold that against him. He was a fraud, but he was also a hero (and *they're* thin on the ground, my darling, as rare as unicorns). We managed without that money anyway. There was a week's kerfuffle at St. Agnes, much toing and froing and whispering behind doors; there was an atmosphere of malaise, panic, and hopelessness. Doctors came and went; Millicent and my mother were thick as thieves, but Millicent was old by then and didn't know what to do, I could tell. Maman wept into that scrap of a lace handkerchief of hers—and I was excluded.

I walked Marine Parade and looked at warships. I talked to the gulls. I couldn't help, all my offers of help were rejected. "You're just a child, dearie, and your mother doesn't want you worried," Millicent said—but I knew that wasn't true. I wasn't a child anymore; I wasn't a woman, either. I couldn't be a doomed boy. I had no function, no gender, no identity; others were making decisions, making arrangements, the females were rallying, I could sense it—and meanwhile I was trapped in a hinterland; I was down there with the unborn and unbaptised, in Limbo.

The next thing I knew, Danny had arrived. She was taking charge—and how she relished it! Danny's always been drawn to crisis; she flies to it the way iron filings fly to a magnet. Suddenly, she'd given up her position, was back at St. Agnes, and was ordering everyone around, me included. Maman was quite seriously ill, she said; she needed a rest cure; all the doctors were unanimous: She'd been overworking, and her nerves were strained from fatigue and fretting about my welfare. Maman needed to rest and build up her health for a few months. It was possible Danny might be able to get her into a convalescent home she knew of; if so, Danny would be going with her, she wouldn't dream of leaving her side. Meanwhile, such excitement, a sanctuary had been found for me. Just for a while, a few months, until Maman was quite recovered, I was to stay with Maman's sister, Evangeline, in her beautiful house, St. Winnow's.

Evangeline had been to see Maman the previous day, it seemed, when I'd happened to be out shopping with Millicent. It was all arranged, there was nothing to worry about. My aunt would pay any nursing home fees; meanwhile, it would be a great opportunity for me. St. Winnow's was a fine establishment; I would move in the best circles, and no doubt pick up all kinds of useful instruction from those two fine young ladies, my cousins Elinor and Jocelyn.

Such an arrant lie. Danny's eyes slid away. I stared at the aspidistra in its brass pot; I dug my bitten nails into my palms. My *aunt*? My *cousins*? They'd ignored my existence since the day I was born—for nearly fourteen years, they'd ignored me. Evangeline had made Maman feel like a pariah. I knew what this lie was hiding: I was being bundled away from some terrible truth. What was it, was Maman dying?

I left Danny there, talking to the walls; helter-skelter up the stairs to the new room where they'd put Maman. She was lying in bed, blue shadows under her beautiful eyes; that cunning locket was around her throat; Tennyson's *Complete Works* lay on the counterpane. I flung myself across her, and Maman held me tight; she stroked my black Devlin hair; we were both crying.

"Darling," she said. "I love you with all my heart. You know that, Becka. You're the only thing that matters to me, and I would never lie to you. I promise you, I'm not dying. I'm not seriously ill. I just need to rest for a while—we'll be together again in just a few months, my sweet, I swear to you."

Fait accompli. Dispatched to St. Winnow's. There, no one explained to anyone who I was. I was just a relation, one of the tribes of Grenville connections. I was camouflaged by vagueness. They walled up my mother, brick by brick; they entombed her in reticence. Maman must never be mentioned; her name was never uttered except by Evangeline, and then only when she was alone with me.

I'm sure they'd never have taken me in, had straitlaced Sir Joshua not been away for months, making a tour of foreign shipping yards. I was put in a cold attic room, and forbidden to speak to the servants. Everyone in this house was half dead; they were dying of anemia. I was expected to sit, to take tea, to sew, to modulate my behaviour, alter my way of speech and reform all my attitudes. I mustn't wear my hair loose. I mustn't face the air without gloves, and a hat, an umbrella or a parasol. I mustn't walk alone anywhere, except in the garden. I mustn't run or raise my voice, and I should speak only when spoken to.

Dearest, I started dying inside. My heart shriveled. Danny sent twice-weekly bulletins and said Maman was too weak to write. Only my anger kept me going.

No one was unkind, exactly. They kept me in the cage, and they fed me regularly—no red meat, though! They put their hands through the bars and stroked my fur and remarked on my odd habits and appearance. I was a very exotic little beast, a *chien mechant*—and they were wary. Who bred this little bitch, with her doubtful pedigree? I might bite the hand that stroked and fed me, look how I snarled, look what sharp little teeth I had! Careful, careful: I might shame them all by some sudden unspeakable bestial barbarity.

What fools! I could mimic them and their milksop ways inside a week. I could do their accents and their gestures within a day. I could speak their language if necessary. And when Evangeline saw that, she grew a little bolder and a little bolder. I was allowed outside the kennel occasionally.

First, Elinor, the elder and sharper of my cousins, took me out on the leash. Elinor was not living at St. Winnow's, she was training to be a voluntary nurse, a VAD, at a hospital in Exeter; on one of her rare visits, she took me to Kerrith, and when I didn't disgrace her in the shops or streets, took me to a house called The Pines, to call on her friends, old Mrs. Julyan, and her soldier son, Arthur. "He's a fine man," Elinor said, striding briskly up the hill. "Two days' leave from his regiment. His wife's expecting their first child. I must inquire after her."

No sign of the wife—too far gone to be presentable, I think now. But Captain Julyan was a *very* handsome man: tall, thoughtful, and lean, with clever blue eyes—I liked him instantly. We took tea in a garden between a palm and a monkey puzzle. Elinor was brusque, but I scented a tendresse; if Elinor had once had expectations that had not been fulfilled, however, she hid them. How perfectly I behaved; scarcely spoke, didn't swing my legs, made myself invisible.

My identity was being smudged again. No one mentioned Maman. I looked at the great billowing banks of roses by the house. They had bloodred heps, big as a baby's fist. Old Mrs. Julyan said they were scions of the famous Grenville roses. Elinor changed the subject immediately.

Captain Julyan was gallant. He looked at me intently. He admired my blue butterfly brooch—and I wouldn't be silenced then. I said Maman had given it to me.

As we left, Captain Julyan took me into his grandfather's study: such a room—books, books, it was barricaded with books, all four walls, floor to ceiling. He showed me the collection of butterflies he'd made as a boy, and there was one just like my brooch. He'd caught it in the Manderley woods, when he was seven; it was a Meadow Blue, not as rare or showy as a Painted Lady or a Swallowtail, but intensely blue, and one of his favorites. Poor *papillons*! They were finished off with chloroform, then pinned through the furry heart; there were thousands in those specimen drawers, as many butterflies as books, my darling.

He packed the Meadow Blue up in a small box, and gave it to me and I treasured it, but it was lost in the rush and confusion some months later, when Danny summoned me, and I had to go to my mother's bedside at Greenways. Or maybe I took a dislike to it and destroyed it. I forget now.

"You're a good girl, Rebecca," Elinor said, striding back down the hill again. "You can behave so nicely when you want, my dear."

"I can act," I said scornfully, tossing my head. "Of course I can act. I've been doing Shakespeare for seven years. Tea at The Pines isn't difficult."

"I would imagine not," she replied calmly. She was not a fool, Elinor, I realized. How old was she, I wondered. Twenty? Twenty-four or -five, maybe.

"Everyone acts, in any case," she went on. "You're not unique in that respect. Nurses have to act, for instance, as I'm learning at the hospital. Nurses have to be *great* concealers of the truth . . ." She frowned, slowed, sighed, then picked up pace. "Still, never mind that. Let's go home, dear. Don't scuff your feet now."

My first outing. My first sniff at this new world. A repetition wasn't risked, not for weeks. Elinor returned to her hospital; younger sister Jocelyn used to talk to me sometimes, but plump pretty Jocelyn was in love, sighing for a subaltern fiancé somewhere in France. She wrote letters to him every day, and sometimes I'd walk with her to the box. Before she posted them she'd kiss the envelope flaps for luck. She was sweet natured but moony and not much use to me. My nosings scared her: "Do you remember my maman?" I said. "Did you meet her when you were little, Jocelyn?"

Jocelyn crimsoned, and looked at me with round blue eyes. She said she couldn't remember my mama, that she wasn't allowed to discuss my mama, her father wouldn't have her name spoken in the house. "Why not?" I cried, stamping my foot. "Why not? She's a Grenville. The Grenvilles go back to kingdom come. Your father's family's nothing to write home about."

"Papa didn't approve of her marriage," Jocelyn blurted. "And you mustn't speak of Papa in that way. It's very rude and wrong when Mama's been so good to you."

"*That* for your mother," I shouted, snapping my fingers in her face. "Damn your father! I hope his ships sink! He's food for worms, he is!"

Jocelyn ran away. She was packed off to stay with friends before the week was out, and it was back to the kennel for me: Obedience lessons with Aunt Evangeline every morning—it didn't do to challenge the authority of the master of the house, you see, and as for swearing . . . No beatings, don't imagine that. Evangeline was not a bad woman or a stupid one; she tried the reasonable approach. We'd sit side by side on the verandah if the autumn day was warm enough. Evangeline would work on her embroideries and tapestries; I would sort the wools and line up the rainbow silks. Vermilion and violet. Down below us, the river Kerr wound; I'd watch its windings, I'd hear Maman's voice reading Tennyson, and imagine the river was winding all the way to Camelot.

"I try to help," Evangeline said, her needle moving deftly back and forth, little flashes of silver, always work in the same direction and keep the tension even, she told me. "But Isolda always was so headstrong! She will not listen to reason. She will rush in where angels fear to tread, you see, Rebecca."

Had angels feared to tread at Manderley, I wondered? Why was Maman banished to France? I asked Evangeline.

"Heavens, she wasn't banished! What a word! It was just felt . . . well, that it would do Isolda good to spend some time abroad. Your mother's very sensitive, and she's easily influenced, and she was terribly distressed by our sister Virginia's death. It made her quite ill. She wasn't herself for a long while afterward. So she went to France, and then she married in France, of course—pass me the mauve silk, would you, dear? I'm going to do this flower next. I must change color."

I passed the silk. "Is Maman going to die?" I said.

"No, no, no," said Evangeline, rising quickly and putting her arms around me. "You mustn't think that. In another few months she'll be quite well again—"

"How many months?"

"In the new year, by February at the very latest, for sure. Now, that isn't long to wait, my dear, is it?"

Not long? It was an eternity. Three more months in the cage. By February, I'd have dwindled to nothing—and I didn't believe Evangeline, in any case. Danny had written to say that I still couldn't visit; all being well, Maman would be moving to a convalescent home in Berkshire shortly—and I knew what that meant. Once they ferried her there, once those gates clanged shut on her, I'd never see her again. She'd go down to join my dead Devlin father in his underworld; he'd reclaim his bride. He'd wind her in his arms, as he sometimes did in my dreams, and there'd be no escaping *that* long embrace. *My father, my father.* Somewhere around that time, I began to fear him.

Did Evangeline see those thoughts in my face? Perhaps, for she tried harder and harder to divert me after that. She fetched out Jocelyn's old dolls; she played the piano for me (a great Steinway: these strings needed no tuning). She gave me silly girls' books to read, when I hungered for the meat and wine of Shakespeare. She produced jigsaws and scrapbooks; she taught me bezique and bridge, and one day, when inspiration was nearing its end, she brought me a pile of fat black notebooks, with strings that tied on their spines. My

mother had had some very similar as a child, she said. I was such an
odd little girl, imaginative, just as my mother had been; maybe it
would amuse me to keep a diary, or write stories?

THOSE LITTLE COFFIN BOOKS DREW ME. THAT AFTERNOON,
while Evangeline was at home to her visitors downstairs, I sat in the
old schoolroom. I took up a steel-nibbed pen and dipped it in black
ink. I thought, I'll write Maman's story and mine. I'll write our history, and, when she's well again, I'll present it to her.

I didn't get very far, my darling. I stuck in a picture of myself with
Midsummer's Night's Dream wings—I'd been proud of that picture
once, Maman had it taken specially. I stuck in a postcard picture of
Manderley I'd bought that hot day Elinor took me out on the leash. I
wrote the words "Rebecca's Tale," and curled the tail of the letter "e"
all the way down the page like a fleshy serpent. It was potent; it was a
python, an anaconda.

What else? I wanted to give Maman our past; our idyll by the sea,
and all the glories of my childhood—they would make her well again.
I wanted to write about Brittany and our foursquare house; the sound
of the waves and the sin in a speck of dust. I felt certain that, if I
wrote accurately enough, Maman would survive. She'd live then, for
sure—but something was choking me. My head felt hot; my mouth
was dry; the pages blurred. I missed Maman, I feared for her, and not
a word would come to me.

In the end, I left the pages blank, telling a tale only I could read. I
closed up the black covers, tied the strings on the spine, and hid it
away. Maybe my failure caused Maman's death, I thought afterward;
maybe I was responsible.

I have that little book still, and it's on the table here now. I took it
out this afternoon to look at it. Such a change! Then I couldn't write;
now I can't stop. I feel such an itch and an urgency; there's so much I
want you to know, my dearest. The memories come at me pell-mell.
I can't write fast enough—my story's eating into me.

Has my mother come back from the dead for you? I hope so. I
want you to know her. Can you hear her voice? I can, so clearly. Now
there are other ghosts to resurrect, and other twists in the tale to tell
you. Not so very many pages left in this book, but enough. I'll tell

you how I first came to Manderley, how my Devlin father came back from the dead—and how I won myself a husband. Now there's a fairy tale, and a Grimm one! Meanwhile, my love, it's late; the sea's silvery.

I'll have to go back to the house for dinner; I must put in appearances occasionally. I'll continue tomorrow, my sweet—husband permitting. I'll have to leave for my London appointment very early the next day, but I'll take you out in my boat, and then finish my tale before I leave, I promise you.

TWENTY-FOUR

Back from your first sail; conditions were perfect. You've seen this bay, the blue diamond in your Manderley crown, my dearest.

You've seen the twin rocks christened Scylla and Charybdis, centuries ago, when Max was a child. You've navigated between them, ventured out into the open sea, and felt the swell of the ocean for the first time. Isn't that intoxicating—feeling that pulse, riding that power? But be warned. Tonight, conditions were calm for this coast; those waves aren't always so obedient, and if the wind alters direction, their mood can change very swiftly.

Such a night! A world made monochrome; a mercury sea, a high full merciless moon; water of such transparency you could see the upper ridges of the sandbar out by the reef—a treacherous underwater bank, so pale and bone colored. Whenever I see that, I think of the nights in the wings when I listened to Oberon; *I know a bank* . . . and, although I understand I must steer away from it, it entices me. If there are sirens in this bay—and I know better than most that there are—it's there that they lie in wait and sing their songs for me.

Tonight, I could hear their voices clearly. In the moonlight, they were sweet, plangent, and powerful. Perhaps I was tiring; suddenly I longed to lie down there and sleep. I felt such a yearning for *oblivion*.

I wanted to rest in peace on that bone-white bank, nestle under the rocks beyond it. I thought, No more striving; O, wind a chain about my wrists, pay me out, and lower me down there. . . .

You should know—I don't mind your knowing—I've had that temptation before, I've been beckoned down *that* route for years. When I was a child, I heard those sirens. They whispered to me once on the Brittany waves, but sirens are great survivors, and can adapt to all manner of habitations if need be. They're ingenious, I've found.

The sea, of course. They like best to be there. But they'll take up residence almost anywhere: on the deck of an ocean liner, or the top floor of a high building; inside razors and gas jets and guns; they fit snugly into a handful of pills; they'll breed like germs on the broken neck of a bottle. They sang out from razors after Maman died—and, in my twenty-first year, when my Devlin father had his neck broken, they were everywhere, the whole house swarmed, it stank of them. I gave in then: I uncorked a bottle I knew was full of them, and I sucked it dry in a locked room at Greenways. I swallowed a milky pint of their poisonous promises then, and I was sure that would satisfy them—but I was foiled. Guardian Danny had the door broken down; I was pumped out in some hospital, and in due course I was glad. I began planning how to marry Max not long afterward. As I said, the ways of death are infinite.

Last year, once last year, just after I'd cut my hair, I went out in *Je Reviens*, and I nearly succumbed to those sirens again. But that was the last temptation, and it was before your advent, so don't be anxious; I know how deathly cold that water is, never fear. I've stopped my ears to those voices, like Odysseus; I've blinded my eyes to those beckoning hands. I won't be joining my sisters by the reef, I promise you—not now I have such precious cargo aboard, my darling.

NOW WE'RE IN HARBOR, AND ALL IS WELL. *JE REVIENS* rides at anchor on the buoy by the breakwater; I had her made by Marie-Hélène's eldest boy, and he named her for me. A lucky name for a lucky boat: For all those who sail in her, safe passage home is assured. Her tender's tied fast at the jetty; her spare sails are stowed, wound as tight as winding sheets; all her brass gleams like gold; her decks are smooth as skin, she's been cleaned and caulked and rigged by expert hands; she's seaworthy, ready for embarkation—why, in this boat, we could go anywhere, we could sail to Newfoundland.

And I'm ready, too. Danny's packed my case for me, I've set an alarm clock on my table here, in case I should oversleep. I leave for London at six. I'll have my hair done when I get there because I want to look my best tomorrow; then I'll have lunch at my club. My grave doctor is so in demand that he can't see me until two. Frustrating! I'd like us to see him at dawn. I may set off even earlier—it's such a long drive. I'm impatient to be there, and above all I don't want to encounter Max when I'm leaving; he's furious that I'm going back to London.

I want to continue with our story, but first I must tell you what happened when I informed Max of my plans, which I did over dinner last night. I'd expected trouble, but what happened was *very* strange, my darling. I'd finished writing, as you know, then I hid my notebooks away. Our boathouse cottage is damp, and the best place to hide things is somewhere ordinary or everyday, so I've been keeping them in an old biscuit tin; then I locked the door and set off up the path. It was about 6:30; the light was pearl, the sky rose-colored, with streaks of garnet. When I reached the top of the path, the scent of the azaleas was heavy and sweet from the evening dew. Manderley lay before me, in all its beauty. In such lights, it looks welcoming and harmonious, but it's a house of many moods, some of them dark, and they can change as swiftly as the weather here. I exult in that—but not everyone, not even Max, agrees with me.

Last night, the windows were lit up by the sun's sinking rays; the long western facade was aflame. I kicked off my shoes and walked barefoot across the cool damp grass toward my home. The thrush that's nesting in the lilacs was singing; a blackbird saluted the beauty of the evening from the yew. I was at the still point of the turning universe, suspended in time, with no yesterday to perplex me and no tomorrow to fear. I could feel your weight in my womb. I could hear the sea moving behind me. I felt the greatest possible joy, my darling.

I went into the house, and it was as perfect as the evening. The branches of white lilac that's forced on every year were blooming in the right vase on the right table; the flames of the fires burned steady; lilac and woodsmoke scented the air. Manderley was so still, so utterly lovely. All the fervor of my old Religion of the House rose up in me. What a hermetic place this was when I first came here—a barracks would have been more welcoming; you couldn't breathe, the air was so old. Now my house has become itself; it's a sanctuary. I crossed into the hall where the cool flagstones caressed my feet, and the thick ancient walls were as pale as alabaster. The oak stair treads were smooth; the bannister fitted my hand. I knew that my work was well done, and Marie-Hélène would have approved of me.

I went upstairs to my bedroom. Danny drew a bath for me, and I washed in the soft fragrant water; she brushed my hair. I put on a sea-green silk dress; I wound some pearls round my neck; I put scent on my wrists, and on my right hand some ancestor emerald Max gave me on our honeymoon. I'd eaten very little today, but I'd only been sick twice, and that was encouraging. I felt cleansed and anointed and calm. I went along the gallery, past all those portraits. I saluted the women of this house: Caroline de Winter, the most tormented of them all, and those three graces, the Grenville sisters, Evangeline, Virginia, and Isolda.

I decided I'd tell Max over dinner that I'd be going to London tomorrow; I'd do it when the servants were there. I fill the house with people for days at a time, you see, dearest, but sooner or later there comes an evening when we have to be alone together. I know Max dreads such evenings—we sit there acting out our rituals for our spectral spectator servants, two castaways, surrounded by wrack, wreckage, and ruin.

God, that dining room's cold when there's just the two of us! I take precautions, insofar as I can. I ensure the fire's been built up with the best oak logs, with heartwood—and the room always seems warm enough when we first enter. The wines are always good; the food is superb. Then I look down that long mahogany table at Max, past the bulwarks of flowers and silver; I look at his stiff white shirt and I look at his eyes; I listen to the conversation we make for the servants' sake and my blood starts to congeal. The pack ice closes in. Icicles form in my lungs. I'd be warmer in Siberia.

Last night, my blue-green dress shimmered in the candlelight; the emerald ring was now loose on my finger. I could see my pale double, and Max's, moving on the polished mahogany. There was a pyramid of dark fruits between us. I was so strung up. My eyes shone. I'm too thin, but I *know* I looked beautiful, sitting there, dying of cold, and I'm almost sure Max had noticed that.

"So soon?" Max said. "It's less than a week since you last went to London."

"It will be exactly a week," I replied. I thought, Am I without powers now?

"And will you be staying overnight?" he asked, for the benefit of Frith and Co., who were standing to attention in the shadows. He gave me a wintry glance. He wasn't calm, but how calm he sounded!

"I don't like the thought of your doing that drive twice in one day, darling," he said. "It's too far. You'll be exhausted. That's how accidents happen."

"I haven't driven off the road yet," I said.

"There's always a first time," he answered.

Terms of endearment for the sake of servants' ears—that always enrages me, and Max knows it. When we were finally alone, and God knows that's hard enough at Manderley, I told him, If he'd like to exile me to my flat, not just overnight but for a week, a month—or evermore, if possible—then he should have the guts to say so in front of Frith. He says it to me often enough; why not let the servants in on the secret? Why not broadcast it to the world, Max?

No answer, but I could feel a groundswell of rage and misery. We were in the library, his cavern of books. It smells male: leather, dogs, cigarettes, old newspapers, old brandy, and old feuds. Max was barricaded behind a newspaper, a new technique of his. I have to goad him a great deal now to get him to react; he's afraid to retaliate the way he once did. If he can, he avoids the blows and bloodletting and we both know why. Anger opens a wide, wide door, and even now sex lies in wait on the other side of that portal.

I sat there in the leather chair opposite him. I smoked a cigarette. I smoked one more. All my own anger was leaching away; I had that weakening bleeding sensation again, the one I had yesterday when I stood outside the estate office. I was tired, bone tired—and I was feeling so sick. I'd scarcely been able to eat any dinner, and that was making me desperate. My thoughts went round and round on a torturer's wheel. First breakfast, then lunch, then tea, now dinner. No one ever told me you could have morning sickness twenty-four hours a day.

I don't want to starve you. The clock ticked; the newspaper pages rustled. I had the strangest sensation that I'd died; I didn't exist; was Rebecca invisible now?

I looked around that room, the dog-fox's den, his refuge: shelves of bloodstock bibles, equine and human. Shelves of other authorities. Precious few females, a tonage of male authors. Christ, there's thousands of them. How they clamor! I haven't touched this room. I left it as Max likes it: plain, shabby. I tried to read the patterns on the dark Turkish rug; what did they tell me? Was there a message in the curtains, in Great-grandpapa's furniture? What did the air here say?

I have a very good critical eye, and I knew: unchanged since the day of creation! Poor Virginia will have sat in this chair; Max's grandmother sat here before I persuaded her to depart to the dower house. Maybe Max's great-grandmother alighted here once, and another mother before her. All those de Winter wives; the line stretched back to the crack of doom—and, just as I was thinking that, the strangest thing happened. There was a new ghost, I realized, she'd come in out of the blue night air, and she was skulking over there by the blue curtains.

Such a stealthy presence, very subdued—but insistent, determined; there's a strength in passivity, and I could sense it now, sidling up to my chair. Max seemed unaware of her presence; I leaned forward to take a good look at her. Such a secretive, bloodless mouse squeak of a ghost! Sweet as sugar, innocent as a schoolgirl, not a scrap of makeup, wearing no scent, lank hair—sly eyes, I thought, but I expect I was biased. I could smell emulation and rivalry; I didn't take to her, not at all, my darling.

She was stroking *my* dog; she had *my* handkerchief in her pocket. A tweed skirt and a twinset, an air of docile desperation; no fire, no chic, no nerve. I thought, Who in God's name is she? How dare she come here?

Did she have a *name*? She put a finger to her lips; no name, apparently. I decided it was Max who was conjuring up this anonymity, this airy nothing; perhaps this hallucination was his notion of an ideal wife, the woman of eternal subservience who might have made the perfect Mrs. de Winter.

That angered me. How could that be? Was I *so* wrong, so ill suited from the very beginning? I gave Max the gift of tumult once. I put lightning in his hand. Such gifts are rare. Had he forgotten that? If so, he was betraying himself; he was a lesser man than I'd thought him; he was paltry.

I felt the blood rush up to my head; I felt dizzy and murderous. Not possible, I said to myself; not possible. I *know* what happened between us; nothing and no one will unwrite that; those words are carved too deep in us. Time started to bend and the room started to move. I stood up. I felt sick, white with anger and contempt; I could hear a noise like cards shuffling; they were being shuffled by a huge and expert hand, packs and packs of them.

I may have made a sound of protest, because Max also rose; he started to move toward me. And then the astonishing thing happened. It wasn't Max who put his arms around me, it was that quiet ghost girl with her wide seeking eyes. She stepped in between me and Max; she held on to me for strength; I saw it was I who'd summoned her up, and I saw she could be my ally. I kissed her on the cheek, like an accomplice, and then on the mouth, like a lover. Blood rushed up into her bloodless cheeks. It was such a deep shocking kiss that we both shuddered. She gave a sigh and vanished into the air. She left as swiftly as she came—and my blind husband noticed nothing.

How do you explain *that*? Who do you think she was, this revenant? Even by Manderley standards, rousing a ghost that equivocal was unusual.

I've been thinking about this vision since, and I've decided it was due to your influence. You're so rooted in me now that you've altered my eyesight forever. I could always see around corners, and over the lip of the horizon, but now I'm perfected. My new powers are extraordinary. I can see to infinity and way beyond; I can see all the patterns in my past that I never saw when it was happening.

So, pregnant with my new powers, I'll continue our story. I must tell you how I came to Manderley, first as a girl, then as a bride, my darling.

It was November 5, 1914; that was the day I first came to Manderley. It was the week of my birthday and it was Guy Fawkes Night. I'd hoped I might be allowed a birthday visit to Maman, but I wasn't. On our way to Manderley, we passed a great mountain of wood that had been piled up on the outskirts of Kerrith; they were going to burn the transgressor in effigy that evening. The little outing had been announced the previous day, without warning, by Evangeline, and I'd been very surprised. True, Evangeline had taken me out on my leash once or twice recently, but to Manderley? That seemed very incendiary.

The preparations took an hour. I was stripped, scrubbed, and disciplined. My rebel hair was flattened and curbed; it was bound up into plaits and coiled on the back of my neck like a dead snake, stabbed with hairpins. A hat was jammed on top of it; my nails were inspected, and the bitten stumps sighed over; my fingers were forced into tight gloves. I was laced into layers of modesty: camisoles and bodices and scratchy starched petticoats. My feet were buttoned up into little boots I'd outgrown, and, as a final insult—none of my own dresses passing muster—I was dolled up in an old frock of Jocelyn's the color of dried blood, surmounted by a cape affair. What a triumph; I looked hideous!

When the maid had completed this assignment, I was led downstairs for Evangeline's inspection. She seemed to approve the effect until she came to my face. She took my chin in her hand, and tilted it up toward her. She looked intently, very intently, first at my mouth, then at my eyes. She sighed, frowned, and shook her head, and I could see these features of mine disturbed her. What was wrong with my mouth? Hothead Orlando had once said, in a teasing way to Maman, that it was kissable, which had put Maman in a temper all day. Were kissable mouths not permitted? And what was wrong with my eyes? "What's wrong with my eyes?" I said as Evangeline continued her inspection. "I can't help them. They're the eyes I was born with."

"There's nothing wrong with your eyes, child," Evangeline said, in a defeated way. "It's just . . . I think it's the *expression*, dear. You always look so bold. And the effect—your eyes are an unusual color, you know, and your lashes are very long and thick—I'm sure you're not aware of it, Rebecca, but it's slightly *immodest* somehow. A young lady does not stare, my dear, and if she feels scornful, she disguises it."

"Shall I stare at my boots?" I said. "I'll stare at them if you prefer it."

Evangeline told me not to be impertinent, and we left with her uniformed driver in her motor car. Up hill and down dale, through tall iron gates, and into the endless drive of my imagination. The Indian summer was continuing. It was hot and thunderous. The leaves on the trees in the Manderley woods had shriveled; great golden heaps were being raked up and burned by gardeners. The gravel hissed and crunched; the air smelled of smoke; when we slowed at a bend I could hear the sea. Ghosts greeted me. Sweet aunt Virginia came out to welcome me. When Evangeline was looking the other way, I fished out my blue butterfly brooch, secreted in my pocket, and pinned it right on the front of my dress. My blazon, where no one could miss seeing it.

We entered the great tomb of the north entrance portal where, returning as Max's bride a decade or so later, I would drop one of my gloves and force Frith to stoop and pick it up—my private revenge on him for those mauve suede gloves he'd packed up to placate my poor Maman, that present from a scoundrel. Frith wasn't butler on this first visit; some other watchdog, some other Cerberus came out to greet us. And in we went to the house of the dead: dark, dark, the air wet with the sweat of centuries of secrets. Welcome to Hades!

A drawing room, dearest: not *my* drawing room, not my lovely creation, but the place it used to be; the windows fastened shut, the light made wintry by these thick ugly barbarous curtains, all festooned and frogged and looped back with silky hangmen's nooses. A miserable little heap of wood expiring in the fireplace; the paneling obscured by great dark mothy tapestries; abominable fat chairs in funereal colors set crabwise across the corners; a thousand little traps and fortifications, baby tables on stilted legs, stunted stools. Trying to find a passageway across that room was like negotiating no-man's-land. One little flick with my preposterous skirt, and I could cause a catastrophe. What a crashing of china knickknackery then, what a tinkling of photograph frames as they fell to the floor. There were ancestral images on every available surface; I knew one of them had to be Lionel—ah, the pleasure in smashing *his* image!

And there, rising to her feet and approaching us, the grandmother, Maman's interfering, arrogant old beast. I didn't intent to look at my boots *then*—I raised my eyes and fixed her with my Medusa stare, I can tell you!

I'll tell you another thing, dearest, and very curious it was: One look, and I *liked* her. At once. Maybe it's those *chien mechant* tendencies of mine, but I think you can always sniff out an enemy or a friend straightaway. I always know immediately if someone's to be trusted or not—and I can't say that old Mrs. de Winter was trustworthy exactly, but she had presence, she had vim, and she had nerve, too. This woman wasn't afraid to be rude. She was not interested in Evangeline, I saw, and she dispatched her inside five minutes. A maid was summoned to escort her upstairs where, the old dragon said, her granddaughter, Beatrice, was resting with her new baby, and would be delighted to see her.

"Now," said the old beast, turning to me the second the door closed. "Do you know why you're here, child? You're here because I wanted to meet you. Let me look at you." ·

She inspected my face as closely as Evangeline had done earlier. "Well, well, well," she said, gripping my chin hard. "A little fighter, I see. Good. Very good. I can't stand women who like being trampled on, never could. Women are the stronger sex; if you don't know that, learn it. I run things here—I expect you've heard that. If it weren't for me, this place would have gone to wrack and ruin long ago. My son's no use at all; a weakling, not a brain in his head. He's dying— did your aunt Evangeline tell you?"

"No," I said, though of course I was delighted to hear *this* news. I looked at her boldly. Tall, strongly built, handsome, arrogant blue eyes: a hungry old gorgon—give her half a chance and she'd eat you for breakfast. Sixty-ish? Seventy-ish? She'd been widowed young, Evangeline said, and I could believe it; this woman could wipe out a man in weeks. I squared up to her.

"Your son's left my mother some money in his will," I said. "So, if he's dying, you should tell him to alter it. Maman doesn't want his money. Neither do I. We wouldn't touch it. We scorn it."

"Do you indeed? Well, you don't beat about the bush, do you? Isolda must have changed her tune! And how do you know about my son's will, Miss?"

"I stole a letter and I read it."

She threw back her head and laughed. "Very good indeed. Always be well informed, whatever it takes, that's my motto. You're small. How old are you?"

"I shall be fourteen in two days' time."

"I see." She gave a frown and mused for a while, looking me up and down. I can see now, though I couldn't then, that she was assessing whether or not I might be a Lionel by-blow. She may well have been assessing something else, too, sizing me up for some future role—I wouldn't put it past her.

I'm almost sure she decided I *wasn't* the fruit of Lionel's loins, because after an interval her face cleared. She reached across to one of those spindly unstable tables and picked up a photograph in a silver frame. She gave an odd gloating smile. "My son," she said. "Tell me what you think of him."

I didn't think much of him, my darling, and I was hugely relieved to see Lionel was everything I'd imagined from his letters: a bloat, a peacock of a man. A self-satisfied smirk; pale wolf eyes; thinning fair curls; a luxuriant moustache; a paunch not concealed by a costly waistcoat. An adulterer to his fat fingertips. I blushed to the roots of my black Devlin hair; how could Maman have looked twice at him?

"I wouldn't trust him as far as that door," I said. "He looks villainous to me—though there's no art 'to find the mind's construction in the face,' obviously."

"You think so?" She gave a frown. She was disconcerted, and she didn't recognize the quotation. But, then, she didn't look to me like a woman who read; she was a bit of a barbarian, probably.

"I don't agree," she said. "Not villainous. Weak, perhaps. Self-indulgent. A disappointment to me—but he's my son, so I forgive him. Do the best I can by him. Clean up the messes he leaves behind—that's what mothers are for, in my view. He's my only child. Very demanding as a boy. I couldn't refuse him anything. . . ." An odd lost look came upon her face. She stared off into the middle distance for several minutes, until I began to think she'd forgotten me.

"So, tell me about yourself, Miss," she said, rousing herself so suddenly she made me jump. "I can see your mother in your face. She's there in the set of your lips. Isolda was always willful. A mind of her own. I liked that in her. Very different from Virginia. Lionel chose the wrong sister, in my opinion—but there, Isolda was so much younger; he overlooked her. Wait a few years till she's grown up, I told him. But he wouldn't listen. Virginia was so accommodating— never you be accommodating, Miss, it's dying by inches. Who's your father? I've heard tales! Take after him, do you?"

"My father's Jack Sheridan Devlin," I said, speaking very fast. "He's Irish. He's an adventurer. He swept my mother off her feet. They met on the Monday and married on the Tuesday, Maman says.

I have his hair and his eyes and his temper. But he's dead. His ship went down off the Cape in South Africa. He'd gone there to make our fortune."

"I see. I see." She gave me such a queer look, my darling! To this day I don't know what that look meant; she looked disconcerted again and thoughtful. Insofar as the old beast had a heart, it softened toward me a little, I thought, and I didn't like that. I won't be pitied!

She looked away toward the windows and the thin rays of sunshine that just penetrated those curtains; a snap of the fingers and she was brusque again. "That's enough questions for one day. I'm glad to have met you, Miss. Give your mama my regards when you next see her." She stared hard at my butterfly brooch. She said, "Who foisted that hat on you? It's perfectly hideous."

"Evangeline."

"Well, take it off, child. Go outside and run around. Young people like to do that. Get some air into your lungs. You see those steps over there? Go that way, follow that path. My grandson, Maxim, went walking that way. He's leaving for his regiment today. The house is at sixes and sevens. All the menservants are leaving. Go and introduce yourself to him. Follow that path and you'll come to the sea. I expect you'd like to see the sea?"

"Yes. I would."

"Then run along. Return in forty-five minutes. I wish to speak to Evangeline."

I went out through the French windows she indicated. I crossed an ugly regimented section of garden, with scarlet-berried plants lined up like redcoat soldiers. I started to run. Down the steps and across the lawn. I yanked off that hideous hat, and I ran as fast as I could, sucking in great gulps of the salt air. I wished she'd never mentioned my father or my mother. I wished Lionel the betrayor would hurry up and die. If I ran fast enough, I knew there'd be no danger of tears, the wind would whip them away or disguise them.

Pell-mell, faster and faster. When I came to the top of the path that leads down here, I came to a shuddering halt. I scrunched that hat into a ball and threw it into the wind. The wind caught it up and spun it away, played with it, then drowned it in a rock pool.

When my vision cleared, I saw this bay for the first time in all its glory. The water was white lipped, aquamarine, and purple. The light dazzled. The waves washed and withdrew, washed and withdrew, endlessly promising, endlessly cleansing. All the aches in my heart began to untwist and uncoil; I looked over my shoulder at the long panthery shape of Manderley, crouching by its woods; I looked back at the suck and flux of the tide, and I knew I'd come home. This place was mine. I spoke its language, and it answered me.

Could I make it mine? Could I wrest it from the de Winters' hands? That would be true revenge for all the injustice dealt out to Maman: an excellent reward for her. But how on earth could *that* be achieved? I frowned, and I puzzled, and I considered my erstwhile successes and stratagems. Ever since Frank McKendrick had paid me that compliment on Marine Parade, clever deformed Richard III had been my favorite character and mentor. At that moment, a very Crookback mood came upon me. I thought to myself, *Can I do this, and cannot get a crown? Tut! Were it farther off, I'd pluck it down.*

And at that very second, my darling—precisely then, so I knew those fixed stars had always intended it—a tall man came into view, wearing uniform. He'd been out of sight, in the shadows beyond the boathouse, but now he emerged into the dazzle of the sunlight. The son and heir, it had to be! There were two children with him, a tall shambling boy in poor clothes, and a tiny wizened girl holding up the corners of an apron that was weighted down with something; they were too far off for me to identify what she was carrying.

I think he was ordering them off the premises—it certainly looked that way. I could see him pointing toward the trees that come down close to the shore by the boathouse. The boy bowed his head and stared at the shingle and scuffed his feet; the shriveled little girl dropped the corners of her apron, and shells tumbled out. Then they clasped hands, and ran off into the trees, and the son and heir, head bent, hands behind his back, turned toward the cliffpath.

I watched him walk up. He wasn't wearing his cap; I approved of his dark hair. I inspected the leather holster on his hip, his gleaming boots and the godlike glint of his buckles. The son and heir. The sun and air. I thought, Aha!

He didn't see me until he reached the top of the path—he was preoccupied, I think, and none too pleased to discover he was being spied on. I introduced myself at once. I told him my name was Rebecca, and I'd come here with Lady Briggs. He introduced himself in return, and briefly shook my hand, but he wasn't remotely interested, he was scarcely listening. His mind was on something else, I'd interrupted some reverie, and I wondered what it was. Was he thinking about his father, dying of my curse in the tower room back there, or about going to a war that was supposed to be over by Christmas?

He seemed undecided what to do, walk on past and leave me, or stand and make remarks for a few regulation minutes. In the end, he compromised. He stood next to me, a few yards away, staring out to sea, frowning and saying nothing.

"Who were those children?" I asked, after an interval.

"What, the children on the beach? Their name's Carminowe. Ben and Lucy Carminowe. Their mother's one of our tenants. They don't mean any harm, but they will hang around down there. My father doesn't like them to trespass."

"What about you?" I said. "Do you mind? It's only a beach, after all."

"True. But it's our beach." He shot me a quick glance. "This bay is private."

"Do you just own the beach, or the sea as well? I don't believe anyone can own the sea. That's impious."

"You may very well be right," he said, with a sigh. He took out a cigarette, and lit it. "In fact, now I consider it, it's ridiculous. Why not say we own the sky? Still, that's the way things are. And always have been."

He lapsed into silence again. I considered him. To him, I was just a dull plain girl in an ugly frock, some appendage of Evangeline's, there this minute, gone the next. I was well-nigh invisible, which is always useful; invisibility meant I was able to inspect him at leisure. He had a fine-drawn sensitive face and good hands. I was fascinated by his revolver as much as anything.

"Is that loaded?" I asked, after a pause in which I'm sure he'd forgotten me.

"What?" I'd startled him. "My revolver? No. It isn't."

"May I look at it?"

"No, you may not. Weapons are dangerous. They're not toys for little girls to play with."

"I've never seen a gun before. I won't touch it, I promise."

I think he was half amused. He gave another sigh, and finally, in a resigned way, unclipped the holster case, and took out the revolver. He showed me how it worked, and spun the bullet chambers for me. The sun caught its dull metal and it glinted. I gave it a covetous look. It was sleek and desirable.

"And when will you use it?" I asked. "Will you kill Germans with it?"

"I very much doubt that," he said in a dry way. "As I understand it, I mount the ladder out of the trench ahead of my men, and lead them forward across no-man's-land to the German position. We negotiate the barbed wire and the shell craters; they open up with machine guns, and I fire this. Unlike a machine gun, it has a short range. It has just six bullets. So it's not the most even of contests. I expect to be dead within the year. Two of my closest schoolfriends are dead already. I've had four weeks' training. I know nothing about fighting, anyway."

"Do you think you'll learn to kill?"

"No doubt. If I'm granted time enough."

I wondered if I should tell him that although he was doomed like his father, he wouldn't die—he couldn't, I had plans for him. I decided he wouldn't believe me if I said he'd survive because I intended it, so I remained silent. He put the gun away—and, of course, that was the very *same* revolver I caught Max oiling the other day in the gun room; imagine his cherishing it all this time! I never have discovered whether he killed any Germans with it. Max won't discuss the war at all, and I never press him. So maybe he's practiced at killing, and maybe he isn't.

"I shall have to go now," I said after a further interval; and I left him standing there by the path, staring out at the reef that runs across the bay. He'd forgotten me by the time I was ten yards away— I wasn't memorable then, dearest, though I've made myself memorable since. I ran back to the house, where Evangeline and the old beast were deep in conversation.

I DIDN'T SEE THE OLD BEAST AGAIN FOR YEARS; A GREAT tract of years went by. The next time I entered her lair, I was twenty-five, tall, transformed, and Max's fiancée.

"You're the butterfly girl, aren't you?" she said to me when we withdrew after dinner—she'd been watching me with her blue raptor eyes, all evening. Maxim and the only other guest, Frank Crawley, had remained at table with their port. This was obviously the ritual moment in which Grandmama assessed the bride-to-be. The next day, at a larger gathering, sister Beatrice was due to inspect me.

Grandmama looked me up and down. She looked at my dress, which Max had bought me; its rich velvet was the color of my engagement rubies; it was the color of blood, as glowing as the heart of a fire. It was exquisite.

"It's a very good disguise, my dear," she said. "Most accomplished—even I didn't recognize you at first. But then you'd disappeared into thin air. No one seemed to know what had become of you—and now, here you are! The little fighter. The eyes are unmistakable. Tell me, did you set your cap at Maxim?"

"No. I despise such techniques. Anyway, I didn't need to."

"That I can believe." She gave me a sharp look. "Three qualifications are required in a wife, as I've told Maxim since his childhood. They are: beauty, brains, and breeding. You have beauty, my dear— and to a dangerous degree. Brains, undoubtedly; I could see just how sharp you were the first time I met you. Breeding? Well now, I remember Isolda *very* well. And I haven't forgotten the Irish adventurer either. Old families require fresh blood from time to time. . . . An unusual pedigree, but not a bad one, all considered." She frowned, mused a little, and beat a tattoo with her fingers. "Of course, I could break this engagement—you do realize that? I've done it before, when Maxim has fallen for some inappropriate girl, and I could do it again. Does that worry you?"

"Not in the least," I replied. She sat down on a funereal sofa, and I sat next to her.

Seventy-ish? Eighty-ish? She was still a magnificent gorgon, but she was stooped now and lined; she was tiring. I had the advantage of youth, and I had another advantage, too: Max was fathoms deep in love with me.

I haunted him. He couldn't breathe for want of me. I've always liked the idea of evermore, and Max used the word "forever" constantly. He said I was the only woman he'd ever loved, the only woman he ever *could* love; he said he needed me and would always protect me. He wanted to be with me all day and all night; all night and all day he wanted to be *in* me. Sometimes he couldn't wait to undress. Hurry, my darling, he'd say; he'd touch me under my skirt, and when he felt how wet I was, he'd groan, and he'd say, Quickly, quickly. He said he dreamed of my small breasts and my pale, pale skin. He'd bury his face in my long black hair and just the scent of it made him hard; he said he drowned in my eyes—he'd die if I didn't marry him, and I'd die if I refused him. All these potent things he said. They were true then—and they're still true. They were as immutable and inevitable as the tides, all the things he told me.

Knowing this, and pitying Mrs. de Winter a little because time vanquishes even the most indomitable of women, I was gentle with her.

"If you tried to part us, you'd fail. I'm more than a match for you," I said. "In any case, you *won't* try. You can't rule Manderley forever. You're old. You need an ally and a successor—won't it be a relief to have the right successor?"

She threw back her head and laughed in exactly the way I remembered. "Very direct. I recall that from the first time I met you. A plain-speaker—up to a point. Does Maxim know you're Isolda's girl? Does anyone know?"

"No. I'm Isabel's child. An actress's daughter."

"And so you are, my dear," she said. "In the blood, I'd say, given your bravura performance at dinner. Don't worry, I can keep a secret, if that's how you prefer it. What about your father? Maxim has no reservations there? Maxim can be fastidious. I'd have thought he might have done."

"My strength comes from my father," I replied. "And Max knows that."

I looked at her lined face; should I tell her my father came back from his underworld when Maman died, then returned there the day I came of age? Should I explain how his love gave me strength? No point. I could see she'd forgotten his name, and I didn't want to waste him on her.

She gone off into another of those musing states. I saw her look around that airless room; her eyes rested on its shadowy corners. "So, how did you meet Maxim?" she asked. "You came upon the scene very suddenly. Did you give fate a nudge? I always did. Men need their minds made up for them."

I saw no reason to lie, so I told her some details, though not all of them, my darling! I'd been in New York with one of the suitors who buzzed around me after my father died—this suitor being especially persistent. We were supposed to be going on to meet his ancien régime family somewhere dull, patrician, and inland, when I heard from a friend that among the passengers on some queenly ship about to sail to England was that catch, the owner of legendary Manderley, Maxim de Winter.

The next morning, I sold a necklace the suitor had bought me the previous week—I had some money of my own, but not enough for a first-class ticket, and I disliked the necklace anyway: icy stones and too tight around my throat, it strangled me. I took myself off to the shipping offices, acquired the last available stateroom, and sailed that same day. I didn't bother to say farewell to the suitor—he'd begun to bore me. And, once on the ship, I made no attempt to waylay the son and heir, or get myself moved to his table—I knew there was no need for ruses like that. I'd been in a bad way after my father broke his neck, but I'd recovered my selves in the years since. I'd been reborn behind the green screens in that hospital ward I mentioned, and I'd made myself into the weapon of a woman I am now, not Becka anymore, but Rebecca.

The son, meanwhile, had inherited; he was still unmarried, and I knew that he was waiting for me. I'd kept an eye on his progress for years—little magazine references, anecdotes from friends. We'd almost met several times, at parties; sometimes I'd hear he'd arrived just as I'd left, but that never worried me. I was becoming famous for being myself by then, so I knew: Sooner or later, if not here then elsewhere, we'd meet—and this time he'd notice me. It was inevitable.

We did finally meet on that ship, two days into our sail; it was a rough crossing, and most passengers had retreated to their cabins. I was standing on deck, leaning over the rail, watching the gray cold swell of the empty Atlantic. The wind was gusting and keening; I didn't hear him come up behind me. He looked much as before, though less interesting minus the uniform and the gun. He was then in his midthirties; people were beginning to remark on his still being unmarried.

"You're not thinking of jumping, I hope," he said, and because I could tell the quiet inquiry was serious, not some witless joke, I replied honestly.

"Not now," I answered.

I wasn't wearing a hat, and I wasn't wearing gloves. He looked at my face, then down at my hands gripping the rail, and I saw him note the narrow band of eternity diamonds on my wedding finger. His expression altered, and he looked so dejected that I had to put him out of his misery.

I explained that my father had given me the ring, made from diamonds he'd brought back from a mine in South Africa. I didn't tell him that my father had put it on my finger the very first day I met him, as a symbol of our reunion, when I came downstairs from the sheeted mirrors in Maman's bedroom. But I did explain that my father was dead now, so I wore it in remembrance of him.

"On that particular finger?" he said, with a small frown.

"It's the only one it fits," I replied, which was true. And the ambition to replace that ring with his own came to him then, right then, or so Max always claimed to me afterward . . .

"And after that, my dear?" prompted the old gorgon of a grandmother beside me. But I didn't answer her that time. It was none of her business!

Max and I weren't apart for one moment for the rest of the crossing. We ate dinner together that night, in a near-deserted dining room; a pianist was playing edgy jazzy tunes; the ship pitched and rolled—it was supposed to have the very latest in stabilizer devices, but they weren't effective on *that* voyage, my darling.

I told Max that I refused to call him "Maxim"; the word had two meanings: it was either an artillery gun or a rule of conduct expressed in a sentence—and neither of those meanings was attractive to me. I prefer small guns that nestle in your palm to large ones, and I despise all rules, especially those foolish arbitrary ones that govern conduct. I think Max liked his new name, and perhaps it influenced him. He came to my cabin that very first night—not his usual "conduct" with women, I'm sure—and we talked all night, never touching once, then walked the wet decks at dawn the next morning.

We only had to look in each other's eyes to know: Everything was already decided; weddings, et cetera, were mere details. Dear Max! He was lonely, I suspect, searching for something and unable to find it. He wasn't at ease in the brave new postwar world. It suited me just fine, but it went by too fast and too carelessly for Max. How scrupulous he was, worrying that I'd misinterpret him, fearing I'd think he'd treat this as a shipboard romance; tempted, but terrified I might view this as a casual seduction on his part. "That isn't what I feel," he said, standing like a lost boy in my stateroom. "I want you to know that."

I told him I knew what he felt—and, if I was wrong, on my head be it. I think he'd have wasted half the night with his English arguments and moral anguish. Well, I had no patience with that. I was wearing an avant-garde witchy dress; a Scheherazade dress; it fitted like a second skin, with hooks and eyes down the line of my spine. I made him undo them; the dress slipped down and made a red pool about my feet. I knew this event mattered, it was like a birthing, so I was nervous then, but only for a second. I stepped out of that pool to the sound of the ship's turbines powering the ship inexorably on—and what happened then, when I relented, I'd never reveal to a living soul, not even you, my dearest.

Max and I meshed. We exchanged bravery for vulnerability. I was a little blind, I suppose. I didn't notice then that he was very possessive. I didn't equate marriage with ownership, so it didn't occur to me that he might. If I had realized, I'd have told him that the idea of owning anyone was impious *and* stupid! I could see I'd revealed pleasures and possibilities to Max that he'd imagined, but never experienced. I gave him carte blanche with my body, though that's nothing special, a man can pay a woman to do that for him. I also gave him carte blanche with my heart and mind—and perhaps that's rarer. Max seemed to think so.

As a result, we were both entranced—and that's no state in which to make decisions. So I was fair; I made Max wait until he was sure what he wanted, though in essence I'd promised to be Rebecca de Winter before we docked at Southampton. It's what I'd intended since the age of fourteen, after all. I always meant to usurp the name, and I always knew it would fit me. *Rebecca de Winter*—and no mealy-mouthed nonsense about Mrs. Maximilian!

I didn't intend to sully any of this by recounting it to the gorgon, so I diverted her away from the truth—which I'm good at, dearest; there's a thousand techniques, and one day I'll teach you them. She listened intently, and an expression came upon her face that I remembered from the last time I'd met her. I think she was anxious on Max's behalf—with reason, as it turned out; but she was also anxious for me, which I found peculiar. There was a certain concern in her old eyes, and a sympathy I couldn't understand, as if she not only pitied me, but feared for me.

"Why do you look at me like that?" I said.

"Because I'm not as hard as I'm believed to be, and you're not as impervious as you pretend," she replied with a shake of the head. And I took no notice of that, as you may imagine. Not only was she aging, as I've said, but with age she was becoming sentimental, and I liked her the less for it. Not impervious? Wrong, wrong, wrong, Grandmama. I'm granite.

"And this *is* what you want?" she said finally. "You're *sure* it's what you want? Manderley makes demands of wives, you know. It requires . . . sacrifices."

What a shivery way that was said! She might have meant "sacrifice" in the conventional sense, but I'm by no means sure she did. I couldn't tell if she was thinking of her dead son, of past sacrifices or future ones. I had a vision of Manderley brides being led in procession to the ancestral altar; there, anointed and accoutred, with a patient acquiescence, they prepared themselves to be offered up to their wintry bridegrooms. Stifled? Strangled? Wedded?

I smiled. Virgins make the best sacrifices, as everyone knows—and my blood wasn't virgin. I had darker powers; I was protected by my own strength of will, a more reliable weapon for a maiden than virginity. Being sexually pure in that limited sense was always a useless defense in any case—at least in the stories I'd read. Manderley held no dangers for me. And this was fact, not hubris.

I told Mrs. de Winter that it *was* what I wanted, and what I was determined to have. She gave me her imprimatur—which was useful, though not essential: Max was so deep in love by then that, even if she'd banned me from the house, he'd have defied her. Or so he claimed; he was never put to that particular test, so the daring remains in question, though if I point that out, Max at once becomes angry. How odd men are! I speak truth, and Max takes it as a slur on his virility.

And so, to come full circle, the bride was approved, and three months after we met onboard ship, Max and I crossed the Channel to my village birthplace in Brittany. We stood by a February sea, the sky wept salt rain, Max stroked my sealskin coat and kissed my eyes. We made our morning journey to the *mairie*; we exulted in each other. I dreamed of my house every night, like a secret lover.

When I came back to claim Manderley, it was spring, just as it is now; there was bridal blossom on the trees; the lilacs were in bud; the earth was waking after winter; the woods smelled rich and fertile. Despite the difficulties of our honeymoon, I took possession of my house on a spring tide of optimism. I made them force open all the windows, one by one. It was the first thing I did.

In gushed the air from the sea. I was certain I must be carrying our child, my dearest, but I proved to be mistaken.

M Y DEAR LOVE, MY SWEET LOVE — HOW LATE IT IS. I FEEL so restless tonight, but I must sleep soon, for both our sakes. In the space of half a page, between the paragraph above and this one, a great wash of despondency came in on the tide; I started to have doubts and fears. In the morning, they'll vanish again. It's always these hours after midnight that are the dangerous ones.

I went out to breathe the cool night air; it's so still, so still. The moon has risen and declined; she's obscured behind the great dark bulk of the house above, but I could see by starlight. The stars tonight are ice bright in a cloudless sky; some giant god has scattered their cold seeds across the heavens; they're profligate.

How close my father is tonight. Even the waves were mourning him. I've scarcely written about him, I know—it's hard to fit a life in a notebook, I've found, much harder than I'd expected. But you can see him circling around in my story, I hope, prowling on its periphery: hungry old wolf, baying at the moon. I'd made such a mythology of him; he was a giant in my mind and the flash of his lighthouse beam lit my childhood—but what was he really?

He came back to England and bought a stockbroker's house—not imaginative! He never explained his quarrel with Maman or his departure to South Africa. He told me he'd always stayed in touch with her and always cared for her in his way; he said he'd taken her in the instant he heard she was ill—but how true was that? I never saw

any letters from him, and Maman hadn't been ill, she'd been pregnant, though it was ten years before I discovered that.

I was so hedged in with lies! *Everyone* lied to me. Maman always
told me my father was dead; Danny told me Maman died of a fever;
they whisked that little half-brother of mine away, and I still don't
know for sure whether it was my father who made Danny banish my
mother's newborn son, or whether she did it of her own volition.
Danny finally confessed the truth to me, years later, not long after
my marriage, not long after I came to Manderley. Was it when I realized I wasn't carrying a child? It might have been. I know I was sad
about something; I think I might have been weeping. I forget. Anyway, she told me about my little lost brother, my mother's baby.

She claimed the foundling home was all her idea, but I don't
believe that. I think it was the Devlin's hand at work. I think that
baby was still in a far room of that hideous house the day I came to
Greenways and Maman died; I'm still certain it was that baby I heard
cry as I sat by her bed—

Danny was wrong; it wasn't me crying, I couldn't cry—I was in a
trance. For weeks afterward I was sleepwalking.

The Devlin was a hard man. He wanted to check the little bitch for
mongrel blood. He'd have banished me like my brother, I expect—and
wouldn't have thought twice about it—had it not been for the fact that
I was the living spit of him, his Devlin daughter, with his eyes and his
black hair. I went down the stairs from Maman's room, and there he
was, back from the dead. His eyes locked on mine, and I thought, He's
air—I'll be able to walk straight through him. I sleepwalked up to him,
and he held me at arm's length, looking at my face. Vain, vain, all he
was interested in was his own reflection, a little chip off the old block,
that's what he wanted to see; and once he did, how his expression
changed! He locked his arms around me. He put his ring on my finger.

Oh, my darling—I won't write about him; I won't. I worshipped
him for a while, and he worshipped me in return. What an idolatry
that was! A ring on my wedding finger, bells on my toes. "I'll make
such a fine lady of you, Becka," he'd say. The hell with him! I've
never allowed anyone to make me into anything. Not him, not Max,
none of them. My daddy tried to saddle me: bit, curb, and bridle—
bring in the governesses, wear this dress, dance to this tune. Never
trust men when they come bearing gifts, dearest, because, believe

me, there's always a price for them, and it's always the same price, too—it's liberty.

I was jealously guarded at Greenways, and that's all you need to know. I was my daddy's princess, the widower's queen; he kept me in his tower, and he was so sweet, so sweet, that it was *years* before I realized he'd taken the key, and he'd never give it back to me. First my cousin Jack was banished—not that I cared too much about that. He's a sleek, weak apology for a man, as I pretty soon realized; a spy, a tittle-tattler with the mind of a vulgarian—and those weaknesses will be the end of him one of these days, you'll see.

Cousin Jack was the child of my daddy's favorite sister, and he was taken in at Greenways for a while—until he looked at me in a particular way once too often. A kiss in a cupboard under the stairs; caresses that made me murderous. I scratched his face, and when my father saw the claw marks, that was cousin Jack, done for. I was glad to see the back of him—though you never really rid yourself of a succubus like that; he's taken to turning up at Manderley, and, not having a forgiving nature, still blaming me for the failures of his life, which in truth are all of his making; he tells Max lies about me, lies that fester.

I'll punish him for that, one of these days; *his* card's marked. He's been stoking Max's anguish nicely for months now, and I'll repay him in kind. He's always after money, so I'll deal him a promissory note with my right hand, and with the left I'll deal him some retribution. My daddy would approve; he banished him from Greenways without a second thought—but then, all males in the vicinity were banished sooner or later. "I won't have them here," my father would shout. "I won't have them sniffing around—you understand me, Becka?"

I had a friend named May, such a gentle girl, clever, and with no airs and graces. May lived in the manor house close by, and I was allowed to see her, but my friend May had brothers, three of them, and my daddy took agin *them*. May showed me endless kindness—and I was able to repay her for that one day, years later, as I'll explain another time, my dearest. My father liked May, but if her brothers were home on leave, if I walked with them, or talked with them, or rode with them, how he watched! And then he'd brood and sulk, and drink. "Tell me you love your old father, Becka," he'd say—and no matter what I said or did to show my love, it never contented him, it never satisfied him.

Old Lear; tawdry old mountebank. He hung a revolver over his desk; there were trophies on the wall that he'd brought back from the bush: the head of a gazelle; the head of a lioness.

"Damn that taxidermist," he said to me once, when I reached up to stroke their powerful heads. "Kaffir. Look what a lousy job he did, Becka." I looked. My daddy was a good shot, famous for it, he said. The great white hunter, the wild colonial boy. So it was a very clean kill; a tiny hole just visible where the bullet went in—but it wasn't well stitched; it was leaking. Where the fatal wound was, the sawdust packing was leaching.

What did I do, the seven years I lived with him? Nothing you need know about, my dearest. He taught me to gamble at cards. I'm a demon at card games to this day; never play poker with me! I'll strip you of your winnings; I'll have the shirt off your back. I can palm aces; I can deal from the bottom of the pack: I have to win, and will cheat every which way.

He told me about mines—and I'll tell you something interesting about mines that I never knew till my daddy revealed it: They have a hidden danger. It's not just that the men have to work in the depths of the earth, down, down, in a tiny seam, so tight and narrow they have to lie on their bellies and they can't stand up; it's not just that the dynamite is unstable, and the roof props might collapse; it's that, down there in the depths of the mine, it isn't cold, as I'd always imagined, it's *hot*, fiendishly hot, so germs breed. Those gold seams swarm with bacteria. They swim into the mouth on saliva. They thrive in the secretions of the throat; they get gulped down into the stomach bag. They worm their way into the lungs, they wriggle right into the cavities of the heart and spawn in the aorta. If you cut yourself down there, the wound infects; it can fester away for months, Daddy said, *years* even. Sometimes it never heals properly, however careful you are with hygiene, however often you change the dressings and swallow, swallow the medicine—

Interesting? There's a message for you, a message in a bottle. Cast it into the sea and watch where *that* comes ashore, Daddy.

I WON'T WRITE ABOUT HIM ANYMORE. HE'S TOO BIG FOR my pen. My page won't encompass him. He wasn't always a mountebank; people don't stay still in that way. Just as Frank McKendrick showed me, they can be Prospero one morning, Mark Antony the next; they can start the day as Miranda, and, hey presto, they're Lady Macbeth or Cleopatra come the evening. Everything's in flux, always. My Devlin father had the heart of a lion; he fought to the bitter end, and no matter what anyone else may ever tell you, my darling, it was the hidden debts and the creditors that killed him.

He couldn't face me with the truth; he couldn't face the shame— that's why he took himself off to the attics, locked the door, slung a rope over a roof beam, and broke his own neck. It was the day the debts were finally being called in, you see.

It was also the day of my twenty-first birthday, as I told you; it was the day I came of age. I've never celebrated my birthday since. I won't. I won't. I'm wild with grief the instant I wake. They aren't birthdays for me, they're deathdays.

No more o' that, my dearest. Enough, enough. I'm on the very last page of my little black notebook. I didn't mean to end it on such a dark chord; I cut all those cords, long ago.

Let's forget ghosts; *future tense* from now on. I want you to know— I want you to know—

How dear you are to me. How much I love you. What joy it's given me these last months to feel you grow, to think of you and plan for you.

When you're born, my little one, it will be late summer, and that's a beautiful season here; there are often long warm benign weeks before the westerlies that herald autumn. You'll be born in my Manderley room overlooking the sea. You'll be able to hear the sea. *La mer, ma mère.* I'll nurse you, and care for you and I'll always watch over you.

All that's bad in me I shall cut out. I want to be the best of mothers, so you grow up in a certainty of love. I'm sure that once Max sees you, he'll come to love you too. He'll come to look on you as his changeling child, just as I do—I'm willing it, it's inevitable. Who knows what might happen with time? Reconcilement? Peace? Anything, anything. Think of all the decades ahead of us.

It's two o'clock. Five hours from now, we'll be on the road to London. As soon as I return here, I'll start a new page in a new notebook and I'll fill in the gaps in my story. I'll tell you more of my father's tale and Max's; I'll translate the braille of my marriage—and of course I'll tell you everything that happens to us in the city, what the grave doctor says, and so on.

How tired I am suddenly! Jasper's restless and unsettled; he's looking at me with such mournful eyes. I think he knows I'm going away; he can always sense it.

I've opened the curtains so the first light will wake me. The alarm clock is set. Can you hear it ticking? I'm going to lie down now, and sleep for a while, my dearest one.

4

Ellie

MAY 1951

TWENTY-FIVE

IT'S A HEAT WAVE, MY DARLING, I THOUGHT TODAY. I was
sitting in the garden, between our palm and our monkey puzzle.

I was writing a letter to Tom Galbraith and it was proving very difficult. I couldn't make the words lie down on the page in the way I
wanted. I knew I had to tell him what happened yesterday, and I suppose there were other things I might have liked to say, too. I'm not
good at concealing my feelings. I still think of him as "Mr. Gray";
after an hour's pen chewing, all I'd written was "Dear Tom," followed
by one pedestrian paragraph.

I had reread sections of Rebecca's notebook this morning, and,
when I couldn't think what to say next in my letter, her words sprang
into my head. I didn't write them down, obviously. It *is* a heat wave—
we've had five weeks of unrelenting sun—but I couldn't use the word
"darling," unfortunately, and, anyway, Tom would recognize the
quotation. He knows that little black coffin book of Rebecca's by
heart, just as I do.

I'd brought a table out into the garden to write. I was sitting
exactly where the young Rebecca took tea in 1914 with my father,
with twenty-five-year-old Elinor, and with my gentle grandmother
(whom I never knew; she died before I was born). On either side of
me, those famous Grenville roses were in full bloom. Daddy hacks

them back and stunts them, but even his punitive pruning techniques can't quell their inbred exuberance. I've been secretly watering and feeding them. They've responded to these weeks of sun, and now there were great billowing banks of them on either side of me, weighed down with glorious crumpled blooms, every shade from the softest blush pink to wine crimson and lavender. The scent was intense. I was in a bower of roses—and I kept telling myself that a bower of roses was no place to be miserable.

I caught this melancholy from Rebecca. It's contagious. Up it came from those pages of hers, the first time I read them. Six weeks later, despite everything that has happened, it still refuses to be exorcised; I drive it out it for an hour or so, then in it comes on the next tide. I think and think about what she wrote—and in this way she's come to haunt me, just as she's always haunted my father. I ask myself all these questions, some of them serious and some, I know, trivial. I think, Did Rebecca ever suspect that it was death, and not a child, that she was carrying inside her?

This morning, examining the stillborn paragraph I'd written so far, other questions sprang into my mind and refused to be dislodged. I looked at my handwriting, which is neat and a great deal more legible than Rebecca's. I hated its neatness. I hated its legibility. If I actually finished writing this letter and sent it, Tom Galbraith would scan it in a cursory way. He'd be interested in only one section: He'd want to hear about the visit to London I'm about to make, because it concerns Rebecca. No doubt he'd read my account of the latest news from Tite Street with the very closest attention—but beyond that my letter would be only too forgettable. Unremarkable pages from an unremarkable woman, the colonel's daughter, the dull dutiful girl on the periphery of the story. How sick I was of being the good daughter, the invisible inaudible woman!

I screwed my letter into a ball. I took it into the kitchen, stuffed it inside the range and burned it. I thought, How do you make yourself *memorable*?

Rebecca had done just that, or so she claimed. In 1914, when she met Maxim for the first time on that visit to Manderley she had been invisible, instantly forgettable; by the time she remet him on board that ocean liner she had transformed herself. Unfortunately, she gave no handy tips as to how she pulled off that particular conjuring trick.

I slammed the range door shut. The kitchen was insufferably hot. Presumably that kind of transformation is easier if you're beautiful.

How silent The Pines was! My father was upstairs, having his pre-scribed afternoon rest. He's been put on new medication by the heart specialist and surgeon, Mr. Latimer, to whom he was referred when he went to Lanyon for those exhaustive tests. My aunt Rose, who arrived from Cambridge for an indefinite stay at Easter, was sitting by the open French windows in Daddy's study, correcting the proofs of her forthcoming book, a weighty analysis of Jacobean tragedies. Today she was working calmly away on the Eroticism of Death sec-tion in her Webster and Tourneur chapter. Rose takes killings in her stride—over our breakfast boiled eggs this morning, we'd been ami-ably discussing incestuous passion, smothering with diamonds, and a fatal kiss bestowed on a poisoned skull—but then the texts Rose teaches are so stuffed with the pyrotechnics of death that virtually nothing shocks or astonishes her. All the time I'd been writing my sad abortive letter, Rose had been covering pages with spidery hiero-glyphs, and changing commas to semicolons.

I couldn't bear to be kicking my heels in the house any longer, and I'd already decided where I needed to go, so I walked over to the French windows. I stood three feet away from Rose, and, after about five minutes, she noticed me.

"Rose, I'm going to take Barker for a walk," I said. "He needs a walk, he's getting fat and lazy. I'll be back in time for Daddy's tea."

"You're going to Manderley, in other words," Rose said without looking up. "Don't worry, I shan't tell Arthur where you've gone. What *are* you writing, Ellie? That's the fifth page you've burned this afternoon. If you continue at this rate, Mr. Galbraith will be back from Brittany before you've completed your outpourings. Then you'll have no excuse to write, which seems a wasted opportunity."

"Not true," I said. "If I don't write to him in Brittany, I can write to him in Cambridge. Once he gets back from France, he's going back to King's, he's not staying in Kerrith. I *told* you, he's given up his cot-tage. And they're not outpourings."

"So you did," said Rose, who remembered all this perfectly well, I knew. "And a very good thing, too. He can't continue with this quest of his indefinitely. He should draw a firm black line under it and get on with his life. As should you, Ellie."

"Thanks, Rose."

"Now, now," said my aunt, looking up from her pages for the first time. "I appreciate your circumstances are difficult. But worrying about your father will not help, and pining for Mr. Galbraith, or indeed any man, is positively counterproductive."

"I'm not bloody well pining."

"Aren't you? Well, something's the matter. You are not your usual self. You're in a most peculiar state of mind. Now, go for your walk, for heaven's sake. I can't concentrate with you sighing and staring at the sea. You're palely loitering, Ellie, and it's unsettling."

I whistled to Barker, helped him into the car, and set off. I didn't bother to reply to Rose; my aunt's frighteningly clever, and would probably demolish all my arguments in seconds, but donnish Rose is better at analyzing texts than she is real-life situations. Rose has never married, never had children, and as far as I know has never been in love. These are limitations.

Rose used to be my mentor, but I had a new mentor now, I told myself, as I urged the car fast round the blind bend near Tom Galbraith's former cottage. *Walk by the sea and you'll feel me*, I thought, accelerating toward the woods of Manderley. I parked by the Four Turnings entrance, and set off with Barker down the drive and into the cool blue shade of the trees. We approached the dark redoubt of the ruined house, but in the past weeks the undergrowth had sprung up, and our way was now barred by stinging nettles and thick arching brambles. I could hear Rebecca's heartbeat in the ruins even so, just as she promised her imaginary child. Feeling as if I were that child, as if I were the *girl-boy* to whom her tale had been addressed (and I'd felt *that*, ever since I'd first read her notebook), I turned toward the place where I knew I'd find her.

I could sense her even before I saw the shore and her boathouse. I knew she was there as soon as I heard the murmur of the sea. I think I'd begun to cry at some point on our walk; Barker sensed the distress welling up in me and came to press his damp muzzle against my legs. That dumb, gentle concern was weakening. A huge choking tide of misery washed up through me then. All my fears for my father and for a future without him rose up; I was frightened of spinsterhood, too, and despised myself for that. I put my arms around Barker and kissed him on the nose. I fought my demons down, wiped my eyes and caught my breath. I walked on past the gorse; it was still in bloom, and thick with butterflies. I reached the top of the path, looked at a lapis lazuli sea, and began to run down to the water. In my way, which is not my father's way or Tom Galbraith's, I was looking for Rebecca—and I felt that, if I could find her, all the knots of my past and my future would undo themselves.

R EBECCA WAS RIGHT ABOUT GHOSTS: THEY DO HAVE AN affinity for the sea. Barker and I sat for a while on the rocks, and I knew he could sense them, just as I could. I could see the ghosts Rebecca had conjured up for me, but I could also see my own. I'm now the age Rebecca was when she died, but somewhere up there on the headland was an Ellie I used to be: twenty years old, fearless, innocent, and gullible—a dangerous cocktail.

I'd nursed my mother, my mother had died—and now it was wartime. My father was away, working on codes and ciphers in some secret establishment—"hauled back into harness," he likes to say, but I think the truth was that he was taken on with reluctance, after endless string pulling and badgering, and then worked in some fairly humdrum capacity. The brilliant men who made the real breakthroughs at that establishment were for the most part a great deal younger, and less rusty than he was.

I had three years of liberty; they ended in 1945 when my father returned to Kerrith, suddenly aged, his health broken by the death of my mother, and, then, late in the war, the death of his favorite child, my brother Jonathan. I knew I couldn't leave him; it never occurred to him that I might. The decision was made in an instant, and I've never regretted it. People in Kerrith talk on and on about how dutiful I am, and what sacrifices I've made. "Sacrifice" can indeed be a shivery word, as Rebecca says, and it's very stupid on their part to use it. I love my father; no sacrifice is— or ever was involved, though people never believe that, no matter how often I tell them.

As for my three years of freedom, how did I use that precious commodity? Hungrily, probably—or so I thought this afternoon. I tried to summon up that time, to remember it in detail, but the details skidded past. I joined the WRAC. I wore a uniform. I had a woman's war: I was taught to type and salute. I drove officers in jeeps. I drilled.

And I fell in love—with an American naval officer, stationed at Plymouth. I made love for the first time, with him, up there where my ghost lingers by the gorse on the headland.

He came from the blue hills of Virginia, which was as exotic to me as Timbuktu or Islamabad. He gave me nylon stockings, his heart (or so he said), and a pretty ring that I wore on a string around my neck; he thought it best to be discreet, and to keep the engagement unofficial. "It's unofficially official, honey," he said—and just as well, really. He had a wife and two children back in those blue hills of Virginia, but they had somehow slipped his mind in the heat of the moment. He wrote a letter to me at the end of the war, and explained. He said he really had meant all those things he'd said to me; meant them from the bottom of his heart. He hoped I wouldn't think badly of him.

And I don't. I never have. Why would I? I'm glad it happened. I'd felt utterly alive for six whole months, and that's a fine gift by anyone's standards.

Barker and I buried his ring in the Manderley woods some years ago. I'd decided on a ritual purging. We made a fire of his letters too, a small fire—there weren't that many of them, I realized, so perhaps I should have seen the warning signals; perhaps I'd been naive. Cross out and carry on, I said to myself then, and I resolved to be more choosy the next time temptation came my way. Temptation then waited five long years, which I felt was unduly dilatory. When it finally manifested itself, it was in the shape of a tall, alarmingly handsome, taciturn Scot. A man with an alias; a man who was not what he claimed to be. A man to whom I'm air: invisible Ellie. *How do you make yourself memorable?* I said to the sea and the rock pools this afternoon. But Rebecca proved as contrary in death as she'd been in life, and no answer was given me.

I rose and clambered back over the rocks to the shingle. With Barker at my heels, I began to walk toward the boathouse—my chief object in coming here. I was feeling much steadier now. The air was still, with not the least breath of wind; the sea was flat calm, as calm as I've ever seen it. Out by the sandbank, where Rebecca sensed those sirens, the water was translucent; above us, gulls wheeled. It was on the northern side of this beach that, as Rebecca mentions, Ben Carminowe's little sister, Lucy, was drowned in one of the rock pools.

I paused to look at the pools, shading my eyes from the sun, and trying to work out where it had happened. Tom Galbraith, as I now know, pursued the sad little ghost of Lucy Carminowe in the course of his investigations; apparently, he spent days trying to discover whether she was alive or dead, and what might have become of her. . . . What a waste of time, I thought now, feeling a familiar rankle of frustration and impatience.

If he'd asked any of the tenant farmers or the fishermen, anyone could have told him Lucy Carminowe's story, though, to be fair to Tom, people in this neighborhood are close, and they don't take kindly to intrusive questions from strangers. He was viewed with a certain suspicion from the moment of his arrival, I know. What I *didn't* know was that there was a great deal of gossip in Kerrith about his habit of taking walks after dark, and the frequency of his visits to Manderley. I learned that this week, when I was waylaid by the appalling Marjorie Lane, who couldn't wait to be spiteful about Tom's leaving Kerrith. "How sad for you, Ellie, when we'd all hoped . . . Are you devastated?"

She claimed the Manack brothers, those descendents of generations of honest smugglers, kept a *very* close eye on his activities, and that either they or their sister's husband, Robert Lane, started the rumor that Tom Galbraith was working undercover for Customs and Excise. So this explains, in part, why he encountered a wall of silence from local people—but I think there were other problems, too, problems of his own making. If you want people to warm to you and open up to you, it helps if you're similarly accessible. He's such a mollusk of a man! When they're questioned by someone as wary and defensive as he is, people clam up. Why can't he see that?

Daddy could have told him Lucy's story, if he'd asked, and so could I; it's brief enough in all conscience. Like her brother, she was rumored to be Lionel de Winter's illegitimate child, though I don't know if that's true. If one credited all the rumors about him, half Kerrith would be his descendents. From infancy, there was some mysterious ailment: Lucy scarcely grew, she failed to thrive. When she was about seven, she was sent to live with an aunt with a farm inland, but she kept running away, and returning here in search of her brother. She drowned in a pool out there when she was nine years old—only a few months after the glimpse of her that Rebecca records in her notebook.

When she slipped and fell she had been trespassing with her brother, and gathering shells. She had a passion for shells. Apart from her diminutive stature, that's virtually all anyone now remembers of her, poor child. But she is buried in the Manderley churchyard. Her stone is lichened and worn, the inscription's almost unreadable; I took Tom Galbraith to it, eventually, but I could have taken him there much earlier if he'd asked. I could have helped him with this part of his puzzle—and with other parts of it, too. The fact that he rarely asked me *anything* didn't help him, I feel. I still don't understand why he kept me at arm's length in that way. Was it so hard to trust me? What's wrong with my testimony?

I blame my gender. It's my sex that's at fault, I think. Tom Galbraith finds it difficult to talk to women; he seems to find them irrational and intuitive, and for him intuition's invalid. He didn't listen to me, and he didn't listen to Elinor and Jocelyn as closely as he might have done, either. I'm not even sure that he's listened—*truly* listened—to Rebecca. I felt a wave of retrospective rancor at this blind male arrogance. In this respect, for all his scholarship, Tom Galbraith was a fool. He just couldn't see an obvious truth: Women are the gossips, the seers, the storytellers. One of these days I'll tell him, Pay attention, Tom dear, because it's women who are the keepers of secrets.

I'd reached the boathouse by then. There were signs of a recent bonfire on the shingle nearby; someone had been burning bits of wood and old rotten material. I poked at the still-warm ashes with my foot; the air smelled singed. Barker flopped down gratefully in the shade by the boathouse walls. I pushed the door open. Sacking had been pulled over the windows; inside, it was dark after the dazzle of the sunlight, and deliciously cool. I knew I was going to make a discovery; I could sense an imminence, just as I could yesterday when I answered that telephone call from Tite Street.

Tom had told me about the search he made of this place, weeks ago now. There have been changes since then. The Manack brothers shipped in one too many cases of undrinkable sherry, I think; so far, they've been too wily to get caught, but Customs and Excise has been making searches of any likely illicit storage premises in the vicinity of Kerrith, including this boathouse. Nothing was found, I gather—any evidence there might have been had been spirited away—but Elinor and Jocelyn told me yesterday that complaints were made to the land agents responsible for Manderley; they were asked to make Rebecca's boathouse "secure." So my visit was timely. Some preparatory clearance work was in progress, as I could see once my eyes adjusted to the light, but—as I'd hoped—it had not been completed. Some of Rebecca's belongings were still here.

The semirotten furniture Tom Galbraith described to me had already gone—it had been burned on that bonfire, presumably. The door into the storage area at the far end had been wrenched off its hinges, and beyond it there was now no sign of the ropes and sails Tom had seen, the sails Rebecca had described as wound tight like winding sheets. I peered into that dark space, wishing I'd brought a flashlight with me; thick cobwebs brushed at my face like hands.

I stepped back into the area where Rebecca had sat writing in her notebook. There was a pile of ashes and soot in the fireplace and a burned smell to the clammy air; my heart was beating painfully fast. I was certain I was standing in the place where Rebecca had been killed. I'm certain I now know what happened to her that night in the boathouse.

Rebecca made Maxim kill her, murder was her chosen method of suicide—I'm sure of that, as sure as if she'd taken me by the hand and told me. In her notebook she claims that she could make him murder, and I believe her. She has a wicked tongue, and I could half imagine how she might have done it, with rage and desire as her twin weapons. Did he kiss her before he killed her? Did she persuade him that death was the ultimate way to possess her? *Cover her face,/Mine eyes dazzle.* I shouldn't have discussed those blood-soaked plays with Rose this morning, perhaps. It's as dangerous for me to have a headful of plays as it was for Rebecca, but they're educative, particularly if your own experience is as limited as mine is. I closed my eyes, and shimmying up out of the bonfire-scented air came a dark and final embrace. It thrilled me a little.

She'd have meant Maxim to die, too, I was sure of that. She'd never have permitted him to escape into a future without her. Would she have tolerated for one second the idea of his living on, remarrying, producing an heir to Manderley by another woman—a woman who wasn't barren? Never. She'd have meant Maxim to hang for the crime, or kill himself, or die of remorse; she'd have meant to drag him down to her underworld—and, of course, she did. No one can inherit Manderley now—it's a burned-out shell, a roofless ruin. Maxim never had a child, and he did take his own life, after years of exile with the second wife. His death was no more an accident than Rebecca's. Did she haunt and hound him to death—or did he smash his car by the Manderley gates because she still lured him after all those years, and he had to be reunited with her?

I opened my eyes. I don't have the unnatural vision Rebecca claims she had—I can't see around corners or over the horizon—but, even so, her notebook's altered my eyesight. How did Maxim kill her? Did he stifle, strangle, or stab—or use that service revolver she'd once eyed so covetously? And how did she bring him to that pitch? Did she whisper secrets about her lovers, or tell him she was pregnant with another man's child? For the owner of Manderley, descendant of the direct male line, that would have been the ultimate transgression. But could Maxim have killed her believing she was carrying a child? That truly would have been a sin. Rebecca's right—if any action could damn a man, that would.

The sea washed against the boathouse wall. I could sense some wickedness in the air, and it stifled me. The belief that I was inches away from answers was already fading. I couldn't arrive at answers, I told myself. At best I have theories, and I've been careful not to confide those theories to anyone. They would distress my father, who seems to see Rebecca as the victim in this story—perhaps because he can then defend actions of hers that he would otherwise find indefensible. They would no doubt irritate Tom Galbraith, who'd scoff at them.

Tom believes Rebecca killed herself, and with Maxim's service revolver. He believes she made it look like murder intending to incriminate Maxim; that she lured Jack Favell to the boathouse in the hope he'd find her body and call the police. But Favell never turned up and it was Maxim who found her, panicked, and tried to dispose of her body at sea, sinking the boat too close in to shore. An unsatisfactory theory: Either Tom doesn't *listen* to Rebecca when he reads, as I said, or he's perverse. All Tom talks about now is the need for "verification" of the notebook; he's begun to mention "discrepancies." It's discrepancies, real or imagined, that have taken him and his Cambridge friend off to Brittany.

I stood in the center of that shadowy room; I pushed Galbraith and my father out of my mind; I refused to consider their misreadings. What do men understand of tending houses or growing babies? It was not the outer truth, but the inner truth of Rebecca's actions that concerned me. I could hear her voice so clearly that it felt as if it were inside me, struggling to be voiced. If I opened my lips, I felt she would speak through me. She would acknowledge me—and I wanted that intensely. I wanted Rebecca to know that she wasn't without heirs after all. The same women's voices she had heard now spoke to me. I, Ellie, was her heiress—and today there was something of the utmost importance she had to tell me.

Where was the last of her notebooks? I knew it must exist; I'd felt certain of its existence for weeks, ever since I'd read that promise of hers on the final page of the notebook we already have. I *knew* that Rebecca would never have left her tale incomplete; she would not have been silenced, not then, when she was facing death. Somehow, I had to find the third notebook, with her last words, her final entry.

I'm still hoping I may find it when I go to London, but it could be elsewhere—it could even be secreted here. Supposing it had remained hidden away all these years? That could explain why the anonymous, still unidentified person who sent the first two notebooks had sent nothing further. I looked about the boathouse. I knew Tom Galbraith had searched it exhaustively, but I've seen how blinkered Tom's searches can be; and today I felt a strengthening conviction that he might have looked in the wrong way, in the wrong places. I felt it could have been right under the man's nose and he still might have missed it.

He does not believe there is another installment. He says Rebecca had reached the end of her story, and that the fragmentary disjointed nature of the last pages of the existing notebook indicate that she had reached, for her, a conclusion. Tom Galbraith says that once Rebecca had seen that doctor in London she had only one task left: to die. And she achieved that within hours of seeing him.

He's wrong. I know he's wrong with every instinct in my body. I looked and looked at the chipped, abandoned, broken belongings that had been left behind in the recent clearance. The shelves Tom described were still there, piled with some dirty crockery. A cracked mirror hung on a nail, reflecting my own splintered face back at me.

Tossed down on the floor was one of the little wooden boats Rebecca had made; the others, presumably, had been fuel for the bonfire. I picked it up and cradled it.

In the corner of the room was a rusty paraffin heater and a kettle without a lid. There was a cardboard carton, sodden with damp, filled with scraps of material too wet to burn. I reached in my hand, and felt about in the mildewed contents. An empty ink bottle; part of a broken pen; I felt indescribably sad. All that spirit, all that endeavor, reduced to these fragments.

But something was lodged behind the carton; wedged between it and the wall was a square metal shape, upended, with scraps of bright paint still adhering to its rusty surface. I stared at it, and I could hear Rebecca's voice spelling out my instructions: *The best place to hide something is always somewhere ordinary or everyday.*

Barker had roused himself and followed me inside; he gave a low whine from the doorway. I picked up the ordinary everyday biscuit tin, which was heavy. I opened it without difficulty. Inside it were four books: a broken-backed edition of Tennyson's *Complete Works*; two tiny editions of Shakespeare plays, one *Othello*, and the other *Richard III*; and a familiar topographical work, written by my great-grandfather: *A History of the Parishes of Manderley and Kerrith, with Walks.*

I stole them, and the little wooden boat—and I did so without the least pang of conscience. I knew I was rescuing them from the bonfire. I carried them back to The Pines with me, and they're beside me now on my desk in my bedroom as I write. I've been examining them for hours; I feel I was guided to them. Now I, too, have my talismans.

The two small red morocco Shakespeares must date from the McKendrick days; they're covered in pencil notes marking cuts, moves, entrances, and exits.

The Tennyson has a faded copperplate inscription on the flyleaf:

For J.S.D., my beloved husband—July 25th, 1900, from his Isolda.

Devlin must have left his present behind when he walked out and sailed for South Africa.

My great-grandfather's *History* also has an inscription on the flyleaf, in my father's handwriting:

Rebecca, hoping this will interest you. With good wishes for your birthday, November 7, 1929, from "Cromwell," alias Arthur Julyan!

That jaunty exclamation mark, and all that it's designed to conceal, breaks my heart. Poor Daddy. The book has not been read, I think; it's damp-spotted and foxed but its spine is uncreased. Folded into its pages, I discovered in great excitement, was a thin sheet of paper with the engraved Manderley heading. Written on it, in two columns in Rebecca's hand, is a list of Christian names: boys' names on the left, girls' names on the right. I've found that list she wrote at her London flat, when she returned there after that sad orgy of baby-clothes buying.

The lists, as I would have expected, are in alphabetical order—*My future's an alphabet. I file it in pigeonholes.* And among the twelve selected names on the female side, I see, is my own name—Ellen.

It's late at night, I can hear the sea sighing away in the distance. Rebecca's ways of thinking are infectious, so I'm going to take this writing down of my name as a sign. I shall regard it as the acknowledgment I was hoping for. I'm not going to wrack my brain writing letters to Tom Galbraith any more—where's the point in that, when the letter's bound to be evasive, inhibited, and unnatural?

No. My father wrote his account of the beginning of these events, and I'm going to write my version of their conclusion.

What shall I call it? It's tempting to call it *Ellie's Tale*, of course—but I won't. That would feel impious.

TWENTY-SIX

I'LL BEGIN AT THE BEGINNING—AND I'LL BEGIN WITH THE
rain. Rose always maintains that when you read, there's a chemical
reaction between the words on the page (which are never inert) and
the state of mind of the reader (which can be, unfortunately). Much
depends on that state of mind, Rose says, and the state I was in when
I read Rebecca's notebook for the first time was a receptive one.

I'd delivered it unread into Tom Galbraith's hands in a downpour;
I drove back in a downpour to the hospital with my father's pyjamas
and shaving kit. When the consultant, Mr. Latimer, had finished
examining him, he announced that he was going to keep him in, not
just overnight as had previously been said, but for an entire *week* of
tests and observation. I drove home, still in a downpour. I was agitated and afraid. I had the headlights on, and the wipers were set at
their fastest speed, but the windscreen kept misting up; I peered at
the road ahead, but all I could see was ten feet of tarmac, and beyond
that a haze of watery reflections and dazzle.

I couldn't drive straight and I couldn't think straight: *Seven days—*
what did that mean? Did that mean grave Mr. Latimer was going to
take me quietly aside and explain my father's condition was terminal?
I knew it was terminal. It's terminal for all of us from the day of our
birth. The question is, *how* terminal? Did my father have a year or so,

a month or so, weeks, hours, minutes? I let myself into The Pines, and the house echoed its emptiness. The rain rattled on the roof; it was sluicing down the hill outside; it sheeted the windows, and made the sea invisible.

Barker and I sat by the range in the kitchen willing the telephone not to ring. Rose always says she stays awake on long flights in order to keep the plane in the air. I've never been on an airplane, but I now know exactly what she means: By staying awake all of that night, I prevented the hospital from calling. I'd forgotten all about Tom Galbraith and the notebook. Early the next morning, I left in heavy unremitting rain for the hospital.

"Has anything happened? Is my father all right?" I said to the starchy ward sister. She said my father was fine, that nothing had happened—but she was wrong. Institutions change people, especially the elderly, with frightening speed, and when I saw what had happened to my father in the space of a night, I felt sick with anger and pity. They'd put him in a hospital gown that was too small for him. They'd somehow contrived to make him smaller, too. The man to whom I'd always looked up, the pillar of my childhood, had been reduced to this: a frail patient with an errant heart, differing from all the other frail men in the ward only in the nature of his symptoms. The terrible anonymity of hospitals was trying to claim him.

They'd wired him up to an alien machine that recorded a graph of his heartbeats. A drip was inserted in his arm, and a colorless fluid fed into his vein. He was the world to me, and his scope was now a metal bed in a narrow cubicle surrounded by floral curtains. For a second, before my father could conceal it, I saw the fear and eddying regret in his eyes; then his gaze steadied and held mine and everything that needed to be said by us was said, as we looked at each other in silence. He rested his hand on mine: "Ah, Ellie," he said. "My dearest Ellie."

I spent a vile morning at that hospital before they finally lost patience and turfed me out. I was exiled to a visitors' room lit by a cold blue fluorescent light, and, while tests were performed, I kept a grim impotent vigil. There was a yellow table piled high with tattered magazines filled with female industry—homely recipes and knitting patterns, how to make a dress or jam, how to help baby through teething problems—they might just as well have been in

Sanskrit for all the sense they made to me. I tried to summon up my father's past; that seemed the only way I could be sure of never losing him. But that past refused to take any orderly or sequential shape. Everything became tangled up in the rush of decades, so the trivial and the significant were equal.

I saw the marriedness of my parents, the striped wallpaper of a house we rented in Singapore, the medals Daddy hides away in his desk drawer; I saw my mother young and strong, my mother dying. I saw my brother declaiming poetry, and Daddy telling him poetry was for pansies. I saw myself fly down the hill to Kerrith on the joy of my first bicycle, and my sister, Lily, dancing in the kitchen at The Pines to some bluesy tune played defiantly loud on her windup gramophone. I saw Barker as a fat puppy chewing a pair of shoes; Rebecca's car roaring up the hill to The Pines. I heard bitter voices behind closed doors, saw my father's face when the telegram came announcing Jonathan's death, and saw—every link distinct—the chain stitch on a tobacco pouch I lovingly made, aged eight, for Daddy's birthday.

Was this a life? My heart ached. I owed my father more than this sad collection of scraps, especially now, when the hospital and death were intent on erasing his identity. I was very angry with myself—and no doubt angry and accusatory with Mr. Latimer when he finally came in to speak to me.

Mr. Latimer is newly arrived from some grand London teaching hospital and is younger than I'd expected, about forty. He's a tall man—not quite as tall as Tom Galbraith, but over six foot, I'd say—and some women might find him good-looking. He has dark hair, an unsettling, steady gray-eyed gaze, and a watchful demeanor. I was prejudiced against him, perhaps. I resented the way he'd overruled my father, and insisted he remain here. The Sister had sung his praises, needless to say, rhapsodizing about what a fine surgeon he was, how distinguished, with such a reputation in medical circles, but I'd watched the nurses flutter and coo and kowtow to him the previous day, and I'd decided he was arrogant.

I've since revised that opinion. He's a clever man and may have sensed my antagonism; it's even possible that he set out to defuse it. Certainly he spent far longer with me that day than I'd expected, explaining patiently what these tests and this period of observation might achieve. He refused to rule out surgery yet—which made me afraid—but he was quiet and understanding, even optimistic in a measured way, though there were many "ifs," as there always are when doctors make an analysis. To my surprise, he wanted to know some of my personal details—my age and so on. And he asked me many close and searching questions about our life at The Pines—far more questions than seemed necessary.

"We live quietly," I told him. "We don't go out very much any more, and my father dislikes visitors. I try to keep to a routine: meals at regular times, a short walk every afternoon. My father tends to dwell on the past, and that can upset him. So, I try to divert him. We play cards sometimes, or I read to him."

Latimer had been watching me intently. I knew how dull this sounded; it occurred to me that he must think me dull, too—not that that mattered. I colored. "Who chooses the books when you read to him?" he asked, with a half smile. I could see sympathy, perhaps even concern, in his steady gray gaze, so I lied. "I do," I replied. I will not be pitied.

It's strange, what good interrogators doctors can make. I'm sure it's because we invest them with special powers, like priests; because we long to believe in their wisdom and insight. I found I was telling Latimer things I've never discussed before—I even told him about the months of broken nights, the cries in the dark, and my father's recurrent nightmares.

"I see," Latimer said, and made a small note on the clipboard he was carrying. Later he quietly asked me if my father had anything "preying on his mind"—that phrase struck me, though for some reason I can't remember exactly how I replied to him.

From now on, Latimer decreed, there was to be a regime of rest—and I was banished from the precincts except for the strictly observed single visiting hour in the afternoon. So I drove back to The Pines, still in sheeting rain, and, for the rest of those seven days, the rain continued. It was an interval in my life, a period unlike any other: I felt *marooned*—and that was the state I was in when, that first afternoon, a white-faced Tom Galbraith turned up at the door, with Rebecca's little black coffin book tucked inside his soaked mackintosh.

He wanted me to read it, but first he had to explain who he truly was and what his own connection was to the events Rebecca described. It was painfully hard for him. Maybe it's the legacy of his orphanage years that has left him so fearful of trust, friendship, or intimacy, but he always behaves as if he's reluctant to risk closeness because, if he did, it would be instantly snatched away. For this reason, perhaps, or other reasons of which I know nothing, he seems to fear the idea of being "known," as if knowledge might give someone power over him.

He found it indescribably difficult to tell me the truth as to why he came here in the first place; when he came to the contents of the notebook, and what he had learned about his parentage and his birth, he spoke very fast, in a cold dismissive way. I imagine he felt this was his best protection.

I was astonished by what he told me, and very happy for him, but we were at odds with each other, I can see that now. I thought that for someone brought up as he had been, with years in a children's home and lasting uncertainties as to his parentage, this notebook must have been a precious gift. I still think that, if I'd been in his position, if I'd known nothing about my mother, I'd have been overjoyed to find her in Isolda, with her beautiful hair, headstrong and courageous, dancing barefoot by the waves. I thought it must gladden his heart to learn that he *was* related to Rebecca, if not in the way he'd imagined. That must give him a sense of belonging and identity, I felt; he had a family now, and a history. Surely that must reassure him, when he'd spent so long seeking it.

"Why, it means you're related to Elinor and Jocelyn," I said. "You're cousins, Tom—how extraordinary! They'll be overjoyed. You'll be the child they never had. When are you going to tell them? Have you told them already?"

"No. I haven't told them—I don't know if I will. Not for a while, certainly. There's a great deal I need to think about."

I checked myself. I still hadn't read the notebook, of course, so I wasn't to know how troubling a document it was, especially for him. There are darknesses in it—it's shot through with darkness, and I began to sense that as I looked at his face. I realized that I was trespassing, that I couldn't begin to understand how he felt. I came from such a normal world, he from such an abnormal one. My mind was filled with death, his with birth. How could I reach across these divisions?

It had been a strange dreamlike conversation. It took place in the kitchen, but I wasn't really sure where we were, or what year it was. I felt we'd both been sucked into some vortex of the past, that we were spinning about in the decades. Looking at his troubled face, I felt heavyhearted and light-headed, sober yet dizzy, as if I were standing on the edge of a cliff and might fall over into an abyss at any minute. All I could think, in a muddled way, was that he needed love—that love was the only possible short-circuiting device here. I almost told him how I felt about him, *that's* how ill balanced and frantic I was; but, thank God, I stayed silent.

I swallowed the sentence down, which made me feel even more choked up with impotent urgency. Tom pushed back his chair and stood up. I stood up, too. The rain rattled, Barker's paws twitched as he dreamed. I was in such a muddle of distress, afraid for my father, afraid for Tom, angry with myself for being normal and inadequate. I think he saw some of these conflicts in my face, and was as concerned for me as I was for him; in a gentle way he put his arms around me. The next thing I knew, I'd begun kissing him. It was the only way I could think of to reach him. I'd kissed him once before, when I delivered the notebook—God knows why—but that was a very hasty casual sort of kiss. This wasn't.

I don't have great experience of kisses, but I can taste desperation. This time he kissed me back, and the kiss continued for a long time. Then it ended. He broke away from me in an odd, ashamed, abrupt way, and left shortly afterward. Since then, we've met often, and he's brought me up to date with everything that he's discovered, but the barriers were back in place the next time I saw him.

At first I thought he was distancing himself because he felt stigmatized by his illegitimacy—which doesn't matter a jot to me, but does to him. Then I realized there was a more obvious barrier between us. I finally understood: He loved someone else, that was why he'd reacted so guiltily. He began to hint that this was the case, but he never spoke of the woman directly, and I wouldn't have dreamed of questioning him, so it was several weeks before he told me her name. Meanwhile, he did seem to trust me more than he had, and began to treat me like a reliable friend, which was progress of a kind. That kiss was not repeated, of course. From his point of view, I suppose, it was an aberration.

I began reading Rebecca's notebook as soon as he left, and I was still reading it, approaching its disjointed end, late that night in my bedroom. Rebecca's words flew straight off the page and into my heart. This winged girl gave *me* wings, I felt—but, as I discovered subsequently, that was not the reaction of others who read her story.

So, perhaps my own state of mind was to blame for my response. If dry, clever, skeptical Rose were to ask me to describe that state of mind now, what should I say? I felt as if death and birth pressed me in on either side, like bookends. Rebecca was writing about giving birth when actually she was dying. Births, deaths, love, hate, the many guises that murder can take. Those forces swirled up at me from Rebecca's pages and my own uncertainties, hopes, and ambitions spiraled to meet them. It was a maelstrom—and, in the midst of a maelstrom, as I shall tell Rose, should she ever bother to ask, *no one's* objective.

MY NEXT TASK—UNDERTAKEN AT TOM GALBRAITH'S SUG-gestion—was to make a copy of Rebecca's notebook. Tom insisted that it had been sent by that anonymous donor to my father, and was therefore his property. When he was stronger, he should be allowed to read it—I agreed with that, up to a point—but Tom also needed to be able to refer to it at will; there were a number of things, he said, that he wanted to check. It was during this conversation that, for the first time, he used the word *verify*.

I didn't like that word—it sounded chilly to me. But I could see how much Tom wanted to keep this story close to him, and I could see other advantages, too, so I agreed to help. Apart from anything else, it kept me occupied.

I spent the rest of that rainy hospital week copying out Rebecca's words. I could have used my old portable Hermes typewriter, but my typing abilities are not what they were. Apart from the WRAC wartime typing pool, I'd had a period of part-time secretarial drudgery in a lawyer's office near here before my father's health worsened. As a result, I associate typewriters with servitude.

I decided to use pen and ink. Handwriting is as distinct as a person's voice, so Rebecca's tale looked very different in my neat legible hand. It looked mistranslated somehow, and its oddities were more noticeable. I'm a careful reader (Rose has trained me), so I'd noticed the gaps in Rebecca's story, but they hadn't worried me at all. I accepted them as part of the timbre of her tale. Now, altered by my own handwriting, those gaps yawned; what had seemed artless to me before now seemed artful and deliberate. I noticed the several references to evading truth, to dealing from the bottom of the pack. That concerned me, but I was convinced that a third notebook must exist, and I told myself that most of my questions would be answered there, in her final entry.

I was a faithful amanuensis. I made only one change. I'd already decided that it would be this copy of her tale that would be given to my father (Tom could whisk the original away). This meant that I could make one small adjustment. When Rebecca wrote that if she were to die or disappear suddenly, she could rely on her "good friend Arthur Julyan" to insist on a full investigation, I edited. I sliced that sentence out. My father already feels guilty enough in this regard; I was determined to protect him from a remark I knew would pain him. I censored, in other words.

By the time I'd completed my task, a week had gone by, and I believed we were due for our next installment. Rebecca's diamond ring, Tom said, had been sent to Jack Favell on the same day the first notebook had been sent to my father. There had then been a seven-day interval before the second notebook arrived. This anonymous sender was oddly methodical! I was convinced that a third notebook would turn up by the first post that Wednesday morning. Barker and I hung about in the hall, waiting for the postman. He delivered a communication from the Inland Revenue and a grocery bill. We waited for the second post: nothing.

I was disappointed and frustrated. I itched to know more. Tom Galbraith was busying himself with his dreary tasks of verification; he'd returned to London in search of backup secondary sources. I was impatient with that. I wanted to tap straight into the primary source, I wanted to hear Rebecca's voice again. Transcribing is a strange process; she'd become my friend and confidante by then, and it's possible that I was especially vulnerable to her seductions: I was lonely at The Pines without my father, and I knew that worse loneli-nesses inevitably lay in wait for me. I wished I could learn how to grab life by the scruff of its neck as fearlessly as Rebecca had.

When no further installment arrived I gave in to temptation. I went into my father's study and looked at the folders he'd laid tidily on his desk before he left for the hospital. Inside them were the fruits of those searches he'd been making these past weeks. He'd not forbidden me to open those folders, but he hadn't encouraged me to do so, either.

I circled his desk. I looked at the ramparts of books. I slid open and slid shut the specimen drawers with their butterflies. With a grumbling arthritic sound, Barker lay down on the hearthrug, and looked at me expectantly. I battled briefly with my conscience, then gave in. I opened the folders and box files. Poor Daddy.

No wonder he'd been so defensive of this "archive," as he likes to call it. No wonder he'd delayed showing it to Tom or to me: His pride would have been badly wounded by such an inspection, for the contents here were pitiful. What did my father's much-vaunted special information consist of? His own account of his "quest" which I'd read another time, if he permitted; invitation cards to Manderley parties; a few scrawled notes from Rebecca concerning local charitable events; the annual programs for the Kerrith regattas in which she always took part; some Manderley recipes that my mother requested.

I felt I was trespassing, but I went on with my search. Initially, the only evidence of interest I found was a photograph of four women in elaborate dresses taking tea in the gardens at Manderley; they were identified on the back, in my father's handwriting, as the three beautiful Grenville sisters and Max's grandmother, the "old beast" of Rebecca's tale.

The grandmother looked magisterial; Evangeline's features were obscured by a huge hat; poor Virginia had averted her face; beautiful Isolda was here aged about sixteen; she was sitting on the grass at Virginia's feet, her lovely hair unbound, and tumbling across her shoulders. I fetched my father's magnifying glass: Isolda's sepia expression was irritable; she was frowning at the camera, her lips slightly parted. In all photographs, there's a secret force, a missing person—the cameraman. Who had taken this picture? Lionel de Winter?

Apart from this photograph, the only other item of interest was a batch of letters from Maxim de Winter; at first these, too, proved dry and disappointing. Then, at the bottom of the pile, I found the last of

them, sent to Singapore, written in a small close slanting hand on
thin air-mail writing paper:

My dear Julyan,
It was good to hear from you—it's excellent news that you and your
family will shortly be returning to Kerrith. Don't worry about being
"underemployed" as you put it. Once you're here, you'll quickly find
that every damn committee of do-gooders will be trying to co-opt you.
A vacancy on the Bench is coming up, I hear, so, if taking on the bur-
den of J.P. and magistrate interests you, just say so and I'll put in a
word. You may regard your appointment as a certainty.

Now, I write with important news. I'm about to be married, so will
be confounding all those confounded bores who'd made up their minds
that I was turning into a crusty confirmed bachelor. I've finally met the
only woman I could ever make my wife. Her name is Rebecca—her
father, now dead, was an expat who made a fortune through mining
investments in South Africa. We have acquaintances in common, and
move in circles that overlap, though Rebecca moves with a faster and
more fashionable crowd than I care for. I first glimpsed her last sum-
mer at various London parties, but couldn't contrive to be introduced to
her. She's the most beautiful creature I've ever seen. I was bowled over
the instant I set eyes on her.

Beyond this, I won't attempt to describe her. By the time you return,
we'll already be married—we plan to marry in some style in France,
where Rebecca has relations, and may honeymoon at a chateau they
own there before traveling on to Monte Carlo in search of sun. We'll
return in the spring, when Manderley is at its loveliest. So, in due
course, you'll be able to see for yourself how extraordinary Rebecca is,
and how lucky I am to have carried off this prize—in the face of some
cutthroat competition, I may say! I think Beatrice wasn't quite sure
what to make of her—you know what a stick in the mud Bee is—but
my grandmother has been utterly won over by her. If I'd had any
doubts (which I didn't, of course), Gran would have scotched them!

I brought Rebecca to Manderley for the first time last week—very
nervous, as you may imagine—and she fell in love with the place the
instant she saw it, which was a tremendous relief. Stupidly, I'd been
afraid that she might find it too remote, or not up to her smart metro-
politan standards; Manderley isn't to everyone's taste, and some

women might find it daunting—but, as I'm discovering, nothing daunts Rebecca.

God knows, the old place is looking rundown. Since the war, I've had my work cut out getting the estate back into good order, and even with Crawley's help it's been an uphill task. When it came to the house, I didn't know where to begin—it's scarcely been touched since my father died—but that doesn't dismay Rebecca; she can see its potential, as I can, and says she can't wait to get her hands on it.

I can't describe the turmoil of these last few months, and the alteration Rebecca's made in my life, Arthur. I remember your once saying to me that marriage was like entering safe harbor. I can't say that it feels that way for me now—more like heading out for the open sea. Conditions there are unpredictable—I'm pulled this way and that by the most powerful currents. To love and to believe that one's loved in return, to feel great joy, but be assailed by a lover's doubts and fears . . . Well, I'm being paid back for years of romantic skepticism, I expect. I'm discovering at last all the agonies I used to scorn; as a result, I cannot write sensibly—or, I see, legibly. Forgive me.

Come and see us as soon as you return, but be ready for some surprises: Rebecca is unlike any woman I've ever known. There is a brilliancy about her, she's as fearless as any man, and she's not, thank God, the kind of conventional woman people expected me to marry. You'll find her manner astonishingly direct—and it may well cause some raised eyebrows here. But, knowing me better than most people as you do, I'm sure you'll understand why I didn't hesitate when I finally met her at last—utterly by chance, on board ship recently, when I was returning from that visit to America. In confidence, entirely between the two of us, and so you're prepared, I'd like you to know that

I turned to the next page. There was no next page. I began shuffling the pieces of paper in the file, but, no, the continuation of Maxim's letter was missing. I was not to learn, it seemed, what Maxim had wanted to tell my father in confidence.

Several weeks later, when I confessed to my father, and admitted I'd looked at these files, I questioned him about this missing page; he claimed it was lost long ago, and merely revealed that Rebecca's mother had been an actress. I'm sure my father wouldn't lie to me, but that day I was suspicious. Could he have censored for any reason, as I had? Could he have destroyed other documents besides this, and might that explain the paucity of this collection?

I looked at the mound of ashes in the grate, but it told me nothing. We'd had fires there every evening until my father went into hospital.

ONCE MY FATHER RETURNED TO THE PINES, AND ROSE arrived to stay, I had to put these issues to one side for a while, until I was sure my father felt settled. Mr. Latimer had ruled out surgery; a multitude of pills had been prescribed, half of which seemed designed to counter the side effects of the others. There was also a rigid regime: light meals at regular intervals, plenty of rest, moderate exercise, no anxiety or excitement. I still had a superstitious fear that my father's illness was partly caused by his guilt about the past, so I let Rose into the secret of the anonymous parcels, but I made both her and Tom Galbraith promise that neither Rebecca nor her notebook would be mentioned.

This was easier than I had expected, partly because Tom Galbraith was frequently away in London on his verification visits, and partly because my father had acquired a new favorite, as I rapidly discovered. Daddy has a suspicion of all doctors, and a deep contempt for medicine; but he'd taken a great shine to Mr. Latimer. Not only did my father swallow down without protest all the pills he prescribed, not only did he invite him to The Pines on several occasions, he also sang his praises at every opportunity. Francis Latimer was a brilliant doctor and a delightful man; he was astute and well-read; his politics were a little radical, but he was stimulating company and "an asset to the neighborhood." What Latimer didn't know about the workings of the human heart wasn't worth knowing; he was solely responsible for my father's much-improved state of health, and above all he "spoke his mind" and "got on with things" and didn't "shilly-shally about"—unlike certain people my father could mention.

Latimer was making a new start after some unspecified difficulties in his life, and was temporarily renting a house close to the hospital, while looking for a permanent residence nearer the sea. He had two young sons, Michael and Christopher. He was also divorced, it emerged, and, given this information, I was even more astonished that he and my father had struck up such a friendship. My father believes marriage is indissoluble; he is inimically opposed to divorce and will usually avoid those he regards as tainted by it. The final rift with my sister, Lily, was caused by her long affair with a married man, and I'd never seen the least indication that Daddy's antique views had modified, despite the anguish that the breach with my dead sister caused, and continues to cause him.

In due course, Francis Latimer was to influence my own actions. Initially, I was somewhat suspicious of him. He visited us at least twice a week in the guise of a guest, but I could see there were deceptions here. I was sure the doctor's motives were professional as well as social. My father's motives were not as altruistic as he liked to pretend. Latimer was keeping an eye on a patient; my father, I saw to my astonishment, was lining Latimer up as a prospective purchaser of The Pines.

Every time he came, my father would take him on guided tours. He'd extol the view; he'd point out the palm and the monkey puzzle. He'd shuffle into the kitchen and sing the praises of the range, which broke down every other week, though that wasn't mentioned. In an airy way, he'd pass over the leaking roof, the rusted guttering, the rotten window frames: "You can see the sea, Latimer," he'd say. "And you can see it from damn near every window."

Francis Latimer, who misses very little, was well aware of the dilapidations, I think; he was amused by my father's boasts, but hid this behind poker-faced solemnity. Once, as we stood at the end of our garden by its crumbling boundary wall, he caught my eye as my father praised the vista behind me; I saw the flicker of amusement in Latimer's intelligent face when he agreed that, yes, indeed, the view was beautiful—unforgettable.

I was puzzled by this new impulse to "get shot of The Pines," as my father put it, when hymning the virtues of snug low-maintenance bungalows. When my father dies—and he's always made this clear to me—The Pines will have to be sold. There is little capital left, so this rickety house is our only serious asset. It's the money from the sale of The Pines that must provide for me in the future, my father says. I shall provide for myself, in fact; I agree with all of Rebecca's remarks concerning women's employment, so I've planned it all out. I shall go to university as I meant to do all those years ago; I'll get a degree and then I shall work—but I've never told my father this. It would hurt his pride dreadfully.

It had never occurred to me that my father might consider selling the house before his death; the only way he'd ever leave it would be feet first, he'd always told me. I couldn't understand why he would change his views now—unless Latimer had planted the idea in his head. And I knew how fatally stupid an idea it was. I could no more imagine my father living in a bungalow than I could imagine him in one of those Manhattan skyscrapers. This house is as important to him as Manderley was to Maxim. To leave here would kill him.

I told Francis Latimer that in due course; it would have been on his third or fourth visit. I didn't want him to get his hopes up—he did seem actually to *like* the house, despite its disadvantages and eccentricities—and this new idée fixe of my father's was now worrying me seriously. I was beginning to see that the stay in hospital had produced many changes in him; he seemed stronger and in better health, but his irascibility and vigor were much reduced, he was occasionally forgetful, and he passed many hours in a gentle, musing, contemplative state that bewildered me. I was glad he seemed tranquil, but this wasn't the father I knew. I suspected that among that myriad of pills was one that calmed his moods as effectively as others controlled his blood pressure.

Francis Latimer's reply interested me. His words marked a turning point, I can see now. He said that he knew it would be disastrous for my father to leave The Pines. He said that nothing he'd prescribed could account for my father's altered state, which he, too, had noticed during the long conversations he and my father had had at the hospital. It was the first I'd heard of these conversations. I began to wonder if Latimer knew more about my father's state of mind than I did, if my father might have made some confession to him of which I remained ignorant. Francis Latimer denied this, too, though doctors resemble priests when it comes to the sanctity of the confessional, so I'm not entirely sure I believed him.

He added, looking at me in an intent way, that I must expect alterations. "People *change*, Ellie," he said, speaking with a sudden vehemence that surprised me. We were sitting on that boundary wall of ours, overlooking the water, and Latimer, unusually for him, seemed restive and preoccupied. I think it was the first occasion that I saw him as a man, rather than as a doctor; I could sense something was troubling him.

"Don't you find yourself changing, Ellie?" he went on. "Dear God, I certainly do. Two years ago, at the time of my divorce . . ." He checked himself, and then, to my great surprise, took my hand. "Never make the mistake of believing that anyone is in stasis, Ellie— especially the old," he said gently. "People your father's age, in his state of health, change at great speed. They advance into territories unimaginable to someone your age or mine. Your father's a remarkable man, and a courageous one. He has a whole lifetime to come to terms with. If he does so calmly, or more calmly than he once did, it's a blessing, believe me."

I liked Francis Latimer after that, though it saddened me to see how swiftly Tom Galbraith had been displaced by him in Daddy's favors; that seemed fickle. And I was influenced by what Latimer said. I can be overprotective. I saw I had no right to hide *Rebecca's Tale* from my father. It was his property.

I asked Tom's advice, then Rose's. With their agreement, I finally gave my father my copy of Rebecca's tale about three and a half weeks after he returned from the hospital. The night before I did so, I stayed awake worrying for hours, looking back through the notebook, searching for any passages that might hurt my father. In the end, I decided to make one further slash with my censor's scissors. Radical surgery: I removed from Rebecca's story the entire section concerning her life with her father at Greenways.

I'd always found that section perturbing, in any case. I found it curiously ambivalent and hard to understand. Why, for instance, did Rebecca write so violently, and at such length, about *mines?* Rebecca accuses her father of imprisoning her, of stealing her liberty—and that made me anxious, for people in Kerrith have made similar charges against my father, in the past. They've claimed he's curtailed my freedom, that he's denied me my chances and so on. Nothing could be further from the truth, of course, but although there's no cause, I know those accusations have wounded him. There is no comparison between Rebecca's situation and my own—none. But if my father read this, in his present weakened state, I thought it possible he might imagine one.

I glanced one last time at the section I'd censored, hesitated, then hid it away in my desk drawer. All those comments about being locked up in a tower! What an ogre of a father! Sometimes Rebecca gets carried away, and overstates her case, I feel. Her tale read better without those fanciful pages anyway, I decided.

MY FATHER'S LIFE IS ROUNDED WITH A LITTLE SLEEP NOW, and it took him such a long slow time to read those pages I'd copied out for him. Nearly two weeks went by, and he still hadn't finished them. Rose whisked them out of his hands one day, as he sat dozing in the sun, and read them in the space of an afternoon—but Rose is a voracious professional reader, and she wasn't caught in the web of these events to the degree that my father was. "Very female," was her comment, and she'd be drawn no further.

"What was Maxim *like*, Rose?" I asked her one evening in the kitchen, thinking of that legendary time just before the first war when Rose was young and lovely, and rumored to be the object of Maxim's affections. Rose, after all, had known most of the characters in Rebecca's story.

"Which Maxim?" Rose replied, tossing salad leaves for supper in the kitchen. "My Maxim? Rebecca's? His second wife's? Your father's? There are umpteen to choose from."

"Yours," I said. "Stop splitting hairs, Rose."

"Afflicted by ancestors, but I liked him well enough. Anchored at Manderley, but always dreaming of voyages. I wasn't in love with him, or he with me, though he may have imagined he was. Does that answer your question?"

"Have you ever been in love, Rose?" I asked, in a moody way, staring out at the sea in the distance. Tom Galbraith had returned that day from another verification visit, this time to the house Jack Devlin had owned in Berkshire, Greenways. He was preparing to leave Kerrith, and due to depart tomorrow for Brittany. I'd agreed to meet him later that evening, to wish him well on his journey. He'd said he would remain in touch, and would certainly visit us again, but I knew that to all intents and purposes we would be saying good-bye to each other.

"Of course," Rose replied. "I was deeply in love with a fellow undergraduate at Girton, Helen, her name was; she's dead now. And later I loved a woman called Jane Turner for years—she used to share my London house in the old days, before I began letting rooms to students. You met her once or twice when you were younger—do you remember her?"

I turned to stare at Rose; I fumbled with a memory. An afternoon at Rose's house in St. John's Wood; a quiet scholarly woman in tweeds pouring tea and asking me about my academic ambitions. I was about to take the Cambridge entrance examination; she gave me a book she'd written on the Brontës, which I still have somewhere. Love? How blind I'd been.

"Oh, for heaven's sake, Ellie," Rose said in a brisk way. "Do you imagine I've lived the life of a nun? How very galling. There's nothing remarkable about it, you know. Sexuality is a matter of taste. Some people like oranges, some people like apples, and some like both. You surely don't believe that morality is involved in that choice? Your father would, obviously, but I expect better from you. Am I to be denied apples because he likes oranges? Is it wicked to like one fruit, and virtuous to like the other? I don't think so. Use your mind, Ellie dear, and peel those potatoes, would you?"

I did as she said. As the skin of the potatoes uncurled, I wondered about Rebecca. Which fruit had *she* liked? She mentioned no liaisons with women in her story, but then there were all those gaps and elisions, and she *had* believed that men were the enemy. I'd already thought of a way in which the most glaring of those gaps might be filled in, and, if it could, I might have the answer to my question. Meanwhile, I put it to Rose, but Rose—who can be infuriating—only considered it briefly. It seemed not to interest her.

"Both? None? I haven't the least idea. Though I did notice she was careful not to tell me. Very difficult to know whom she loved, I thought—apart from Manderley, obviously."

How obtuse Rose can be! "What nonsense, Rose," I said, tipping the peeled potatoes into their saucepan. "She loved her mother. She loved her father. I think she loved Maxim, too, though she hated to admit it—"

"What an innocent you are!" Rose said, giving me a sharp glance. She dropped a kiss on my brow. "We must have a little seminar, you and I, one of these days. Your critical powers are getting rusty." She pushed me toward the door.

"Now, tell your father that supper will be ready in twenty minutes. He's wandering about the garden again with Barker."

I WENT OUTSIDE INTO THE LIQUID LIGHT OF A BEAUTIFUL evening. After the heat of the day, the air was just beginning to cool; there was a salt breeze from the sea; little boats, their bright pennants fluttering, were tacking back and forth in the harbor-mouth below, and the calls of the sailors echoed across the water. The sky was rose colored, milky, and mauve at the horizon. My father had taken up his customary station, sitting on our low boundary wall, his loyal shadow Barker at his feet. He was leaning on his cane, a quiet stooped figure, looking out toward the ocean.

He had finally come to the end of Rebecca's tale, as I could tell immediately. His eyes were moist, and his expression was one of sadness and resignation. Although he'd turned to look at me, it was some while, I think, before he registered my presence. I held out my hand to him; he clasped it tightly, and drew me down beside him. We sat in the still of the evening, looking at the wash of the waves. I said nothing, but I marveled at his tranquility.

Were his hauntings over? I'd been so afraid that Rebecca's notebook would reawake all the demons of his past, but there was no sign of that. For weeks now, ever since his return from the hospital, he had slept through to morning without waking once, his rest uninterrupted by nightmares.

Yet this last year, those nightmares of his had been terrible. There was one particular dream he had, which recurred several times, and which haunted him afterward: In a snowstorm, he was driving in a black car up that endless twisting approach to Manderley. Although he sat at the wheel, the car propelled itself, and seemed to steer itself, its gears meshing soundlessly. Beside him, on the passenger seat, was a tiny coffin, which it was his task, he knew, to deliver safely.

Somewhere on that drive, that little coffin would begin to move, and a child's plaintive voice would rise up from it. *Let me out, oh, let me out now*, it would wail. *Let me out at once*, it would demand, becoming peremptory, and my father, recognizing Rebecca's voice, would try to stop the inexorable car, and try to unfasten the butterfly screws that held down the lid of the coffin. But the car would continue on through the blizzard, and the bright brass butterfly screws would refuse to budge. The cryings out at this confinement and the pleas for release would mount, becoming more and more frantic, and my father in a paroxysm of fear would finally wake, sometimes calling out my name and sometimes Rebecca's.

My father has forgotten he ever told me this dream, which I've never recounted to anyone; these past weeks, I'd begun to see that the dream itself had been forgotten, too. All the time he'd been reading Rebecca's tale, I'd been waiting for signs that those old anxieties would resurface, but they never had. My father had dozed, read, drifted off into a dreaming musing state; sometimes I thought he was watching some film of his own, and comparing its images with those on the page; at other times, he'd shake his head, as if in disagreement. For the most part, he responded to the words of a woman he'd loved as if they came from the far distance, from an imagined world, like a novel.

Once he'd said to me, "That's just how she was, old Mrs. de Winter. The old Termagant, that's what my nurse, Tilly, used to call her. Though my grandfather always did say her bark was worse than her bite. Tilly came from London, you know. She was good to me when my father died. How it all comes back to me!"

Another time, a part of the story—I'm not sure which—had made him tearful, but he never explained why, and he brightened again soon afterward. "I always *thought* she was the butterfly girl," he'd said to me. "I remembered her mother Isolda from my boyhood, you see. I'm glad Rebecca kept that Meadow Blue I gave her, Ellie—kept it for a time, anyway."

No sign of shock or anger; I was mystified. Many of Rebecca's actions flagrantly contravened my father's creed; she had no patience with conventions and beliefs that have shaped his whole life, yet he seemed unaware of that, or indifferent. That evening, as we sat looking at the sea, the cooling air fragrant with roses, the little boats tacking back and forth, and the light dimming almost imperceptibly, he finally began to speak, in the musing way he does now. He even asked me questions: What did I think of this passage? How did I interpret that one?

"Poor child," he said. "That time she came here to tea, Elinor took me to one side, you know, and said we mustn't mention her mother under any circumstances. Such an embattled little girl! And she became a brave woman. Taking on the de Winters and Manderley— that damned house wasn't kindly disposed to anyone, I always felt, but she tamed it. How I hated that place as a child, Ellie! How I loathed Lionel de Winter. I'd heard the rumors about Lionel and Isolda, you know, and there was a time when I feared . . ."

"Feared what, Daddy?"

"Nothing. Nothing." He hesitated, and looked away. "I remember his final illness, that's all. How he looked when he died. I was a witness to that last will of his. Not an incident I'm proud of. Can't undo it now, of course." He gave a sigh and patted my hand; below us, the waves whispered.

He continued to speak for a while, winding down the avenues of the past. Sometimes he referred back to events Rebecca described in her tale, but I could see they were already inexact in his mind; they were transforming even as he spoke; they were entering a twilight where they merged inextricably with his own complementary, confirmatory, or contradictory memories.

"I don't think Rebecca quite says that, Daddy," I said gently at one point, and he gave a smile and a shake of the head.

"Doesn't she?" he said, in his new, quiet way. "Ah, well, I expect I'm getting muddled. Losing my marbles, damn it. Never mind. Let it be. It's done my heart good to hear her voice after all these years of silence. But I shan't look at it again. It's all over and gone now. I'm old. It was a long time ago. I've more urgent things to think about now—tell me what you've been up to, Ellie."

So distant to my father, and so close to me. We ate our early supper— early suppers being part of the new regime—then I left my father playing cards with Rose. I rushed upstairs and changed into a newish dress, crept out the back way so no one would see me in the embarrassing finery of an unfamiliar frock, took the car, and drove to Tom Galbraith's cottage.

He suggested we drive over to Manderley church, and walk by the river. We did this, and, while we were there, he told me several surprising and significant things, among them what he'd discovered when he went to Greenways.

TWENTY-SEVEN

Rebecca's father didn't commit suicide, Ellie," Tom said as we walked between the grassy hummocks of the grave-yard toward the winding of the river.

We walked side by side; Tom didn't look at me, but at the water ahead of us. It was low tide, so the river had thinned to a narrow channel; birds were feeding on the mud banks—my father could have identified them, but I couldn't. As we approached, the flock rose, twisting and glinting in the low angle of the light, black and silver, a sudden sparkle in the air like diamonds. We sat down on a bank thick with buttercups; I wound a wiry stem of sweet grass round my finger. After a pause, Tom continued.

"I've known that for some time," he went on. "I checked his death certificate at once, obviously. Quite apart from anything else, Rebecca's version of his death didn't tally with the one Jack Favell had given me. I wanted to be sure of all the details, and now I am. There's no doubt, Ellie."

How thorough he'd been! He'd double- and triple-checked every-thing. He had all his beloved evidence, all the documents. He had the death certificate; the obituary report in the local Berkshire news-paper; the records of the inquest. He'd written to the couple who purchased Greenways when it was sold after Jack Devlin's death, a couple who were elderly now, but still living there. He'd been shown around the house and stables. He'd spoken to people in the village who could recall the events surrounding Devlin's death, and he'd visited the small country graveyard at Hampton Ferrars where both Jack Devlin and Isabel-Isolda, side by side, lay buried.

"Was it a black marble tomb?" I asked, looking out across the silvery mudflats. I knew it wasn't the most pertinent question, in view of what he'd just told me, but for some reason, for me, it was the most urgent one. I wanted that detail, which had mattered to Rebecca and must matter to him, to be accurate.

"What? The tombstone? Yes, it was. Black marble with gilded lettering. Devlin's taste, presumably." He gave a frown. "Have you been listening to what I've said, Ellie?"

"And which name was on it—Isabel or Isolda?"

"Isabel. Ellie—I knew this would upset you. I know you set great store by what Rebecca wrote, but you must see: I had to check. This matters to me too much to leave room for any uncertainties."

"Tell me again," I said, though I could remember what he'd already said perfectly well. I wound that grass stem around my finger. I wanted to give myself time to think, as much as anything.

So he told me again and, indeed, there was no possibility of mistake. Jack Devlin had been deeply in debt and close to bankruptcy, and he had died on Rebecca's twenty-first birthday, that was all true, but he had not hanged himself at Greenways, and his death had been accident, not suicide. He'd gone for a ride on the Downs behind the house early that morning, accompanied by Rebecca and by one of the stable boys. A mile or so from the house, on a high, isolated area of the Downs, Devlin's mount had bolted.

The weather was clear and bright, but the ground was hard after frost, not ideal riding conditions. Devlin was thrown, his neck was broken. There was nothing the other two riders could do; he was already dead when they reached him. Rebecca had been too ill to attend the ensuing inquest, but the stable boy, whose name was Richard Slade, had given evidence. The coroner's direction was clear, the jury members did not bother to retire, and accidental death was their verdict.

"Let me tell you about Richard Slade," Tom continued. "He was twenty, a local boy. He'd worked for Devlin for four years, and was well regarded. Though there seems no reason why he should have done so, he appears to have blamed himself for the accident—certainly his behavior altered after it happened. He began drinking heavily. He was taken on by the new owners of Greenways, but became a liability. After nine months he was dismissed. A year after the accident to the day, he hanged himself from a roof beam in the stables there."

"There's no question of that, either?" I asked, though I knew what the answer would be: It would have been triple-checked by the man sitting beside me.

"None at all. I've seen all the official records. Two of Slade's brothers are still living in Hampton Ferrars and I also spoke to them. I asked them about the accident. Jack Devlin was an experienced horseman, and I wanted to know if he was riding a difficult horse that day, as Favell had suggested to me. Apparently he wasn't. I also wanted to know why his horse might have bolted. Richard Slade hadn't been able to account for that at the inquest; not surprisingly, neither could his brothers."

"There's scores of reasons why a horse can bolt, Tom." I thought of Rebecca's words: *Daddy tried to saddle me; bit, curb, and bridle.* I said. "Accidents like that happen all the time, even to experienced riders. I don't understand. What are you implying?"

"Nothing."

He kept his face turned away from me, resting his gaze on the band of water beyond us. The tide had turned, and the water was flowing upriver again; almost imperceptibly the channel was widening. We sat there in silence for some time, until Tom spoke. "Why would Rebecca do that?" he asked. "Why merge those two deaths in that way? Why conflate her father's story and Slade's? I can't understand it. In the notebook, that passage sounds—" He seemed to check himself, and glanced at me. "Well, it begs a number of questions, but it sounds heartfelt—at least I thought so."

"She was *ill*, Tom," I said. "She had a breakdown after her father died—she tried to kill herself. Writing about her father was difficult for her, and you can see that very clearly in the notebook. Maybe the only way she could deal with her father's death was to alter the details. Maybe she felt the accident was willed, that it was a form of suicide—in the circumstances, that's possible. If so, she told the truth obliquely. She often does that, or I think so, anyway."

"That's one possibility. The other is simpler. She's a liar."

That word shocked me. It angered me, too. I'd been remembering Rebecca's remarks about "debts being called in," and for some reason they made me uneasy. "You don't believe that," I said sharply. "What other lies have you caught her in? Next you'll be telling me her father and that stable boy were Rebecca's victims. You're starting to take sides, Tom, do you realize that?"

"Aren't you?" he replied, equally sharply.

Was I? I didn't feel as if I was taking sides; sooner or later, people do; I've watched the process at work in Kerrith for years. All black or all white. People line up to defend the husband or the wife, and they always vindicate one at the expense of the other. The authorized version supports Maxim, and paints him an innocent: He probably *didn't* kill her, and, even if he did, he had just cause, and she drove him to it. I've never understood why it should be morally acceptable to kill a woman because she's promiscuous, but apparently it is—at least according to the gospel of the males of this parish. They've never silenced the opposition though, I notice, and I wouldn't let Tom Galbraith silence it now.

"I'm not taking sides, and I'm not passing judgment, either," I retorted. "All I'm doing is trying to *listen* to Rebecca."

"And I'm not?"

"Not at the moment, no. You're allowing prejudices to influence you."

"I'm allowing my own past to influence me, actually," he replied, in a stiff way. "And if you must know, I'm being influenced by my adopted mother. May Galbraith was very careful to keep me at arm's length from Rebecca, I can see that now. She permitted that one meeting, and, after that, nothing. Why? It's always puzzled me. May wasn't a possessive woman, or a jealous one. I used to think she was insecure, perhaps, but now I wonder. Maybe she kept me away from Rebecca to protect me."

"Protect you? Why would you think that?"

"Because men associated with Rebecca seem to suffer fatalities with astonishing regularity," he replied. "A boy in Brittany, who may or may not have died in a storm at sea—and maybe I'll discover the truth about that once I go there, though I doubt it. Maxim de Winter. Her father. A twenty-year-old stable boy. Even my adopted mother's brothers—you remember Rebecca's brief reference to May's three brothers? They all died young, Ellie: one in the first war, one in a so-called climbing accident. The third killed himself not long after May adopted me—in other words, not long after Rebecca's marriage. I'm not saying she had the evil eye, obviously, but she seems to have been a femme fatale, and she certainly had a death wish."

"Tom, you can't blame Rebecca for a man's getting killed in the first war—*millions* of men died in that war. I can't believe you're thinking in this way."

"Neither can I," he replied, with something approaching a smile. He rose to his feet. "Let's not talk about it any more, Ellie. I've decided, I'm going to Brittany, then that's it. I shan't pursue this any further. There are a hundred questions here that are never going to be answered, by me or anyone else. I wrote out a two-page list the other night. For instance: Was Jack Devlin Rebecca's father? Why did he walk out on his wife? Did Maxim de Winter ever discover the truth about Rebecca's parentage—and the question marks surrounding it? If he did, given Lionel de Winter's past and the nature of his death—"

"Tom, the answers are there, insofar as she knew them," I said, interrupting him. "I'm sure Devlin was her father—almost sure, anyway. I think Devlin found out that Lionel de Winter had been Isolda's lover—he could have seen those letters from Lionel. Maybe he believed the child his wife was expecting wasn't his, so he broke with her."

"That's one reading. There are others." He glanced at me, and again I sensed he checked himself. He hesitated, as if about to say more, then his tone altered. "I'm sorry," he said in a resigned way. "I look for certainties, I know, and I also know that if we had Rebecca and her husband standing here right now, and we interrogated both of them, my questions still wouldn't be resolved. Shall we walk back via the church? I'd like to do that."

I could see he wanted the subject closed—a wise decision. We were close to quarreling, and I didn't want an argument to mar the last evening I was likely to spend with him. I didn't want Rebecca to drive a wedge between us when there was so little time left.

Tom held out a hand to me and pulled me to my feet. I think he, too, regretted the disagreement between us; certainly it was from that moment that his manner began to change, or so I think, looking back. I followed him toward the church, lingering by the gravestones as we walked. It was such a calm, still evening, and I wanted to spin it out like the finest gold thread, so it lasted for as long as possible. The clasp of his hand had disarranged my defenses; I couldn't look at him without experiencing that painful sensation for which I think the word is "yearning," and that made me edgy. I was as capable of reticence as Tom was. I didn't want to weaken and confess my feelings— that would wreck the evening every bit as effectively as any quarrel.

We wandered back between the tombs in the still twilit air, the river winding silver below us; the church clock struck the hour, and I tried to change the subject. I asked Tom Galbraith about his return to Cambridge and his work there; to my surprise, he actually answered.

As he began describing it to me, I tried to see the bookish monastic room in the first court at King's, where he said he had his rooms on the first floor on the first staircase. I tried to see him in the libraries where, in a wry way, he said he spent too much of his time searching for truth in the small print. If, in the future, I couldn't meet him, I wanted to envisage him.

His images of Cambridge mixed with those already in my own mind, and I saw it as it was one winter when I was visiting Rose, its pinnacles rising up out of the pale mist of the Fens, snow lying on the beautiful banks of the Cam, the air bitterly cold in an east wind, the lights of the colleges shining and promising. He lived and worked there; for me it had been a mirage. I did not say that.

We went into the church, and bent over the brass memorial to Gilles de Winter. I gripped the sides of an oak pew, thinking of Tom Galbraith as a small boy, thinking of Rebecca's sea-colored eyes, and her presence in the crypt beneath us. Both Tom and I, I knew, were aware of lost opportunities, and how haunting *they* are. I could sense their sad insubstantial presences all around us.

We walked out past the font, in which, I used to believe, my children would one day be christened; I touched it superstitiously as we passed. We went back outside to the soft light of the chuchyard. All the words I would have liked to say to Tom Galbraith rose up in my heart, but I checked them.

For the first time, he began telling me about the man who was to join him in Brittany, Nicholas Osmond, a fellow don at King's, his closest friend, whom he'd known since they were undergraduates.

Osmond, whose special area of interest was medieval French literature and the Romance tradition, had been giving a series of guest lectures at the Sorbonne. He was recently widowed; his wife had died of
leukemia a year ago.

Tom came to a halt; we were just outside the church porch; the gold
of the evening light was now fading. I tensed. I could sense something
unspoken beneath his words; I could hear the undertone of emotion.

"How terrible," I heard myself say in the usual way one makes such
inadequate statements. "How sad for him, and for you. Was she your
friend, too, Tom?"

"Yes. I knew her well. We were all three very close. The illness . . .
well, it was very brief, and very sudden."

"What was her name?" I asked, keeping my tone neutral, keeping
my gaze on tombs.

"Julia," he replied, and that one word answer told me everything. I
could hear the strength of feeling banked behind it, and, for a second,
before he could disguise it, I glimpsed it in his face. I knew then for
certain that if I was invisible for him, it was not solely because of my
own inadequacies.

I'll confess: There was an instinct, mercifully brief, to question him.
I wanted to know all the usual stupid things one can't bear to know,
yet can't resist asking: Was she beautiful? Did she return his love, this
wife of his best friend? Had anything happened, or had nothing happened? Then I regained control. I had no right to ask; he wouldn't tell
me if I did—and it was better not to know. If I've learned anything
these past months, I've learned it's useless to fight against the claims
of the dead. The dead are unchanging and therefore too powerful.

I said nothing more, though I felt much. Taking his arm, then letting go of it, I led him between the larger tombs and the smaller,
tilted headstones toward the high ground of the churchyard. From
there the sea was visible in the far distance. "I'll show you Lucy
Carminowe's grave before we leave," I said. "You remember you
couldn't find it? It's just over here, Tom."

The light was fading fast. I walked ahead of Tom, who followed me
more slowly. I sensed that I'd broken off a conversation he might
have wanted to continue, that perhaps he'd had more to say to me. I
didn't want to hear it. I quickened my pace, peering for the familiar
granite memorial; the grass was so tall, and growing so thickly that at

first I couldn't find it. When I did, I drew back sharply. This grave had been visited, and visited recently. The lichen had been scraped off the low, lozenge-shaped stone, and in front of it, where the tussocky grass had been parted and flattened, an offering had been left: not flowers, but shells, a whole heap of shells, a basketful of them or, I thought with a shiver, an apronful.

I knelt down and touched them. There were scallop shells, limpets, barnacles, hinged cockles like castanets, mussels like mermaids' fingernails. I traced the spirals of a perfect unbroken whelk shell with my finger, then lifted it to my ear. I listened to the sounds of the sea secreted inside it, then replaced it.

Beside me, Tom stood staring down at the grave, and I knew he was thinking, as I was, of that azalea wreath laid at Rebecca's boathouse. "Do any of the Carminowe family still live in this neighborhood?" he asked. "Relatives—friends? Who would do this?"

"No relatives, not now. And no friends that I know of. She's been dead nearly forty years, Tom."

"Well, someone's remembered her," he said quietly. "I'm glad of that, Ellie."

I was glad, too, puzzled but moved, as I could see he was—and I think that these shared feelings helped to break down both his habitual reserve and the constraints between us.

I drove him back to his cottage, which looked very bare and sad now that all his books had been packed up.

He returned the key to the Manderley gates that my father had given him. Then he showed me that eternity ring of Rebecca's for the first time. I held it in my palm. It was tiny—how narrow her fingers must have been!

He poured me a glass of whisky, and we sat outside for a while, watching the last of the light fade, the little ring glittering on the stone step next to us. "I wrote to that girlfriend of Favell's about this ring," he said, after an interval, his gaze on the sea. "She says it's unlucky. She doesn't want it back under any circumstances. What am I going to do with it, Ellie? I don't feel I should keep it."

"I don't see why," I said; I was feeling much calmer now. "If anyone should have it, it's you. I think that's what Rebecca would have wanted."

"Ellie," he said, and hearing the sudden alteration in his voice, I realized too late that for minutes now he'd been struggling with the need to say something, and the fear of expressing it. "Ellie, before I leave Kerrith. There's things I must say to you, things I want you to know—"

"I expect I do know them," I said quickly. I rested my hand on his arm. If he started to tell me about Julia, I felt I couldn't bear it. "And you don't need to explain anything, Tom. Truly. We're friends, aren't we?"

"Of course, and that means a great deal to me. But I want you to understand—being here has changed me. *You've* changed me, Ellie."

"*I* have?" I turned to look at him in surprise.

"Of course." He hesitated, then took my hand gently. "Ellie, you possess so many qualities I admire and envy. Candor, a capacity for trust—I wish I shared it. I wish that very deeply. But I find it hard to trust, hard to talk about my feelings. 'Entombed in reticence,' that's Rebecca's phrase for it. A very English affliction. I'm not the most forthcoming of people, and I do know that. So I made up my mind: Before I said good-bye to you tonight, I'd be as honest with you as you've been with me."

"Oh, Tom, I haven't been honest, not really." I said before I could stop myself. "I expect you know that. I'm not very good at disguising my feelings."

"Why should you disguise them?" he said gently. "Why do any of us try to do that? It's only self-protection, or false pride—I should know, Ellie: When it comes to defensiveness, I'm the expert." He hesitated. "I must say this—and, no, don't interrupt me. Years ago now, I found out exactly how it feels to love someone, and be unable to express that love. I learned how agonizing that can be. I know how you *hope* in that situation; how you go on hoping, longing, to be told the love is returned, and the joy you feel when you sense a response."

He paused again, looking out toward the sea, and I could sense the effort it cost him to speak in this way. "I won't talk about that," he went on quietly, "I make it a rule not to do so. But I will say this: In that situation, I know the uncertainty causes more pain than almost anything else. So I don't want there to be any uncertainty between us. I like you and I admire you deeply, Ellie. I hope we will always be friends, and that I'll never do anything that might cause you to withdraw that friendship. But you have to know: I care very deeply for someone else—and that won't change. I loved that person for most of my adult life, and even now, despite everything, I still feel the same unwavering love. Can you understand that?"

"I can," I said quietly. "Of course I can, Tom. I just wish . . . you sound so sad. I wish you could be . . ." I stopped. What did I wish for him? Happiness, of course; that he might be less lonely. I hoped that, in the future, he'd find a woman who could console him—and I felt sure that, one day, he would. I was unsuitable, that was all. He was not attracted to me. I didn't say this, I couldn't find the words, but he read my mind anyway.

"Ellie, I'd feel this about any other woman, I want you to understand that," he went on—and I knew we'd now reached the part where a kind man let me down gently. "To be involved with anyone else would feel like a betrayal. I can't alter the way I feel, you see, no matter the circumstances. So it cannot be more than friendship between us, Ellie. You have to know that. It's not possible."

I'd never heard him speak with this degree of emotion; these were set speeches in a way. I could see he'd prepared them. But the strength of his feelings broke through even so, and I was moved by that. I suppose he thought, now I knew Julia was dead, that I would hope—and he was right; the tiniest vestige of hope did linger on for some days after this conversation, though I'm stronger now and determined to conquer it. That was why he spoke in such a definite, unequivocal way, and I was grateful to him for that. But I felt pain, obviously, and embarrassment, too, so when he began speaking again, and I realized that there was more he intended to tell me, I interrupted him.

"Tom, don't say any more," I said hastily, draining the last of the whisky, and rising. "I understand—truly, I do. I know how hard it must have been to say this. You've been kind, and you've been clear, and you've trusted me. And you're in no danger of losing my friendship, either now, or in the future. Meanwhile, friends don't need to explain things. 'Never apologize, never explain.' . . . Rose is always quoting that at me. . . ." I hesitated, feeling a great fool. "Besides, if anyone should apologize, it's me. I don't usually go about kissing men without warning—I hope you know that."

"I had realized that. I had no doubts on that score, Ellie." He also rose. If he'd then made any ritual remarks about how I deserved better than him anyway, or how I'd make a good man happy one day, I couldn't have borne it. But he didn't; he's too intelligent and too sensitive—and for that I silently blessed him. He looked down at me and, in the last of the light, I watched his face change while he hesitated. He looked affectionate, torn, and undecided; finally he risked putting his arms around me.

I could sense the ghost at his shoulder. I didn't want to offend her, or him, so I was scrupulous. We said a sensible good farewell. I promised to look into his cottage and forward any mail that arrived for him. He promised to come to see me and my father as soon as he returned from France. He said he would miss us both, which I think was true, and, finally, as I turned to leave, he drew me toward him and kissed me good-bye.

It was a kiss I shall always remember, gentle and regretful—a brotherly kiss. And that is how I've resolved to think of him from now on, as a replacement for the brother I lost in the war. I've decided to regard my former feelings for Tom as an *affliction*, and I've set about curing myself. I've prescribed remedies for myself, Latimer style. I've swallowed the pills of common sense and distraction; there have been side effects—but I've told myself that's only to be expected. I expect *time* is the surest cure, and I also place faith in *absence*. I refuse to believe it makes the heart grow fonder—that's a myth, it's an old wives' tale.

A week after Tom left, I received a postcard with a bright image of a Breton fishing village. A week and a half after he left, I called into his cottage to check on his mail for him, and found the telephone ringing. The caller was a woman Tom had described to me when he told me about his visit to Tite Street; her name was Selina Fox-Hamilton.

She was in an excited state, and disappointed not to reach Tom (or Terence Gray, as she called him), but once I'd explained who I was, we had a long and interesting conversation. There have been developments at Tite Street, and it's Selina, among others, who I'm going to see in London tomorrow.

I've arranged to stay overnight at Rose's house, and will return the next day. I know I'm going to make discoveries—I can feel that imminence again. If I can rely on what Selina told me, and I believe I can, tomorrow I should discover who the anonymous sender of these parcels is. Once I've done that, it can only be a matter of time before I lay my hands on Rebecca's final notebook.

TWENTY-EIGHT

I TOOK THE EARLIEST POSSIBLE TRAIN, AND, SHORTLY after midday, reached London. I hadn't made a trip of this kind since my father's heart attack last autumn, so just to make the once-familiar journey was exciting. I leaned up close to the train window and watched the suburbs inch us into the heart of the city. The noise of the crowds and the bustle at Paddington were foreign and exhilarating. I was wearing a stripey full-skirted dress my father bought me for my last birthday; it looked very smart in Kerrith and very old-fashioned here, but I didn't care. It was a very hot day; in the Underground the heat was infernal. I came out at Sloane Square, and walked toward Tite Street imagining how it must be to live here in the capital; why, you could go to theaters and concert halls and art galleries every day of the week. How astonishing that must be—though I'd miss the sea, obviously.

I felt very carefree and excited, walking up the King's Road. I was imagining how I'd describe this day to Tom, when he returned from France and I explained that in his absence I'd made extraordinary discoveries. This mood of elation and optimism carried me as far as Tite Street. It was only as I approached the tall house where Rebecca had had her river flat that my mood began to alter. That street brought back memories of my sister, Lily, whom I still miss very much, and I lost heart a little. I felt nervous at the task ahead of me, also.

I could see a small removal van drawn up outside the house, and I guessed that the slim girl wearing slacks, who was standing on the pavement giving directions to the removal men, must be Selina. Tom had described her poorly I saw, as I drew closer. She had long dark hair, as he'd said (that day it was drawn up in a ponytail), and she was wearing interesting eye makeup. Tom had been disparaging about this eye makeup, but I longed to copy it. The most noticeable thing about Selina was that she was very pretty indeed—and that he'd neglected to mention.

I think she was a little taken aback when she saw me, because I looked such an old-fashioned country mouse, I expect, but I took to her and I think she took to me almost immediately. The removal men had finished packing up her things, and they departed, but as arranged Selina took me into her flat, and I sat on a tea chest talking companionably to her cats while she made us instant Camp coffee. I tried to imagine how it would be, living in a room of your own, coming and going as you pleased. To me the bare white space was glamorous.

"Pack the kettle last and unpack it first," she said, returning. "I've been making tea for the removal men all morning. You don't mind the cats? They're getting very jumpy. They can't wait to leave here, and neither can I. I can't believe I'm finally going to escape this place."

She stretched out on the floor, lit a cigarette, and examined me narrowly. "So, handsome Mr. Gray's taken off for Brittany, has he? Have you had any luck with him? I tried my damnedest: One long conversation here, then I sent a postcard. I called him at least twice. Result? Precisely nothing. I thought I must be losing my touch, but now I've met you I begin to see, maybe I didn't have a hope from day one. Are you and he . . . you know?"

"No," I said. I considered, then added: "Unfortunately."

"Ah, well, plenty of other fish in the sea," she remarked in a nonchalant way. "Too many minnows, of course, but there you are. Cigarette?"

I took the cigarette (I smoke occasionally, when I want to look modern). The ice seemed to have been broken, and we talked for some while. Selina told me about the new flat she'd found, and her work at the gallery—she made it all sound so easy. She'd just walked in there one day, and talked her way into a job. "You could do it, Ellie," she said airily. "A pretty girl can always get a job—it's fun what I do, but it's not difficult. Mostly I send out invitations, organize the private-view parties. You're not thinking of coming to London, are you? I'm going to need someone to share this new flat of mine—unlike this place, it's pricey."

I explained that I couldn't contemplate anything like that; I explained that my father needed me, and that if anything did happen to him, I had my life mapped out: I was going to pick up where I'd left off and go to university. "Cambridge," I said. "If they'll still have me."

Selina gave me a very queer look. "Don't tell me you're a bluestocking," she cried. "Give me strength. One of those women's colleges? Why not go the whole hog and lock yourself up in a nunnery, Ellie?"

I'd never thought of myself as a bluestocking before, but I suppose it could be true. There's Rose's influence to consider, and I do read passionately. I don't consider Girton a nunnery, either. It's a palace of learning, a passport to the future—though I could see it might not suit Selina. We discussed all this, I asked Selina how she contrived those marvellous sooty Egyptian eyes (she fetched something called eyeliner and demonstrated). Finally, after about half an hour's frivolous talk (I'm starved of frivolity, so I enjoyed it very much), we got down to business. In more detail than she had on the telephone, Selina explained the developments that had brought me to London.

The week before, a package had arrived, addressed to the upstairs flat, the first mail—as far as she knew—that had ever been delivered to its tenant during her own tenure. She found it when she returned from work one day, a brown envelope addressed to a "Mrs. Danvers." She'd inspected it, then placed it on the shelf for mail in the hall; she'd tried to call Kerrith at once, but received no answer from Tom's cottage. Four days later, the package was still lying there unclaimed, though she knew that the flat above was not empty—the eerie furniture moving noises had been continuing intermittently.

On the fifth day, Selina risked the stairs, and knocked on the black door on the landing. She called through the door, using the name

"Mrs. Danvers," to be met with the usual silence. She was certain the woman was there listening, so she announced that a package had arrived, and she was leaving it outside the door, on the landing. Two days later, curious to know what had happened, she crept up the stairs to check. The package was still lying exactly where she'd left it. That was the day she had called Tom's cottage again, and I had answered. This morning, shortly before I'd arrived, she had checked one last time. The package had disappeared, so it had been claimed at last, presumably.

"Which means she must be there," Selina went on, "Yet she's been totally silent ever since I took that package upstairs. For three whole nights, not one sound!" She made a face. "I was used to the noises, so the silence felt worse. I thought, maybe she's *dead*, or maybe she's planning some new routine, creeping downstairs in the dead of night, or something. . . ."

She gave a shiver. "Are you sure you want to go through with this, Ellie? You're sure you don't want me to stay here while you go up? I will if you want—she's not going to open that damn door, so it won't take long anyway."

I *would* have liked Selina to remain—I'd looked carefully at the staircase as she showed me in. It was ill-lit; a cataract of bloodred carpet poured down from the landing above; I could see why Selina and her cats avoided it. But I knew I'd never succeed unless I was alone in the house. "I think if she hears you leave or sees you leave I have a better chance," I said. "You're probably right, and she won't open the door—but if she does, she has no reason to harm me."

Selina looked unconvinced. "You're sure, Ellie? Whoever she is, we know one thing about the woman up there: She can't be too sane."

"If it's who I think it is," I said, "she was never too sane anyway."

I finally convinced Selina that I meant what I said. I helped her pack up the last of her belongings and persuade her cats into traveling baskets. Selina gave me her front door key; I promised to let her know what happened, and we exchanged addresses. The cats began to yowl piteously as soon as the flaps of the baskets shut. Selina left, banging the front door loudly behind her. I could still hear her cats yowling as I stood in the hall behind the closed front door, and Selina loaded them into her car outside. I heard its engine start up, then draw away until its sound merged with that steady background hum of traffic.

The hall was cool; a thick grayish radiance from the fan light lit the black-and-white tiles and the winding staircase. There were faint creaking noises in the air, which I told myself were movement in the fabric of the building; the slanting light from above the door was thick with motes of dust; they eddied about, as if there were a draft source somewhere, yet I could feel no draft anywhere.

I walked to the foot of the stairs, hesitated, then slowly began to mount them. I knew that Tom Galbraith had failed to get any response from the occupant above, and that I would fail, too, unless I could think of the right words. What would be the "open sesame" here? I thought Rebecca's notebook might have given me the answer.

My footsteps on the red carpeted stairs made no sound. They were silent on the carpeted landing. I stood outside the black painted door at last; there was a faint scent of burning. I felt watched—and had to tell myself that no one could be watching, that no one could see through wooden door panels, that there were no spy holes or crannies through which someone could squint at me.

I counted to ten, then tapped lightly on the panels. I said: "Danny, are you there? Please let me in. I must talk to you."

There was silence. The air felt clammy against my skin. It may have been my imagination but the smell of burning seemed to intensify. I forced myself to tap on the panels once more. I said in a sharper, more authoritative voice: "Danny, open the door at once, please. I don't intend to stand here on the landing all day. Open it immediately."

There was a pause, then I heard that noise Tom described, like the soft brush of material against a skirting board. There was a sliding and a turning sound; bolts were being drawn, and locks unfastened. Slowly, the door swung open. The hall beyond was bathed in a bright glaring light from a window at its far end which faced directly into the afternoon sun. The sudden glare after the dimness of the stairwell and the fear and excitement I felt dazzled me. Then I began to see, to read, the figure in front of me.

Standing silhouetted in the light was a woman with white hair; I'd only ever seen her with dark hair dragged back into a tight bun, but this thin white hair was loose on her shoulders, giving her a shocking girlishness. She was as still as death, with a waxwork pallor; but, just as Rebecca described, I could sense the peculiar energy that emanated from her. She was attempting to speak. Her pale lips moved soundlessly. Even in my childhood, this woman had dressed in the style of dead era; she was wearing similar clothes now, as if her clock had stopped in 1918. Her long black skirt just cleared her ankles. In my dismay and shock, I found myself looking for the little meticulous darn in her stocking that seven-year-old Rebecca had seen. These stockings had holes in them. She was painfully emaciated, but I knew this was Mrs. Danvers.

She appeared to be staring over my shoulder; she'd begun to tremble violently. For a moment or so, she remained still, then she did a terrible thing. She leaned toward me, very, very close. I thought, Dear God, she's trying to *smell me*.

I could smell *her*—as soon as she moved a sour sickly grave smell came off her clothes and her breath; I recoiled. Could she see me? I wasn't sure. Her eyes were milky white, they looked as if the skin had grown across the irises, and I had to tell myself it was cataracts. "Your hand, give me your hand," she said, in a dry grating voice, atonal and very low, as if she were unused to speaking.

I was afraid, but I did so. She clasped it very tight, making a broken crooning sound in her throat. She began to stroke it, and I saw her face change. My hands are narrow, though not nearly as long and narrow as Rebecca's were, but I suppose her desire was great, and the wait had been very long, so the mistake she then made was understandable.

She made a choking sound, and to my horror, went to kiss my fingers. I snatched my hand back; at once, in front of my eyes, a transformation took place. I could sense the mechanisms of her willpower grind. She crushed her emotion, and shaking with the effort, tried to turn herself back into a servant.

"At last, at last," she said in that harsh disused voice. "I knew you'd come. I knew you'd never fail me. Everything's ready for you, just the way you liked it. Your favorite flowers, all your lovely furniture and pictures and books. You remember that special tea you liked? I have it here, all ready. All I have to do is boil the water—come in, come in—how was your journey, madam?"

She led me down the corridor before I could say a word; we went up a short flight of steps; she stood back, and I passed through an archway into a huge and appalling room. I felt as if I were sleepwalking. It was the room with the great arched studio window that's visible from the street below, and I'm not sure I can describe it. I was overcome with confusion, with dismay, and pity for her—and with fear, too, because it's frightening to be that close, face-to-face with the unmistakable evidence of a mind gone awry long ago, and a willpower so intense that I could feel it scorching the air around me.

"You've let your hair grow long again," she said, leading me toward a chair. "I'm glad. I always preferred it long. Do you remember how I used to brush it for you? 'Hair drill, Danny,' you'd say. 'You maid me better than anyone, Danny,' you said. I've looked after everything; when I left Manderley, I couldn't bring very much, but I brought your favorite dresses, the sea-green silk, you remember that? And that sealskin coat—it wasn't costly, not like some of the others, but I knew that was the one you'd want, and it's here. But I couldn't find your ring, your little diamond ring—I looked and looked, but I couldn't find it anywhere." She began crying.

"Mrs. Danvers," I said, as gently and quietly as I could. "Mrs. Danvers—please. You're ill. Won't you sit down for a moment?"

"I'll fetch the tea," she said, regaining control. I'm not sure whether she failed to hear me, or refused to hear me. "I'll fetch the tea, now. You sit there. I won't be a moment, madam. Then I've something to show you—a surprise for you. . . ."

Before I could prevent her, she turned and left me. I heard her footsteps go softly down that short flight of stairs. A door closed. The heat in the room was stifling. The chair I'd been led toward was crawling with moths. I backed away and looked around me.

The studio room was double height, opened right up into the roof beams; it must have been beautiful and would once have been white, but now the walls were yellowish and scabrous. It was crammed with an insanity of things, but they must have been rearranged so often during those long night rituals that any purpose they'd had was inverted. Tables were upended; cushions hung from hooks on the wall; pictures were stacked with their faces to the skirting; books had been made into barricades, sectioning the room into quarters. I thought of Rebecca's Religion of the House. Was this what that worship led to? I edged between the book barricades, toward the far corner, where there was a piano.

Something scuttled out from under it as I approached; I nerved myself to go nearer, though the smell in that part of the room was fetid and turned my stomach. The piano had been gutted: its lid was propped open, so I could see into its entrails. The strings had been sliced; it looked as if someone had taken a knife to them, then caught hold of them, and attempted to pull them out. The result was a writhing tangle of wires and loops, like metal intestines. Something—a rat, a mouse—had got trapped in there long ago; I could see a dusty mummified darkness in the depths of the wires. I could smell old decay from three feet away.

I stepped back, feeling hot and sick. Who had done this? Mrs. Danvers?

"Don't you fret about that, madam," said a voice behind me. "Now you've come, we can get that piano mended. I would have done it before for you, but I don't like men coming here—and I wasn't sure, maybe you preferred it that way. When I first came here—after you left—everything was so lovely, just as it always was, except for that. I knew you must have done it after you saw that doctor, madam. Shall I get it mended, I thought? Then I decided to wait, until you gave me instructions. Oh, look, oh, look—" She made a choking sound. I turned to her and saw her face contract. "I've brought the tea, madam—and I don't have lemons. I should have bought lemons. . . ."

Her distress was very great. When I called her "Mrs. Danvers" it seemed to distress her more, so, in the end, pitying her deeply, unsure what to do, I called her "Danny" again, and told her the tea was delicious as it was. I lifted the dusty cup to my lips and pretended to sip. The tea had been made with cold water.

"Will you be needing a fire, madam?" She said, looking around the room in an anxious way; the temperature there, at the top of the building, under the roof, with the windows fast shut and the sun blazing in, must have been well into the eighties. I told her I wouldn't be needing a fire, and turned to look at the fireplace. She had been burning books, I saw—perhaps they were her only fuel in the winter months. There was a great mound of ashes in the grate, and the singed remains of half-burned pages and calf bindings. On the chimney-piece shelf above, an exquisite china figure in a *bocage* of flowers stood next to a stopped clock. The looking glass behind them had been sheeted.

"Oh, madam, how it burned!" Mrs. Danvers said, gazing over my shoulder. "All that paneling, such dry tinder, and up it went in a sheet of flame, just the way I knew you wanted. You could see the flames from ten miles away, like a great beacon. You could hear them, too— a noise like roaring. It raced from one end of the house to the other, so fast; I couldn't believe how fast it was. I said to myself, That's my darling, she's done for them. Miss Rebecca never would let anyone get the better of her—then I came here. You take care of the flat, Mrs. Danvers, he'd said, You make the arrangements. . . . *He* never cared what happened to this place and all your lovely things. Too busy trying to forget you. I knew he never would. He could marry a hundred women, but he'd never replace you. You marked him for life—I could see that when I looked in his eyes—even if *she* couldn't. It was killing him—being without you. Shall I show you your surprise? It came just the other day, or the other week, I forget. First the azalea, then this. I knew they were harbingers, I knew you were coming. I can't tell you the joy. I knew I hadn't much longer to wait. Look, madam."

She reached across to me and laid her thin fingers on my arm; she began to tug at me, and although she had almost no physical strength, the force of her will was mesmeric. I followed her, then halted. Of all the evidence of the past that I might have found in that terrible place, the last thing I would have wanted to see was this, yet there it was, laid out on the only table in the room that was upright.

Two smart boxes, once white, now yellowed, their lids removed, and the tissue paper folded back for my inspection. Inside, carefully folded, baby's clothes just as described: tiny matinee jackets, nightgowns, bonnets, and booties, a gossamer shawl, fine enough to pass through a wedding ring. The smallest pearl buttons, faded threads of ribbon, exquisite hand stitching, knitted of the finest wool, on the thinnest needles: a wardrobe for a child never born. It was recognizable, but pitilessly moth eaten. Lying on the remains of the shawl was a blue enameled butterfly brooch, and next to it, carelessly tossed aside, the brown envelope it had arrived in, addressed to "Mrs. Danvers."

I stared at the baby clothes and the brooch; I couldn't bring myself to touch them. I suppose I'd known from the instant she opened the door to me that there was no possibility Mrs. Danvers could have sent those notebooks or that ring of Rebecca's to anyone. She was too frail to break out of her obsession in that particular way; someone else must have sent them, and sent this, too, I thought, looking at the brooch that had been Rebecca's talisman, her blazon. I felt jerky, sick, and trapped. I no longer cared who had sent these things or why—all I wanted to do was escape from this woman and this place and breathe air again.

But I couldn't leave her. I couldn't just walk away and do nothing. It repelled me to look at her, but I made myself do so. I could see she was desperately ill, physically as well as mentally; the emaciation was very advanced. How long had she been shut away here? How did she eat? How did she exist? "Danny," I said quietly, "how do you manage here? Do you go out to the shops? What do you do for food?"

She looked at me as if I were the insane one. "Tins," she said, making me jump. "Cupboards full of tins. I went on working until last year, madam. People always need housekeepers and companions. I always left a message here for you, so you'd know how to reach me. I looked ahead; I was careful with my money and, when I was stronger than I am now, I laid in the stores—I never knew when you might come back, you see, madam. And I still go out even now—sometimes, not so much recently." She gave a little grimace. "During the day—when *she's* out, that spy downstairs. I wait till she's gone, I'm in and out—I don't like her to see me. I don't like anyone to see me. It's more difficult now. The pain's been bad these last weeks. And my eyes aren't what they were—I expect you can see that, madam." She turned her milky gaze in my direction. "I can see you, though—oh, yes, I can see you. I remember that dress. Your daddy bought you that dress, one day at Greenways."

"Danny, do you have a doctor?" I asked. "Is there a doctor you see? Someone who might help if you fell ill . . ." I hesitated. "Or, say, if I did?"

If I hadn't added that last suggestion, I'd have met with a blank dismissal, I knew—but putting it that way seemed to convince her.

"Oh, yes, oh, yes," she said, looking around her. "I *was* ill last year, madam. Sick, so sick. I couldn't seem to eat, and the pain was terrible. I saw a doctor then—well, I had to. And I was in hospital for months; until this January. I had the very finest treatment—I have a card somewhere, madam. Let me see, where did I put it?"

I thought of the periods of activity Selina had described, and the periods of silence. Did this hospital stay explain that?

Mrs. Danvers finally found the card. It was inside a vase filled with shells on the same table as the baby clothes. She picked up the butterfly brooch as she passed it, and to my dismay and shame, pinned it on my dress. She gave the doctor's card to me in a childlike trusting way, and I saw that the only way to proceed was to tell her firmly what to do; the sad instincts of feudalism remained with her still. The instant I gave orders, she seemed much less uneasy.

In this way, I persuaded her back downstairs. Even then, she insisted I see "my room," which she'd kept as I'd always liked it. She opened a door, and I looked into a large square chamber, dominated by a four-poster bed. The blinds were down; the light in the room was thick and shadowy. The disorder upstairs was not repeated here. Apart from the thick silvering of dust on every surface, this bedroom must have been just as Rebecca left it.

There were silver hair brushes on the dressing table; on a chest was a small triptych of photographs in a blackened silver frame. I moved hesitantly toward it. Under a veil of dust were the photographs of Rebecca's mother that Jack Favell had described to Tom; here was Isabel Isolda as eternal understudy, as lady-in-waiting and as Desdemona; here was the final resting place of that shrine to her mother that Rebecca had erected at Greenways. "So beautiful and so gifted," said that low voice behind me. "When she died, it made my blood run cold. I'll never forget it. It's branded on my memory."

Was she thinking of Isabel's actual death, or Desdemona's—or Rebecca's? I couldn't tell. I was beginning to feel dizzy and light-headed; the room felt hallucinatory. I turned to look at the bed. What I had taken for thin muslin hangings were spiders' webs; the bed was sheeted with cobwebs.

I closed the door on that room, and persuaded Mrs. Danvers that she must lie down and rest. I could see that the very last of her energy had been exhausted. She leaned on my arm, and I helped her into a little dark cupboard of a room nearby; I assumed she had used it when she left Manderley, but its importance to her went back further than that, I discovered.

"Do you remember when we came here after your daddy died?" she said, staring at air as I folded back the coverlet. "I had my savings, you sold those bracelets, and you said to me, 'There you are, Danny, that will buy us a refuge.' I found this place and I took out the lease and I brought you here. How ill you were—I was beside myself with worry. Night after night, those terrible dreams—how he haunted you, your daddy. But I was always here. I sat up with you night after night. You were like a daughter to me, my own little girl—you knew I'd never leave you. 'Now I'm going to mend myself, Danny,' you said. 'One piece at a time. You're going to help me, and we're going to make all the joins invisible.' And you did, too. I loved your mother, but she was nothing to you. I've never known anyone with a quarter your courage and willpower."

Tears had come to her eyes. Taking her hand, I told her she must rest. She was fretful and bewildered at first, but I managed to make her lie down on a narrow bed, and drew the musty coverlet over her. I tried to open the window to let some air into the place, but it wouldn't budge an inch. I went in search of a telephone, but there wasn't one. I found my way to the kitchen, and fetched her a glass of water. I opened one of the cupboard doors and there were battalions of tins, some prewar I think, just as she claimed; I wanted to weep when I saw them. When I returned with the water, her eyes were shut. I stood, afraid, in the doorway, then I saw the slow rise and fall of her chest, and knew she was breathing.

I know some people find it very hard to be close to illness, or close to the old and the infirm—they can't deal with the smell of sickness apart from anything else; I was like that once, but I'm not now. Nursing my mother and looking after my father has cured me of that kind of fastidiousness. So I went back to that bedside, and took Mrs. Danvers's hand in mine. I explained that I was going out briefly, but would return, and I was taking the key to this flat with me.

I don't think she heard or understood any of this; but I'm glad that I took her hand, in view of what happened afterward. She clasped it tight in hers with surprising strength. Her milky eyes flickered open, and fixed on a vacancy behind me. I think the last of her energy and the last of her will had been used up in admitting me, talking to me, and fetching that stone-cold tea. Now, her lips moved, shaping words, but no words were spoken. A ghost of some gladness came into her face, then her eyes flickered shut, and I saw that she was sleeping.

The details of what happened after that don't matter. The logistics of finding that doctor, persuading him to see me, persuading him that action was necessary, and persuading him, eventually, after endless delays, to come back to the house with me, are just that, logistics. He administered an injection, and then took me aside into that studio room. Its insanities seemed scarcely to bother him; maybe, with a busy London practice, and many poor elderly patients, he saw similar decay and confusion on a daily basis. He certainly made no comment on it. The cancer, he said, had been already advanced when surgery took place last October; it had brought some months of remission; Mrs. Danvers had been first in hospital, then a nursing home until January this year. He was very definite about these dates, to which I paid careful attention. They meant that whoever Selina had seen on the stairs in last November's fog, it could not have been Mrs. Danvers.

Consulting his notes, he said he had last seen her in February at his surgery, by which time it was clear to him that the cancer had spread; when no further contact was made, he had assumed she'd died, or left London. He was surprised that she could have survived another three months—but I wasn't.

I knew what had kept her alive; I knew *who* had kept her alive. I knew that the end couldn't be long delayed, and it would be easier for her now she believed she'd been reunited with Rebecca. Did I feel guilt at the deception on my part? Of course not. I've spent the last ten years of my life with the old and the ailing. I know: Truth can damage, and deceptions can be a blessing.

Mrs. Danvers did not wake from that last sleep of hers; she did not recover consciousness, and I was glad. I thought it merciful. She was taken to a hospital in Chelsea, but when I went there the next day, still wearing that butterfly brooch, I was told she hadn't made it through the night. She had died at three in the morning, in what Rebecca called the dangerous hours after midnight.

How I wanted to leave London then. I'd spent the night before at Rose's St. John's Wood house, talking to the women students who rent rooms there. I'd said nothing to them about how I'd spent my day, and I must have disguised my feelings, for they seemed to notice nothing. They were friendly and kind; they talked about lectures and examinations, parties and men, and they seemed to believe that this world they conjured up could be mine for the asking. I nodded and smiled, but I could feel that world receding further and further away from me. Its gestures and delights came from the other side of a thick glass pane. I couldn't join the young women the other side of it, I was over there in another world with the old, the haunted, the sick, and the dying.

It would have been wicked in me to regret that, I felt—but I went to bed tied up in knots of yearnings, desires, and duties. The following morning, leaving that hospital, all I wanted to do was rush to Paddington, get on a train, and escape home to The Pines and the sea. Once I was there, I felt I might forget that terrible studio room and forget all my disloyal conflicts. But I'd arranged to talk to those artist friends who had shared a house with my sister Lily, and who had told Selina those ghost stories; they still lived in Tite Street. I'd once known them well; they were looking forward to seeing me; I felt I couldn't cancel the visit.

They occupied a large bohemian house, a short way along the street from Rebecca's flat. For as long as I could remember, that house had always been crammed with visiting friends, with mistresses, wives and ex-wives, with tribes of children of confusing parentage, all of whom came and went very amicably. I found it little altered since I last saw it, just before the war, when Lily was leaving London with her married lover to make a new life in Australia. It still had the same rich, gypsyish beauty that had so fascinated me in my teens: There were still the same bright rugs, the vivid blue and scarlet painted rooms were still crammed with pictures. In the kitchen, the still life of an eternal convivial meal lay on the long scrubbed kitchen table; a fat jug spilled dog roses and scarlet poppies; I could hear the sound of a violin from upstairs, and the shouts of children from the garden.

They led me out into that garden, and it was still an Eden, just as I remembered it, a long country garden in the midst of London, weedy, overgrown, and beautiful, heady with the scent of roses and orange blossom. I was kissed and hugged, introduced to new occupants and reintroduced to old ones. I was led to a rickety wooden table shaded by a scarlet Japanese parasol; there was a large bowl of ripe strawberries on the table. A woman I didn't recognize from before, with a long rope of auburn Pre-Raphaelite hair, brought the men cigarettes and a jug of red wine. She was heavily pregnant, rapt, and majestical; she was wearing a vivid peasant skirt and a careless silky shawl embroidered with flowers and butterflies. I looked enviously at her from the other side of my pane of glass; she smiled at me, then wandered back to the kitchen. In this household, for all its liberality, I reminded myself, women had always been treated as muses—and servants.

In the bright sunlight, still behind my pane of mysterious glass, I looked at Lily's former friends, who had also at one time been Rebecca's friends: Everything in the house was the same; they were the same; there was only one difference—I remembered them young, now they were in their fifties.

The three men who had been closest to Lily, who had been the fixtures in the caravansary of this house for thirty years, were known as the "Three Rs": Their names were Richard, Robert, and Rayner. The first two were painters, Rayner was a sculptor. They sat with me at the table, lit cigarettes, poured wine—and talked. How they talked! They told me tales of Rebecca that I'd heard years ago from Lily, tales that they'd clearly been repeating ever since. Those anecdotes had been altered, embellished, improved, touched up, rubbed down—they were now myths, and, although they were well told, even wittily told, with many interruptions, much laughter, and squabbling about who said exactly what, where, when, and to whom, they were meaningless, meaningless. Somewhere in the forests of those tales, I'd glimpse a brightness I knew was Rebecca, or a patch of cool shadow, and I'd think, yes, that's her; then she'd slip away unseen again, lost in the undergrowth of digression and detail.

I had thought they might know about those one-a-month men, and might even be able to identify the poet of Irish extraction Rebecca mentioned. But they couldn't. Did I mean that fashionable photographer, perhaps—or the rich American she was involved with for a time? There had been a Scottish earl, the Hotspur of the North, they'd called him—but he hadn't lasted long. There was that witty insolent novelist, what was his name? But a poet? No, they couldn't remember a poet, or an Irishman—but it could have been anyone, men couldn't resist Rebecca. "We were all in love with her at one time or another. *Everyone* was in love with her," said Robert, a man who'd once been going to have a golden future, but hadn't, though he didn't seem bitter about it. "She was a glorious woman, *glorious*— a law unto herself. Ah, the days of wine and roses," said Rayner, lifting his glass and smiling.

Off they went into another anecdote, tumbling with names famous and names forgotten. Richard went indoors, rummaged around, and found a pencil sketch of Rebecca he'd once made; he was a clever portraitist, a protégé of Augustus John. The sketch was delightful, but it looked nothing like her.

When I'd set off from Kerrith, I'd had a list of specific questions I wanted to ask—I wanted to know what Rebecca had *done* during the period of roughly four years between the death of her father and her marriage to Maxim. She'd said that she went out and "earned"—but how, exactly? I suppose I also wanted to know about her sexual preferences and whether she had ever been in love, but most of all I just wanted an answer to that eternally unanswerable question: What was she *like*? What happened to her in the period to which she never referred, the years between Greenways and Manderley?

Did I get straight answers? No, of course not. Both Richard and Robert had been conscientious objectors in the first war; they'd worked on a farm on Richard's father's Sussex estate, then moved here when the war ended. They remembered Rebecca's arriving at Tite Street three years later; both could remember a period of ill health, one claiming it lasted a few months, and the other hotly denying this, and claiming it was a year at least before she recovered, to become feted, courted, envied, and emulated.

Richard was sure she'd worked at the French Embassy in some social capacity; Robert said she been the brains behind a little couture business run by two fashionable titled women, a business that had been the last word in chic for a brief period. Rayner said a financier friend helped her gamble on the stock exchange and invest in property. They all three agreed that propelled upward by beauty, wit, daring, a droll way of speaking, and charm, she had become, overnight, as it were, a necessary adornment in a long dizzying chain of Jazz Age parties.

"She was a muse!" cried Rayner, who'd had more wine to drink than anybody else. "I was so young! It was an inspiration just to look

at her!" "Ah, those eyes, those *dangerous* eyes," said Richard, or perhaps Robert—I forget. And I knew that, fond of them though I was,
this was all a gossamer weave of indulgence and fabrication, wefted
with truth perhaps, but warped by nostalgia.

As I rose to leave a group of children, as grubby as gypsies, as
plump and hungry as puppies, emerged from the shrubbery at the far
end of the garden. They piled into the kitchen in search of food, and
in a tranquil unhurried way the lovely, heavily pregnant woman I'd
seen earlier began laying bread and fruit on the table. She lifted a
pitcher, and poured milk into glasses, the children scrambling around
her. As I was about to pass by, she laid a hand on my arm.

"You're wearing her brooch," she said, in a low voice, glancing
over her shoulder at the group of men who were still in the garden
doorway, arguing over an event that might have happened in 1921 or
1922, or might never have happened at all. She was older than I'd
realized, I saw. Something in the way she spoke, or something in her
eyes, made me pause.

"You knew her then?" I said, and I watched her face light.

"At one time, very well," she replied. She glanced back at the men,
and smiled, a slow smile, of great warmth. "Insofar as anyone knew
Rebecca," she added in a final way, then she turned away to attend to
the children, and I left the house shortly after.

I CAME OUT INTO HOT, AIRLESS TITE STREET. I STILL HAD
the keys to Rebecca's house. I could have let myself in, and looked
through the belongings there like some thief; I could have searched
for that last notebook—though I was sure I wouldn't find it. I suppose I could have rescued that little shrine of photographs to her
dead mother, but I couldn't bear to set foot in that death space again.
So, rightly or wrongly, I stepped back and distanced myself. Let
someone else deal with that flat and its contents; let someone else
dispose of the relics. Yesterday I'd seen the sickness an obsession with
the past can inflict. I'd met a woman *dying* of the past. I wanted no
more talismans.

I dropped the keys at the agents for the building, then I left London. Once on the train, I could see my double moving on the glass
whenever we passed from sunlight to shadow. I could see the butter-

fly brooch pinned on my dress. I didn't feel like myself: I felt *other*. I
tried to think about what I'd seen and learned on this visit, but the
details fragmented. Why had Rebecca attacked that piano after her
final visit to that London doctor? I thought of the piano at her childhood house in Brittany, with the strings that perhaps needed tuning.
The carriage became hotter and hotter as we jolted westward; the
strap for fastening the window was broken, and the entire train felt
sealed and airless.

I told myself that Tom Galbraith was right to curtail his searches
and I should do so, too. Everything of importance I had to learn of
Rebecca I already knew; the rest was detail. I would probably have
honored that resolve, but as I was about to discover, the past is capri-
cious. Sometimes you pursue it, sometimes it pursues you—and,
when it does, you cannot ignore it.

"Good news," said Rose when she met me at the station in our car.
"Your Mr. Galbraith telephoned from Brittany yesterday. He's coming back to England in four days' time. He and that friend of his are
going to call in and see us."

"He isn't 'my' Mr. Galbraith, Rose," I said, winding down the window. "Do stop calling him that. How hot it is."

"And Francis Latimer's coming for supper tonight. I sweet-talked
the fishmonger. We're having sea trout."

"Tonight? Oh, Rose, I'm exhausted. I feel as if I've been on that
train for a week. Whose idea was that? Yours?"

Rose gave me a pitying look. "Ellie, do you know me at all? No.
Your father's."

Rose said nothing more until we'd negotiated the narrow roads
inland, winding our way between the banks and hedgerows that are
so tall here they make the lanes into rich green tunnels. The scents of
summer flooded the car; the despondency of my day began to slip
away. I looked at the woodbine and the dog roses twining in the
hedges; I thought of Tom Galbraith's return, and my heart lifted. We
reached the brow of the hill behind Kerrith, and the great blue
panorama of the ocean opened out for us. The horizon shimmered.
Anything's possible, I said to myself; think of the weeks, months,
years ahead of us.

"Oh, and by the way, we've had a visitor," Rose said. "A woman.

She arrived yesterday afternoon, when your father was having his rest. She was somewhat odd. I haven't mentioned it to him."

"A woman? Who was she? What did she want?"

"I don't know. I didn't recognize her, and she didn't leave a name. Her manner was evasive. She said she might call again, or she might not. She'd hoped to see your father."

"She didn't leave a name? How strange. What did she look like?"

"Not very memorable," said Rose. "Dowdy. Gray dress. Gray hair. Mousy."

Someone from the parish council, I thought, or one of the innumerable do-gooders who are always trying to rope my father onto some committee. I forgot the incident almost at once, and wasn't to understand its significance for several days. I was slow, but then my mind was elsewhere; I was thinking of Tom Galbraith's return, and, as that anonymous woman might have told me, such preoccupations can be curiously blinding.

TWENTY-NINE

THE INFORMATION THAT TOM GALBRAITH WAS RETURNING, albeit briefly, spread around Kerrith with astonishing speed. Within a day of Rose's giving me the news, I found it was common knowledge. I went into the chemist's to renew my father's prescriptions and they smiled at me knowingly. The day before Tom and his friend were due to arrive, when I went into Kerrith to buy food for the lunch Rose was planning, I could see the shopkeepers were measuring me up for a wedding gown; I fled as fast as possible from their assumptions. I didn't manage to avoid dreadful Marjorie Lane, however. She rushed out of her bijou cottage as I passed, and clasped my hands. Fizzing with suppressed spite, she said she wanted to be the first to congratulate me.

"I knew he'd be back!" she cried. "Tomorrow, I hear. How thrilling! One or two people here—I'll mention no names, Ellie—said he wasn't interested in the first place. Well, my dear, I set *them* straight. I told them, Ellie wears her heart on her sleeve. Dear Mr. Gray must have known how she felt; why, it was obvious to everyone! He wouldn't have made a fool of her for the world. You mark my words, I said, he'll be back! Tell me, Ellie dear, have you made any definite plans yet, the two of you? I can see it must be difficult—a man can only take on so many responsibilities. What *will* you do about your father?"

"You're mistaken," I said. "These rumors are all nonsense. He'll be here for a day at most. It's just a brief visit, to see my father mainly. Excuse me."

"Of course, Ellie, if you say so! How is your dear father? I bumped into him the other afternoon with your aunt—did she tell you? Rather crisp, isn't she? Quite short with me, I felt—I couldn't hide my shock when I saw your poor father's state, such a rapid decline! Perhaps she felt I should have hidden my reaction better—but you know me, Ellie, what I think is what I say; I've no time for subterfuge! And I'm so fond of your father, with his funny little ways. It quite broke my heart, dear, to see him so absentminded—and so thin! It can't be long now, I said to Jocelyn Briggs, I just hope poor Ellie's prepared. You'll be putting The Pines up for sale, I imagine. A little bird told me Mr. Latimer might be interested in it. That's not all he's interested in, I said. He's divorced, of course. But I expect you know that?"

"Certainly I know that. I also know that if my father's stronger now, which he is, it's entirely due to Mr. Latimer. I really must go, Mrs. Lane—"

" 'Marjorie,' dear! I don't stand on ceremony—all my friends call me 'Marjorie.' "

"In that case, I'll continue to call you 'Mrs. Lane,' " I said, and wished her good morning.

I FELT THAT REMARK AT LEAST LEVELED THE SCORE, BUT what she'd said hurt me, as she'd certainly intended. I went straight to see the Briggs sisters—I've never been in any doubt as to where most of the rumors in Kerrith originate.

I was fortunate in that I happened to find Elinor alone—it's always easier to persuade the sisters to listen to you when they're separated; when they're together, it's difficult to get a word in edgeways. Jocelyn was visiting a friend; Elinor was in their exquisite garden, exterminating greenfly. She seemed pleased to see me, and settled me in the shade of their terrace with a cool glass of homemade lemonade. She had the grace to blush when I put my accusations to her.

"Heavens, where do these rumors start? That Lane woman is an abomination. I'm sure it can be nothing *I've* said. Why, I'm the soul of discretion—I haven't breathed a word about Tom Galbraith, and who he truly is, for instance—well, he made Jocelyn and me promise that we wouldn't. No, no, I'm afraid Jocelyn must be the culprit! She's so fond of Tom—even before we knew who he was, we took to him! Such a thoughtful young man—he brought us chocolates from London, and our favorite violet creams, too; so clever of him! And then we're devoted to you, Ellie, so of course when we heard Tom was returning to Kerrith, we both hoped . . . Yes, I feel Jocelyn must have dropped a tiny hint—and then people have jumped to their own conclusions." She gave me a small glance. "And, who knows, they might be correct, dear."

"Elinor, they're *not* correct. They couldn't be more wrong. And I wish they'd stop. Can't you make them stop? I'm fed up with it. We're friends, that's all. I don't even want to get married. I'm perfectly happy staying single. What's wrong with single, anyway? I'm used to it. It suits me."

"Of course it does, Ellie. We shall say no more about it. I shall make the situation known, have no fear. Still, I expect you'll be looking forward to seeing Tom, and hearing his news from Brittany— Jocelyn and I certainly are. Did he tell you, dear—he showed us part of that notebook of Rebecca's? Well, not the notebook itself, you understand, but he copied out the sections about her time at St. Winnow's, and her comments on dear Mama and so on."

"I didn't know that. You haven't mentioned it, Elinor."

"I know—and there were reasons for that. We couldn't decide quite what to make of it, my dear, to tell you the truth. Jocelyn was very upset—she doesn't like to discuss it. In the Manderley days, we were both so fond of Rebecca, you see—and we'd never once suspected she had any connection with that strange girl who stayed with us—but then Jocelyn and I scarcely saw her, we'd forgotten all about her. I met her that one time when I took her to tea at The Pines, and Jocelyn was in a dream of love then, poor dear—writing all those letters, and her fiancé was killed, of course, the following year. . . . But the way Rebecca wrote, it was so hurtful and *inaccurate*, Ellie. That's what I can't understand."

"Inaccurate in what way, Elinor?"

"Well, she says she was put in a 'cold attic room,'" she cried, in a burst of indignation. "And that's certainly not true. Mama wouldn't have dreamed of doing such a thing. Put her up in the attics with the servants? What nonsense. She slept in the old nursery, Jocelyn's almost certain, or in one of the guest bedrooms. And it wouldn't have been cold. Mama would have made sure she had a fire there. She says she was forced to wear an old frock of Jocelyn's that day she went to Manderley—when the truth was she arrived at St. Winnow's with the shabbiest clothes, most of which she'd outgrown, and Mama took pity on her, and thought she'd like to wear something pretty. . . . At least, that's what we think must have happened, though neither of us was there that day, obviously."

"Maybe she just confused the details, Elinor. She was under great strain when she was at St. Winnow's. She was afraid her mother was dying—and she does mention how kind Evangeline was to her."

"And so I should think! Mama was the kindest woman imaginable. She went out of her way to make her welcome—obviously the situation was difficult, but she didn't make it any easier, believe you me, dear! She was a very difficult child indeed, prickly and rude, with all these fanciful ideas, the strangest manners, and the most peculiar way of talking! She says we were 'dying of anemia.' We were very hurt by that. What can she possibly have meant, Ellie?"

I knew exactly what she meant, but I couldn't very well tell Elinor.

"In short, Jocelyn and I are extremely glad that we read only that one section. We told Tom, that's quite enough, we don't wish to see any more! If she can be that misleading and unfair in just the course of a few pages, heaven only knows how inaccurate the rest of it is. Even Tom had doubts; he admitted it. He said he'd read her notebook very carefully, and it was filled with evasions and suggestions. Apparently there are several references to guns—is that true, Ellie?"

"There are three or four at least, yes."

"Tom says she makes great play with the fact that she'd seen Maxim cleaning his service revolver shortly before her death—and, as Tom pointed out, that kind of detail is impossible to check, which is convenient for her! By placing it as she does, she plants the idea that Maxim might have been *planning* to kill her. And I can't believe that. We've sometimes suspected he might have been involved in her death, but we always thought it must have been, well, a kind of *crime passionnel*, Ellie. What do you think, dear?"

"I think it depends where Rebecca was killed, and how," I replied carefully. "If she was killed at her boathouse, which seems likely, and if she was strangled, or attacked with a weapon that happened to be to hand, then it might be a *crime passionnel*. But if a gun was used, it would have had to be taken to the boathouse, which suggests premeditation." I paused, frowning out toward the sea. I was hurt that Tom Galbraith had spelled out his doubts to the Briggs sisters in greater detail than he ever had to me.

"We'll never know, Elinor, in any case," I continued, turning back to her. "If Rebecca's body had been found quickly, then presumably the postmortem would have shown exactly how she died. As it is . . ."

"Well, I don't see how a gun could have been involved anyway," said Elinor, on an argumentative note. "I may not know much about firearms, but I know a great deal about wounds. I was a nurse in the first war, remember. When I was sent to France, I nursed men with the most terrible injuries. I said to Tom, if she's suggesting Maxim's gun was the murder weapon, you want to look into it, my dear, because bullets smash bones, they leave *traces*. Tom must have been thinking along the same lines, because he'd consulted a pathologist in London on that very question—and he confirmed what I'd said: It would be *very* unusual for a bullet wound not to be identified at a postmortem, even allowing for decomposition. A bullet wound to the skull would be obvious, and even a chest wound would almost certainly show up—there'd be damage to the rib cage. If no bone damage was found, the man said, then almost the only way a fatal wound could have been inflicted was if the bullet hit soft tissue only, and passed straight through the body. If the gun was fired at the stomach, in other words."

"A stomach wound?" I stared at her. Elinor, who had not read all of Rebecca's notebook, could not see the significance of that, but I could.

"Exactly. Which, as Tom said to us, just goes to prove that the idea of Maxim's gun being the murder weapon is *extremely* unlikely, whatever Rebecca may hint. Maxim fought in the war. He'd been used to guns since childhood. He'd have known that if you want to kill someone quickly and effectively, you aim at one of two areas. The heart or the head. You don't fire at the stomach, which causes a slow, agonizing, bloody death. Tom feels that detail virtually *proves* Maxim's innocence. And I must say, I'm coming around to his point of view."

"That's the most jesuitical argument I've ever heard," I said hotly, though I was angrier with Tom Galbraith, who knew the details of these events, than I was with Elinor, who didn't. I had a sudden vision of Rebecca, lying bleeding on the floor of the boathouse. Had she died quickly? Had she been dead when she was taken out to her boat and *Je Reviens* was scuttled? "Elinor," I said, "what's happened to you? We're talking about someone who was almost certainly murdered. You were always such a staunch defender of Rebecca."

"I know. But that was before I knew all this. It was before I read all those unkind remarks about Mama and St. Winnow's. Quite apart from the inaccuracies, I didn't like her *tone*. All those comments about dogs, and kennels, and red meat. I found it lacking in all taste, Ellie, to be frank with you. Strident and exaggerated—altogether unwomanly." She paused, having become quite pink. "What does Arthur feel? I shouldn't like to think of his being as upset by all this as we are."

"He's not upset—he's finished reading the notebook now. If anything, he seems calmer than he was. And Rebecca writes very kindly of him."

"Well, I'm glad she writes kindly of someone!" Elinor said with a sniff. I think she sensed my hostility and uneasiness, for she changed the subject. And it was then that she gave me information that would prove crucial, though I didn't realize that immediately.

"Ah, well, let it rest," she went on. "And speaking of letting things rest, Ellie, have you heard the latest tales in Kerrith? We have a new ghost, my dear! James Tabb's little grandson saw her at the Manderley graveyard just the other evening."

"A new ghost? No, I hadn't heard that. I was there not so long ago, Tom and I were there, in fact, and we didn't see any ghost."

I hadn't been paying close attention; ghost stories in Kerrith are two a penny, and besides, I was still considering the significance of our earlier conversation. I was thinking about fatal wounds, and the images in my mind now were dark and disturbing ones. I was angry with Elinor, too, and had been about to leave; now I hesitated, thinking of that heap of shells on a dead girl's grave.

"The poor little boy imagined it, obviously, but he was very frightened indeed. He said this strange woman rose up from behind the gravestones, as he was passing by in the lane, and she *beckoned* to him.

He ran home to his mother as fast as his legs would carry him. And didn't sleep a wink that night, apparently."

"A strange woman? Strange in what way?"

Elinor smiled. "No one seems too clear on that point, my dear. I was imagining some splendid ghoul, but apparently she was *gray*. A gray dress, gray hair—not a very memorable ghost! But there's a rash of sightings already. The grocer's wife is claiming she saw her by the Manderley gates, and Jennifer Lane—you remember her, dear? Robert Lane's daughter, a redhead, like her mother; she works at St. Winnow's, she's old Frith's favorite nurse, I hear—well, she claims she saw the woman yesterday, standing in the gardens there, looking down at the river. One minute she was visible, the next she'd disappeared. Isn't it absurd? Oh, must you go, my dear? Before you leave, I must find those jars of chutney Jocelyn and I put up. I've been meaning to give them to you—I know how fond your father is of our chutney."

I left Elinor as quickly as I could; I'd suddenly remembered that unidentified visitor who'd called at The Pines. I hurried through Kerrith and stopped halfway up the steep hill to our house. With one kaleidoscopic twist, the pieces of this puzzle that had most perplexed me began to re-form into a new pattern.

I thought of Elinor's description of the "ghost"—and of the places she had chosen for her visitations. I thought of the azalea wreath, of the heap of shells on Lucy Carminowe's grave; I thought of the notebooks and Rebecca's diamond ring, the butterfly brooch, her personal effects—and I reconsidered the question that had puzzled Tom, my father, and me from the very beginning: Who could have had access to these objects? Mrs. Danvers, possibly—but, if she was ruled out, who else was a candidate, who, in fact, was the *only* possible candidate?

Rebecca's description of the revenant she'd seen at Manderley came eddying into my mind: *Such a secretive, bloodless mouse squeak of a ghost* . . . Until I read that, it had never occurred to me that anyone could be haunted by the future, yet Rebecca had been. I had recognized that ghost as soon as I read her description; I recognized her again now. I turned, and began to run up the hill. I burst into the kitchen, where Rose was preparing lunch.

"Rose," I said, "that visitor who came here the other day. The one who didn't leave her name—describe her again for me."

"Heavens, I don't know—just an ordinary woman. Pleasant enough, though she seemed nervous. Gray haired. In her early forties . . ."

"Was she carrying anything?"

"No. Well, a handbag, obviously."

"You're certain of that? Nothing else? Not a book—or papers?"

"No, just the handbag, I'm sure. A sensible bag—quite like mine, actually."

I looked at Rose's handbag, which was propped against the table. It was large; since Rose never goes anywhere without a book, and a book will easily fit in this bag, she finds it invaluable. That decided me. I was certain I now knew who the anonymous sender of Rebecca's notebooks was—and I knew why she had come to The Pines, too. She had come in person to make her final delivery.

I bolted my lunch; after that, I was press-ganged by Rose into helping prepare the food for the next day, when Tom Galbraith and his friend Nicholas Osmond were expected. I whisked egg whites and melted gelatin for a mousse; I diced cucumber for the iced soup that is one of Rose's specialties, and all the time I longed to escape; I wanted to go in search of our mysterious visitor. At three, when my father had been settled for his afternoon rest, I was finally able to leave. I pushed Barker into the car, and drove straight to Manderley.

I waited within sight of the shore and the house itself for nearly two hours, but no gray lady of a ghost manifested herself. Disappointed and frustrated, I drove home via Manderley church, which was deserted, and St. Winnow's. I saw Frith, seated in his wheelchair, keeping up his eternal vigil on the veranda where Rebecca had sorted tapestry silks and watched the windings of the river.

I questioned the little red-haired nurse, Robert Lane's daughter. In the space of a few hours, the story as related by Elinor had already developed new and macabre details, but I learned nothing that was useful. I returned to The Pines, put the car away in the garage, and went into the house by the back door. Rose was sitting at the kitchen table, a book propped up in front of her; she was reading while she hulled strawberries. As I entered, she looked up: "She's *here* again," she said. "That woman visitor—she turned up about an hour ago. Your father let her in, and she's with Arthur now, in his study."

"He didn't ask you to join them? He didn't introduce her?"

"Conspicuously not," Rose replied, and returned to her reading.

I edged out into the garden, Barker following me. I hesitated between the palm and the monkey puzzle. The French windows into my father's study were open. I could hear the low murmur of a woman's voice; my father was silent. I removed Rebecca's butterfly brooch, which I'd been wearing ever since my return from London, and put it in my pocket. I walked up the steps and into the book-lined room beyond, my eyes taking a moment to adjust to its shadows.

"Ah, here's my daughter now," my father said. I could hear relief in his voice. He struggled to rise to his feet, and I moved quickly to his side, laying my hand on his arm to prevent him.

I turned to look at his visitor. She was seated opposite my father, a middle-aged woman in an unflattering summer dress patterned with twining gray vines and miniature flowers. Her fine, straight gray hair was parted on the side, and cut in a schoolgirl bob—a hairstyle that had often been described to me, which presumably she had never altered. She was seated on the edge of her chair, back straight and hands clasped in the manner of some applicant at a job interview. She was looking at me with the forced and bright attention that shy people often adopt to conceal their social nervousness.

When she'd first come to Manderley, I knew, she'd been very young, a twenty-one-year-old with the demeanor of a schoolgirl, according to the Kerrith gossips. Nearly two decades after her brief sojourn here, they still spoke of her gauche manners, of her relentless questions about Rebecca, of the fact that she'd been half her husband's age, young enough to be his daughter.

This woman was no longer the slip of a girl described by the tittle-tattlers of Kerrith. With age had come a thickening of the waistline made more noticeable by her matronly dress. Her pale face was lined, but she had fine eyes, sweet eyes. Lying on the table next to her was a pair of summer gloves, and under them, a familiar black shape: I knew that it had to be the last of Rebecca's notebooks.

"Let me introduce you, my dear," my father said. I could hear a note of warning in his voice. "Mrs. de Winter, this is my daughter Ellie. Ellie, you've heard me speak of Maxim's wife: This is Mrs. de Winter."

As soon as we shook hands, I sensed that Maxim's widow was anxious to escape. Whatever the nature of the conversation she'd been having with my father, she was clearly reluctant to continue it in my presence. I could see she was looking for an excuse to extricate herself, but she seemed to lack this elementary social skill; instead, in a shy flustered way, she snatched at the first remark that came into her head. It was not a fortunate one.

"Ellie. How do you do?" she said in a bright tone. "Of course. Of course. We never met—but I remember your father spoke of you. You play golf, don't you? That was it, golf. You loved the game. You were awfully good at it."

"That was my elder sister, Mrs. de Winter," I replied, with a glance at my father. Lily had never been any good at golf, and had taken it up out of boredom, in the hope of meeting men. I couldn't think why Mrs. de Winter would suppose Lily had been expert. She seemed unaware that Lily was dead. She frowned, shook her head as if puzzled, then brightened again.

"Oh, yes—that's right, I remember now. There were two daughters. And a son. I remember your talking about him, Colonel Julyan. He wrote poetry, didn't he? I think you were rather concerned about that."

"He wrote poetry for a while when he was a boy," I said quickly. Seeing the expression on my father's face, I knew I had to stop her before her remarks caused further damage. "He was killed in the war, Mrs. de Winter."

There was a silence. Mrs. de Winter gave me a most peculiar look, as if she doubted the truth of what I'd just told her. Then she blushed. "I'm so sorry. If I'd known I would never have said that— please forgive me." She turned back to my father with a pleading childlike expression. "I forget sometimes how long I've been away, Colonel Julyan. I behave as if nothing's changed—when, of course, everything's changed. And I'd always imagined your daughter on the golf course, and your son, writing his poems—I could see it so clearly!"

"Perfectly understandable," said my father in a tone that I knew meant the very opposite. He bent forward to fondle Barker, thus concealing his expression. "I don't recall mentioning my children to you," he added, in a gruff tone.

"Oh, but you did!" Her color deepened. "It was the day you came to Manderley for lunch. We talked about the Far East, and your children." She glanced at me. "It's a dreadful habit of mine. I seize on a little fact someone tells me, and I go off into a dream, and before I know it, I've made up an entire life story. I even do it with complete strangers, sometimes. People in cafés, other guests at an hotel—I imagine their histories, and they're probably all wrong, just silly fictions, but they feel so right at the time. Maxim used to tease me about it—"

She came to an awkward abrupt halt, her hands twisting nervously in her lap. "What a dear sweet dog," she went on, her tone so relentlessly bright I almost pitied her. "I miss having dogs. They're such loyal companions, aren't they? They never have moods, they never reproach you and they're always glad to see you. . . . Goodness, is that the time? I really must leave. I'm returning to London tomorrow, then flying back to Canada, so I have to pack—and I'm afraid I'm a bit disorganized about packing. I mislay things. It used to infuriate Maxim. . . ."

She gave me a flustered sidelong glance, fumbled for her gloves and handbag, and rose to her feet. My father also rose; I could see his face was gray with strain and exhaustion. As Mrs. de Winter, in a flurry of nervousness, dropped her glove and bent to retrieve it, my father's eyes met mine, and a silent message passed between us. "Mrs. de Winter came over here by bus," he said in a firm way. "She's staying at an hotel just along the coast—The Rose, Ellie, you know it. Ellie will be delighted to run you back, Mrs. de Winter."

As I moved toward the door Mrs. de Winter began on some polite protest, but I ignored that; I knew she'd have to consent to being driven by me, and to being alone with me—my father may have been ill, but, when necessary, his will remained formidable.

ONCE WE WERE IN THE CAR, WITH THE WINDOWS DOWN, and the warm sweet evening air flooding in, we drove for some way in silence. I waited until we had left Kerrith behind before speaking. I was very aware that our route would take us past the Four Turnings entrance to Manderley.

"Mrs. de Winter," I said finally, as we crested the hill behind Kerrith, "I've read the notebooks of Rebecca that you sent to my father. I knew there must be a third. Have you left it with him?"

"Yes. Yes, I have. Oh, I can imagine what you must think of me," she replied, speaking with sudden rapidity. "Sending them anonymously like that—it seems so underhand, rather hateful, I realize that now. I did think of enclosing a letter, and then I couldn't work out what to say. I wasn't even sure if your father would remember me. People don't. I'm afraid I always was a rather anonymous person—not like Rebecca!"

She gave me a little sidelong glance, as if she expected me to demur; then frowned. "I didn't want to keep the notebooks myself, you see, and Rebecca refers to your father as her only real friend, so I thought he would be pleased to receive them. Then I heard he'd had a stroke recently—someone was discussing his health in one of the Kerrith shops the other day—and I felt dreadfully guilty. I decided I must make amends. I don't expect I have. All those stupid remarks about your brother. I've made things worse, probably."

I decided to accept this explanation, though I wasn't at all sure I believed it. "I'm sure he understood—you weren't to know," I said, and accelerated; we were approaching the gates of Manderley. The "accident" in which Maxim had been killed occurred on this stretch of the road. I glanced at Mrs. de Winter; she was looking at the blue shadows of the woods, her face pale and set.

"Are you in a great hurry, Miss Julyan?" she asked suddenly. "Would you mind if I walked in the woods for a short while? I shan't come back here again, you see. I dream about this place so often. That's how I've spent half my life, I think sometimes. Dreaming and daydreaming."

I stopped the car. I could hear the tears in her voice before I saw them in her eyes. Mrs. de Winter climbed out. She stood by the gates, her face averted, the breeze ruffling her straight gray hair. She was twisting her wedding ring—the only jewelry she was wearing—round and round on her finger.

I waited for a few minutes; she had produced a key but seemed unwilling to open the gates. I went to help her. I was shocked by the desolation in her face as I reached her. She looked like a bewildered child—and the signs of age on her face made the childlike nature of her grief all the more poignant.

"I must tell you about those notebooks," she said, leaning against the gates, and looking through at the trees. "I meant to tell your father, but then we began talking of other things. Perhaps you would explain to him? I found them after Maxim died—that is, I found the metal deed box they were in. It was in a locked drawer in Maxim's desk at the house we'd bought in England. Such a lovely house—as far from the sea as it's possible to be in this country, and quite large— I hoped for children, you see. . . ." She checked herself. "Did you know we moved back to England after the war, Miss Julyan?"

"Yes, I did, Mrs. de Winter."

"I took that deed box with me to Canada," she continued, as if I hadn't spoken, her eyes fixed on the drive ahead of us. "I still hadn't opened it—it was locked, and the key was lost. But I wanted to keep everything of Maxim's, so I kept that, too, thinking the key would turn up eventually. Then one day, last year, I opened it. I had to break the lock with a screwdriver, and I cut my hand. I was missing Maxim so much—it comes in waves, you know, grief. Some days, I manage quite well, and other days . . . I wake up and I feel so dreadfully bereft.

"I had no idea what I was going to find," she continued. "I was sure it would be something that would remind me of my husband. Old photographs, records of his boyhood, perhaps. It never crossed my mind that I'd find anything connected with Rebecca. Maxim's first marriage was deeply unhappy, you see—it came very close to destroying him. So the last thing I expected to find was any belongings of hers. It was a dreadful shock to me."

She pushed back the gate I'd unlocked for her, and walked through; I hesitated, then followed her. Ahead of us, the trees met in an arch creating a tunnel of shadow; I thought of my father's dream, of that tiny coffin. Mrs. de Winter walked in silence along the drive, looking around her with a dazed expression. Coming to a fallen tree trunk, she sat down, and I went to sit beside her. We had reached the bend in the drive where my father always likes to pause, where the sea is audible in the distance. Mrs. de Winter appeared not to hear it. After a while, her pale tired face still averted, she began speaking again.

"There were five things in the box," she went on. "The three note-books, a tiny diamond ring—far too small for any of my fingers—and a blue butterfly brooch. I didn't understand the significance of the ring and the brooch, not until I'd read the second notebook. I'm afraid I read that notebook again and again. I could recite it by heart. I always wanted to know what Rebecca was really like, you see. Well, I know now."

"Mrs. de Winter, you don't need to talk about this—not unless you want to. I can see this is painful for you."

"Oh, it *was* painful at first," she said in an earnest way. "I was desperately upset to begin with. I couldn't understand why Maxim would have kept her things. He hated to be reminded of Rebecca. So, why would he have kept them? I was bewildered and miserable. I was sleeping badly; I began to have hateful dreams about Rebecca, just as I did when I first came to Manderley. That's when I decided to come back. I had to confront my past. That's what Rebecca would have done, I decided. And if she could, I could. I didn't want to be cowardly."

In a disingenuous way, still keeping her gaze fixed on the trees, she then told me about her visit to England. At first, she said, she'd been intent on finding out more about Rebecca—for all she knew then the entire story Rebecca told could have been one long fiction. So she had visited libraries, found the McKendrick autobiography, and checked what details she could. But she began to realize: This was not curing her unhappiness, it was deepening it.

She resolved to rid herself of the belongings of Rebecca's that she'd been carrying around for weeks; she felt she couldn't destroy them, so she decided to send them to appropriate recipients. The notebooks went to my father. The ring went to Jack Favell—who'd been easy to trace—because it was his uncle who'd brought it back from South Africa. The brooch went to Mrs. Danvers, who would remember Rebecca's mother—but it had taken a long time to find her. She had seen her one day, she said, completely by accident, when she happened to be standing outside Rebecca's flat in Tite Street, and Mrs. Danvers came out of the house. Though she was greatly aged, she had recognized her. "I found the address in one of Maxim's old diaries. I would have known Mrs. Danvers anywhere," she said. "I could never forget her. She made my life at Manderley a misery. I'm sure I'd have managed so much better if she hadn't been there."

I thought this explanation concealed as much as it revealed and I wondered just how often Mrs. de Winter had revisited Tite Street, to stand outside Rebecca's London apartment. I noted that the more obviously obsessional details of this search went unmentioned. Nothing was said of azalea wreaths. . . . Just as I thought that, as if she could read my mind, Mrs. de Winter raised that very subject. She had left a garland in remembrance of Rebecca at her boathouse cottage, she said, and later she'd left shells at the grave of the little girl Rebecca had seen. The reasons she gave for doing so surprised me.

"I think they were alike in some ways, you see," she said in a hesitant way, with a little glance at me. "Rebecca and Lucy Carminowe. Neither of them could *grow*, neither of them ever grew up. I pitied that child, and it was when I saw the similarities between them that I first began to sympathize with Rebecca. It's very sad, to be as filled with certainty as she is, and to be so *deluded*—don't you agree, Miss Julyan?"

"Deluded, Mrs. de Winter?"

"Oh, yes." Her face brightened. "Rebecca sets such store by her willpower, she never stops boasting about it. But she couldn't will Maxim to love her, could she? It was me Maxim loved, not Rebecca. She claims she made herself so memorable, but once Maxim and I left this place, he very rarely thought of her. I realized finally: *That's* why Maxim kept those belongings of hers—he felt sorry for her in the end, just as I do. Her father's ring, and her mother's brooch: Rebecca was childish, that's what I've decided. She may like to think she made herself tall, but she never really grew up, not emotionally. She even writes in a childish way, don't you think?" She looked at me eagerly.

"I wouldn't say 'childish,' " I replied. "She writes in an odd way, certainly."

"Oh, I think it's *very* childish. It's just like some silly fairy tale, with curses and ogres. I was surprised by that. I'd expected her to be sophisticated."

She gave a frown. "She can't have been at all normal, can she, to behave as she did, or write as she did? I can see now why she made Maxim so miserable; he was a man of such high principles—and she had no principles at all. She was callous and cynical, and so terribly *restless*. Maxim would have hated that. He liked to live in an orderly way. He liked peace and security and companionship. Rebecca would never have understood that, or cared. She was stuffed full of all these selfish romantic notions. I told you: She was *childish*. Infantile. I was quite disappointed in her. She wasn't *nearly* as interesting as I'd imagined her to be.

"Shall I tell you what I decided?" She looked at me in a solemn way. "I decided she was really rather pathetic, writing to some fantasy child, when all the time she was barren. That sounds unkind, but it's true. She was barren in many ways, I think—barren of normal affections. Not warmhearted. Not womanly. Once I realized that, I felt so much better, so much stronger, Miss Julyan. I knew it was true, you see: Maxim could never have loved her."

I'd been feeling uneasy even before Mrs. de Winter launched herself on this speech; now I was angry. I didn't believe Rebecca was pathetic, callous, cynical, or unprincipled. As for Maxim's being honorable, he had almost certainly perjured himself at the inquest into Rebecca's death; he had almost certainly killed his wife and escaped justice. The sweet-faced woman sitting beside me must know the truth about these events, if anyone did; if so, in legal terms, she was an accessory after the fact. Her prime concern might be whether or not Maxim had ever loved Rebecca; it wasn't mine.

"Mrs. de Winter," I said quietly. "I wish I knew the truth. Did your husband kill Rebecca?"

"Oh, yes." To my surprise, she replied without hesitation. "I can say this now, because Maxim is dead, and there can be no possible repercussions. In any case, I don't regard it as murder, and I never have—it was suicide, and Maxim was merely the instrument. He went down to that boathouse cottage of hers, the night she returned from London. He thought she might have taken a man there, one of the lovers, her cousin, Favell, probably. He took his service revolver with him—the gun Rebecca writes about—because he wanted to frighten them. He'd decided, he wouldn't tolerate Rebecca's behavior any longer. She was *shameless*, he told me. He didn't care what she did in London, but he wouldn't have her bringing men to Manderley. . . ."

She paused. "He found Rebecca alone—and she taunted him, taunted him in the most wicked hurtful way, Miss Julyan. She told him she was expecting another man's child, and she intended to pass it off as his. She said her bastard child would inherit Manderley, that all the tenants would rejoice, they'd been waiting for an heir so long. In the end, Maxim lost control. He aimed the gun at her heart and shot her. She died instantly. Then he had to clean up all the blood—

there was blood everywhere, he told me. He had to fetch seawater, and clean up the floor of the boathouse. Then he took her body out in her boat, meaning to sink it in deep water, but something went wrong, I'm not sure what went wrong. Poor Maxim must have been in turmoil, the wind was getting up, he hadn't sailed for some years. Anyway, he was losing control of the boat, so he opened the sea-cocks, and drove holes in the bottom boards, and climbed into the tender.

"*Je Reviens* keeled over, and went down just clear of the reef, by the sandbank. It was too close in to shore—if only Maxim could have reached deep water he'd have been safe. The boat would never have been found then, and Maxim and I would have stayed at Manderley. We'd be living there now. We'd have children, and a future. I often think of that future we didn't have. I can see it so clearly. I wanted two boys and two girls. I'd be sitting in the drawing room at Manderley now, and I'd hear their voices, calling to Maxim in the garden. . . ."

She swung around sharply, as if she had just heard a voice calling behind us. She bent her head and soundlessly began crying. After a while, she reached in her pocket for a handkerchief, and dried her eyes. To my astonishment, she then seemed to regain her composure; when she turned to look at me, her sweet tired face bore that same expression of earnest and resolute brightness. That expression shocked me as much as anything she'd told me.

"I explained all this to your father today," she said. "So, no doubt he'd have told you when you went home anyway. But I prefer you to hear it from me directly—as I told Colonel Julyan, it's very important to understand the *details* of what happened. Rebecca was lying to Maxim that night. She knew she wasn't expecting a child. She knew she was dying. She deliberately provoked Maxim into killing her, she just *used* him, Miss Julyan. She would have died within a few months anyway, that doctor told us, so, in a way, Maxim's act was a merciful one. He saved her from months of suffering and agony."

"Yes, but he wasn't aware of that, Mrs. de Winter."

"Oh, I know." She ignored my tone, and waved my objection aside. "But that's irrelevent. No jury would ever have found Maxim guilty of murder, not if they'd known what Rebecca was like, and the misery she'd inflicted on him. As it was, it never came to trial, thank God. And for that, we have your father to thank, in part anyway. Oh, I know he didn't have any evidence against Maxim, I know there was no proof—but Maxim and I always believed your father guessed what he'd done. Your father was merciful, Miss Julyan, and that was the real reason I came to see him today. I wanted to tell him how grateful I was. Maxim and I were married for over fifteen years, you know—if your father had pressed matters we might never have had those years of happiness. I wanted him to know that before I leave England, and before he—"

"Before he dies, Mrs. de Winter?"

"Well, yes. Of course. He has been ill, and he's not a young man. I didn't want to keep him in ignorance. I wouldn't have wanted that on my conscience."

Her conscience seemed oddly accommodating to me, so I wasn't sure why it should balk at that, but I let it pass. Rising to her feet, she stood looking toward Manderley, then, as if coming to a decision, turned back toward the gates. We began to walk slowly along the drive. Mrs. de Winter walked beside me with every appearance of serenity. Occasionally she would tilt her head on one side, as if she were hearing sounds inaudible to me, and sometimes she would look through the trees, and smile, as if someone she recognized were coming toward her. I think she was still watching that future of hers that never happened, and I think it was utterly real to her.

I said nothing. I was thinking of the implausibilities in the story she had told me; it was hearsay, in any case, her version of Maxim de Winter's version of events—and to me there were many weaknesses in it, not least the question of the weapon. Why would a man used to guns and aware of their dangers, take a loaded revolver to the boathouse, if his sole purpose was to surprise Rebecca with a lover, and threaten them? Maxim de Winter might have claimed that he "aimed at the heart," but where, exactly, had the wound been inflicted? Did someone shot through the heart, someone who had "died instantly," bleed copiously? Bleeding stopped, I knew, once the heart ceased beating. And what exactly *had* Rebecca said to Maxim that night that caused him to lose control? That reference of Mrs. de Winter's to the Manderley tenants had reminded me of Maxim's paramount need for an heir; it had planted a new idea in my head. Two marriages without issue: Could Rebecca that night at the boathouse have accused her husband of some sexual inadequacy?

I knew there was no point in raising these issues with the woman next to me; it would have been cruel to do so. I could sense that Mrs. de Winter was less serene than she seemed, and less convinced of what she had told me than she appeared. Her control was tenuous. I noticed that she began to quicken her pace as we approached the gates; she passed through them without a backward look, and, once we were in the car again, she reverted to the question of the notebooks.

"I know when my husband found those notebooks, Miss Julyan," she said, as we continued down the road, the estate walls and the woods to the left of us. "It was after the fire at Manderley, the last night we were ever here, the night before we left for Europe. Maxim wanted to go for a walk on his own to say his last farewells to the place—and I know he went down to the bay. He was away hours. When he came back, I saw the sand on his shoes, and I knew where he'd been. He was so silent and white-faced—I knew something was terribly wrong, but I told myself it was because we were leaving Manderley. I see now, he must have gone into that boathouse, and found Rebecca's notebooks. All her belongings were there—it was untouched, that boathouse cottage, just as Manderley was. I never understood that; it was as if Rebecca had just gone out for an hour or so, and would return at any minute. You'd have thought Maxim would have had that boathouse cleared—Rebecca had been dead for over a year, after all."

She risked a sidelong glance at me; her hands had begun to twist nervously in her lap again. "Why do you think he kept those note-books, Miss Julyan? Oh, *why* did he keep them? And that eternity ring of hers—it was on her finger when they brought up her body— did you know that? They found that ring and her wedding ring. It was the rings they identified her by. Why did Maxim keep the eter-nity ring, and not the one he'd given her?"

I hesitated. I thought of Rebecca's comment that, from the first moment Maxim had seen Jack Devlin's eternity ring on her finger, his ambition had been to replace it with his own. Presumably Rebecca's wedding ring had been interred with her, so Maxim's ambi-tion had been achieved in the end. It seemed kinder not to say this to his widow. "I can't answer that," I replied. "Your husband was the only person who could. No one else can say what it meant to him."

"It wouldn't have meant *anything*," she said, with sudden force.

"None of it could have mattered to Maxim. I told you, he never loved her, he *hated* Rebecca. Once he found out what she was really like, he could scarcely bear to be anywhere near her after that. If you'd known Maxim, you'd understand—he was very protective to women. He expected a woman to be . . . well, all the obvious things. Gentle. Pure. Innocent." She reddened.

"There are different kinds of purity, perhaps," I said, as mildly as I could. "I find Rebecca pure, judging from her notebooks. She is what she is—and it's unadulterated."

"I can't think what you mean," she replied in an obstinate tone. "I don't believe half of what she writes there, anyway. I told you, I've decided: She's to be pitied if anything—she can't be blamed for her upbringing. But she had no sense of *proportion*. She writes in such a silly exaggerated way. . . . Saying she gave Maxim the gift of tumult— I was so upset when I read that. But I see now how absurd it was. Maxim hated that kind of unrest. He liked peace and quiet and regular routines. . . . If you'd turn left here, Miss Julyan, the hotel's just along on the right."

I turned where she indicated, and began negotiating a high-banked narrow lane that led us down toward the water. I could see its blue glint ahead of us; the hotel Mrs. de Winter had selected was set up above the sea; it was a small, modest, traditional place, much favored by elderly visitors.

"I'm staying here under my maiden name," she said, as we drew into the car park. "I prefer to be anonymous. Maxim and I always kept ourselves to ourselves. There's really no point in getting to know people, is there, if you're going to be moving on shortly? And besides, people are so inquisitive."

She hesitated. "I miss my husband so much, Miss Julyan. I only ever had one ambition in my life: to make Maxim happy, and I know I did that. I know it in my heart. Maxim and I were rarely apart, you know, he became utterly dependent on me—but, of course, I don't have him to talk to anymore. So sometimes I feel lonely. That's why I like small hotels like this one."

She turned to me, her face brightening. "It reminds me of all the lovely little places we stayed in France. Sometimes, in the evening, I sit here on the terrace, and I imagine Maxim's beside me. I tell him little stories about the other guests, and he pretends to be bored, and

gives me gruff answers just the way he used to do—but I know he's
there with me in spirit, and he's not bored at all, he's just teasing me.
He's happy, terribly happy, just as we always were."

As she had done earlier, she swung around suddenly, as if she had
heard a sound inaudible to me. She stared out to sea. "Did you hear
that?" she said in a nervous way. "I thought someone called to me."

I told her I'd heard nothing, but she looked unconvinced. "I expect
it was gulls," she said quickly. "Yes, I expect that's what it was. Some
seabird. They can sound quite eerie, can't they? Well, I must be
going. I have a long journey tomorrow, and, when I'm back in
Canada, I've resolved: I'm going to put all this behind me once and
for all. I'm going to make a new start, go out more, make an effort to
meet people. I may even get a job—I don't need to work, of course,
Maxim saw to that, but I'd like to be useful. I thought, something
with a charity perhaps. They always need helpers, don't they?"

That relentless brightness had returned to her face, but her eyes
had a lost look, and I could hear the panic in her voice. I pitied her
then, and I think she saw that, for she colored, fumbled for her bag
and gloves, and opened the car door, ready to escape. She gave me a
shy glance.

"This was so kind of you." She clasped my hand. "It was good of
you to listen to me as you did. I was glad to see your father again. I
hope I did the right thing. . . . I hope I didn't tire him out. . . . Goodness, it's past seven. How time flies! I must go. Thank you again.
Good-bye, Miss Julyan."

I watched her walk up to her hotel, an ordinary unremarkable
middle-aged woman. She nodded to some of the other guests, elderly
couples returning from walks; on the terrace, I saw her pause, her
gray dress merging with the pearl of the evening sky; she was looking
toward the sea. I turned to follow the direction of her gaze; when I
looked back, she had vanished.

I released the brake, swung the car round in a tight circle, and
accelerated back up the hill. I wound down the window, letting the
sea air flood the car, and I drove fast. I wanted to leave Mrs. de Winter behind as swiftly as I could—and I think I know why: I'd suddenly
seen the possibility that I could turn into her. It was one of the
options that could lie ahead of me after all; I'd hoped for love, like

most people, but, if this was what wifeliness meant, I wanted to escape it as fast as possible.

When her sole ambition had been to make her husband happy, had she foreseen the long days of her widowhood? Did the gift of his love compensate for his being a murderer? If this was where love led a woman, I feared it. I no longer wanted to listen to the second wife, it was the first wife's voice I needed now—and I knew it was waiting for me back at The Pines, inside the covers of that last black notebook. Rebecca was about to tell me the truth about her father and her husband. She was going to *translate the braille of her marriage*.

When I reached The Pines, I left the car in the yard, and went straight to my father's study. He and Rose were sitting there, deep in conversation. Rose looked concerned and anxious; my father's face was pale and drawn. Without a word, my father handed me the black notebook. I weighed it in my hand. Even before I opened it, I could feel that this little coffin book differed from the previous two. It was lighter.

I undid the ties on its spine, and opened the black covers. On the first page, which had been torn in half, was the date, April 12, on which Rebecca died; under the date, in Rebecca's hand, the writing visibly under stress, was the single word "Max."

Below that, the fragments of a first sentence were just visible; I could see the broken arches of individual letters, but the tear had been made in such a way as to make the words unreadable. The rest of that page, and a whole further section of the book had been removed. All the remaining pages were blank. Rebecca's final entry, her last communication, had been addressed to her husband, and someone had destroyed it. No last message; no last words. In the end, Rebecca had been silenced.

"Who did this?" I was shocked and angry, my hands unsteady. "Maxim?"

"Possibly." My father sighed. "Or Mrs. de Winter, though she denied it."

"Rebecca herself could have done it. You certainly can't rule that out. But I know which of the three candidates I favor," said Rose. "Very foolish: Silence always speaks volumes," she added.

THIRTY

THAT NIGHT, MY FATHER—TO MY RELIEF—SLEPT soundly, though I did not. In the morning, I took him breakfast in bed, but found him already up. I'd been expecting questions about Mrs. de Winter—there had been remarkably few the previous night—but my father's new capacity to dismiss the immediate past had already reasserted itself; these last weeks he'd made himself learn the art of forgetfulness. He had focussed his mind on the lunch that would take place that day, and the arrival of Tom Galbraith and his friend Nicholas Osmond. Preparations were already under way. Several of my father's suits lay on the bed, he was holding a fistful of ties, and staring beakily at his wardrobe.

"Have to look presentable. Best bib and tucker. Francis Latimer's joining us—did I mention that, Ellie? Thought he might liven things up a bit. Now—I need a woman's eye. Which suit, Ellie—this one or that one?"

Francis's presence had certainly *not* been mentioned, as my father well knew; both the suits he was proposing were of heavy tweed. It was nine o'clock in the morning, the sky was cloudless; the temperature was in the seventies, and rising. I tried to guide my father toward one of the lightweight suits that dated from his Singapore days, but he was having none of it—and I knew why: He hates people to notice how thin and frail he's become, and the tweeds disguise that. I gave in, and he finally selected a bristling greenish tweed with a clashing regimental tie.

"Just the ticket," he said, holding them up. "Looking forward to this, Ellie. What time are those two whippersnappers arriving?"

"Twelve-ish, Daddy."

"Ish? Ish? In my day, people were punctual, made a point of it. Still, better get a move on. I must see to the drinks, have a rummage about in the cellar. . . . Can't seem to find that bargain sherry of mine. I know there are a couple of bottles left, and I can't damn well find them anywhere."

I hurried downstairs. I hid the bottles of bargain sherry in an even more effective place, then Rose and I moved the lunch table into the shade of the monkey puzzle. "Tweeds," I said. "The green tweed at that. . . ." I placed a jug of flowers on the white tablecloth; the air felt full of expectation, the sea sang, and the future beckoned. "Oh, Rose," I said, "what a glorious day."

"How pretty you look," she said. "I hope your father's not going to be difficult. When I serve the mussels, don't say a word—that Mr. Galbraith of yours promised to bring me some garlic."

Tom Galbraith was a man of his word. He arrived with his friend, in his friend's exotic car, at five minutes past twelve exactly. They'd come off the ferry from St. Malo early that morning, and they came bearing the fruits of France, all of them unobtainable in Kerrith. There were bottles of champagne and some glorious young wine; there were bunches of pink grapes, baskets of black cherries, a plaited string of rosy garlic, bundles of pungent thyme, marjoram and rosemary, a bag of black coffee beans, and, in an exquisite box tied with ribbons, a collection of tiny handmade biscuits shaped like palm leaves. Rose fell on these delights as they were unpacked from a hamper in our kitchen; I stared in wonderment, first at this luxury, then at Tom Galbraith and his companion.

Two weeks in Brittany had transformed Tom, who was sunburned, smiling, more at ease than I'd ever seen him. And his friend? I could only stare: I had been expecting a dry scholar, a sad widower. Nicholas Osmond was a golden young man, probably the most beautiful man I've ever seen, or am ever likely to see. He had golden hair and golden skin; his eyes were the clearest sapphire; when he stood still—which he rarely did—he had the poise, perfection, and gravity of an angel in an Italian Renaissance painting. He didn't belong in a kitchen, by a range that broke down every other week; he belonged under a fresco blue sky, handing a lily to the Virgin Mary.

Even Rose was rocked; when she was introduced and shook hands, she was visibly stunned, and had to divert quickly to the joys of that hamper, and the cunning way it had been packed, with containers for ice, and straw, and wax papers. "May we open the champagne, Dr. Julyan?" Osmond said to her, lighting the room with his smile. "It's just about cool enough, I think—one of the stewards on the boat gave us fresh ice this morning. And we must celebrate—I've heard so much about you all. . . . What a marvelous house! What a glorious day! Miss Julyan—that's no good, I can't call you that—may I call you Ellie? Ellie, where's your father? How is he? I'm longing to meet him. Tom's told me so much about Colonel Julyan, I feel I know him already."

I knew where my father was; he was skulking in his study. I persuaded him as far as the French windows. "Good to see you again, Galbraith," he said, shaking hands with Tom—and then he was introduced to the angel. I saw him resist: I saw the cold blue stare that was bestowed on the golden hair, which curled unashamedly, and touched Osmond's collar. I saw the cold blue glare fixed on Osmond's open-necked shirt and lack of tie; both my father and his suit bristled.

Osmond, joyfully unaware of this, clasped his hand. "I'm glad to meet you at last, sir. Tom's told me so much about you," he began— and then he spied Barker. "Oh, what a magnificent dog," he said. "I love dogs like that. A Newfoundland cross, sir? I had one as a boy— they're always highly intelligent—we went everywhere together. It's Barker, isn't it? No, don't get up, old boy."

Barker, who is always aloof with strangers, was rising arthritically to his feet. Osmond crossed to him and held out his hand. Barker sniffed it, looked up at him, sniffed again, and licked him. This, at first meeting, was unheard of. Osmond sank to his knees and cradled

Barker's malodorous head. I looked at my father. The blue glare was vanishing away; a glint of amusement had come into his eyes, and he was smiling broadly. The angel, I told myself, had conquered.

IT WAS A WONDERFUL LUNCH. WHEN I LOOK BACK ON IT now, I can recall few of the actual details, and I certainly can't recall any signs that might have indicated to me then how much my life was to alter afterward.

Before we sat down, Tom drew me to one side; taking my hand, and with no sign of his usual constraint he told me that he'd finally decided what he must do with Rebecca's eternity ring—he'd decided where it belonged. Would I come to Manderley with him and his friend that afternoon? He needed to talk to me. "It's so good to see you again, Ellie," he said, putting an arm around my shoulders. "We have so much to catch up on."

Indeed we did, and the prospect of this visit was enough to color the meal that preceded it. I don't recall how long that lunch lasted; a couple of hours, I suppose, but they seem to be held in a golden haze that is timeless.

I can see my father seated at one end of the table, with Rose on his right hand, and Nicholas Osmond to his left; I can see myself, seated at the other end, between Tom and Francis Latimer, who arrived late from some emergency at the hospital. I can recall the food—Rose is a very good cook—so I remember the iced soup, and the fish mousse, the salmon-trout fresh from the sea that morning, and the mussels, which my father ate without complaint, seeming not to notice that they'd been adulterated with garlic. I can remember the strawberries, and the palm-leaf biscuits, and the strong wonderful coffee we drank. I can remember the wine, which tasted of summer, and the shadow of the monkey puzzle blueing the white cloth, but all these are background components. What I chiefly remember is intangible, and it was happiness.

It was at that lunch, I think, that I understood the gift of charm. For years, when people had spoken to me of Rebecca, they had emphasized her charm—and I, too, could remember it. But I'd forgotten how truly powerful a force it can be, and how rare it is, until I encountered it that day again in the person of Nicholas Osmond. When people speak of "charm" they can mean something synthetic, a mere manipulative technique; true charm, I think, is a gift from the gods, it is never conscious and is always natural. It comes welling up from a person, and its effects, akin to magic, are irresistible.

Nicholas Osmond did not set out to charm, any more than Rebecca did. From both of them emanated a pure joie de vivre that affected everyone. Watching him that day—and it was difficult not to watch him, just as it had been difficult to drag your eyes away from her—the details of a day altered. The ordinary became extraordinary, the light that shone on us all was crystalline. I had the sensation, which I cannot explain, that Rebecca watched over us.

I can't remember now what we talked about—Brittany, certainly; Cambridge, I think; cabbages and kings, probably. Even watchful Francis Latimer fell under the spell—I know I learned more about him at that lunch than I had in weeks of previous visits. He had seemed ready to dislike Tom Galbraith when they were introduced— maybe he'd heard gossip in Kerrith about Tom, or my father may have made some comment about him; but, during the meal this hostility vanished, though I noticed he watched both Tom and his friend very closely. Francis's presence, as always, put my father in a good humor. He forgot to be testy, and told tales of Singapore that I hadn't heard in decades. He ate his small portions of food with enjoyment, and none of his usual complaints about "fancy cooking." "Not for me, Galbraith," he said, when Tom attempted to refill his wineglass. "Under doctor's orders, you know. I'd risk a second, but he's down there at the other end of the table, blast it, keeping his eye on me."

"Not true. My attention is elsewhere," Francis replied with a smile, and I saw a small glance pass between him and my father, as if the two of them were enjoying a private joke, from which the rest of us were excluded.

"Look here, Osmond," my father said, in a magnanimous way, as the meal drew to an end, and he prepared to retreat indoors for the regulation rest. "Come and see us again, won't you? Make Galbraith there drive down with you one weekend. If the weather's good, Francis will take you out in his boat—he's teaching Ellie to sail, you know. We can put you both up. Be delighted. Too many bedrooms in this damn house. Never get used, half of them. Ellie, you persuade them."

Rose's eyebrows rose. Apart from her, no one has stayed at The Pines since the end of the war; six people for a meal was a ten-year record. I frowned: I couldn't see why the sailing lessons needed to be mentioned; I'd only had two of them.

I went inside to see my father upstairs. In his room, I opened the window and went to draw the curtains. I could see Francis Latimer in the garden below; he had left the other guests, and was standing alone near our boundary wall, watching the sea. As I watched, he began to pace back and forth, as if something were agitating him; I saw him glance at his watch and then back at the house. He looked up toward my father's window, then turned abruptly away. The sun would have been in his eyes, and I'm not sure if he saw me.

I half drew the curtains. Barker settled himself on the hearth rug. My father removed his terrible tweed jacket and his brogues, and lay back on the bed. He closed his eyes at once, and I thought he was sleeping. I tiptoed toward the door, and just as I reached it, he opened his eyes, and fixed me with a blue glare.

"Want to see you settled, Ellie," he said. "That's all I want now. Once I know you're settled, I can die happily. Shan't turn up my toes until I'm sure—I hope you realize that."

"In that case, I'll keep you waiting for a good time yet," I answered.

"None of your impudence," my father replied; he gave a sigh. "Listen to the sea, Ellie. The tide's coming in."

I turned to leave him, then I stopped. I could hear the sea, and I suddenly felt right on some edge, tears and happiness in absolute equilibrium. I went back to the bed, and kissed his forehead.

"That was a good lunch, Ellie." My father's eyes were closing. "I took to that Osmond chap. A widower, I hear . . . Needs a haircut. Galbraith was in very good form, I thought. Hardly recognized him when he walked in. Latimer enjoyed it, I know. Never seen him look so happy. Pity Rose put garlic on those mussels, they're much better without it. Where are you off to this afternoon?"

I evaded this question, asked on the edge of sleep. I said Nicholas, Tom, and I were going for a walk; they were then going to see the Briggs sisters, but I'd be back for tea. Francis Latimer was staying. Another sailing lesson was planned for this evening.

"You're a good girl, Ellie," he said, and clasped my hand. "Willful, of course—always have been, always will be. Mind of your own, a bit too damn independent to my way of thinking, and secretive, too; play your cards very close to your chest. Your mother was just the same. But she'd be proud of you, Ellie, I know that. I'm proud of you. Don't know what I'd have done without you. That's the long and short of it. Off you go now."

I WAITED UNTIL I WAS CERTAIN MY FATHER WAS SLEEPING peacefully, then I sped down the stairs, and out into the sunlight. It was a glorious afternoon, the sea calm, the sky unclouded. I touched Rebecca's butterfly brooch, which I'd pinned to my blue dress that morning. I wanted to run, or sing.

"You look happy. It suits you, Ellie," Francis Latimer said with a smile as I passed him by the monkey puzzle.

"I *am* happy," I replied.

"Where shall we take the boat this evening? Upriver, or out to sea?"

"Out to sea," I said, dancing past. All questions have a right answer and a wrong one and I knew this answer pleased him—I saw his face alter. I left him talking to Rose in the garden, and we set off in Nicholas Osmond's low-slung car; I sat in the passenger seat next to the angel, and Tom crushed his height into the tiny jib seat behind us. The tonneau cover was down, the air rushed past. I'd never been in a sports car before; I'd never known it could be this exhilarating.

We drove fast round the blind bend near Tom's former cottage, then up the steep hill toward the woods of Manderley. We parked at Four Turnings, pushed back the heavy gates, and entered the cool blue shade of the trees.

"You've brought the ring with you, Tom?" Osmond asked. Tom nodded, and I saw a small glance, a silent message, pass between them.

"I might just wander off and look at Manderley itself," Osmond said. "I have to see it, after imagining it all these weeks. I'll meet you both at the beach, shall I?"

He disappeared between the trees, and I tensed. I was now alone with Tom Galbraith—and in no doubt that this had been pre-arranged between them. Had Tom been as reserved as he usually was,

I would probably have remained tense, but even now we were alone his new mood of confidence did not desert him.

I wished I knew what had caused this transformation—he had the air of a man who'd made up his mind, and was now at peace with himself; but I quickly forgot that as we began to walk through the trees. I could hear the sound of the waves, inviting us forward, and I began to tell him what had happened in his absence. I described my encounters with Mrs. Danvers and Mrs. de Winter. I told him about the books I'd found in the boathouse, the list of children's names, the butterfly brooch, and the last, censored notebook.

He listened intently—and he questioned me, as I'd expected. But, by the time we were reaching the edge of the woods, with sunlight ahead of us, I'd become aware of a certain distancing in him. Even when I told him of Mrs. de Winter's revelations regarding Rebecca's death, his response was curiously muted. He was interested in what I was telling him—but not as interested as he would once have been; I could sense his mind was on something else. Once or twice I saw him glance at me with an amused affection, but I knew he was preoccupied.

I decided I'd been dwelling too long on these details, and all the questions they raised; he must want to tell me—and I wanted to hear—about Brittany, and what he had discovered there.

"Well, as I said at lunch, we had a wonderful time there," he said, as we came out into the sunlight, and turned toward the sea. "The coast is very similar to this. I could see at once why Rebecca felt she'd come home when she first came here. Nicky and I found some very beautiful fishing villages, quite untouched. The churches are interesting—"

"But you went to St. Croigne Dulac itself?"

"Eventually. We drove about for a bit first. Nicky needed a break, and I wanted to get my bearings. So we made our way down the Brittany coast quite slowly. We went to St. Croigne our second week."

"You waited a whole week? Heavens—I'd have rushed straight there. Oh, Tom—did you find Rebecca's house, the foursquare house set down by the shore?"

"Oh, yes. Well, you couldn't miss it, really. St. Croigne's a tiny place. That house is set apart from the rest of the village. You step out of the door, onto the sand. It's exactly as Rebecca describes it, I suppose, but the house was empty, and shuttered up, so we couldn't see inside. We did hope to track down the key—one of the fishermen acts as a *gardien* for the place—but we never quite managed it. We kept missing him."

"And where did you stay? Did you see the church, or the cousins' chateau? Were any of Marie-Hélène's family still alive? I thought, maybe the son who named *Je Reviens* for Rebecca might still live there."

"We put up at a little hotel—a guest house, really. The wife was a marvelous cook. She took to Nicky—well, everyone does, I expect you've seen that. We didn't manage to track down any of Marie-Hélène's family though. The son had died in the last war. And we never did establish the truth about that boy who died in the fishing-boat accident—well, I didn't really expect that we would. That coast is highly dangerous; there are too many accidents, too many drownings. . . ."

Something was wrong. This, from the man who triple-checked everything?

"Not that it was a wasted journey," he went on, glancing over his shoulder toward the house. I could see Nicholas Osmond in the distance, the sun glinting on his godlike hair. Tom and I began to descend the path to the beach. The tide was coming in fast, now; soon the rocks of the reef would be invisible.

"I hope not," I said, feeling my elation begin to seep away and trying hard to hold on to it. "I'd so like to have seen it—I'd so like to go there."

Tom took my arm. "Don't sound so sad," he said with a smile. "It's just as Rebecca described it, I promise you. No discrepancies there." He hesitated, then said gently, "In some ways, you know, Ellie, you see a place better with your mind's eye anyway. Imagination gives you 20/20 vision—that's what Nicky always says, anyway."

Our footsteps crunching on the shingle, we walked across to the boathouse, but the land agents had completed their task of making it secure. The windows were boarded, the door padlocked. Looking at the building, I felt the conversation with Mrs. de Winter the day before had changed nothing. She had given me answers of a kind, but the questions—and many questions remained—were more interesting. We turned away, and began to walk back along the beach. I increased my pace, Tom slowed, and gradually a distance opened us between us.

I kicked off my sandals, and walked at the edge of the waves, letting the water wash over my feet. I could feel the promise and energy of the day emptying out of it. I stopped and turned to look at the sea. Rebecca had died in this place. Her body had lain under the water directly in front of me. Once that had mattered to Tom Galbraith as much as it did to me—but I was no longer sure that was the case. He had moved on, I could sense it. Maybe he was right to do so. Maybe all these events were of such importance to me only because the rest of my life was so constrained and limited.

Did I believe that? I watched the waves; no, I didn't believe it. The past matters. The dead matter. And I wouldn't have expected this reaction from a man who searched for truth in the small print, either.

"You've lost interest," I said sadly to Tom as he drew alongside me. "You no longer care as much as you once did. That's why you've brought that ring of Rebecca's here today, isn't it? You're going to consign it to the waves, then go back to Cambridge and forget the whole thing. Oh, Tom, it will just be an episode for you, I know it."

"Ellie, don't look so downcast. It isn't that, I promise you." Taking my arm, he drew me toward him. "I couldn't go on being as obsessed as I was—it wasn't healthy. Going to Brittany and talking to Nicky made me see that. That visit, well, it's shown me what my priorities have to be. I can't spend all my waking hours thinking about the dead—neither can Nicky, and neither should you. I want to get on with my life, make plans for the future. I feel as if I know who I am now. It's what a person does that determines who he is, not who his parents were—that's what I believe now, at least I think that's what I believe. Ellie, look at me—please. There are things I need to say to you. . . ."

I turned to face him. He was looking down at me with an expression of concern and there was a tenderness in his face that I'd not seen before. "Ellie, listen," he said, "there's something I want you to know. I've changed, Ellie, I've been changed by the visit to Brittany. Rebecca's influenced me, you've influenced me—but it's more than that. A month ago, I couldn't have said this to you. Two weeks ago I tried, but I couldn't say it. Now I can. I expect you can tell what I feel in any case—it's obvious, at least I feel it is. I can't hide it."

He stopped. Behind him, Nicholas Osmond was just descending the cliff path; he shouted Tom's name, and Tom swung around to look at him. My mind was trying to follow Tom's words, but my heart was swifter. In two weeks, I hadn't entirely cured my propensity to hope, after all. I felt a rush of joy, as sharp and immediate as a jolt of adrenaline—and then I saw Tom's expression.

He was looking at his friend, and he was transfigured. I suppose I knew then—or began to know. I saw love in his face, as I should have seen it before—and indeed when love is felt to that degree it is unmistakable. It lit his eyes, and I stepped back from its radiance. I looked at the figure of his friend descending the path, I looked at his bright hair and I knew that if Tom was changed it was nothing to do with me or with reading Rebecca's notebooks. He might choose to believe that, but I thought it was the angel's influence.

Halfway down the path, Osmond broke into a run, and in a carefree joyful way leaped down onto the shingle and approached us. He had mistimed his return, but it didn't matter. I didn't need Tom Galbraith to tell me what he felt, I could see it in his face and in his friend's. No one looking at them could have been in any doubt that this love was reciprocated.

I think Tom knew there was no need for further explanation, he saw the comprehension in my face. "Ellie," he said awkwardly, turning back to me. "You do understand now? I should have told you, but I didn't know how you'd react. If I've done or said anything that misled you—"

"You haven't. Of course you haven't," I said, speaking fast. "And I'm glad for you. I'm glad for you both. I told you before: You're my friend, Tom. I hope you always will be."

As soon as the words were uttered, I knew they were true—I *was* glad for him. I still felt pain, so perhaps I hadn't succeeded in relinquishing him as fully as I'd tried to do; I felt embarrassment at my own stupidity, too, but those emotions were unimportant, and, oddly enough, the happiness I felt for Tom and his friend almost wiped the pain out—at that moment anyway. I hugged Tom, and when the angel came closer, I embraced him, too. "The ring, the ring," said the angel, who seemed to take the embrace in good part. "Hurry up. The tide's coming in—another ten minutes and the rocks will be underwater."

We all three set off across the shingle and began to clamber out across the rocks, Tom some way ahead, Nicholas Osmond and I behind him.

"I see Tom told you. You don't disapprove?" Osmond said, glancing at me with those sapphire eyes.

"No. Why should I?"

"Most people do. It's a hanging offense, virtually." He came to a halt, and I saw him hesitate. He looked toward Tom, moving across the rocks ahead of us.

"I always have loved him," he said. "Almost from the day we first met. I'm sure my wife knew, though I never told her. I never told Tom, either. I'm not as brave as he is, you see, Ellie. That's the great difference between us. I used to be afraid to admit what I was—Tom never felt that. I thought that if I married, maybe I could turn myself into someone else, be what everyone had always expected me to be, and I did try. . . ."

He hesitated, then his face lit. "Then Tom wrote to me, and asked me to go to Brittany for him. As soon as I opened the letter, I knew that wasn't what he was really asking. I was being given a second chance. I'd promised myself I'd never live a lie again—so I took it."

"Come on," Tom shouted from the rocks ahead of us. Osmond rested his hand on my arm and looked at me closely. "You're not hurt, Ellie? Were you in love with him?"

"I don't know," I replied, and as I said it, I realized it was true. "It felt like being in love. I've only been in love once before, so maybe I'm not a good judge. Tom told me not to be, in any case—he was very scrupulous about that. But it's not so easy to stop, is it? Maybe it will be easier now. I'm sure to make a full recovery in due course. People do. Meanwhile, I don't intend to pine away, I promise you."

"Oh, I think pining away is a very unlikely fate," Osmond replied, with a smile. "I was watching you at lunch and I rather thought that consolation was close at hand. Come on, Ellie."

Taking my arm, he led me across the rocks. I thought about that word "consolation." We clambered over rock pools, until we were as far out into the bay as we could reach. We stood next to Tom, who had taken Rebecca's tiny ring from his pocket. To our left, we could see the reef curving out into the water in a scimitar shape, and beyond it, bone white under the translucent water, the sandbank where *Je Reviens* had gone down, the bank where Rebecca had listened to her sirens.

Above us, gulls wheeled and cried; behind us, the low dark bulk of Manderley crouched by its woods; there was a salt breeze off the water; the air smelled newly created. I looked up at the milky haze of the sky, then down at the azure of the sea. The waves washed and withdrew. I moved a little apart from the two men. I looked up at the path where fourteen-year-old Rebecca had seen this place for the first time and known she spoke its language. I looked at the tiny ring, glittering between Tom Galbraith's fingers; I thought of who had given it to her and when, and what it might mean to her. I summoned her up, all her brightness of spirit—the water moved against the rocks with a new restlessness. Tom spun the ring high up into the air. It arced against the light, glittered and became invisible, sparkled one last time, then disappeared beneath the green-blue water by the sandbank.

I thought, I shan't come back here again; that's it, it's over and done. I was wrong, in fact—I have been back once since then, but at the time I couldn't have foreseen the circumstances.

I turned, and we clambered back to the shore. We climbed the path, passed the gorse at its crest, and walked back through the blue woods, reaching the gates as the heat of the afternoon began cooling. Tom and Nicholas Osmond drove me back to Kerrith, dropping me, at my request, by the Briggs sisters. They went in to say good-bye to Elinor and Jocelyn. Glad to be alone, I walked back through the town, and up the hill toward The Pines. I had no premonition, no sense of what was going to happen next, though I'd imagined this moment many times, and always believed that I would have.

I was looking at the honeysuckle and the dog roses entwined in the hedgerows; I was letting the events of the afternoon lie down in my mind, and an ache was settling about my heart. I could relinquish Tom, I realized, but it was hard, very hard, to relinquish Rebecca. Below me, in the mouth of the harbor, little boats were tacking back and forth; a future I'd allowed myself to imagine was eddying away, but I knew there must be another, over the edge of the horizon. I looked out toward the shimmer of the ocean; then I realized someone was calling my name. I looked up the hill and saw Rose standing at the gate of The Pines, her face a white blur of fear and anxiety. "Ellie, Ellie," she cried. "Oh, thank God. Come quickly . . ."

I began to run. I ran up the hill, past Rose, who could scarcely speak, and then down through our gardens. I ran past the Grenville roses, between the palm and the monkey puzzle, toward a shape, a huddle, at the end of our garden. Francis Latimer was kneeling by our boundary wall, holding my father in his arms; my father was lying on the ground, half slumped against the wall, and his face . . . ah, his face was terribly altered.

I couldn't speak or cry out—but I wasn't turned to stone, and I could move. I knelt down, and put my arms around my father. His eyes were still open, and he was still breathing, though very shallowly. I think he knew I was there, and I think he did sense my touch, though I could see from his face that he was traveling very fast to a place where I couldn't reach him. His eyes were watching this place approach, and the journey there seemed to be taking all his energy and all his attention. He didn't turn to look at me, but even so I'm sure he knew I was there, and my presence seemed to ease his passage a little. Some tension left his face; his hand jerked, then rested on mine. He said what I think was my name, though the syllables gave him difficulty.

Then he gave a sigh and rested in my arms. I waited for him to speak again, because I knew he must speak now, that it was of the utmost importance and urgency that he did so. The flood of love in my heart was so full, I knew it must revive him, so I held him tight and tried to instill it into him. I began to see he was asleep, and I couldn't understand why he would sleep with his eyes open. Then Francis Latimer quietly put his hand on my arm and said, "It's over. He's gone, Ellie."

"No," I said. "No—you're wrong." But of course, he wasn't. It had happened so stealthily that I still don't know when exactly my father stepped through that door and it closed in my face. He left me, without words, between one quiet breath and the next, while I was holding him. Gone forever. I didn't understand, or wouldn't understand until, from the house where Rose had shut him in, my father's shadow, his silent loyal companion, began barking.

THAT WAS THREE MONTHS AGO, AS I WRITE. NOW I CAN smell autumn in the air in the early mornings. The weather is warm; we've had weeks of long balmy days; we're in the midst of an Indian summer. It's the time of year when Rebecca believed she'd give birth to her girl-boy.

I am learning to live alone, to think of my father but pass my days without him. There were no further revelations after his death; there was no hidden cache of letters, no document that answered my questions and removed my uncertainties. I was glad of that. I was grieving, and I'd come to believe that uncertainties, not answers, were truthful. With the loss of my father, Rebecca's story, for me, was over—but her influence was not.

In the time that's gone by there has been a funeral, and many people have written letters to me about my father; sometimes I recognize the man they describe, more often I don't, but I was prepared for that by the months I'd spent trying to rescue Rebecca from people's stories and memories. The Pines has been sold to Francis Latimer, to whom I've grown close since my father's death. He is a man who encounters grief on a daily basis at the hospital, and he understands that its processes are slow and labyrinthine.

During the summer, I spent many hours in his company. He told me the story of his life and his marriage; the hours I spent with him and with his two young sons—walking, picnicking, and sailing—were healing ones. In practical terms, too, Francis was the greatest possible help to me. My father had always protected me, as he had my mother, from the day-to-day realities of life. He had always flatly refused to involve me in, for instance, his financial affairs, claiming this was not a matter for women. So I was woefully ignorant, and ill prepared to deal with that great tangle of affairs, investments, probate, tax, and so on that inevitably attend a death. Suddenly I had to deal with a battery of supercilious lawyers, bankers, and executors, whose faintly impatient politesse did not disguise the fact that they expected me to do as they said, sign on the dotted line, and not bother "my pretty little head" (as one of them actually said to me) about the details of these male mysteries.

Here, Francis was invaluable. He explained, and, when I didn't understand, explained again; he was endlessly patient, and if I wished he hadn't seemed amused sometimes, as if this were just a temporary game we were engaged in, I put that thought out of my mind. It seemed ungrateful. "Don't humor me, Francis," I said to him once. "This is serious—I have to understand it."

"Of course you do," he said, giving me a thoughtful glance. "It's unusual, that's all, Ellie. Most women are content to leave that sort of thing to . . ." And he paused. "Well, to their fathers. Or their husbands."

"Maybe I'm not like most women, then," I replied, perhaps a little sharply.

"Now, that I agree with," he said in a quiet way, and took my hand. He then kissed my hand—and there I was at once, pushed right to some edge, still raw with grief, longing for the protectiveness I knew he was offering, and at the same time fearing it.

Francis is intelligent, and he is subtle. He knows, I think, the dangers of overt opposition; he knows how that can make a person entrench, and I suspect—he mentioned it once in a teasing way—that my father had told him I could be obstinate. So, when I explained my plans to join Rose in Cambridge (she returned there late that summer), he always listened quietly and with sympathy—and he always found a way of changing the subject. The last time we discussed it, we were in my father's study, packing up his books, some of which I was to keep and most of which—there were so many of them—would have to go to a saleroom.

I was kneeling on the floor, stacking Aquinas and Homer in packing chests; poor bereaved Barker was half asleep in front of a swept empty fireplace; Francis, who had been helping me, was due back at the hospital shortly; now he was pacing back and forth, only half listening to me—or so I believed. I should have realized that this pacing, and his slight air of edginess signaled something more than anxiety about time, but the task I was engaged on was a painful one. I can see now that it made me slow to understand a state that would have been obvious to most women.

I was explaining the plans I'd nursed for so long; I explained I could sit the entrance examination this autumn, taking up my place— if I was awarded the scholarship I hoped for—the following year. I'd tried before, on other occasions, to make Francis see these plans as I did. I'd tried to tell him about that time I'd visited Rose, and the great ache of longing for a future I'd had to abandon that I'd experienced walking by the Cam, looking at the lights of the colleges. I'd sensed a faint male impatience then, so this time I kept the details dry, quick, and specific. I'd study; I'd actually use my brain at last,

before it conked out completely like some rusty disused car; in three
years, I'd have my degree, and I could—

"Do what, Ellie?" he said, and he stopped pacing.

"I don't know yet," I replied, looking up to meet that alert, intelligent gray gaze, still not seeing, even then, what was about to happen.
I felt a sudden jab of emotion, right to the heart. "That's the whole
point, don't you see, Francis? Anything could happen. I'd have a
choice. For the first time in my whole life, I'd have a *choice*. I've never
had that luxury. Can you understand that?"

"You have a choice now," he said, in an odd abrupt way, with a sudden roughness of tone that startled me. Then he moved swiftly
toward me, and knelt beside me. He knocked over a pile of books—
Austens and Brontës, I think, not that it matters; I dropped a fat
leather-bound complete Shakespeare; Barker growled. I'd seen the
expression in Francis's eyes by then, and, inexperienced as I am, there
was no mistaking it. I knew what was about to happen.

He pulled me toward him and, with none of his customary gentleness, he kissed me. I'm not used to desire; I'd forgotten how sharply,
and how swiftly, it digs in its claws. Ten minutes later, when we were
both in its grip, standing in an empty dusty room, in a sea of books,
the sunlight striping the walls, the sound of waves moving, moving in
the distance, Francis asked me to marry him. We looked at each
other, white-faced. "Marry me, Ellie," he said. I was shaking; his
hands were unsteady. It was the week before I was due to move out of
my father's house and he was due to move into it.

WHEN YOU'RE IN THAT STATE, YOU CAN'T THINK—AND
Francis knew that. He took advantage of it with a ruthlessness I'd
never have expected of him. "Every time you use the word 'think,'
Ellie," he said to me, "I shall kiss you. I don't want you to think. You
don't need to think. I love you. If you haven't realized you love me
yet, you will. I'll make you. I've waited months for this. I've been
patient and forbearing and understanding, and I'm sick to death of it.
Can you understand that?"

"I think I can," I replied—with an inevitable result. Such games are
seductive—but it was more than a game, and I knew that, so I
wouldn't give in, and I wouldn't let him rush me. When I was with

Francis, I wanted only one thing; when I was apart from him (I didn't tell him this) I wanted something else. It was hazy this thing that beckoned to me. I used to ask myself what Rebecca would have called it—freedom, liberty? For want of a better word, I called it independence. How Francis disliked *that* term! If I used it, he could become irritable. He'd push it to one side; he'd tell me how he wanted to protect me and take care of me. . . . And into my head would come Rebecca's voice, reacting to Maxim's very same promises. "I've been taken care of all my life, Francis," I said to him. "I can take care of myself, you know."

And then he played his trump card—how I wished he hadn't! "This is what your father wanted, Ellie," he said. "Darling, he knew I could make you happy. He and I talked about this—we talked about it often."

That touched me—and it frightened me. Day by day, hour by hour, I bought myself time. It was finally agreed that I'd give Francis my answer on the day The Pines was due to be handed over. I bought a one-way ticket to Cambridge that I could use that same morning— or not. Before I made up my mind, there was something I had to do, an act Francis would not have understood. I had to make one last visit to Manderley.

I'D SET MY ALARM CLOCK, BUT EXPECTATION WOKE ME; AS dawn was breaking, Barker and I were walking through the quiet of the Manderley woods. My trousers were soaked with the dew from the long sweet grass; the brambles barring the approach to Manderley itself were weighted down with black fruit. Through the trees, we watched the skimmed milk sky warm to rose on the eastern horizon; the sun was rising behind the dark shape of the house. Emerging from the woods, we walked toward the sea; the shore below was still in shadow, and the water in the bay was restless, its color metallic.

The wind was freshening; I sat down in the shelter of the gorse, and watched the many ghosts that inhabit this place, Rebecca's, my father's, and my own. I touched her blue butterfly brooch, which I'd pinned to my collar, and, instead of looking to the past, as I had so often here, I waited to see my way through the future. I looked at two fair prospects: on my left hand, love; on my right hand, liberty.

I tried to look at the options in a dry unemotional way. I could

become Francis's wife—was I ready to be a wife? That possibility
brought with it everything I'd been taught a woman should aspire to,
including children; I should like to have children. I could take my
beloved university route, as I'd always hoped and planned. I could go
to London, find a job—share a flat with Selina perhaps; after my
father's death, she'd written urging me to do that. With the money
from the sale of The Pines, I could do almost anything and I could go
almost anywhere. I could blow the lot if so inclined; I could sail to
America or Africa, and see what happened. I stared at the sea, my arm
around Barker's neck. When you're not used to freedom of choice, I
was discovering, it's bewildering.

I knew which course of action my father would have advised, and I
was tempted by it because he would have approved it. Even though he
was gone—because he was gone—I still sought to please him. I looked
out at the reef and the sandbank where Tom had thrown that glittering ring that day. I was washed this way and that on a tide of indecision.

Impatient with myself, knowing I needed guidance, I stood up, and
turned back toward the house. I walked as close as I could, looking up
at the broken crenellations of the walls, the dark empty windows
almost invisible now behind the fingerings of ivy. I picked a handful
of brambles; the dark fruits were cold with dew; they tasted sharply
sweet; they stained my hands with their juices. I thought of the
promise Rebecca had made to her child. I stood very still, as close to
the walls of Manderley as I could get, and I listened, listened, listened
for that voice, for that heartbeat.

WHEN I HEARD IT, AND HEARD IT FOR SURE, I RETURNED
home. I was methodical. I packed up the very last of my belongings,
including the faded snapshot of Rebecca and the creased photograph
of my mother that I had found folded together in my father's wallet.
I packed Rebecca's childhood notebook last. Before I did so, I looked
at its blank pages, which told a story only she could read, she'd said. I
felt they also told my own. I traced the faint outline of that winged
girl's wings, then I closed the notebook, and fastened my suitcase.

I went downstairs to empty rooms. I stood in my father's study,
where the shelves had been emptied of books. I waited there for
Francis Latimer, and when he joined me, I refused his proposal.

It was very difficult to do that. He's a good man, an attractive man, and an honorable one; I am not without feelings for him, either—if I had been, the decision would have been a simple one. He took it harder than I had expected; it was the first time I'd ever seen him lose his composure—and that pained me deeply.

"It's too soon—is that it?" he said. "Ellie, please tell me it's that. Should I have waited longer before I asked you? Dear God, I wish I hadn't waited one minute now. I should have asked you the day we first talked at the hospital. I wanted to. Didn't you realize that?"

I stared at him. I hadn't realized. It had never crossed my mind. I said, "Francis, please try to understand. This is very hard for me. I'm not ready to be a wife. I'm thirty-one years old—and I've only just stopped being a daughter."

"I'm not asking you to be *a* wife, I'm asking you to be *my* wife," he said in a harsh way, and I saw I'd hurt him. "Darling—come here. Look at me. Don't do this. I love you. Darling, please, listen to me."

I listened. I listened to Francis, the man my father had chosen for me, and I listened to the other voices that had spoken to me so often these past months: to the second Mrs. de Winter, whose one object in life had been to make her husband happy; and to Rebecca, who warned of men who came bearing gifts, and extracted a price for them. The more I listened to all these voices arguing away, the more muddled and distressed I became. It went on and on—what a cacophony! But I'd made a decision, and it seemed feeble and wrong to go back on it, so when Francis was calmer, and I was much less calm, I refused him a second time.

There was a long silence. Francis moved away from me; my vision was blurry, and my mind a mess of indecision and inconsequentiality. I thought: It's 1951—what will happen to me, where will I go, what will I become in the second half of this century?

Time ticked; Francis gave me a long, slow, measuring look. "Very well," he said finally. He might have been amused; he might have been angry. "In that case, I'll wait. And then I'll ask you again, Ellie."

"No, no, no," I said. "You mustn't do that. I might weaken."

"That was the idea," he replied in a dry way, and he then took me out to see his sons, who were waiting in the car. He knows how fond of them I am, so I thought this was a little devious of him.

The two boys greeted me, then ran into the house. I heard a sound

I hadn't heard in twenty years at The Pines: the sound of children. I heard their footsteps run up the uncarpeted stairs; I heard their shouts from the bedrooms. They opened one of the windows, and leaned out to look at the sea. I looked at the sea, too, one last, long, painful look while I made up my mind. Then I fastened Barker's lead, kissed Francis good-bye, and turned my back on my home and my childhood.

I left for the station and my new life; for work, and the room of my own in Cambridge. Barker sat at my feet in the back of the taxi; we swooped down the hill into Kerrith; we passed through familiar streets, but my tears obscured them. The cottages, the harbor, the stations of my childhood. I could walk here blindfolded. I wound down the window and let the fresh salt air flood the car; at once I began to feel stronger. As we mounted the hill toward the Manderley headland, I found my tears had dried, and something had begun to creep along my veins, something new and alive that felt like exhilaration. Its energy was very rich. It was as intoxicating as wine, as shocking and powerful as freedom.

We were about to pass the Four Turnings entrance. I leaned forward to the driver. "Stop here, please," I said, "Stop here for a moment."

I climbed out and ran toward the gates. Suddenly the light was like diamonds and the air smelled of the future. My heart was beating fast, and my hands were shaking. The sea is inaudible from there, but that morning I could hear it. Had I made the right choice or the wrong one? I had made a *beginning*, I decided—and to begin felt perilous and joyful. For the first time in my life, I was answerable to no one. I was neither daughter nor wife; from now on, for better or worse, I alone would determine my future.

Beside me, Barker made a low whining sound. I felt the soft fur rise on his neck. I bent to reassure him, and then, as I straightened up, I saw—I'm almost sure I saw—someone moving through the trees toward me. She was very swift. I glimpsed only a passing brightness, a quick glitter of movement—but I felt the burn of her glance and it gave me courage.

I think a final salutation passed between us—I certainly felt it did, though I might have imagined it. I waited. When the air was ordinary again, I returned to the car, and told the driver to take me to the station.

THE HISTORY

BEHIND

THE STORY

RESURRECTING REBECCA

BY SALLY BEAUMAN

"I suppose you want another novel," Daphne du Maurier wrote to her publisher, Victor Gollancz, in the spring of 1937, from Ferryside, her house in Cornwall, where she was awaiting the birth of her second child. And, in her first reference to *Rebecca*, the novel that would make her famous, she went on to give Gollancz an outline of her next book: it would be a "sinister tale about a woman who marries a widower . . . psychological and rather macabre."

Gollancz was indeed hoping for another novel (it would be her fifth) from his thirty-year-old author. True, du Maurier's previous novels had produced a mixed response, with the third, *The Progress of Julius*, a harsh account of an incestuous father-daughter relationship, being met with widespread condemnation. But du Maurier's nonfiction work had been well reviewed, and with *Jamaica Inn* the previous year, she had struck a chord: the book had outsold all her previous fiction. So Gollancz was not merely hoping for another novel, he was hoping for a bestseller—and with *Rebecca*, of course, he got it.

Du Maurier gave birth to her child (a second daughter) that April. In July, leaving her children behind in England, she returned to Egypt with her husband, Frederick "Boy" Browning, a career soldier and officer in the Grenadier Guards, who had been posted there as commanding officer of his battalion. In Alexandria, which she loathed, she was expected to play the role of the commanding officer's wife— one she detested, and performed ineptly. She was constantly homesick for England—so much so, she wrote, that her longing for Cornwall was "like a pain under the heart continually." It was in her room in Alexandria, in the appalling heat and dust of an Egyptian summer, sweating so much that her fingers stuck to her typewriter keys, that du Maurier began writing *Rebecca*. After a false start she described as "a literary miscarriage," she found the narrative voice and the setting (Cornwall, though it is never identified as such) she needed. She found Manderley, and inside that resonant unforgettable house, she placed Maxim de Winter and his two wives, the dead but ever-powerful Rebecca and her successor, the famously (and fascinatingly) anonymous narrator of the novel, the woman whose identity, like her name, is determined by her husband: the daydreaming, fantasizing second Mrs. de Winter.

In creating Manderley, ancestral home of the de Winters, she created a house that—as Hitchcock remarked when he came to film the novel—is as powerful a force in the book as any of the characters. The setting of Manderley, so minutely detailed in the novel, is that of Menabilly, the hidden, half-ruined house on a wooded peninsula near Fowey that du Maurier had discovered some years before, and in which she was later to live for more than twenty years. Menabilly was a male preserve (as the first syllable of both its name, and its fictional counterpart Manderley, suggests); it was entailed and had passed down through generations of the male line of a distinguished Cornish family; it was a house that was to obsess du Maurier, light her imagination, and fuel her fiction for years—but she was able only to lease it, never to own it. The private name she gave Menabilly was "the House of Secrets," and when she placed it at the heart of *Rebecca* (five years before she went to live there), she created an elliptic, shifting, and deeply secretive book. The plot of *Rebecca* hinges on murder and masquerade, and the text itself (as well as the characters) can don disguises.

By the time she came to write the book, du Maurier had mastered the techniques of popular fiction; she could create both atmosphere and suspense—*Rebecca* is brilliantly structured and plotted—and so her novel came well disguised as the bestseller material Gollancz had hoped for. An intriguing tale of love and murder, in which two female archetypes, the "good" and the "bad" woman (or the "Healer" and the "Destroyer," as du Maurier herself termed them), do battle for a man, with the sweet, pure, self-effacing second wife apparently winning—this was, in modern parlance, a guaranteed page-turner. When they received the finished manuscript, Gollancz and his editors were unanimous: they were jubilant. Greeting it as "an exquisite love-story," planning to promote it as a gothic romance, they predicted a huge success for the book. In the run-up to publication, there was only one fearful and dissenting voice: du Maurier's.

Learning how much Gollancz was spending on promotion, she wrote to him foreseeing "an awful flop." The novel was "gloomy" and its ending was "grim," she felt—and she was, of course, correct. *Rebecca* is a grim—or Grimm—novel: examine it closely, and you discover a perturbing, dark construct, part fairy tale, part myth, part Freudian family romance. The novel's "hero," Maxim de Winter, is, as his name suggests, a cold and authoritarian man, whose idea of a proposal is to say, "I'm asking you to marry me, you little fool." He has not only murdered his unconventional and transgressive first wife but also (as he believes) her unborn child. De Winter, first cousin to Bluebeard, albeit in the guise of an English gentleman, is a perjurer who escapes the gallows only with the connivance of the novel's "heroine," that very unreliable narrator, his sweetly tenacious second wife. Such details would be dangerous in a popular novel now: in 1938 they were, as du Maurier saw, profoundly heretical. Yet when the novel was published, du Maurier's anxieties proved groundless and Gollancz's predictions proved correct.

True, the reviews were poor. *Rebecca* was promptly attacked for its echoes of *Jane Eyre*—Manderley, like Rochester's Thornfield Hall, is burnt to the ground at the end of the novel, and the poetic agent of the fire is de Winter's indestructible, errant (and, he claims, sexually voracious) first wife. Rebecca might not exactly correspond to Charlotte Bronte's "madwoman in the attic," but their literary kinship is clear and intended to be so. Such gothicisms, as far as most critics were concerned, were too much. Some reviewers were prepared to admit the novel had a certain odd power; nevertheless, reactions were withering. It was a mere notch up from "servant-girl fiction." It was a book written by a woman, about women, and aimed at women—and as such critics felt able to dismiss it with that telling female diminutive that spells literary death: *Rebecca*, they chorused (and, yes, most of the reviewers were male), was a "novelette."

As for du Maurier herself, well, she was a "romantic novelist," and having shoved her into that particular wastebin, the critics could duly wash their hands of her. Thus was du Maurier "named" and categorized as a writer, much to her resentment. The tag was lazy and inaccurate, and the question of how women are named and categorized (and the ironies and inexactitudes inherent in that process) was, of course, central to the themes of *Rebecca*. Not one of the reviewers, busily pigeonholing, noticed that. Did these reviews affect sales? Not one jot.

Rebecca became an instant bestseller in America and in Great Britain. Two years later, came the Hitchcock film version, starring Joan Fontaine and Laurence Olivier, which won the Oscar for best picture in 1940. Hitchcock's version, particularly strong on the sexual ambivalences of the book, has become a cinema classic, but—revealingly—Hitchcock made alterations to the plot: if it was risky to present an apparent hero as a murderer in a novel, it was unthinkable in a Hollywood movie. Accordingly, Maxim de Winter's crime was reduced to that of manslaughter; wicked, promiscuous Rebecca was not shot but fell and hit her head, thus conveniently absolving her husband of all guilt, and retaining sympathy for Olivier as de Winter (very fetching in a camel hair overcoat).

Boosted by the success of the film, demand for the book increased. *Rebecca* went through twenty-eight reprints in four years in Britain alone, and after the war, it continued to attract a worldwide readership. Over the decades since, while other novels of its period, both literary and popular, have been forgotten, *Rebecca* has continued to fascinate, to provoke debate, and more recently, assisted by the interest of feminist critics, to launch a secondary literary industry. It has been adapted innumerable times for radio, stage, and television. Nearly seven decades after it was first published, the "novelette" reviewers so derided has never been out of print.

This is unusual. The lifespan of most popular fiction is brief. First it dates, then it dies; usually it endures, at best, for a couple of decades. Yet *Rebecca* has escaped that fate; it has made the strange and rare transition from bestseller to cult to classic. Three million copies of du Maurier's work are in print worldwide; *Rebecca* still sells, on average, thirty thousand copies a year in Great Britain, and more in America. Visit the du Maurier website, and you will find a flood of praise for, and argument about, the book, much of it from readers who are clearly young (many are students). *Rebecca*, set in a lost world of rigid class distinctions and frigid sexual codes, a world where tea is served on the lawns at four-thirty (and by a footman, at that), a world in which a woman's hardest decision is whom to call upon that afternoon, and her role in society, like her status, is determined by her husband—this is a world that still speaks to an emancipated, sexually liberated cyber-generation. Why is that?

I first asked myself that question some six years ago now, when I wrote an article about du Maurier and *Rebecca* for *The New Yorker*. I've asked it again, many times, over the past two years, while I've been writing my own novel, *Rebecca's Tale*—a book that is deeply indebted to du Maurier's, but which is, I hope, freestanding. I began writing it sixty-one years after *Rebecca* was first published, very aware of the sea change that has occurred in our attitudes toward women, wives, sexual morality, and sexual transgression. Writing in 1938, du Maurier both questions and subverts the attitudes of her era to such issues, but the conventions of her time force her to do so obliquely. Her narrative is handed to that voice of conformity, Mrs. de Winter: you can hear the clarion call of the opposition if you pay close attention to the subtexts, but Rebecca, the voice of female disobedience and rebellion, never actually speaks; she has been silenced by the husband who murdered her. In writing *Rebecca's Tale*, I wanted to return to Manderley and examine that strange place from *her* perspective. Rebecca is one of the most fascinating and elusive characters in twentieth-century fiction. I wanted to give her a voice; I wanted to resurrect her.

It is one of the great feats (and great curiosities) of du Maurier's novel that a woman who is dead before it begins, who never appears, whose character and actions are reported only by others, comes to dominate the book that bears her name. It is her pallid successor who conjures her up, of course, and from the second we glimpse her (in the shape of her handwriting, in a dedication to a book), Rebecca rises from the dead with terrifying speed and vivacity. Like the woman in Sylvia Plath's poem, "Lady Lazarus," who promises "Out of the ash / I rise with my red hair / And I eat men like air," Rebecca proves to be eternally indestructible. Neither a bullet through the heart nor burial at sea can quench her vampiric power—a female avatar, she returns from the grave to wreak havoc on the husband who killed her.

Like her literary ancestress, the first Mrs. Rochester, she destroys a male domain. When Manderley goes up in flames in the final chapter, the novel comes full circle. Maxim de Winter, unlike Rochester in Bronte's novel, is left physically unscathed: he is neither injured nor blinded. But the reader has been given a glimpse of his post-Manderley future and can be in no doubt that Rebecca's revenge on her husband is complete. His powers have gone: perhaps literally, certainly spiritually, de Winter and all he represents have been rendered impotent.

This is not the sort of message one would expect in a lightweight novel allegedly aimed at undemanding readers—but then *Rebecca* is not a lightweight novel, though it is, in the most laudatory sense, an intensely female and feminist one. Du Maurier herself would have distrusted, and probably disliked, the term *feminist*. She was a deeply divided woman, and it is those divisions that fuel and fire all her writing. On the one hand, she was independent, bisexual, and free-spirited, dedicated to her work, disliking fame, and with a fine contempt for convention. On the other hand, despite infidelities on both sides, she loved and remained loyal throughout her life to her very different and far more conventional husband. Throughout her life, she was torn between the need to be a wife and the necessity of being a writer, and she regarded those demands as bifurcating and irreconcilable. Half accepting her society's (and her husband's) interpretation of ideal womanhood, yet rebelling against it, she came to regard herself as a "half-breed," and "unnatural." To her, both her lesbianism and her art were a form of aberrance: they both sprang from "the Boy in the Box" that she believed lived inside her. Sometimes she fought against this incubus—and sometimes she gloried in him.

Given those beliefs, which bedeviled her all her life, the dualism, the gender blurring, and the *splitting* that are so noticeable in *Rebecca* become more understandable. Du Maurier was wrestling with personal demons here, and she gave aspects of herself to the two women who are the polar opposites and the twin pillars of her narrative. She gave her own shyness and social awkwardness to the second Mrs. de Winter. She gave her independence, her love of the sea, her sexual fearlessness, and even her bisexuality (strongly hinted not spelled out) to Rebecca. She also gave Rebecca an ability to rise from the dead, to influence others long after she had ceased breathing—and that kind of immortality, of course, is enjoyed by, among others, artists and writers.

But if aspects of Rebecca strongly mirrored du Maurier herself, she made one very significant change. The question of female fertility is central to *Rebecca*'s complex plotting and themes, and must have been uppermost in du Maurier's mind as she wrote the book (she had just given birth, after all); yet she chose to make Rebecca infertile. Keeping her barrenness secret, lying to her husband and claiming she is pregnant with another man's child, a bastard whom she intends to pass off as his heir, Rebecca is able to goad her husband into killing her: she is sinning against the laws of primogeniture, and in the world of Manderley, that is the ultimate transgression.

Recently, in his fascinating and highly entertaining essay "Where Was Rebecca Shot?" John Sutherland has examined in rewarding detail the riddling circumstances of that death and its many narrative implications. He stops short of examining that invented phantom pregnancy. I think it rewards further exploration, and in my own novel, I've made it central to my account of Rebecca. In a sense, Rebecca, with her rebelliousness and her refusal to live life by male-dictated rules, *was* carrying a child, and a female one at that. In her, in embryo, one can see the new species of women that could and would be born—though for such women to flourish, male preserves of the kind Manderley symbolizes had first to be dismantled.

Would du Maurier have approved such changes? Where did her sympathies ultimately lie—on Rebecca's side, or Mrs. de Winter's? To questions such as these, du Maurier resists giving answers. In *Rebecca's Tale*, I have resisted answers too: the one quality of du Maurier's I wanted above all to honor was ambivalence. I think of my book as approaching a familiar place by a different route—not a new technique, of course. In 1966, Jean Rhys published *Wide Sargasso Sea*, her account of Bertha Rochester's early life. The same year, Tom Stoppard rediscovered Elsinore through the eyes of two attendant lords, and since then, interest in the reverse-angle shot for fiction has increased rapidly. Recently, Elsinore has been revisited again, in John Updike's *Gertrude and Claudius*; Sena Jeter Naslund has built upon a passing reference in Melville to write *Ahab's Wife*; Peter Carey used the Magwitch of *Great Expectations* for his novel *Jack Maggs*; *Lolita* has spawned the irreverent *Lo's Diary*; and Alice Randall, author of *The Wind Done Gone*, a novel that looks critically at Tara from the point of view of a black slave, is being sued by the Margaret Mitchell estate.

When I began planning *Rebecca's Tale*, most of these books had not yet been published; I was familiar with Stoppard's play and Rhys's novel, but if a fashion was developing, or (worse) a trend, I wasn't aware of it, nor did I care. As I discovered once I began writing *Rebecca's Tale*, it is very interesting indeed to alter a literary compass bearing: Manderley may appear familiar if you approach it from, say, the south, but how does it look if you steer north, or north-north-east toward it?

The perspective alters at once, and readers may or may not like this. They may say, "Oh, but we liked the old view much better," or "Well, this is a *really* weird angle," or "Good God, there's a bloody great tower there, I never noticed that," or "Can't we go home? I never wanted to come here in the first place." They may also feel, of course, that trespassing is involved. And I thought long and hard about *that* issue. Resurrecting any of another writer's characters and merging them with your own is dangerous; if you admire the writer concerned (and why would you bother otherwise?), it's especially so. When I came to resurrect Rebecca herself, I had huge freedom because du Maurier reveals virtually nothing about her circumstances ckground. But writing her section (one of four in the novel) was ghostly experience. I sometimes felt as if I were taking dictation, writing very rapidly, yet scarcely able to keep up with her voice.

That has never happened to me before, and I certainly wouldn't want it to happen again. It was, as du Maurier might have said, "macabre"—exhilarating, but deeply unnerving.

RECOMMENDED BY SALLY BEAUMAN

Books lead readers to other books—that is one of their most delightful and rewarding characteristics. I recommend the following books about Daphne du Maurier:

The first full, authorized biography of du Maurier remains the best at present: Margaret Forster's *Daphne du Maurier* must be read. It gives valuable new insight into du Maurier's sexually troubled and conflicted private life, but it is written from an oddly narrow, puritanical point of view. Flavia Leng provides a less judgmental portrait of du Maurier as a woman and writer in *Daphne du Maurier: A Daughter's Memoir*. The second of three children, Ms. Leng paints a sensitive portrait of her mother (not the most maternal of women) and an unforgettable account of childhood at Menabilly, the remote house in Cornwall used as the setting for *Rebecca*.

Du Maurier published several nonfiction books about her family: *Gerald* (an unconventional biography of her father) is interesting, as are *The du Mauriers* and her autobiography, *Myself When Young*. But the book I find most captivating is *Enchanted Cornwall*. Published the year she died, and including photographs taken by her son, it records the places in Cornwall that spoke most passionately to her. It also reveals much about her books—and more about their intensely reticent, secretive author than she perhaps intended. I drew extensively on this and on *The Rebecca Notebook and Other Memories* when writing *Rebecca's Tale*.

The lighter side of HISTORY

AND ONLY TO DECEIVE
A Novel of Suspense
by Tasha Alexander
978-0-06-114844-6 (paperback)
Discover the dangerous secrets kept by the strait-laced English of the Victorian era.

DARCY'S STORY
Pride and Prejudice Told from Whole New Perspective
by Janet Aylmer
978-0-06-114870-5 (paperback)
Read Mr. Darcy's side of the story.

PORTRAIT OF AN UNKNOWN WOMAN
A Novel
by Vanora Bennett
978-0-06-125256-3 (paperback)

Meg, adopted daughter of Sir Thomas More, narrates the tale of a famous Holbein painting and the secrets it holds.

REVENGE OF THE ROSE
A Novel
by Nicole Galland
978-0-06-084179-9 (paperback)
In the court of the Holy Roman Emperor, not even a knight is safe from gossip, schemes, and secrets.

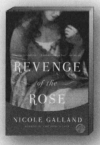